the last ARCHANGEL

A NOVEL

ADVANCE PRAISE FOR
THE LAST ARCHANGEL

"Everything in *The Last Archangel* works on several different levels. I give it an A+ for pacing. When you get this book, you'll want to clear your schedule for the next couple of days. At the very least, leave a note for your loved ones explaining that you're fine, just lost in an excellent story."

—J. Lloyd Morgan, author of *The Hidden Sun*

"*The Last Archangel* delivers quite the entertaining read with enough action and interesting characters to keep me more than satisfied. Xandir rocks!"

—Frank Cole, author of *The Guardians of the Hidden Scepter* and *The Adventures of Hashbrown Winters*

the last ARCHANGEL

A NOVEL

MICHAEL D. YOUNG

BONNEVILLE BOOKS
SPRINGVILLE, UTAH

ISBN 13: 978-1-59955-894-3

Published by Bonneville Books, an imprint of Cedar Fort, Inc., 2373 W. 700 S., Springville, UT 84663

Distributed by Cedar Fort, Inc. www.cedarfort.com

LIBRARY OF CONGRESS CATALOGING-IN-PUBLICATION DATA
Young, Michael, 1984- author.
   The last archangel / Michael Young.
      p. cm.
   Summary: Xandir, an archangel assigned as a watcher angel over mankind, disobeys heavenly law
by interfering with humans. As punishment, he is reassigned as a destroying angel.
   ISBN 978-1-59955-894-3
   1. Angels--Fiction. I. Title.
   PS3625.O9673L37 2011
   813'.6--dc22

   2011012191

Cover design by Angela Olsen
Cover design © 2011 by Lyle Mortimer
Edited and typeset by Megan E. Welton

Printed in the United States of America

10 9 8 7 6 5 4 3 2 1

Printed on acid-free paper

FOR MY WIFE

Per Sempre—Für Immer

CONTENTS

PROLOGUE

"Xandir, approach the bar."

A figure cloaked in a gray robe spotted with black and crimson stains stepped forward. Golden chains, which glowed with a dull light, trailed from his arms and ankles. Before him stood three massive columns of light, each pulsing and letting off a low hum. The voice had emanated from the center column.

"Pronounce your sentence and be done with it," said Xandir. "Cast me out if you must, but let us be done with it."

The center column flared brighter. "That would be too light a punishment, Xandir. You must be properly instructed as to your place, and such lessons require a great deal of time."

The center column dimmed and the right one glowed brighter. "Xandir, you did knowingly abet the rogue angel Azazel, and along with your fellow Watchers, you did stray from your duties and did willfully reveal the secrets of Heaven to humankind."

Xandir lifted his head. "They were kept in bondage! In utter ignorance. I—"

"And furthermore," the voice continued. "you did enter into illicit relationships with humankind, which folly served to create the race of Giants, an abominable race that would have proved the end of humans if left unchecked. For this—"

Xandir reared up and struggled against his chains. "Left unchecked? You slaughtered them! They deserved—!"

1

The golden chains flared with energy, and Xandir writhed against their stinging grip. A faint dark mist escaped from the folds of his robe.

"For this," continued the voice. "You shall be consigned to the role of Destroying Angel, which sentence shall be served until the End of Time."

Xandir raised his head. "The End of Time? But that—"

All three columns flared in unison.

"Silence."

Twin shafts of light shot up in front of Xandir, each leaving a slender sword in its wake. The swords hung in the air around Xandir and then suddenly fastened themselves with a chain about Xandir's waist. At once, Xandir felt himself falling, tumbling through swirling mists, buffeted by darkness and pain.

He gained speed, tumbling impossibly fast and unaware of time or direction. Then, without warning, it was over. Everything around him stood still, and for many minutes, he made no attempt to move. When finally he did stand, he found himself on a barren plain: the earth beneath him riddled with cracks. He glanced around in every direction and settled on a group of huts in the distance. His hands rested on his new weapons, and he set off.

"The End of Time," he muttered. "We shall see about that."

ONE

FAREWELL TO POMPEII

POMPEII, ITALY 79 AD

Xandir pondered the bustling city below him. He sat with his legs folded, his head propped up with his hands, taking in every detail of the city and the face of every person. He felt a momentary twinge of remorse as he considered Pompeii's citizens, but the feeling soon fled, replaced by a calm resolve that burned away all inhibitions. His dark cloak was wrapped around him and covered all of his shiny mahogany-colored armor. A pair of iridescent wings that normally billowed out behind him, now folded close to his body to create a cocoon. They only became visible when touched by light. Then they shimmered like sunlight passing through rain. He ran his fingers through his long, unruly platinum hair and sighed. "It's time."

However, before he could act, he sank again to the ground, a familiar twinge tugging at his heart. His next sigh came even deeper, and his scruples returned. "It's not time. It will never be time."

Just then, a brilliant shaft of red light announced the arrival of a messenger. The imposing figure stepped out of the light and scrutinized Xandir. The figure opened his mouth to speak, but Xandir beat him to it. "Honestly, I'm flattered," he muttered. "They don't send a High Seraph on just any ordinary business. But before you deliver your message, tell me, are the gates still as pearly as ever? I've been dying to know."

The High Seraph sniffed and wagged his head. He stood at over seven feet tall, with a mass of wavy brown hair, piercing blue eyes, and a white robe that revealed his muscular chest. An olive garland circled his head, and a gleaming sword, crackling with energy, hung strapped to his side with a simple golden belt.

"It is time," he said, in a voice that caused the earth to tremble around them as if with a chill.

Xandir raised a single eyebrow. "That's it? What do you take me for? I already knew that."

"You are stalling," asserted the High Seraph. "Do not forget the terms of your probation, Xandir. You have done your duty many times before without incident. What makes today different?"

Xandir pursed his lips and dipped his head. He didn't have anything to say, as the High Seraph could sense his feelings.

"Do not tell me that you have given in, Xandir. I have heard the rumors, though I do not wish to believe them. If you hesitate now, what tidings about you would I have to bring? Do you not remember what happened the first time, to the Giants? What a catastrophe that was? You know the consequences better than anyone."

Xandir shot up, extending himself his full height, only slightly less than the High Seraph. "Of course I know them. In all the millennia I've served, this has never been a problem. My performance has been beyond reproach, and I don't even get to sit high and mighty on cloud nine, eating Ambrosia all day like some people. This isn't right!"

The High Seraph's eyes flared with indignation. "You dare question your mission? Who are you to judge the matter? Their time is up, and their fate is sealed. Complete your task."

The High Seraph reached for his crackling sword, but Xandir placated him with an outstretched hand. His gray eyes flashed a tinge of red as he reached to his left and drew out one of his long, slender swords. Though pale light fell on its ebony surface, it reflected none of it; instead the blade slurped it up like hot pavement in a summer storm. In a movement almost too quick to register, he flicked the sword into the sky and thrust it hard into the earth.

The earth split and groaned beneath his blow, sending a rippling tremor through the ground, which suddenly bucked like a rolling wave and sent both Xandir and the High Seraph scrambling to take to the skies. Satisfied with Xandir's work, the High Seraph vanished in another burst of intense light. Xandir, on the other hand, shot into the air, gaining as much height as he could before the worst of the catastrophe hit.

Even from high above the earth, the explosion still sent him careening out of control as tons of ash and noxious gas erupted into the air with cosmic force. He flew as fast as he could from the scene but couldn't help glancing down one last time at the doomed town below. His eyes mellowed to a deep shade of black, and he spoke a piercing whisper that cut through the din. "Farewell."

NEW YORK STATE, 2011

The pearl earrings hit the mirror, and Eden only had time to snatch one before the other disappeared down the drain. She let out a frustrated cry and stared forlornly at the place where the other one had gone. There was no helping it now.

"Why did I just do that? Stupid!"

She had been unable to remove the back from one of the earrings and had given in to the impulse of flinging away her problem. With a sigh, she opened her jewelry drawer and selected her next best pair. Again, she struggled with the clasps, and in the end settled on a chintzy pair of clip-ons.

"Why am I so clumsy?"

Eden reaffirmed her assessment when she leaned over to look in the mirror and knocked over a picture frame. She righted it and smiled. Her husband Daren stared back at her as he had appeared when they first met at school. His grin was so bright that every look was contagious. Her smile faded, however, when she caught a glimpse of her hair in the mirror. She snatched her comb off of the dresser and launched a full-scale assault on a very poorly timed bad hair day.

After several minutes of frantic urging, it became obvious that she had made as much progress as possible. She let the brush clatter to the dresser in defeat. She gazed blankly into the mirror at the hair, the make-up, the dress and decided that she didn't like any of it. She swung around, unable to hold her own gaze any longer.

"What else is new?"

Eden sauntered into the kitchen and saw everything still in readiness for their romantic evening. It was a surprise she had been planning for months, set on the day they had first met at a homecoming dance her freshman year as an undergrad. His copper skin and wide, dark eyes, coupled with that crooked smile, never ceased to play a jazzy tune on her heartstrings.

She gave the room a once over to make sure everything was perfect. Her nose wrinkled as she caught sight of something on the table that should not have been there.

"The rolls!" she cried, realizing she'd left the tray of uncooked rolls on the table. Softly berating herself, she clopped over to the oven in her red high-heels and slid the rolls in.

Hoping that she hadn't forgotten anything else, she ran over the list of details over and over again: the dress, pizzas with extra bland sauce, the cheap electric candles, the red-and-white check-ered tablecloth. . . .

She placed a hand to her temple and tried to clear her head. There was something else missing.

She turned around, and it hit her. The music! How could she forget something as integral as that? She went over to the CD player and pressed the play button. A moment later, the first cheerful bars of a song from *Bye, Bye Birdie* filled the room.

"Gray skies are gonna clear up . . ."

She closed her eyes and went through the list one more time. Perfect. She had even stopped by the restaurant and swiped a stack of their signature napkins with a cartoon Italian twirling a pizza in each hand. It was the perfect touch.

Just then, the garage door clattered to life. Eden rushed toward the entry from the kitchen to the garage, ready to surprise him at once. She heard the engine cut off and the door slam. He was only seconds away now.

Her stomach clenched, and the door swung open to reveal her

husband in a collared shirt and tan slacks, his tie already hanging at half-mast.

"Hey, honey."

He walked past her without a second glance, dropped his keys on the counter, and disappeared into the living room. For a full minute, Eden could not force her legs to move. Her breathing quickened, and she felt a line of sweat forming on her brow, ready to massacre her makeup at any moment.

Calm down, She told herself. *He's probably just had a really terrible day at the office. He works so much.*

She took a few moments to compose herself and then followed him into the living room. Daren lay slumped over in one of the chairs she had set around their special dinner table. His eyes were fixed on the plate in front of him, bearing an expression as if she had just served him straight from the dumpster.

Eden cleared her throat. "Doesn't this look familiar? I thought . . . I . . . I thought we might do something special tonight just you and me. You've been working so hard with that new project, and I—"

"What's with my pizza?"

Eden felt like she had just swallowed a mouthful of laundry detergent. "What do you mean?" she asked, feeling her composure teetering again, close to the edge.

Daren wrinkled his nose. "There's nothing on it. Your pizza is covered with toppings, and mine barely has enough cheese to cover the sauce."

Eden unconsciously took a step back. "I was just trying to recreate things as they were. I mean, that is what you ordered, right? Plain cheese, go light on the cheese? Don't you remember? I poked fun at you for it. Remember the cheesy show tunes and those awful napkins."

Daren rose suddenly and swept his plate from the table. Eden yelped involuntarily as Daren advanced, an anger in his eyes that she had never before seen.

"What are you talking about? Napkins? I've never heard anything so stupid."

He raised a hand and struck her full across the face. She yelped again and raised her hands to shield herself. The next blow came only seconds later.

Frantically, she stumbled back and fought her way toward the kitchen and the keys sprawled on the kitchen counter. "Daren, stop! Daren, this isn't you! Why are you doing this?"

Her husband said nothing but continued his relentless attack. He backed her into the kitchen, and she lunged for the keys. He was next to her in an instant, pinning her against the counter and readying another strike. She grasped the keys with one hand and lashed out, striking him full across the face and drawing blood. He released his hold, and she bolted for the garage. She fumbled for a second with the keys, then threw herself into the driver's seat. She jabbed the button to open the garage door, and it began its agonizingly slow ascent.

Daren appeared in the garage, hefting a shovel that had been left near the door. He took a swing, and the car's headlight shattered in an explosion of glass. Eden jammed the keys into the ignition, started the car, and flung it into reverse. Another blow struck the windshield, and she knew she didn't have time to wait for the garage door.

She slammed the gas pedal to the floor, and the car barreled backward. It cleared the garage door but then rammed into a pair of trash cans on the curb as she turned out on the road, sending them crashing into the street. She jerked to a stop just in time to see Daren sprinting down the driveway, still brandishing his weapon.

She jammed the car into gear and shot forward, narrowly missing an oncoming car. Speed limits and seat belts forgotten, she raced down the road with no other thought than to put as much distance between her and her house as possible.

Her mind rattled about, unsure of what to do or where to go. *There's always my mother*, she thought with resignation.

Out on the interstate, her heart slowed to its usual rate, and the enormity of the night's events crashed onto her like an avalanche. She could hardly believe them herself. Daren's temper flared up once in a while, but it had never been anything like this.

Her hot tears destroyed what little remained of her makeup. She didn't have to sort this all out now. Her mother would know what to do. She always did.

Two
FLOWERS AND OPERA

NEW YORK STATE, 2012, 9 MONTHS LATER

Eden heard the knock at the door and at once wondered if she had made a terrible mistake.

Everything was in place for her second attempt at recreating the romantic dinner of their first date. Eden's mother had left her the house to herself, and this time, Eden was determined not to let things go wrong.

Mustering up all of her courage, she gripped the door handle and turned. "Daren, it's good—"

She had expected to see Daren standing on the porch. Instead she saw a stranger, holding a bouquet of flowers. "Delivery for a Mrs. Eden Fortuna?"

"That's me," Eden said, accepting the flowers. They were a bundle of multi-colored carnations, interspersed with Baby's Breath. It was her favorite combination and the first arrangement Daren had ever given her. "Thank you."

The delivery man nodded, and Eden shut the door as he bounded off the porch.

Instead of simply waiting by the door, Eden took to pacing, going over the preparations time and time again in her head.

Another knock sounded, and Eden's heart palpitated at an uncomfortable rate. She decided to reserve any greetings until she was sure who stood behind the door. When she flung it open, there stood a man in a tuxedo whom she had never seen before. His easy smile and bright brown eyes exuded the refinement of a gentleman. "Pardon me, ma'am, but would you be Mrs. Eden Fortuna?"

"Y-yes," she stammered. "are you here with a delivery?"

The man shook his head. "No, ma'am, more of a performance on behalf of Mr. Daren Fortuna. He asked me to sing you this song and to tell you that he too remembers that special night."

The stranger drew himself up in a regal stance and opened his mouth. From his lips came the most beautiful rendition of Eden's favorite Italian aria, one that had played over the radio at the restaurant on her and Daren's first date.

When he finished, Eden burst into an enthusiastic round of applause. Tears streaming down her cheeks, she cried. "Bravo! That was fantastic. What is your name?"

The man took a bow. "I am Alfred Olsen. I sing with the Met."

Eden gasped. "You mean the Metropolitan Opera? How—"

Alfred waved a silencing hand. "Your husband and I are old friends. He wanted to sing something himself, but then we both realized that it would be better if I stood in for him."

Both he and Eden chuckled. Daren loved to sing, but his skills left much to be desired.

"Thank you, Alfred," said Eden. "I think I'll try to attend the opera more often from now on."

Alfred flashed a broad grin. "Let me know. I can get you tickets."

Both heads turned as a car drove up and stopped in front of the house. "That must be him. I'll leave you two alone." With a parting smile, he bowed, left the porch, and disappeared."

Eden held her breath as Daren exited the vehicle, dressed in an impeccably tailored suit. She could only stare as he came up the walk and met her on the porch.

"Hello, Eden," he whispered. "I'm back."

Eden swallowed hard. "So you are." She took his hand with her own trembling one. "To stay, I hope."

Daren stepped forward and took Eden into a tight embrace. "Always," he whispered, repeating the word he had whispered so often during their courtship.

Eden felt the tears returning as his familiar touch and sweet scent enveloped her. His skin was so warm, and it seemed to radiate a soft heat that traveled directly to her heart.

"Everything is ready," said Eden, gesturing to the door.

Daren stepped through. "Yes, everything is."

Eden shut the door behind them, feeling for once that things were going to be all right.

THREE

FALLING

THREE MONTHS LATER

Eden stared out at the rain, wishing it would stop so that she could see more clearly. She could hear her mother's voice, warning her not to move back into the house with Daren, warning her with every possible argument and angle. She had barely heard.

Midnight had come and gone, and there was still no sign of Daren. He had told her that morning that he might stay late at work, just like he had so many times before, but this was something else. He had never been home this late, not by several hours.

Her stomach tightened as she thought how distant Daren had become. Their first romantic night back together had been a taste of heaven, but the dust and drudgery of life had settled back onto them both. Daren spent more and more time away, often without explanation. She glanced over at the phone, willing it to ring. Even as she did so, she knew it was hopeless. He never bothered to call.

A lance of pain drove through her heart. She wasn't sure if she had been more miserable during the nine months they had been apart or now that he was back in her life.

A pair of headlights cut through the murky night outside the window. Frantic, she ran to the front door and flung it open, letting in the angry elements. The car stopped in front of their house, and Daren emerged, dressed in a long dark raincoat with the hood drawn up. She rushed out into the rain toward him.

"Daren, where have you been? I—"

He held up a hand to silence her. "Don't come any closer, Eden. I don't have much to say, but you need to hear it."

Eden nodded. "Go on. Say what you have to."

"I have always loved you," he began, his voice raspy as if he were developing a cold. "But now there's someone I love more."

Eden wanted to scream, to cry, to tear toward him and claw at his face, but fear froze her to the spot. Something seemed odd about him, and it took her a moment to realize what it was. The rain sizzled and turned to steam as soon as it touched his long rain jacket, creating a strange, curling mist around him.

"I'm leaving, and I don't want you to come looking for me. We're through, you hear that?"

Her jaw wagged loose, and her mind raced to find something, anything to say. A strange fear, far beyond rational thought, clamped her mind shut, and she could only manage a weak. "I hear you."

Daren nodded, and she imagined that only his gleaming teeth shone out from under the hood. "Good. I don't care about any of the rest of this junk. Don't worry about getting a lawyer."

His speech given, he hopped back into his car and sped off into the night.

Eden choked back the tears and flung herself on her empty mattress. She tangled herself in the bedclothes and finally let out her emotions in an explosion of sadness. From her vantage point, she could still make out the outline of the swinging front door as lightning flashed and the rain pelted the house with unrelenting fury. She made no attempt to close it, though the rain formed a puddle in the entryway.

In a sudden burst of rage, she snatched the nearest pillow and ripped the case in two with a fierceness that surprised even herself. She took another pillow and flung it at the nightstand, toppling an expensive picture frame and sending a pair of reading glasses flying. She snatched everything within reach, flinging objects across the room until the entire bedroom looked as if the storm had struck inside rather than outside.

Her energy spent, she collapsed again on the bed, her long, red tresses falling over her face. For a long while, she muttered incoherently, gazed off into space, and made no attempt to brush away the hair that concealed her face. The blackness closed in on her like another heavy blanket, interrupted only by occasional streaks of lightning.

Slowly, the storm lost its bluster. Eden returned to a sitting position, then leaned over the bed to retrieve the discarded picture frame. She lifted it reverently, brushing away the jagged shards of glass that clung to the edges of the frame. The man in the picture smiled back at her, the moment frozen in time as if they would always be together. Another wave of pain welled up in her, and she slammed the picture down on the dresser just in time to stem the flow of tears.

Eden made up her mind in an instant. She burst from the bedroom, nearly taking the bedroom door off of its hinges, and snatched up her car keys from the shelf by the door. Neglecting to even close the front door behind her, she dashed into the storm, jumped into her battered blue station wagon, and sped off into the night.

Eden stood at the edge of the precipice and gazed into the rushing waters below. Her only regret was that she had not left a note, and so it would be some time before her fate was discovered, if ever.

Not that many will care. So much for second chances.

She closed her eyes in resignation and grew accustomed to the darkness. She leaned forward and released herself into the air. With a rush of wind, she hurtled through the air, expecting the frigid embrace of the river at any moment.

The splash never came.

A brilliant arrow of light arced through the sky and snatched her out of the air. Her breath caught in her throat, and she suppressed the urge to scream. For an instant, she caught the image of a striking man with blazing eyes, trailing white hair, and flawless skin the color of storm clouds. The vision, however, ended abruptly, and she found herself deposited on the south bank of the river, trembling, but unharmed.

She stumbled to her feet and glanced around for any sign of her strange savior. Only the chirping of crickets and the flowing water broke the silence. She rustled through the thick grass up the bank and had almost made it back to the road when a loud hissing sounded from the weeds. She leapt back in horror as a vicious crimson snake sprang from the grass, baring its gleaming fangs. The snake lowered its head, preparing to strike, and with barely a second to think about her reaction, she raised her foot and struck, driving her heel into the snake's head. With a sickening crunch, the snake's head flattened, and its body twitched several times before lying still.

Her breath came in heaving gasps, and all at once, she realized that she wasn't at all ready for the awful journey that she had just tried to inflict on herself. She broke into a limping run, reaching her car in only a manner of moments. Jumping in, she jammed the keys into the ignition just as the clouds released another torrent over her car. She let her hands drop to her lap and released her own storm of tears.

Shivering uncontrollably, Eden paid little attention to the minor lake that had formed in her entryway. A trail of watery footprints followed her from the entry back to her bedroom, where she sat on the disheveled bed. Dazed, she tried to make some sense of the events of the night without a single shred of success. Strange as the details were, however, more than anything else, she couldn't get the face of her rescuer out of her mind. It had been so compelling, so strikingly different than any she had ever seen. Had she truly gone insane? She wasn't sure whether she should discuss the occurrence with a priest or a scientist.

A twinge of pain from her stomach interrupted her thoughts, sending her scrambling for the bathroom. She reached it just in time to wretch and empty the contents of her stomach into the toilet. Miserable and groaning, she sank to the tile floor, clutching her stomach and trying desperately to gain control of her body.

This is it, she promised herself. *If he shows up again, I'm calling the police, no matter how many flowers or opera singers he sends me. I'm not going to let him hurt me again. I'm not going to let anyone do that anymore.*

She rose and studied herself in the mirror. Her hair hung in damp, matted strands across her face. One eye was nearly swollen shut, and her lip was cut from where she had slipped and fallen on her face on the way to the bridge.

She frowned, and her thoughts drifted to the strange figure that had saved her life. She had always believed in angels but had never imagined she would ever see something so like one in this life. Perhaps he was her guardian angel—the male version of a fairy godmother. A fairy godfather, perhaps? If that was true, both the storybooks and her imagination had gotten it all wrong.

"Hm," she muttered to her reflection. "Why would anyone want to save you?"

From his vantage point on the bridge above, Xandir could see into the front windshield of an old, blue station wagon. His eyes lay fixed on the woman inside, and, try as he might, he could not bring himself to look away as a curious mix of emotions washed over him. "It was my duty, nothing more," he muttered to himself, trying to shake the apprehension building in his chest.

However, as he gazed at her, he knew he could not ignore the facts. The river had been her idea, but the snake—now, that was something else. He knew an adversary when he saw one, but the whole situation made no sense.

Fumbling around his neck, he managed to grasp the talisman that hung there. As his fingers closed around it, he finally gathered the willpower to shut his eyes. "Remember the Giants," he muttered before he took off into the stormy night.

FOUR
LONG-HAIRED ROGUE

NEW YORK STATE, 2012

His perch atop the skyscraper afforded Xandir a spectacular view of the bustling metropolis below. From the building's highest spire, he waited motionless; his twitching left eye the only indication of his growing impatience. He scanned the heavens, searching from the telltale sign of the coming messenger. As a low whistle and a brilliant shaft of light severed the clouds overhead, he straightened up to his full height.

The light faded, revealing the usual High Seraph messenger, this time accompanied by a shorter figure swathed in a brilliant white hooded robe and crowned with a slender gold circlet. His slight build and childish features marked him as a cherub, one of the very young heavenly servants-in-training. Xandir scowled inwardly but betrayed nothing in his countenance.

"So," he began. "Why do we always have these meetings so high up? Closer to home?"

The High Seraph did not react to the comment. "I am pleased to find that you have not lost your joviality."

He indicated the cherub at his side with a slight smile. "This is Jarom, your new apprentice and assistant. Congratulations. Call me a doubting Thomas, but I did not suppose you ready for this honor in this century."

Xandir stopped masking his scorn. He had never thought much of cherubs, especially since he once made the mistake of calling Cupid "cute." He still felt the sting of being on the wrong end of a volley of less-than-loving arrows.

"Hm," he muttered to himself. "Love hurts."

"What did you say?" inquired the High Seraph.

"Oh, nothing. I was just wondering to myself to what I owe this honor. It's surely not reflective of my track record. You know I prefer to work alone."

The High Seraph sighed. "Contrary to the rumors and your profile in the Book of Life, I would say that you have proven an able servant to the Kingdom. The ease with which you carry out your assignments is nothing less than remarkable. Consider this your next real challenge."

The High Seraph glanced Heavenward, as if making to leave. Xandir raised a hand. "Wait, before you go, I do have something to report," he interjected coolly. "Last night, on a mission, I saw an adversary. It took serpent form and nearly compromised my mission. I thought you should know."

The High Seraph nodded gravely. "Duly noted."

He looked to the Heavens once more and made a gesture with his hands that Xandir found oddly familiar. "Xandir, I need not remind you of the terms of your service. But let this call to your attention what is at stake. Fulfill your duties for a short season longer, and all of this shall once again be your domain."

The clouds parted above them, and it was as though another layer of the sky peeled back like the opaque skin of a luscious fruit. Before him stretched the Heavenly Citadel, more glorious and pure than all that Xandir had seen on Earth. Wave after wave of glorious light and music streamed down on him, touching every corner of his soul and driving out the dust of everyday life.

In an instant, it was gone again, and the mortal world settled in around him like a noxious residue.

The brilliant beam of light once again shot from the sky and retrieved the High Seraph, leaving the gawking cherub standing across from Xandir. For several moments, they surveyed each other in silence. David could not have appeared any more diminutive before Goliath then the cherub before the towering angelic warrior.

"So, where are you from, kid, Cloud Nine?"

The cherub shook his head, his wavy locks flying freely around his face. "Ah, no, sir. It is actually more around the Elysian Fields. I was a part of the Order of Ambrosia, you know, the bakers union, but there has been a sort of Heavenly draft, so even cherubs have been pressed into service. Seems like they are preparing for something major."

Xandir's ears perked up. Perhaps this assignment would not be as boring as it had first sounded.

Jarom reached into a small satchel around his waist and extracted a bundle no larger than his fist. He offered it to Xandir. "Here. It is an offering I bring to you as my new master."

Xandir accepted the bundle between two fingers. "And this is?"

The cherub shied away, struggling for words. "It isn't much, really. It is a specialty of my family: Ambrosia-filled manna. They may not look like much, but they are really popular."

Xandir lifted the edge of the cloth and glimpsed a layer of flaky, white crust. "So, it's like a Heavenly jelly donut. Thanks."

"I-it is supposed to have incredible medicinal properties. Even angels sometimes need that down here, right?"

Xandir shrugged. "I guess. I don't usually let my enemies get close enough to do any real harm."

Jarom's eyes fixed on Xandir's dual scabbards. "It doesn't look like you were ever in the Ambrosia business. Where did you get those swords?"

Xandir sighed and pulled the handle of his left sword so that a few inches of the ebony blade could be seen. "I'm part of the reason you have so many new tenants up there, Lil' Halo. These blades were given me when I accepted my initial assignment after the War in Heaven. The one on my left is called Dark Judge and the one on the left is Bright Advocate. With them, I hold justice and mercy—and often life and death—in the balance."

He sheathed the sword and folded his arms. The cherub gawked at him as if he'd just announced that the sky was going to be orange from now on. "Does that make you one of the destroying angels?"

Xandir frowned, wincing a bit at the title. "Some people call us that, but it's just so melodramatic," he began, his voice cool. "I don't think that it's a very complete job description either."

When the cherub only stared blankly back, Xandir unfolded his arms and pointed to the distance. "Follow me, kid. I'll show you what I mean."

The cherub was about to protest being referred to as a kid, but Xandir had already shot off into the distance, forcing the small angel to follow as fast as his tiny wings would carry him.

The two of them flitted over the heads of a dense crowd, and Xandir gave his apprentice no break when it came to their flying speed. Much to Xandir's chagrin, the tiny angel kept up while betraying only the slightest amount of strain. He gazed wide-eyed at the throngs below them, taking everything in as if seeing it for the first time.

"What's the matter Lil' Halo? Never seen a city before?"

The cherub shook his head absently. "Ah, no. Not really. This is my first time going Earthside. Why can't they see us?"

Xandir sighed. This was going to be a long day. "They are mortal, and their eyes are dull. We angels are made of a different kind of matter than they are, and unless we want to be seen, there's no way that they can tell that we're here."

They flew along in silence for several moments before Xandir added. "That is, most of them can't. There are some of them who have a special gift. They can see things that mortal eyes normally can't. But don't worry. If we run into one of these people, we'll know. Most people don't take them very seriously anyway."

They buzzed along rapidly, until Xandir suddenly halted over a busy intersection. The cherub, who had built up too much momentum, whizzed past and had to backtrack to follow his new mentor. Xandir floated motionless with one hand behind his ear and his face fixed in a look of concentration.

Suddenly, he lowered his hand and withdrew the gleaming white sword at his right. The sword flashed in the morning sun as he extended it and slashed the air in the direction of the intersection, calling loudly in a language that the cherub did not recognize.

A sound from the intersection drew Jarom's attention from the sword, and he glanced down just in time to see a car run a red light, causing an oncoming car to swerve to avoid a collision. The second car missed the first by inches; however, its sudden movement sent it on a direct course with the sidewalk, where an elderly pedestrian had been walking, oblivious to his impending doom.

Just when it seemed that the car would topple the man, he shot to the side with incredible speed as if snatched up by an invisible hand. The car barreled past him. At that same instant, Xandir removed the other sword and sliced into the air, eliciting a sound like the separation of a mile of Velcro. The car rapidly changed direction, jumped the curb, and came to rest on top of another man who had just emerged from a shop, brandishing a gun in his gloved hands.

The driver leapt from the vehicle and stooped over the crumpled figure. The driver bent down, established that the armed man wasn't breathing, and retrieved his cell phone from his pocket to make the emergency call. In a matter of minutes, police cars circled the scene, having initially responded to the report of an armed robbery.

Xandir sheathed both swords and perched atop the streetlight. He studied the scene with cool calculation for several minutes before Jarom spoke up. "What just happened? Did you do that?"

"No," he replied quickly and softly. "No, not really. I was just a tool. The order came from somewhere else."

The cherub wrinkled his face. "But why did this have to happen? Why did that one man get to live? Why did the other have to die?"

Xandir gave a grunt. "I don't know." He said so softly it was almost a whisper. "They never include their reasoning with the instructions. It's part of the role I play—can't ask too many questions. They claim it is all for the greater good somehow . . ."

Xandir shook his head in annoyance, shedding the thought like an unwanted piece of debris. "Who am I to question the will of the Almighty?" His voice trailed off forlornly as he stared once again at the unfolding scene. He remained completely motionless for a full minute. "Come on, Lil' Halo. You've seen enough. No rest for the righteous, I suppose. Follow me, and try to keep up."

Words formed in Xandir's mind, and his hands shot to the space behind his ears. "We have a rogue angel. Accosted him stockpiling illegal weapons. Fled from the scene. Track him to possible enemy haven. Bring back unharmed."

Xandir did not share their mission with the cherub, who was looking flustered enough already. He smiled, relishing the thought of a chase and thinking that this was the most interesting mission he had received in a long time. Just as long as his little friend did not slow them down.

Xandir shot away, leaving the cherub to flounder. Jarom pursued as fast he could, silently cursing all the centuries he had spent growing fat on Ambrosia.

A mental image formed in Xandir's mind, detailing the projected location of their quarry. He changed his course, heading out of the city and into the wooded countryside, his senses alert for anything out of the ordinary. He blinked once hard, and when his eyes opened again, they glowed red, allowing him to make out heat sources in the foliage below.

At first, only the shapes of deer and other small animals drew his gaze, but then, in the distance, he caught sight of a much larger being, moving quickly just below the canopy of trees. With only a short glance behind him, Xandir stretched his wings to their full span and shot off after his target. Though the rogue angel moved quickly through the trees, he was no match for Xandir's superior speed. Xandir quickly reached his target and hovered just over the trees, waiting for a chance to dive down and strike. Just as he readied himself, a tongue of flame shot from the trees, grazing his left wing and tarnishing its surface. "Hm," mumbled Xandir. "and here I thought I was so stealthy."

He wove in a serpentine flight pattern as the attacks from below continued. Reluctantly, he pulled his ebony sword from its sheath, knowing that the effect might be more potent than necessary if he was supposed to bring back his opponent in one piece. Flying lower to the canopy, he slashed wildly with the blade, causing the air to pop and sizzle around him.

Only moments later, an entire house-sized section of the woods collapsed on itself, burying his opponent in a twisted mass of leaves and branches. Thankfully, he could see that his opponent was still alive, although completely caught in the mass. He sheathed his sword and turned to face his apprentice. "Now that, Lil' Halo, is how it's done—"

His words caught in his throat as only empty space greeted him. The cherub was nowhere to be seen. He soared higher in order to get a better vantage point but couldn't see anything. Cursing his luck, he shot back down to the mass of trees to finish the job. "Blast. They'll demote me to guardian angel of poodles for this."

For a moment, he hung motionless in the air, debating within himself whether to finish the job he'd been given or to go looking for his apprentice. The consequences would be dire either way if he failed. However, as he glanced again at the twisted mass of forest under him, he decided not to hesitate. With a single beat of his wings, he lighted on the forest floor in front of his captured foe.

"Quit your useless struggle," he called into the mess. "I have you in my corner, and that's that. Come with me now, and your only problem will be how to get all those leaves out of your hair."

At the sound of his voice, the twisted mass stopped shuddering, and the entire woods fell into an eerie silence. After a long moment, a voice replied out of the tangled branches. "Well, then it's good to be in your corner again . . . Xandir. I can't recall the last time I was."

Xandir wrinkled his brow. The voice sounded maddeningly familiar, and yet all his good sense told him he was being lured into a trap. "I don't know or care what you're babbling about," he said. "I'm taking you in."

"Suit yourself," replied the voice. "But I think once you see me, you might change your mind."

Undeterred, Xandir began the methodical work of hacking away the tree limbs that buried his prey. He stayed poised to strike in case his opponent resorted to desperate tactics. The other angel remained silent throughout the ordeal, barely stirring the leaves around him. At last, Xandir broke through the last layer of leaves and placed a sword at the throat of his opponent. However, true to his opponent's prediction, Xandir paused when he saw his face.

It was smooth and fair, with shining blue eyes and a veritable wreath of deep brown hair. The rogue angel grinned, cocking an eyebrow in smug satisfaction. "You see? Wouldn't you rather hear what I have to say?"

Xandir shook his head. "Absalom. You were the last person I expected to see. Never thought I'd find a straight arrow like you in a situation like this. It's almost too much. Forgive me if I savor the moment."

Absalom grinned. "Even the straightest arrows have to fall to earth sometime. You can't fight gravity forever, you know."

Xandir studied the angel, trying to judge whether he was being serious. "All the same, that's an awfully long way to fall. Surprised you didn't leave an impact crater."

Absalom sighed, swinging his mane from side to side. "Oh, Xandir, you haven't changed a bit. But as much as I'd like to sample your wit for old times' sake, I have something much more interesting to discuss."

Xandir narrowed his gaze, keeping his sword level with Absalom's chin. "Keep it quick. You're not the only nuisance on my agenda."

"Yes," continued Absalom, leaning back on the branches as if in a hammock. "I know it may sound like ancient history, but do you ever wonder about the Giants?"

Xandir starred. "No. I try to think of them as little as possible," he claimed. "That was a nasty business."

Absalom leaned closer. "I wouldn't believe everything you hear about them. In fact, I think they are quite misunderstood."

Xandir exhaled in exasperation. "What's the point? This seems hardly the time to discuss Giants. I'd be far more worried about your own hide, if I were you."

Absalom turned grave. "I was sent by one of them. He wishes to speak with you immediately. He has an offer I'm sure will tempt you."

Xandir pressed the sword into the skin of Absalom's face.

"And what if I refuse? In the first place, I don't believe you, and in the second place, even if it were true, I've had offers enough."

Absalom jutted out his chin. "Then you will never see your little friend again. My distraction was quite clever, don't you think? Jarom, was it? Such a spoiled little cherub. He might actually manage to slim down a bit where we've sent him."

Xandir gritted his teeth. Like it or not, he'd have to go along now. He slowly lowered the sword but kept his gaze fixed on Absalom. "All right, you little snake. Take me to this Giant. I'll hear him out, nothing more."

Absalom grinned and stood. "Splendid. Follow me. Do try to keep up."

The rogue angel spread his wings, shrugging off the branches as if they had been twigs, and shot toward the heavens. Seeing no alternative, Xandir burst into the air after him.

FIVE

GIANT PROBLEMS

They flew in close formation, heading deeper into the forest. They abruptly changed directions many times and for no apparent reason. Xandir scanned the horizon, trying to keep his mind calm, though he felt like he might burst from anxiety at any moment.

Finally, Absalom plunged into the trees like a diver, followed in sync by Xandir. The trees grew more densely in this part of the forest, blocking all but the most intrepid of sunbeams from reaching the ground. Silently, Absalom beckoned Xandir to follow him deeper into the woods. After a minute or so, a large mound of sandy rock came into view, which revealed an entrance near its base. The two crouched through the entrance and stood immediately as the hole opened up into a much broader tunnel lined with meager torches on both sides.

The tunnel's walls were smooth as though carved by mortal hands. In the distance, they heard the sound of running water from an unseen spring. Xandir followed in silence until they reached a crudely fashioned wooden door at the end of the tunnel. Absalom paused and knocked soundly three times. After a moment, the door swung open, seemingly of its own accord, bathing the two in a stream of brilliant light.

They stepped into the room, momentarily blinded. However, as Xandir's eyes adjusted, he found himself in a sparsely furnished room with little more than a polished wooden table and a smattering of chairs, all much larger than normal. An enormous seated figure in the center of the room stood and fixed his gaze on the newcomers.

Xandir blinked, unwilling to believe his eyes. Unconsciously, his hand wandered to the hilt of his sword. "Well, well, well. Ganosh, I really didn't think I'd ever see you again."

The towering figure grinned, displaying perfectly straight, gleaming teeth. A mess of light auburn hair spilled in all directions over his head and a simple green tunic barely contained his muscular body. Strangely, one eye shone red as ruby, while the other could have passed for obsidian.

When he spoke, it seemed that the earth trembled at his deep, rumbling voice. "Neither do most of you angels. I'm sure they told you that we had all been exterminated. Some say none of us even survived the Flood. Is that still what they're saying up there?"

Xandir nodded. "Yes, but it seems that we've all been misinformed. You look plenty real to me."

He took an additional step back, watching the Giant's every move. "You'll be pleased to know," boomed Ganosh with a menacing grin. "that I hold no ill will against you for our treatment. After all, you were always very civil to my father, before and after the War."

Xandir nodded coolly, completely unable to see where the Giant's train of thought was leading. "Forgive me for asking," he began levelly, "but aren't you looking pretty young for being thousands of years old? I mean, I know you're not like the run-of-the-mill humans out there, but I thought that even your kind had an expiration date."

Ganosh's grin became even wider as he flexed his rippling muscles. "Observant as ever, I see. There are, of course, always ways around such pesky things as mortality. The purges failed to do me in, and I don't intend to let age get the best of me either. But that's a matter for another time. I brought you here for reason."

Xandir raised an eyebrow. "I can hardly believe it's for a parlor chat, especially since you've seen fit to take my apprentice as your 'guest.' And I don't see anything suitable to eat. Just what did you have in mind?"

The Giant stretched and reclined into his massive wooden chair. Xandir took his cue and sat in another chair across from his host.

"Xandir, do you ever wish the War had turned out differently?"

The question took him completely off guard. This wasn't a subject he delved lightly in. "Perhaps," he said. "But at the moment, I can't really imagine things any other way."

Ganosh snorted derisively. "Yes, you always were the fence-sitter. You were just lucky enough to fall on the right side of the fence when the dust cleared. But think just how easily you could have tipped the other way."

Xandir's brow furrowed. "Don't think for a moment that my situation is ideal. Thousands of years of servitude haven't exactly been a vacation. Those events are a blur in my head. Every time I try to bring them up, they float away like mist on a mirror."

The Giant leaned in closer, scrutinizing his guest. "Just how long is your term of service again?"

"Until the End of the World," replied Xandir coolly. "You know that as well as I do. Why are you wasting my time with this useless banter? Don't you have underlings or someone whose job it is to listen to you ramble on?"

Ganosh remained unfazed by his guest's irritation. "Yes, that is a long time. Who knows when the 'End of the World' will finally arrive?" The Giant leaned closer. "Then again, have you ever thought of trying to speed up the process?"

Xandir remained silent, pondering for some time. Throughout the years, the idea had crossed his mind many times. But every time, he had batted it down as a crazy fantasy. After all, those sorts of thoughts had landed him in his current position in the first place, and he had no desire to have his punishment worsened. He had often watched eagerly as the Signs seemed to indicate the world coming rapidly to a close. Most recently, World War II had gotten him particularly excited. But each time, as he held his breath, civilization picked itself up from its ashes and life continued. Eventually he had learned not to get his hopes up, no matter how poor the world situation appeared at the time.

And then there was that glimpse of Heaven the High Seraph had given him to think about. His body tingled with delight as he called up the image in his mind's eye. It faded again all too quickly.

"Of course," Xandir admitted out loud. "But you're going to have to convince me that such a thing is possible. I tend to doubt it after all I have seen. I've had a lot of time to think. I can't say I like my position, but then again, if there is one thing I have learned over the millennia, it's that I can't halt the inevitable. Such control is merely an illusion. Sure, you can change the little things just enough to make you think you have some degree of control. But that's all. Now you're telling me you found the magic bullet that cuts through all that? Forgive me if I'm skeptical."

Ganosh's stony face revealed little emotion. "Xandir, Xandir, Xandir. You may claim you're different, but you've fallen just as far as the rest of us. If my memory serves me correctly, it was that same lack of faith that got you into this mess." The Giant paused for a moment, bringing a beefy index finger to his chin. "Or maybe it was one of your other prized virtues," he mumbled sarcastically. "But which is it? I simply can't remember."

Xandir's fragile patience snapped. In an instant, he whipped out both gleaming swords, bathing the chamber in contrasting shades of intense light. His eyes blazed with fury as an old pain shot to the surface. "Do not tempt me," he seethed. "I'm not feeling inclined to display any of my virtues at the moment."

Ganosh retained his eerie serenity, a subtle smile creeping up the side of his face. "In my book, Xandir, anger is a virtue."

Xandir's intense stare softened as he lowered his blades. "Okay," he said. "Convince me."

Ganosh's small smile finally broke into a sadistic grin. The Giant beckoned with one meaty hand. "Follow me, and I will erase all of your doubts."

Ganosh led the way down a passage to the banks of a pool that was fed from above. Unlike normal water, this water glistened and sparkled of its own accord, its flow almost musical to the ears.

Reaching the pool, Ganosh stooped, filled his cupped hands with the water, and drank deeply. "Try some, Xandir. You won't be disappointed."

The water looked inviting enough and didn't seem harmful, so Xandir complied and took a deep sip of the water. It bubbled slightly going down, and as soon as it passed his throat, it sent a wave of elation and energy tingling through his entire body. His eyes opened wide. He suddenly felt like he had just arisen from a long, satisfying rest.

"Amazing." Xandir muttered. "I think from now on I shall thirst for nothing else. What is it?"

"A fountain of youth, of course," replied Ganosh. "Seems like Cortez was looking in all the wrong places. Obviously, it's not the only one, and it's not the best one either."

Ganosh gestured to a side tunnel running parallel to a stream that broke off from the main pool. "This is good, but the main attraction is this way."

They followed the tunnel for several hundred feet before emerging in another open cavern where the stream spread out into a dozen smaller irrigation ditches surrounding a large and beautiful tree. The bark of the tree itself was a brilliant white, the leaves a very pale gold, and the fruit a lovely shade, which changed constantly as he looked at it. An intoxicatingly sweet smell permeated the entire room, refreshing the senses with every breath.

Several gray-skinned people surrounded the tree, apparently in the act of caring for it and plucking some of the low-hanging fruits. Xandir's eyes opened even wider in surprise. This was a tree that everyone who had ever lived in Heaven recognized. "Don't tell me it's a—"

"Tree of Life?" finished Ganosh with a smile. "Yes. Though it will never be what they have in Eden, the principle is the same. The one in Eden is surrounded by four rivers such, and here we have but one. Its fruit will not bestow eternal life, but it will prolong a mortal life. That is why the Achillians here have been around for so long, not to mention me and many of my associates."

Xandir wrinkled his brow, considering the implications. "If

it's such a commodity, then why do these Achillians let you have it? It seems your circumstances are not as simple as they first appear."

"Quite right. As usual, you are quick to observe. These people are not called Achillians for nothing. As a race they are a hearty folk—cunning warriors able to withstand a great deal of punishment. Thus, they have guarded their secret for centuries, growing stronger, since they die off only occasionally. As a whole, however, their race has one weakness, which they never reveal, for it could be the undoing of them all."

Ganosh grinned wickedly, relishing in his words. "Luckily, my associates and I just happen to know their little secret and hold it over their heads. Not a bad arrangement."

Xandir considered the tree, smiling despite himself. More than anything, he wanted to reach out his hand and pluck one of the fruits but decided it would be unwise.

Ganosh allowed Xandir to study the tree for several moments more before continuing. "And of course, you are well versed in the principle that everything has its opposite, true? If you'll step into the boat, I will prove that this is even the case with this tree."

As if on cue, a small but sturdy-looking craft floated up to them in the stream. They entered the boat and road along the stream away from the tree and into another corridor. The light from the tree dimmed as they sailed along, and soon they found themselves in another room much like the one they had just left. But this room was anything but pleasant.

The water around their craft had darkened into a muddy gray, which roiled and churned like the contents of a bog. An acrid stench rose from the stream, which seemed to dull the senses with every breath. True to Ganosh's word, in the middle of the putrid stream towered a grotesque parody of a tree, a ghastly counterfeit of the one they had just left. Its black bark and leafless branches twisted in every direction like wisps of smoke blown by the breeze. The branches were gnarled and twisted like an arthritic hand and bore a scant number of green, rotting fruits.

"Let me guess," mused Xandir, "a Tree of Death."

"Almost," began Ganosh in a hushed tone. "Growing a Death Tree was our intention, but unfortunately, it's never been done before on this earth so far as we can tell. This fruit will cause violent illness but not its desired effect of painful death. It was nearly achieved once, but that attempt was lost."

Xandir shook his head, scarcely able to believe that something so sublime and something so abhorrent could exist in such close proximity to each other. "Lost? What do you mean? Who else could have tried something like this?"

"Xandir, have you ever heard of the city of Hennoch?"

Xandir nodded. It seemed like an obvious question, though he couldn't see the relevance. "Of course I have. A city so righteous that the entire thing was taken up into Heaven with all her inhabitants."

"Yes, good for you. You know your history," mused Ganosh. "However, there is another example that the history books won't mention. While there were cities that didn't have to wait until the final judgment to meet their Maker, there are other cites that took the opposite direction."

Xandir arched his eyebrows. "I'm not sure what you're saying. Wicked cities are as common as flies to a carcass; you know that as well as I do. It's pretty clear what happens to them as well. Take Sodom and Gomorrah, for instance."

Ganosh waved a silencing hand, his eyes gleaming wildly. "Oh no, I'm not talking about them. There was one city, in particular, that would make Sodom look like a monastery. A city so corrupt and foul that it was doomed to a fate opposite to that of the city of Hennoch."

Xandir furrowed his brow, his insides lurching uncomfortably. "I've never heard of such a thing. Are you saying that instead of being raised to Heaven, it was sunk to Hell? Surely you can't be serious."

"Oh, but I am," replied Ganosh. "You'll be pleased to hear that almost everyone has heard of this place. I'm referring, of course, to Atlantis."

Xandir couldn't suppress a derisive laugh. "Atlantis? The city that sank into the ocean? Come now, we all know the Greeks made that one up."

Ganosh arched an eyebrow. "Oh, did they? Seems to me that

Heavenly education is getting more and more selective these days. I'll admit, it wasn't originally called Atlantis, but it is the city that inspired the legend, so one can hardly separate the two anymore. The original name was Serche, and since I'm an old timer, I prefer to use it."

Xandir wrinkled his forehead in frustration. "For your information, I didn't exactly go to Elysian University, and if you're trying to impress me, you'll have to try harder. When it comes to that time period, I know what I'm talking about."

Ganosh grinned sardonically. "I should say that you do. If I recall, you had a firsthand source. What was her name again? Semper, Simper . . . ?"

Xandir's face contorted in anger, his hands flying to his swords. He flung them out and held both tips only inches away from Ganosh's face. "Don't you ever let her name pass your filthy lips! You know what she was to me."

"Indeed, I do, and I wouldn't bring her up if she wasn't actually relevant to the current conversation. Put down your little knives and hear me out."

Xandir reluctantly sheathed both swords, folding his arms across his chest. "I'm listening," he grumbled, "but my patience is already strained. Spit out what you're going to say already, and I'll be on my way."

"As you wish," muttered Ganosh. "The Sercheans were a cruel people, but their worst sin, the one for which they were punished, was their attempt to create the Tree of Death. It is said they worked under the direct supervision of the Devil himself and created a fruit so powerful that it could strip the very immortality from angels. However, before they could complete the project, the city was sunk and its inhabitants with it."

Xandir shrugged coolly. "I guess that's life, or death, rather. There are some things that were never meant to be tampered with. Besides, what does it matter to us if they are all, let's say, a little more than six feet under?"

"Because," replied Ganosh, "they are not quite there. You see, right before the sinking of the city, a foolhardy man entered Serche in a vain attempt to reclaim the people to the path of reason. It is against Heavenly law that a righteous man should be confined to Hell, and so the city sunk only to its Jaws, what you might call the opposite of the Pearly Gates. At this point, the city isn't going anywhere until the balance is tipped. Either the city must recant its wicked ways, or that one man must give in to the temptation to join the rest of the Sercheans."

"So, let me guess," said Xandir. "You want the secret of the tree. And as long as Serche hasn't entered Hell, then theoretically it could still be reached."

Ganosh laughed wickedly, causing the boat to shake with his considerable girth. "Ha, see! You're not so dense after all! Yes, Xandir, that's what we want, and the way I see it, you're a prime candidate for the job."

Xandir narrowed his gaze. "What makes you think for a moment that I'd go along with this crazy scheme? There's no way I could pull that off without drawing attention to myself. I'm not exactly a free agent here."

"We'd make it worth your while. Remember, you are bound until the End of the World. It should be no large stretch of the imagination to see how this particular secret would facilitate this end, and you would finally be free. For helping us, we would make sure that you would be spared any unfortunate consequences of our discovery."

Xandir sat still in contemplation for a long minute with nothing but the noxious splashing of the putrid water against the side of the boat. "It seems to me like the world is spiraling downward anyway. I really think it will end any day now. You'll have to do better than that."

Ganosh's face remained calm and collected despite Xandir's confrontational tone. "I figured you might say that, and I have prepared for such a circumstance." He lifted his gaze, glaring sidelong at the angel. "What if I told you that we could bring her back?"

Xandir let out a grunt of derision. "Who are you talking about? I'm sure you don't mean who I think you mean."

"Indeed I do," replied Ganosh swiftly. "You requested that I not speak her name again. It may sound strange, but it is true. We can bring her back."

Xandir clenched his jaw, narrowing his eyes menacingly. "You think it's amusing to mock me? I should cut out your lying tongue. She's dead. End of story. I . . ." Xandir paused, his eyes awash with pain. "I am certain. I did it myself."

"So," continued Ganosh in his smug tone, "you've been up to the Heavenly Realms lately? Paid her a visit, have you? I didn't think that was allowed under the terms of your probation."

"Of course I haven't!" yelled Xandir, his temper flaring. "You know I can't! But I killed her myself. She's gone, and you can't bring her back."

The boat came to a stop on a shore of black sand. Ganosh gave the signal to disembark, and Xandir obeyed, eager to distance himself from the foul stream. As soon as they were both out, Ganosh called into the darkness. "Bring out our distinguished guest!"

From the dark corridor in front of them came a short, dark-haired, olive-skinned boy flanked by a gray-skinned attendant. The boy wore a plain green tunic tied with a simple leather belt. The pair approached them and then stopped a few feet away. "Xandir," began Ganosh, "I would introduce you, but I think that you two go back a long time."

The boy stepped into the light, and Xandir stumbled back a step. He furiously blinked his eyes, trying to assure himself that they were not deceiving him. "You! But I, I—"

"Killed him too?" offered Ganosh. "Perhaps you were mistaken. If her brother is yet alive, why not she as well?"

Xandir shook his head, refusing to accept this version of reality. The guilt of what he had done that day still haunted him, even so many years later. Though it was true that he had been compelled to a certain degree, he always thought there must have been something more that he could have done to save those he cared so much about. The only ones he cared about.

"I don't believe it. He's an illusion—some sort of trick you've conjured up. Even if he did survive that disaster, how would he still be alive?"

Ganosh broke in with an explanation. "He's still mostly mortal, I'm sure you know. And no, we did not feed him on our marvelous fruit. We simply woke him up."

Before Xandir could object again, Ganosh continued his explanation. "You see, your swords chose a very fitting method to destroy the people of that city. Most of them ended up encased in ash, frozen in place like living statues. Ironically, the Judgment went even further than that. The victims of the ash remained encased in the statues, alive, but just barely, caught in a state between life and death until the End of the World."

Ganosh turned his attention to the boy. "We rescued this lad here with a technique I will not divulge unless you agree to help us. Ask him anything you want, touch him, anything you like. I assure you, he is not an illusion."

Xandir stepped toward the boy, scrutinizing him closely. The boy appeared just as he had last seen him, his dark features seemingly untouched by the march of time. Recalling the boy's native tongue, he addressed him, keeping his voice calm and level. "Luis, do you know who I am?"

The boy was quiet for several moments, and then he slowly and deliberately nodded his head. "I do," he replied.

"When did you last seem me?" continued Xandir.

"Just yesterday," came the reply. "You came to see my sister. I remember you flying in through the window, and it startled me so much that I nearly dropped the jug of water I was carrying. You talked for a while, and then she left crying. She would not tell me what was wrong." The boy's features softened, and Xandir saw tears forming in the young boy's eyes. "I—I want to see her. Is she here too?"

Xandir glanced over to Ganosh, deferring the question to him. Slowly, the Giant nodded, causing Xandir's heart both to soar and sink at the same time.

"Yes, Luis, she's here. Perhaps we'll see her in a little while."

The boy fought back his tears and nodded, the tiniest flicker of a smile crossing his face. Ganosh clapped his hands once again, and the attendant led the boy back out of the room from whence they came. He then returned his attention to Xandir. "I trust that was enough of a demonstration, even for an old cynic like you. Before you say anything, let me remind you that we have also taken your little friend as an extra measure of security. So, as I see it, the odds are sufficiently stacked against you."

Xandir closed his eyes, bringing memories to the forefront that had not surfaced in centuries. The boy was indeed convincing, and the account of their last meeting had been accurate. It would be a difficult task to keep from the High Seraph, probably impossible. If he was found out, he would surely be denied entrance to Heaven forever. Then again, what would be more like Heaven than having her back in his life after so many years?

Xandir opened his eyes and met Ganosh's gaze. He extended his hand, palm outstretched and facing the ceiling. Ganosh raised his hand, his palm facing the opposite direction and stretched it forward until it hovered over Xandir's. As their palms aligned, a brilliant red spark shot between the two hands, causing both figures to glow momentarily with eerie red light.

They both retracted their hands. The covenant had been sealed.

SIX

BURNING QUESTIONS

Eden paced with her cordless telephone clutched to her ear. The phone continued to ring, and she was about to hang up when a voice finally sounded on the other end. "Hello, Fortuna residence."

She swallowed hard to clear her nerves and began to speak. "Hello, Phillip? This is Eden. How are you?"

"Oh, just fine," replied her father-in-law in his normal cheerful tone. "To what do I owe the pleasure of this call?"

Eden paused for a moment before continuing, choosing her words carefully. "I—Your son, my husband. Have you seen him?"

Now it was Phillip's turn to be silent. He continued in a very cautious tone. "No. Haven't you?"

"No," replied Eden sorrowfully. "He left in a huff a few nights ago, and I haven't seen him since. He's been, well, not really himself lately. I mean, he's usually so understanding."

She paused, having to hold back the tears that were prying at her eyes. "Then again, I really have been a wreck lately. It's probably my fault."

She could hold it back no longer. The sobs wracked her body as she held the receiver slightly away from her face in embarrassment. After a minute, she regained her composure and continued. "I'm so sorry, Phillip. I didn't mean to."

Phillip lowered his voice, full of compassion. "Don't worry, and don't blame yourself. He's a bit of a hothead. To tell you the truth, we haven't talked to him in a very long time ourselves, which is odd. He used to call at least once a week, and Heaven knows how much his mother misses hearing from him."

Eden nodded to herself. That would be only one of the many strange changes she had witnessed in the past few months. "He has been spending an incredible amount of time at the lab. He tells me that it's an important research project, but I can't get another word from him about it. He barely gets any sleep, but it doesn't seem to affect him at all. I've already tried calling his cell phone, the lab, and anyone else I can think of. I didn't think that he'd drive all the way out to see you all, but it was worth a shot."

"Sorry," continued Phillip. "We're just as much in the dark here as you are. If you do find him, please let us know. We'll do the same."

She thanked him and replaced the receiver in its cradle. Alone in their bedroom, she stooped down, first on one knee and then to both. Bowing her head, she offered a quiet prayer to the Heavens. "O, please bring us together again. Please, just let things be like they were."

The day passed slowly, and Eden remained restless and agitated. The conversation with her father-in-law had done nothing to reassure her, and she was trying to untangle the knot of events that her life had become.

At first, she had felt liberated being by herself, free from her husband's strange behavior. However, as the days drew on, she found herself hoping that he would call or contact her in some way.

Finally she decided to launch herself into housework to get her mind off of her other pressing concerns. She mopped, swept, dusted, and scrubbed until her hands felt raw and her muscles ached. Finally, seeking a diversion, she crumpled onto the sofa in front of the TV.

Finding no remote after several moments, she lay there, unmotivated to make any effort to find one, when an interesting sight caught her eye: her husband's open day planner, which had fallen under the coffee table. Sitting up, she retrieved it, thumbed through it, and studied the final entry. On the day Daren left, the only thing written was a bold, circled entry in the midnight slot, made in bright red ink: "THE END."

Eden cocked an eyebrow. "The end of what?" she muttered to herself, suppressing a shiver.

She flipped back through the other pages and found them overrun with notes, appointments, and scribbles, very much at odds with the final page. As much as she stared at the frantic writing, she could make little sense of it, as if her husband had used some sort of cryptic shorthand. Feeling a headache coming on, she set the book down and rested her chin in her hands, deep in thought.

That night surely seemed like the end, but how could he have known that in advance? Surely he wasn't planning an exact date to walk out.

A moment later, a familiar sound broke the silence, and Eden shot up. She used to hear the tune almost every day. It was one of her favorite songs—the one her husband used as a ring tone. She searched around for several moments without locating the source, but then she happened to thrust her hand under the couch cushion she was sitting on and retrieved the still ringing phone. She glanced at the display and didn't recognize the name or number— M. Mahan: 666-1205390-4903.

She furrowed her brow for the second time in a few minutes. Not only was the number too long, but she had never heard of someone having such an ominous area code.

She set the phone on the table and let it ring. Seconds later, she wrinkled her nose as an acrid smell filled her nostrils. She peered down at the phone and to her amazement, tendrils of smoke rose around it, growing thicker and thicker with each successive ring. Fearing that her table would suddenly burst into flames, she bolted off toward the kitchen to snag the portable fire extinguisher they always kept under the sink.

When she returned to the living room hefting the extinguisher, the phone had stopped ringing and smoking. Deliberately, she lowered the extinguisher to the floor and then rubbed her eyes to make sure she wasn't simply seeing things.

Just imagine if that happened while it was in your pocket.

Eden crept over to the phone and examined it. To her surprise, she found that it was again cool to the touch but that it had burned a charred scar into the table's surface. The phone itself, however, seemed fine. Tentatively, she picked it up and it flipped open. The screen remained intact and displayed that there was one missed call.

Eden accessed the phone's voice mail. To her surprise, the phone had accumulated no less than 15 messages. Feeling only a twinge of guilt, she pressed the button to play the first message and held the phone close enough to her ear, but far enough away that it would not burn her if it decided to heat up again.

The very first message piqued her interest. "Hey Daren, this is Mike from the office. Listen, we are all down here waiting for you. If you don't show up in the next fifteen minutes, the boss is going to start chopping heads. Don't bother calling back, just come. You know you can't keep doing this and get away with it. She'll find out eventually, and nobody wants that to happen."

Eden clutched the phone tighter to her ear, trying to figure out if she was hearing correctly. The second message made her stomach lurch.

"Mr. Fortuna, this is Mr. Richards. I'm sorry to say this, but in light of your chronic truancy, we have no choice but to terminate you. If you bother to respond to this message, clear out your desk by close of business tomorrow, or we will simply dispose of anything you leave."

Eden played the message back to make sure she had heard the date correctly. She had. "But that was nearly three weeks ago," she whispered to herself. "Why didn't he tell me?"

More important, she wondered what he had been doing with his time when he had supposedly been going into the office. He had simply gotten ready every morning and left for work as usual with no indication of a problem. True, he had come home late many of those nights, but he had written this off to a special project just like he'd done many times in the past.

Eden held her breath as she waited for the next message,

wondering what else her husband could possibly be keeping from her.

The next message, however, revealed nothing at all—she couldn't understand a word. The voice on the other end was guttural, a perfect match for whatever language it spoke. It was unlike anything she had ever heard. The person spoke hurriedly for about thirty seconds and then hung up. The next message returned a similar result, as did each of the remaining ones. Each remaining message was delivered by the same grotesque voice that sent shivers of terror down her back.

"End of messages."

The sudden return to English startled Eden, causing her to drop the phone, which landed with a crack on the table. She reached for it but fell back, grasping her stomach as a sudden pain shot through it. The pain, however, quickly subsided, leaving her mind once again clear to contemplate her singular situation.

The obvious conclusion was that her husband had been having an affair. It would explain the long nights, his loss of interest in her, and perhaps his absences from work. And though it seemed like an easy conclusion, she couldn't settle on it as the only one. If there had been someone else and he'd been determined to leave, why hadn't he mentioned that as part of the reason? And it didn't explain the strange voice on the answering machine. He had made up entirely different excuses.

On a hunch, she walked over to her personal computer and brought up their bank statement. She looked over the register for anything out of place. Strangely, the register showed that her husband's paychecks had been deposited at the normal time and for the usual amount, even during the time that he was supposedly unemployed. She browsed through each expense, trying to spot any other anomalies but found nothing except the usual day-to-day expenditures. Perplexed, she ran through the list a second time, and this time, she noticed a new trend.

For as long as she had known him, Daren had always preferred bland food. Anything more than a little table pepper was too spicy for him. He usually avoided ketchup on his hamburgers, much less anything like chips and salsa, however mild. But the register indicated that he had eaten at an Indian curry house no less than a dozen times in the last month. Eden wrinkled her nose, thinking of the last time he had sent back a plate of spaghetti at an Italian place because he had found a solitary slice of green pepper in the sauce. Eden couldn't imagine Daren even walking into an Indian restaurant.

Perhaps he's having a mid-life crisis, she mused. *Or I've finally driven him over the edge.*

Eden returned to the living room and sank into the couch. Crushing despair pressed down on her, as it did so often, and for several minutes she couldn't think of any good reason to get up off the couch. Her muscles lagged, and she hung in a thoughtless state between asleep and awake.

She managed to stand, retrieved her purse, and rummaged through until she found her phone. Browsing through the contacts, she selected the number of an old friend and raised the phone to her ear. *She'll know what to do.*

Eden glanced at the car's clock as she sped down the freeway toward her destination. She had phoned an old professor whose extensive knowledge of languages made her a prime candidate to help her begin to unravel the messages on her husband's phone. Judy Meinecke had been a professor of linguistics for almost as long as Eden had been alive, and Eden figured that Judy was her best chance at placing the strange language.

They had known each other during Eden's college days when she had taken her beginning linguistics course and had been chosen to accompany the professor on a research excursion to the Holy Land. There they had fostered a warm friendship and since then, they had lunch together to discuss things as often as their hectic schedules would allow.

Eden had suggested that they meet at the Indian restaurant that had shown up on her bank statement. She exited the freeway, drove through a tangle of side streets to a poor district of town, and parked in front of the restaurant. It was a yellow brick building with a glass storefront. A large sign with red letters and a picture of a snake charmer proclaimed "Taste of Bombay."

Outside the store sat a row of wicker baskets displaying coiling ceramic snakes.

Wanting to breathe some fresh air, Eden exited the car and stood out in front of the shop. She cast her eyes from side to side, hoping to spot Judy. She glanced down at her watch, smiling to herself. "Well, well, I'll have to get on her for being late," she muttered to herself. "Not once did she give me a break in class."

She folded her arms and tapped an erratic rhythm with her foot. Behind her, one of the lids of the wicker baskets stirred. It lifted about an inch, and a pair of yellow eyes peered out from the crack, shifting this way and that. The lid fell back into place for a moment, then continued sliding away.

A brilliant dark green cobra coiled from the basket, never removing its caustic gaze from its intended prey. It reached its full height and flicked its forked tongue, hissing too softly for Eden to notice over the buzz of the street. " 'Tis them, I am sure."

In an instant, the snake coiled back, bared its fangs, and struck. The snake's fangs shot forward, and another object shot downward, crushing the head of the snake in mid-strike. Eden jumped forward, startled by the sudden movement, and whirled around to face her friend Judy, who was still brandishing a navy blue umbrella like a short sword.

It took Eden several moments to begin to comprehend what had just happened. She glanced down where the bloodied snake writhed in the throes of death. Without a second thought, Judy brought down the heel of one high-heeled shoe on the snake's head, snuffing its life out. She glanced back up at Eden with a calm expression. "We're going to have to talk to the management about that. Killing off customers—that's bad for business."

Judy just barely topped five feet in height and had a slender frame to match. She wore her voluminous brown hair up to compensate somewhat for her lack of height. Today, as with most days, she was impeccably dressed in a businesslike navy blue skirt and jacket and had an umbrella to match. A pair of stylish sunglasses hid deep blue eyes, which often sparkled with wit when visible.

Eden's mouth tried unsuccessfully to form words for several

seconds. "Why on earth did you think to bring an umbrella?"

Judy glanced heavenward and shrugged her shoulders. "Thought it might rain today," she muttered.

"But Judy," Eden protested. "There isn't a cloud in the sky, and it's not on the forecast."

Judy grinned and gestured with her umbrella's point to punctuate her words. "Ha! That's what all those people said to Noah right before the flood, and look where it got them. Treading water for a living, with no land in sight. You'd be in a similar predicament without my foresight."

Eden shivered even though the sun shone. Death didn't appear nearly as inviting as it had just the day before. "What just happened?" she managed, her mood turning much more somber.

Judy wagged her head, her lips pursed in righteous indignation. "I don't know, but I intend to take it up with the manager right away! Come inside. You never know what might be lurking in the rest of those pots!"

Judy flung open the door to the restaurant and stormed inside, raising her voice in a language Judy figured must be native to India. One of the workers scrambled for the manager and brought him out to deflect the disgruntled customer. A heated argument ensued with Judy using enough hand gestures and body language for Eden to get the gist of what was being said. The manager seemed on the defensive the entire time and appeared to claim ignorance of having any live snakes.

I have to hand it to her, Eden mused. *What she lacks in size, she surely makes up for in spunk.*

Suddenly Eden remembered the reason that she had decided to meet here in the first place and stepped over to tap Judy on the shoulder. "Judy, could you also ask him about my husband? I would really like to know if he's actually been coming here."

Judy just nodded and, without missing a beat, continued her conversation. After several more minutes of frenzied words, the two finally cooled off, and the manager calmly showed them to a quiet booth and presented them with menus.

"I'm deeply sorry, ma'am," began the manager in accented

English. "Your meal today will be free. You may order whatever you like."

Eden smiled graciously, sat, and glanced at the menu. Her mind, however, couldn't even begin to think about food, and she changed the subject.

"So," she whispered excitedly, "what did he say?"

Judy sighed. "He claims that he didn't know anything about a live snake in any of the pots. He says that maybe it was one of the neighborhood boys playing a prank, but I don't buy that. I could see boys playing with a garden snake, but that particular specimen was a full-grown Indian Cobra! You would have been dead within minutes! The nerve, blaming it on some juvenile delinquents!"

Eden sank down in her seat. She had expected as much.

"He's lucky he's getting off with a free lunch! We should be suing for all he's worth! I've got half a mind to—"

Eden placed a calming hand on Judy's arm. "What did he say about my husband?"

Judy settled into her seat, took a sip of water, and composed herself. "Also very interesting and more believable. He says that he recognized the man from the description as a regular. Says that he always came in around the same time of day—early afternoon, right during the lunch rush—and ordered the same dish each time: noodles with one of their spiciest curries."

Eden wagged her head. Daren had not only taken to eating at an Indian restaurant, but he regularly ordered a dish so spicy that few Americans would risk eating it for fear of losing half of their taste buds. It made no sense.

"But wait, there's more," continued Judy. "According to the manager, he never came in alone. He always met and shared his lunch with the same person, a man who only started coming at the same time as your husband."

Eden raised her eyebrows in surprise. "Interesting. That actually fits pretty well with the mysterious voice I heard on Daren's cell phone. That person started calling a few weeks ago. Why don't you listen to it and work a little bit of your magic?"

Eden selected the voice mail and offered Judy the phone. At

first her face remained expressionless as she listened to the messages in English, but as the other messages started to play, her face registered surprise, which faded into frustration. She listened to each of the remaining messages, sometimes replaying them several times. At last her patience gave out, and she closed the phone with an irritated snap.

Eden felt her heart sink into her stomach. She had seen this look on the professor before, and it had always been the prelude to bad news. After a short pause, Judy pursed her lips and then began, choosing her words with effort.

"I—I don't understand it. It doesn't sound like anything I've ever heard." She stretched her face in a pain as if this concession stung her mouth.

This certainly wasn't something Eden had ever heard Judy say. "What? You mean you can't even pinpoint what language it is?"

The professor shook her head dourly. "If I had to hazard an educated guess, which all of my guesses are, I would say it sounds like a variant of Aramaic or Hebrew. The sound systems are similar to those languages, but as far as I can tell, the vocabulary and grammatical structure are completely different."

She shook her head in frustration, fingering the phone with a manicured finger. "Would you mind if I took this back to the university and had a few other experts listen? I hate to admit it, but there are some things that others might have a better chance at figuring out."

Eden reclined back in her seat. "Whatever you need. You can call me on my own cell phone as soon as you find anything. This is really starting to creep me out. I don't know what scares me more—the thought of my husband being involved in some awful scheme or hearing you finally admit there's something you don't know. I never thought I'd hear you say those words."

"I never thought I'd say them," said the professor, "but maybe it's good to be humbled once in a while. I'll make this my top priority until I can make that annoying reality go away." Judy sat back and unfolded her menu. "Now let's see what this place has to offer. I'm famished after all this excitement."

Eden took up her menu and glanced over the selections. "All

right," she began, "but make sure that you don't get anything too spicy. It seems that you can breathe fire just fine without any help. I'm surprised you didn't singe the poor manager's eyebrows off."

They both laughed heartily and relayed their selections to a nearby waiter. Despite Eden's warnings, they both chose a robust curry and vegetable dish over rice that made their tongues smart and their eyes water. For a few minutes, they forgot the unpleasantness of the day and took time to simply catch up on each other's lives. However, the more pressing matters of the day could not long escape their attention, and eventually they were forced to return to them.

"So," Eden sighed contentedly after spooning the last of the curry into her mouth. "What's my next step? I can't let you do all the work in figuring this out."

Judy took a long swig of her drink and considered the question. "Try to get in contact with your husband's boss or coworkers to find out what happened there. The fact that they continued cutting his paychecks seems pretty suspicious, so maybe they'll reveal something important."

Eden was about to agree when her cell phone rang, startling her almost out of her seat. Fumbling through her purse, she retrieved the phone and flicked it open in one fluid motion. "Hello?" she managed breathlessly.

"Eden," said a familiar voice on the other end of the line. "This is Daren. I know you are looking for me. Don't. You'll be very sorry if you do."

By the time she finally got her wits about her enough to respond, she realized the line had gone dead.

The phone clattered to the table. Eden felt the contents of her stomach threatening to revolt. Her hands shook uncontrollably in a tremor that quickly spread to the rest of her body.

Judy shot up from her seat and was at Eden's side in an instant. "Eden, calm down, honey. Come with me." she whispered, leading her with one arm toward the ladies restroom, away from the prying eyes of onlookers.

Judy held her hand, and Eden's breathing slowed as she steadied herself against the wall. Gradually the shaking subsided. Her face flushed with embarrassment and pain, and as she took one look at her friend and mentor, she burst into tears.

Judy stepped forward and encircled her friend in a sympathetic embrace. "Let's get you out of here. You need to lie down."

Eden nodded, realizing, to her shame, that this wasn't the first time that the professor had had to rescue her in this fashion. It had happened once before during a class, and she had vowed to herself that she would never let it happen again. Eden's heart filled with despair and hopelessness. "What's going on?" she moaned. "Why is he doing this to me?"

Judy gritted her teeth as she led Eden toward the door, the fire returning to her eyes. "I don't know, but I intend to help you find out, though I pity him that man if he ever actually crosses my path again . . ."

The two made their way back to Eden's car, and the professor took the driver's seat. Exhausted, Eden handed over her keys and collapsed into the passenger seat. "What about your car?"

Judy smiled. "Never fear, my dear. I took the bus. Where am I headed?"

Eden considered the question for a moment and then retrieved her cell phone. "I want to go see my husband's former coworker. The one that called and left that last message on his phone. I'm not sure how much he'll know, but you said yourself that he might be a good place to start."

Judy quickly shook her head. "No, we need to get you home. You're a nervous wreck and you need rest. He'll still be there after a nap."

Eden sighed deeply. "Are you so sure about that? I'm not sure about anything anymore. I mean, I just about got bitten by a cobra for goodness' sake!"

Eden's face flushed with color as it had so often when arguing with her husband. She was quickly losing control of her temper.

Judy pulled back a little in her seat. "Now, Eden, calm down. Let's get you home—"

"No!" she snapped. "That's the last place I want to be! I almost took my own life yesterday because of what happened in that place. My life has been completely destroyed, and I want to know why. Now start the car, and let's go find out."

Judy started the car and pulled out onto the street. "Where am I going?" she asked softly.

Eden settled into her seat, her breathing shallow and swift. She closed her eyes and concentrated on calming down. "Gruenewald Industries," she replied, her voice subdued. "Take the freeway."

SEVEN
TUBAL'S TUNNELS

THE REALM OF NOD, 2012

Jarom sat and shivered in the darkness, wrapping his arms around his thin robe for warmth. His first day on the job was turning out horribly, and he could not figure out what he had done wrong. Every time he thought about it, he couldn't help blaming Xandir for leaving him in the dust, but then again, how could Xandir have known it would all turn out so badly? Very few full-grown angels took cherubs very seriously, and he had expected that sort of behavior from his new master.

Jarom had been snatched out of the air and knocked unconscious. He'd woken in a dark cell full of chilly dripping water. Though he couldn't see much, he imagined rows of jagged stalactites and stalagmites jutting from the ceiling and ground like rows of teeth ready to tear him to pieces at the slightest provocation. He found himself longing for the light and sweet smell of the Elysian Fields, where he had worked so many centuries with his family. His recent transfer to Earth had made little sense to him in the first place, and now that he was doomed to rot in a dreary cave, it made even less sense.

He found himself asking the question that he had sworn to himself he would never ask: Why? His father had constantly reminded him that everything that happened, even the unpleasant things, were for the best. Granted, in the Heavenly Realms there had not been a great deal of problems or conflict, but there had still been things he had found unpleasant.

Even when he had witnessed terrible things happen to others, he had accepted his father's admonition. He remembered watching the earth flood in the time of Noah. At first, he thought what a terrible thing it was that all those people had to die. As he stood there weeping, his father took him aside and explained, "So, do you think that everyone should have a chance to make good choices and make it to Heaven?"

"Of course!" Jarom replied. "That is the idea, right?"

"Then this is a sad but necessary step. You see, almost everyone on the earth has become wicked, and that means that most of the children being born will be brought up by families who will not teach them what they need to know. By flooding the earth, civilization will get a fresh start, and many more people will have the chance to learn what they need to know while they are still alive."

Jarom nodded, but the frown remained on his face. "Yes, that makes sense. But it still hurts."

His father placed a large hand on his shoulders and looked directly in Jarom's eyes. "Jarom, sometimes we have to endure pain in order to grow."

His father's words had been a comfort then, but now, faced with incredible pain and loneliness, Jarom couldn't see a single opportunity to apply them. "What good could possibly come of this?" he muttered bitterly. "It will be a wonder if anyone ever finds me again."

Finally tiring of standing still, he decided to fly around to see if he could find anything to break the monotony. For some reason, he found flying much more difficult than usual. His first attempt brought him crashing to the rough floor with a groan. After several attempts, he found that he could manage it, though much more slowly than usual. Not that he wanted to fly around too quickly in this place.

He closed his eyes and flew out with outstretched hands. "Please let me find a way out of this," he muttered.

He repeated the mantra many times, all the while succeeding in securing a few hard knocks on the head. The minutes droned on in bleak monotony, but as he traveled farther along, he came to one realization: the cavern was getting lighter. In the hint of gray light that slowly filled the cavern, he could just barely make out the twisting rock formations around him and was able to better avoid any unexpected collisions. He found that the cavern branched off in many tunnels in separate directions. Each time he came to such an intersection, he paused for a moment until finally deciding which path felt right. Sometimes he would set down a path only to be suddenly overcome with a feeling of dread and confusion. He took this as a sign to retrace his steps and try again.

For hours, he did not see or hear another living thing, and so when he caught the sound of voices in the distance, he hid himself behind a rock formation. As the voices drew nearer, he saw that they also carried torches.

The men who approached him were enormous—much larger than he had ever seen before. Their faces were covered with coarse dark hair and they wore matching dark robes with hoods and long sleeves. The taller of the two carried a blazing red mark on his forehead, like the gash of an open wound that glowed artificially bright in the torchlight. As the man raised his arms, Jarom could see that they were covered with patterns and designs of all shapes and colors, but Jarom couldn't make sense of any of them.

The other massive man possessed similar features to the first but looked considerably younger. "It is true, Master. The angel has agreed to help us on the condition that we release the Italian woman and that pipsqueak of a cherub. It appears everything is going according to our schedule."

The Master nodded approvingly and stroked his black beard. "Excellent, Tubal. I trust that your scouts have pinpointed the location of Serche then? Has it sunk any lower?"

"We have the location, my Lord. The island is holding steady, but only because it is about as low as it can sink. It appears that the flames are slowly eroding the island itself, but it isn't in any imminent danger. How would you like to proceed?"

The Master closed his eyes for a moment and then suddenly flicked them open to reveal glowing pits of amber light. He rolled up one sleeve and studied the marks on his arms. Satisfied, he opened and closed his eyes once more, returning them to normal. "Keep track of him. Have someone follow him wherever possible. He may have agreed to help us, but you know his vacillating nature. He may demand further proof that we have the prisoner before he'll become cooperative. Move her to my chambers for now. She'll make a fine statue."

Tubal bowed and turned to leave, but he was held back by the firm grasp of his master. "One more thing," he muttered, almost inaudibly. "I'm afraid Dusteater might require your assistance. His subtlety has grown weak as of late."

Tubal executed a writhing hand gesture and nodded. "It shall be done."

Jarom shivered as he watched the two enormous men part ways, the Master moving away from him, and the one called Tubal toward him. Jarom ducked farther behind the rock, barely daring to breathe as Tubal passed. As soon as he saw the back of the black-robed man, he was struck with an idea. With the stealth characteristic of his size, Jarom flitted through the tunnel, always staying just beyond the reach of the torchlight. He followed Tubal upward and, Jarom hoped, toward his chance of freedom.

He pondered the strange conversation he had just overheard as he followed his target. He couldn't imagine any angel helping this awful group, whoever they were, but he feared the worst. Hoping against hope that it wasn't his new master they had been talking about, he kept his eyes on Tubal, wondering if they would ever leave this musty cave.

The passage came to a dead end, and Tubal halted. Unprepared for the sudden change, Jarom stumbled for the first time, crashing into a pillar of rock and dislodging a handful of stones, which clattered to the ground. Tubal whirled around, his dark eyes wide with surprise and anger.

"Who's there?" he barked. "Show yourself, or I'll find you and tear you limb from limb!"

To punctuate his last statement, he withdrew an impossibly long, glimmering sword from within his robes. The air hummed around the blade as though an electric current were coursing through it, and Jarom saw that both of its silvery sides were perfectly sharp.

Jarom held his breath, not daring even to blink, *Too bad*, he thought, *I was just starting to believe I was going to get out of this alive.*

Jarom mulled quickly over in his mind whether or not it would be futile to attempt an escape. The towering figure clamored loudly toward his hiding spot, his obviously keen senses instinctively sensing the intruder. Jarom clamped his eyes shut and pictured his father's face. He had not wanted it to come to this, but it seemed he had no choice.

He reached back into the folds of his cloak and retrieved the item that was the defense of all cherubs. The weaponed remained invisible until he drew it, so his captors had not known to take it from him. Though his fingers trembled, he nocked an arrow on his miniature bow and took aim at his assailant.

He had selected a slumber arrow from his assortment, which included everything from the Cupid-style amorous arrows to the swift Artemis arrows, named after the famous angelic sharp shooter. This one might not take down such a formidable opponent, but it would certainly slow him down, maybe giving Jarom time to escape.

Nervous, he squinted, waiting patiently for a workable shot. He didn't have to wait long. In moments, the light from the man's silver sword illuminated the passage all around them both, leaving Jarom feeling naked. For an instant, the man's back was to the cherub, who took aim and sent the dart flying.

The cherub winced as the dart whizzed forward and planted itself in the deep folds of Tubal's robe instead of his momentarily exposed neck. The burly man whirled around and lashed out in Jarom's direction. Jarom bolted out from his cover just in time, narrowly missing being cleaved in half by the blow.

Darting like a hornet, he fumbled in his pouch for another round. The silver sword flicked through the air, sending white sparks dancing in every direction. The rocks around them crumbled into nothing as the sword split through them, mingling their choking dust with the blinding flurry of sparks. Working as fast as his tiny fingers would allow, Jarom flung arrows at the Giant but to no avail. His thick cloak shielded him from most of the assaults, and even when the darts struck skin, they barely left a mark on the calloused surface.

Despite Tubal's expert swordsmanship, he couldn't keep up with the cherub's erratic flight. As the skirmish wore on, however, Tubal's frustration peaked, and Jarom began to tire. His reflexes lagged as he retreated farther into the tunnel, his opponent keeping pace with superhuman endurance. Jarom panicked as he reached back and realized that his supply of arrows was exhausted. He had even used the amorous ones, figuring that at least they would help to stop the fighting.

Guess I'm going to have to do this the David and Goliath way.

However, as he swooped low to pick up a sharp-edged stone, the Giant's sword changed direction and sent him sprawling back. Though the blade did not make contact, the Giant followed through with his massive arm and slammed his elbow directly into the cherub's stomach. Jarom flew back like one of his arrows, hurtling into a jagged stone wall with crushing force.

Jarom opened his eyes a slit, his entire body writhing with pain. It was moments like this that he was grateful that he wasn't exactly mortal, but even so, he cursed the provision that he was still subject to pain and injury. He didn't want to find out what would happen should Tubal's sinister silver blade find its target.

As he looked up with blurry vision, Jarom became aware of two things. The first, as he had expected, was the hulking figure of Tubal approaching, giving himself plenty of time to gloat over his victory. The second, however, he had not expected in the least. A flawless, dark stone statue of a woman kneeling in prayer loomed over him, its dimensions accurate for an actual person. It was one of the most detailed statues Jarom had ever seen, from the folds of her simple dress to her cascading hair and deeply sorrowful eyes.

Jarom nodded in resignation. It seemed to him that the statue had probably been an actual person at one time. And though he believed he would soon meet a similar fate, his only regret was that such a beautiful piece of art should be confined to such an obscure place.

The cherub snapped from his reverie to find Tubal towering over him. "Who are you?" he barked. "One chance—speak now!"

Jarom's voice caught in his throat as he attempted to croak out an answer. "Jarom, from Elysia. Apprentice angel."

Tubal considered the answer for a moment and swung his sword around. "Well, Jarom, you must be that runt we're holding over Xandir. Technically, I have orders not to harm you. But I don't see how I can let you live, not now that you've seen the woman. Perhaps I can make your death look like an accident."

Jarom winced as he prepared to be slashed in two, but as he waited, he noticed something else—a beautiful strain of music that sounded like it was being plucked from a small harp. The music trickled through the air like a bubbling spring bouncing off smooth stones. It enchanted Jarom's senses so that he could think of nothing else, not even his impending doom. To his astonishment, the music appeared to have a similar effect on his opponent. Slowly, Tubal lowered his sword, sank first to his knees, and then to his back, and fell promptly asleep.

When Jarom awoke, he found himself staring into another hairy face. This person looked very much like Tubal but appeared more refined and well-groomed. Stunning blue eyes peered out from deeply set sockets. Those eyes seemed to observe every detail of all they surveyed. Like Tubal, this man wore a dark robe, but instead of a sword, this man brandished a harp molded out of gold and inlaid with tiny gemstones of various colors. The strings themselves shone brightly as tiny specks of light danced up and down their surface.

Seeing that Jarom was awake, the other man spoke in the most melodious voice Jarom had ever heard. "Good day to you, little cherub. I am Jubal, and I must apologize for the rash actions of my brother. He is prone to such outbursts by nature, but that's no excuse. I trust you slept well?"

Jarom rubbed his eyes and sat up, realizing that he did feel pleasantly refreshed. "Yes, very well indeed. I don't remember the last time I slept so soundly."

Jarom surveyed his surroundings and found that they still appeared to be underground, though in a much different setting. This cavern glowed with a reddish light, and the air pulsed with wave after wave of intense heat. He watched the cavern walls move quickly past him, and he realized that he was standing on the gray stone deck of a ship. Nervously, he took a few steps toward the side of the deck and, to his horror and fascination, saw that the vessel sailed atop a roiling river of molten lava. He glanced up. Instead of sails, an enormous gray smokestack spewed great clouds of steam into the surrounding space.

"It's really an ingenious craft," said Jubal. "The entire ship conducts heat from the lava, which evaporates the water in the holding tanks, which turns the pistons, and then it condenses again to fill the tanks. It's a perfect vehicle for our kind, though I doubt that any mortal could set foot on it."

Jarom, impressed as he was at the ship's engineering, wasn't so sure that he felt privileged to be a passenger. "If you don't mind my asking," managed Jarom, "where exactly are we going? What are you going to do with me?"

Jubal laughed harmoniously and fixed his gaze on Jarom, who could feel the subtle hypnotism in his stare. "You will see soon enough. I could tell you, but that's not what our Master wants. For now, if I were you, I would enjoy the ride and do what you can to keep away from Tubal. You're small enough without being split in half by his sword."

Jarom gulped as he remembered his close encounter with that particular sword. He was happy to be alive, no matter how strange his circumstances. Satisfied for now, he slunk back and tried to stay out of the way. Eventually he would try to find out what was going on, but for once in his young life, he was in no particular hurry.

EIGHT
UNDERGROUND ECHOES

THE REALM OF NOD, 2012

"Okay, I've agreed to your plan," said Xandir. "Now where's the cherub? I can't exactly head back without him. They'll start asking awkward questions, which I'm sure we'd both like to avoid."

Ganosh nodded. "I suppose it is the least we can do as a gesture of good faith. He clapped his meaty hands, and again the attendant appeared. "Fetch the cherub," commanded the Giant, "and be quick about it."

They waited there in silence, and Xandir felt his hands grow warm. For several minutes, he tried to ignore the growing heat. But it soon became unbearable, and he snuck a glance at his hand. The instructions were all too familiar. Return and report.

Xandir gritted his teeth, knowing that any delay would cost him a tongue-lashing at best. However, returning without his companion would surely prompt a much harsher response. He needed a distraction.

"How do I contact you? Surely there are other things that we will need to discuss."

Ganosh nodded and approached. He stretched out one meaty finger and placed it behind Xandir's ear. A momentary chill spread where he touched, and Xandir could feel the lines of a Communication Mark like the ones on his hands, tracing themselves onto his skin.

The Giant stepped back. "That should be an inconspicuous

spot. Simply touch the Mark, and your message will be relayed to us. When you feel it grow cold, you can touch it again, and our message will be relayed back to you."

"I'm assuming that you have a timetable for this little operation?"

Ganosh nodded gravely and rubbed his hands together. "Yes, but for your sake, just try go get things done as soon as possible. It's the most we can expect from such a delicate operation."

The attendant returned, his gray face turning pale, his features strained. He obviously did not have the prisoner with him.

"Speak up!" roared Ganosh. "Out with it! Where is the cherub?"

The attendant averted his gaze. "He's gone, sir. Nowhere to be found."

Ganosh flung an enormous fist into the ground, creating a huge depression. "What do you mean? Didn't Jubal lull him to sleep with his harp as instructed? How could he be gone?"

The attendant took another step back, cowering in the Giant's presence, apparently not too keen to stand in range of his fists. "I'm not sure if Jubal got to him in time, sir. He must still be in the labyrinth somewhere. I can start a search party if you—"

Another impact from Ganosh's fist sent the attendant sprawling to the ground. The Giant paced back and forth. "Of course, you imbecile! Why are you still here? Go, go!"

Xandir looked on disapprovingly. "Looks like we're off to a great start with your end of the bargain. I'm starting to think you don't even have the cherub or the girl."

For once Ganosh looked short on words. "We do, I swear it! I can prove it!"

Xandir narrowed his eyes. "I'm through with waiting around. I'll go find him myself."

Xandir unsheathed his ebony sword and trained it on the Giant. Ganosh dropped to his knees, writhing in pain. Xandir unfurled his wings and soared into the acrid air. Before Ganosh could come to his senses, Xandir propelled himself toward the attendant and snatched him up with both hands. With another beat of his wings, he disappeared from the room.

He held the struggling attendant. "Tell me where to find this labyrinth."

At first, the terrified attendant said nothing and struggled harder against the grip of his captor. "Tell me what I want to know," he soothed, "and I will set you free from their service. I can take you to a much better place."

The attendant stopped struggling. Finally, he stopped his struggles and spoke in a timid voice. "Many years have I served the Fellowship of Nod. I do not know if I would be a fitting servant for the Kingdom of Heaven."

"Don't worry. They are much more forgiving than any you would find here. Believe me, they have definitely gone over the prerequisite seventy times seven with me."

Xandir tried to keep his voice calm, but the mention of the name of Nod chilled him to the center. He tried to shove the implications aside with only limited success.

The attendant hesitantly extended a finger. "That way, sir. All the way down."

The attendant stayed with Xandir, mostly out of the desire to save his own skin. They trudged on in silence for about an hour as he led Xandir through the twisting caverns toward their unnamed destination.

Finally, Xandir's curiosity got the best of him. "Do you have a name?"

The attendant paused momentarily, scratching his head in thought. "Yes," he replied. "But names are not often used here. You may call me Philio, if you like."

Xandir pondered this a moment before continuing. "How did you end up working for this rabble? I've heard your people are formidable warriors."

Philio sighed and did not answer for a while. Xandir allowed him his distance.

"We *were* a race of formidable warriors, if anyone can remember back that far. For the most part, we lived under the earth and left everything else alone that stayed out of our way. But then we were betrayed. Our own king sold the secret of our vulnerability in return for the promise of eternal life. But even this promise was hollow. While the Giants can extend life, they cannot do so indefinitely."

"Really?" asked Xandir. "Why is that? Couldn't you just keep drinking from the spring?"

Philio shook his head. "You could, but it's not that simple. The power of the tree does not come out of nothing. It must be fed."

Xandir raised his eyebrows, considering the ominous meaning of Philio's words. "I really hope that doesn't mean what I think it does."

Philio kept walking. "Life cannot be created out of nothing. It must be transferred from one being to another. They must feed living beings to the tree to give it the life necessary to infuse the water around it with its special properties. All sources of life are not equally useful either. Those who lived corrupt lives contribute only little to the tree's power, while the pure and saintly contribute a great deal." He remained silent for a moment before continuing. "So you see, the process would be difficult to prolong indefinitely."

Xandir's face darkened as the words sunk in. This was sinister to the highest degree. It was one thing to live forever but quite another to do so at someone else's expense. "I'm not sure I want to know too much, but how have they accomplished this? I can't imagine that it only takes a few pour souls to make it happen."

Philio raised his head as if to answer but fell silent as a faint sound echoed through the caverns. They both stopped and craned their ears to listen. The sound drifted in from the distance, the harsh scraping of metal against stone moving in their direction. Xandir dropped his hands to the hilt of his swords. "Something I should know about?"

Philio nodded, his expression stern, and whispered two words. "Cave Sentinels."

Xandir rolled his eyes and slunk deeper into the shadows, pulling the Achillian with him. Squinting into the darkness, he eased his swords out with barely more noise than a puff of smoke wafting into the sky.

He lay in wait like a hunter ready to pounce, the scraping

sounds growing closer as the Cave Sentinels closed in on their position. Finally the gleam of metal flashed in the faint torchlight, and the first of the great lumbering things came into view.

The Cave Sentinel appeared as a mountain of metal, constructed in a vaguely human shape. Its armored skin was a patchwork of jagged pieces of metal that stuck out in every direction. It lumbered along on four ungainly limbs with a lopsided gait, causing its many pieces to shift and grate against one other and its surroundings. The resulting racket was terrifying. In the area of the head, a makeshift face had been fashioned with a gaping black gash of a mouth and nose and two lopsided scarlike eyes, which glowed faintly in a different color with each step.

Xandir tensed at the first one, and then an entire patrol of eight such creatures appeared and halted, pinning angel and Achillian in from all sides. As soon as they had found their positions, the largest one spoke in a garbled, grating speech.

The patrol each lifted a limb in unison with their leader and held them unflinching in the air. Xandir and Philio remained still, unsure of what was to follow, but ready to act at any second. With a sudden staccato burst from the leader, all of the metal limbs came crashing down like a chorus of sledgehammers. The cavern rocked as the impact echoed through it, sending showers of jagged rocks raining down.

Xandir leapt into action, springing with his outstretched swords at the nearest foe. His dark sword met the nearest sentinel, sending a volley of shrapnel and sparks whizzing through the air among the falling rocks. He lashed out repeatedly and scored several more direct hits before the creature responded. The Sentinel swung its limbs in a whirlwind of motion, striking Xandir with crushing force. He twirled in the air and swung his light sword, striking it deep into a column of rock and absorbing most of the impact. In an instant, he pivoted about and used the column as a springboard to catapult himself back into the action. He shot like a missile back toward his target, his light sword ready for another blow.

The sentinel poised again to strike but stumbled as Xandir stopped several yards in front of his target. Xandir flourished his light sword in the air, and the creature in front of him groaned as each of its metal limbs fell away from its body. For a split second, Xandir caught the faintest glance of a human face peering out from the darkness of the creature's head. It was a man's face, his features strained and his deep green eyes wracked with pain.

He flourished the sword again and ignored the rain of rubble that continued to fall around him. Entire sections of the creature's body sloughed off like layers of a croissant, and once again a face appeared in the space in the creature's head. This time it was a woman's face, whose piercing blue eyes shone like headlights in the darkness, her mouth fixed in a soundless scream.

With a final flurry of his sword, the entire creature came apart, disintegrating in a contained burst of flame. Xandir caught a glimpse of a whole group of ghostly figures who leapt from the wreckage and disappeared from sight.

Before he had time to ponder the strange scene, a speeding projectile from the darkness alerted him to his next attacker. He bounded toward the attack, just as two more objects whizzed by his head. His bold advance stopped, however, as another strange sight met his eyes.

Philio was locked in combat with one of the sentinels, having produced a short, macelike weapon from his belt. He hacked away at the creature's resilient skin, and though he fought fiercely, it was clear that he was gravely wounded and would soon give in.

Xandir looked on, and the creature landed a direct blow to Philo's chest, sending the Achillian splaying to the ground. The creature loomed over him in an instant, but instead of striking again with its powerful appendages, it brought its head close to Philio's and emitted a high-pitched whine. In an instant, Philio's features blurred together as if they were melting, and his entire body disappeared through the gaping hole in the creature's face.

The momentary distraction was all the creatures needed. With a renewed effort, they circled Xandir and again pounded the ground in concert. The cavern shook, and chips of stone fell faster and faster from the ceiling. With a mighty roar, the roof collapsed, burying Xandir deep under a mountain of stone.

As Xandir's world faded to black, he wondered sadly whether he or Philio had been dealt the bleaker fate.

NINE
BURNING SECRETS

Judy and Eden rode in silence as they proceeded down the freeway toward Daren's former workplace. The company was located in a remote section of the city because it entailed working with potential biohazards.

They drove up to the gate and received a visitor's pass from the security guard on duty after announcing whom they wished to visit. They received directions from the guard and located a parking spot.

As they approached the building, Eden finally broke the awkward silence that had persisted between them since leaving the restaurant. "Judy, I'm sorry I talked to you so harshly about going home. It's been a bad week, but that's really no excuse. I just feel like I can't control myself sometimes. I'm so embarrassed."

Judy smiled warmly, placing a comforting hand on Eden's shoulder. "Think nothing of it. I'm only sorry I thought to question you in the first place. I've had you as a student long enough to know that trying to change your mind is about as futile as trying to catch smoke in a birdcage."

Eden managed a feeble smile. A little humor was very welcome.

"Okay, then," Judy continued. "We're here. What are we going to say to this guy?"

Eden bit her lip, pondering what she could say. She had been so distracted that she hadn't yet formed any sort of plan. Still, her pace didn't slacken as she approached the front entrance. "We'll just have to see if he's noticed as many strange things as we have. From the sound of his phone message, Daren wasn't exactly acting normal at work either."

Judy held open the door to let Eden step in. "Fair enough."

They made their way through the maze of corridors and stairwells until they located a discreet office located on the third floor. The nameplate on the door announced that it was the office of Michael Westover, the man they sought.

She rapped on the door a few times and was answered quickly. The door opened to reveal a blond man in his thirties wearing a white lab coat over a dress shirt and blue tie. He surveyed the two women without showing any recognition.

"Uh, can I help you?" he asked.

"I surely hope so," replied Eden. "I'm Eden Fortuna, Daren's wife, and this is my friend Judy. I left a message on your cell phone. We just wanted to ask you a few questions."

Though he looked puzzled, Michael opened the door wider and motioned them in. "Of course," he said. "I'm guessing this is about Daren. What's he up to now? We miss him around here."

The scientist showed them to two plush red armchairs that sat in front of his desk. The office was furnished with dozens of leather-bound books interspersed with framed artwork that would have looked at home in a modern art museum.

Michael took his place behind his polished wooden desk and turned in his swivel chair to face them. "So," he began cordially, "what is it you want to know?"

Judy remained silent, content to let Eden do the talking.

"Well," said Eden, "we're just trying to piece together my husband's strange behavior. I found his cell phone and heard the message that you left him about not showing up to work. How long had that been going on?"

Michael pursed his brow, his eyebrows meeting in the center of his forehead. "Only a few weeks. As far as I can remember, he never missed a day of work before that. Our supervisor always commended him for being punctual and efficient, but somehow it all just went out the window one day."

He sighed, his eyes allowing a bit of sadness to bleed through. "We worked together quite a bit, Daren and I. He was always so upbeat. But about the time he started missing work and coming in late, I noticed that he just wasn't his normal cheery self. When he did show up, he would hardly say a word to anyone, except to take a call on his cell phone once in a while."

Eden's eyebrows shot up at the mention of the cell phone. "Did you ever hear who he was talking to? The rest of the messages on his phone are very strange."

Dr. Westover shook his head. "No, unfortunately not. He would always leave the room, and he spoke very quietly." Michael's eyes glazed over and then sparkled in recollection. "Actually, there was one time I did overhear something. I was working late one night, and I found him wandering around the halls with his phone plastered to his ear. He didn't know I was watching, but strangely, I couldn't understand what he was saying. He never told me he spoke another language. Does he?"

Eden shook her head. This conversation was confirming all of her suspicions. "If he does, he never let me know about it. Did you notice anything else strange about his behavior that might help us figure out what's going on?"

"Well," he continued, "surely you noticed the burn marks." Dr. Westover retrieved a set of spectacles from his breast pocket and adjusted them nervously atop his nose.

"No," admitted Eden, her stomach once again turning queasy. "What do you mean?"

Dr. Westover cocked an eyebrow. "You must have noticed something. They were all over his hands and arms—even his lab coat was singed. I tried to ask him where they came from, but he wouldn't tell me."

Eden closed her eyes and tried to think back over the past few weeks. Try as she might, she couldn't remember anything even remotely like burn marks.

"This may sound crazy," admitted Eden, "but I don't recall seeing that at all. I will agree, though, that he hasn't been himself at all lately, and now I don't even know where he is. He contacted me again today and told me not to look for him."

Dr. Westover's face turned grave. He walked to the windows, drew the blinds, and then went to the door to make sure that it was locked.

Standing in front of his desk, he spoke barely above a whisper. "I wouldn't mention this if I didn't think it mattered, but I think you have the right to know. Before a few weeks ago, we were working on pretty routine stuff—pain medications and such—but then, just a few weeks ago, he was assigned to a new project without me. I thought that was a bit strange, seeing as we have always worked in tandem before, but I was never afforded an explanation. He would split his time between the labs here and the classified high-security labs underground. I'm not really supposed to know anything, but I've heard rumors that they are working on something really nasty down there . . . a sort of thing that could cause an epidemic if it fell into the wrong hands. So you can see why it would be alarming if he's missing."

Both Eden and Judy leaned in closer, their eyes wide. "Do you think there's a chance that anything happened to him? Could he have been infected with something down there?" asked Eden.

Dr. Westover shook his head. "I don't think so. Most of the stuff down there is fatal. If he had been infected, it wouldn't take weeks to kill him. To tell you the truth, I'm really as much in the dark on this one as you are. Who knows what experimental pathogens are capable of?"

Eden bit her lip as an idea pushed its way to the forefront of her mind. "What about his office? Have they cleaned out everything yet?"

Dr. Westover shrugged, his eyes once again darting to the window and the door. "I'm not sure, though I don't think I've seen anyone else move into that office. I'm sure it would be worth trying to see if he left anything there. Come on, I'll let you in." They all rose and made for the door. Dr. Westover opened it just a bit and glanced nonchalantly out into the hallway just in case.

Seeing that the coast was clear, he motioned for the two women to follow him but to keep their voices down. "Maybe I'm just paranoid, but I don't want to attract any attention."

Eden and Judy entered the hallway, trying to act inconspicuous as they followed their guide just down the corridor and around the corner. They reached another door much like the one they had just left, with the name of "Daren Fortuna" printed on the plaque. Dr. Westover retrieved a key card from his wallet and inserted it into the slot next to the door's handle. A light blinked red by the card slot, and the door remained locked. He repeated the process several times with similar results and mounting frustration.

"I don't understand!" he groaned. "This card should grant me access to every room on this floor. Why would they change my security clearance?"

On a hunch, he tried the neighboring doors and found that his card opened them as normal. He shook his head in disgust. "I've never been much for conspiracy theories, but I'm running out of explanations here."

Judy chimed in for the first time since the meeting had begun. "Is there any other way into that room? From the surrounding rooms perhaps?"

Dr. Westover fidgeted with his glasses for a moment before answering. "It would be a tight fit. Good thing the two of you don't look as fond of junk food as I am."

He knocked lightly on a neighboring door, and, when no one answered, he used his key on the door. The door creaked open, and he slipped quickly into the darkened office. After a few tense seconds of silence, a whisper came through the cracks. "Follow me into the room. No one is supposed to be here right now, so I can't risk turning on the main light."

The two women complied and closed the door behind them. The darkness, however, lasted only a few moments as Dr. Westover turned on a dim desk lamp. He then made his way to the wall that the office shared with Daren's and removed a grating from a ventilation duct near the ceiling.

Eden cast a disparaging glance at the opening. "Wow, I appreciate the compliment, but I don't know if I'm that thin, especially after the lunch we just had."

Judy walked over to the hole and sized it up. "Looks like I'll have to go in alone," she announced, smoothing her slightly ruffled hair. "Get me something to stand on, quickly."

Michael moved an office chair under the opening while Eden collected a stack of sturdy books from the bookshelf to make up the difference. Together, the stack gave Judy just enough height to stretch up and reach the edge of the vent. With a little help from Eden, she succeeded in lunging herself upward and into the space.

"Hm," she grumbled. "I never thought I would be so glad to be so small. It's not often it's such an advantage."

She disappeared into the darkness of the narrow passageway. A few moments later, there was a clang and a dull thud as first the other grate and then the professor hit the ground on the other side. Dr. Westover and Eden held their breaths as they listened to the professor rummaging about the office. The minutes passed slowly, and the noise from Daren's office died down completely. Something had gone wrong. At last, Eden could take the suspense no longer and climbed up on the chair to speak through the grate.

"Judy," she called as loudly as she dared. "What do you see? Did you find anything interesting?"

For several moments, she was met with only silence. She called again, with no result. Panic swelled up in her, and all at once, she felt very dizzy. The room spun around her, and she flailed out her arms in a vain attempt to regain sure footing. Then, in an awful instant, she completely lost her balance and fell from the chair, landing soundly on her back.

Dr. Westover immediately crouched down to her side, his face a picture of deep concern. "Are you all right? I was watching the hallway and didn't see you fall. What happened?"

Eden closed her eyes and concentrated on how she felt. Her stomach threatened to be sick at any moment, but otherwise, she didn't feel anything seriously wrong.

"I don't know what happened. One moment I was fine, and the next moment, I was about to faint. I— My stomach is doing cartwheels."

Dr. Westover placed a hand on her forehead, his concern etching deep creases on his own brow. "You're burning up! We need to get you to a doctor."

Eden nodded groggily, thinking that she could use a good day or two—possibly a week—in bed. "Judy, we have to find out if she's okay."

Michael nodded and rose to his feet, walking over to the scattered pile of books around the chair. But before he could hoist himself up on the chair, Judy's head popped out of the hole, her glasses askew. "Help me out," she whispered tensely. "We should get out of here. I hate to admit it twice in one day, but I think I'm in over my head on this one."

Judy first handed down several manila folders before Dr. Westover helped her out of the ceiling. She rushed over to Eden at once. "What happened?"

Dr. Westover balked a bit at Judy's sudden intensity but quickly composed himself.

"She fainted," he explained. "She was standing up on the chair trying to talk to you, and she just fell. She's burning up. We should get her to the hospital as soon as we can."

Judy slid her arms under Eden's and lifted her with unexpected strength, leaving the manila folders on the floor. Her small frame groaning under the strain, she shot a knowing glance at Dr. Westover. "Grab those folders, or this will all be for nothing."

Michael shuffled over to the folders, stooped down, and paused, frozen suddenly in place. He stood in an unnaturally stiff position, as if rigor mortis had set in mid stride.

Judy stared, unsure of what to think. "Dr. Westover," she whispered desperately. "What's wrong?"

He answered her a moment later as he rose slowly to his feet, his arms stretched out like a scarecrow. In one hand, he held the manila files, and from the other hand dangled a sleek, red and black snake, its fangs sunk deep into the flesh of his hands. As Judy gazed on in horror, a black spot spread from the site of the bite through his hand and toward his arm. The folders dropped from his hands, and Judy made a move toward them.

"Stop right there."

Judy disobeyed, snatching the folders with one hand and then backing away immediately.

The voice that came from Dr. Westover's mouth was still his own, but it had been twisted in a cruel mockery of his natural voice. It sounded as if someone had thrown a bag of nails down his throat, which had mutilated it beyond repair.

Judy stood frozen with fear as Dr. Westover turned and fixed his vacant gaze on her. She took a slow deep breath, knowing that the next few moments might be crucial not only to her, but to everyone she had ever known.

TEN

A CARBONATED SHOWER

NEW YORK STATE, 2012

Crushing fear kept Judy rooted to the spot for only a moment. Almost immediately, she pushed it aside and carefully set Eden down next to her. "What do you want?"

The face that stared back at her appeared only vaguely human. The flames had traveled up his arms and surrounded his head, though they did not seem to harm him beyond turning his skin dark. The same grating voice replied to her, sparks spitting from his mouth as he talked.

"Give me that which you took from the office, and I will turn it to ashes. It wasn't meant for you to see."

Judy clutched the folders tighter to her chest with one arm, and fished around on the bookshelf with the other. "And if I refuse? I think it's a bit too late. I've already read each folder, and my memory's sharp as my rapier wit."

"Then you will share this man's unfortunate fate."

As he spoke, the fiery snake on his arm squirmed and writhed without ever releasing its grip on the man's arm. Before her eyes, the snake split into two serpents, the second one identical to the first. It dropped to the floor with a hiss and slithered toward her.

Judy reached behind her, grasped a heavy medical journal, and heaved her arm forward with all her might. The book hurtled toward the snake on the ground. With surprising speed, it dodged the blow, and the book fell open to the ground.

75

Adrenaline coursing through her, Judy whipped out an entire shelf of books in a matter of seconds, aiming some at the approaching snake, and some at the one hanging off Dr. Westover's arm. The books that hit the man burst into flame, and had little effect. She managed, however, to land a few blows on the advancing snake, deterring it temporarily. At last, she dropped a Webster's Comprehensive Dictionary right on its tail, and the creature retreated under the desk.

Judy seized the momentary reprieve and slid the documents under one arm. She hoisted Eden out of the way and placed herself between her former student and the man on fire. She hunched down low to the ground, brandishing a small bronze statuette and waiting for the snake to show itself.

Breathing heavily, she started across the office, her eyes watching for any sign of movement. Her nose wrinkled as the scent of burning wood assaulted her nostrils. She swiveled around to find the source, and at that very moment, the snake leapt from its concealment among the shelves.

Judy rolled out of the way, just missing the snake's fangs by inches. The snake continued its decent, and the fangs found a mark: Eden's right shoe, a navy blue high heel. Judy gasped as the shoe burst into flames. Thinking little of her own safety, she plucked the shoe from Eden's foot and flung it across the room.

As if guided by an invisible hand, the flaming shoe flew true. The protruding heel clipped the hanging snake and snatched it from the man's arm. The flames that had engulfed his body immediately fizzled out, and Dr. Westover fell lifeless to the floor. A thin, acrid smoke hung in the air, turning Judy's stomach over with nausea.

She let out her breath in a rush, but her relief was short lived. The scarlet snake hit the ground and immediately split again in two, bringing her foes to three. She glanced behind her and saw that her supply of weapons had severely diminished. Clearly another strategy was in order.

Her enemies wasted no time in regrouping. The three snakes first converged, each flaring brighter as it came in contact with the others, before branching out again. Each came at their quarry from a different angle. They left trails of flame in their wakes, and the books strewn over the floor quickly flared up beneath them.

Judy struggled with the cabinets around her, searching for more options. She wondered why a smoke detector or fire alarm hadn't been triggered. The ceiling was now obscured by smoke, so she knew that they had only minutes before being overwhelmed. The first two cabinets refused to budge, even under a firm tug, and she fell back when the third one gave way without a struggle.

As she fell, the snakes found their moment to strike. They leapt through the air from separate directions, streaking across the room like flaming arrows from a crossbow. Judy rolled and cried out as a stinging sensation scalded her skin and burnt streaks into her clothing. Anticipating another attack, she rolled again, swiftly bringing herself back toward the open cabinet. In another quick motion, she thrust her hand inside and was greeted by a truly strange and unexpected sensation: cold.

Judy turned just in time to see a serpent flying toward her unprotected face. Her reflexes kicked in, and she shot down as quickly as she could manage, slamming her face into a smoldering pile of debris. The snake flew just over her, but she felt the searing heat as it passed overhead.

Judy raised her head, and her vision blurred. Sweat poured down her brow, and a blanket of heat and smoke enveloped her. In the midst of the oppressive heat, it was only a moment until she realized what she was now clutching in her hand.

It was a can of ice-cold soda, retrieved from the well-disguised fridge when she had dodged the snake's last attack. With the serpents closing in, she knew there was only one thing that she could do. She shook the can with all her might, fumbled for the tab, and ripped the top off the can.

The resulting explosion had the desired effect. The refreshing liquid calmed the flames around her, and she felt the snakes rushing away from her, slithering to get out of the way of the cold mist.

Fumbling back the way she came, she thrust her hand back into the fridge and retrieved several more cans of soda. Now armed, she shook a can vigorously in each hand and sought out her attackers. She didn't have to wait long.

They stuck together, latching themselves to her clothes, burning them, and tearing with their fangs at her sleeve. In a moment of panic, she felt one of their searing fangs break through and plunge into her skin. Her head swam, her vision blurred even more, and she felt the tug of unconsciousness pulling her relentlessly down. With her last conscious thought, she raised a can above her head and pulled the tab.

ELEVEN

UNEARTHED

THE REALM OF NOD, 2012

Xandir didn't stir for many hours. The weight of the cave that had fallen on him would have snuffed the life out of a mortal. Even for Xandir, the painful weight was bad enough. With his arms pinned down so that he couldn't reach either of his swords, he was powerless, and the crushing silence and blackness all but devoured any hopes he had of escape.

Left with only his thoughts for company, his mind began to wander, and scenes from his drawn-out existence passed before him. *Funny*, he mused, *I thought this was only something that was supposed to happen to people before they die.*

He had often pondered death but knew only too well that it wasn't really an eternal sleep as so many people supposed. Though to him, it seemed that it would at least provide a respite from the servitude.

Too bad it's not really a possibility. There aren't many ways to kill an angel.

A particular scene from his life passed his mind, and he remembered what he was living for. He was still not sure whether the images were real or simply conjured up in his mind's eye, but the scenes played out as though he were watching himself from a distance.

He glimpsed a brilliant night sky, with a full moon smiling down on row after row of pleasant vineyards. At the head of the vineyards sat an impressive villa of light-colored stone. He saw himself flying through the sky, briefly eclipsing the moon before landing gently on the balcony of the villa. A robed figure was already waiting for him there, the moonlight creating a halo around her honey-colored hair.

Slowly he stepped forward and tenderly took her hand, but she lowered her gaze and couldn't meet his eyes. For a long moment, neither spoke.

"I'm afraid," she began, her voice choked with emotion, "that this is it, Xandir. You must not return."

She lifted her head slightly, and her tears gleamed like falling pearls in the moonlight.

"I was afraid you might say that," replied Xandir, his voice even. "But forgive me if I do not understand, nor agree. I can tell it's not really what you want."

She shook her head, her wavy locks tousled by an evening breeze. "No, of course it isn't, but it is how it must be. You know what they think you are, what they think I am, what that means."

Xandir raised an eyebrow in amusement. "One of their pagan gods? Who are they saying I am this week? Jupiter? Neptune?"

She met his gaze, desperation clear in her voice and eyes. "Xandir, this is serious! You know they can't explain your power! You and I know the truth, but we're the only ones! If they think I am your chosen acolyte, they will kill me because they think my sacrifice will win your favor! Is that what you want?"

"No!" he replied, his voice rising with emotion. "You know I don't want that! But you also know that I cannot simply turn my back on you forever! You must understand. For centuries and centuries, I have thought the world a cold and solitary place. I have seen more lonely sunrises and sunsets than you could ever imagine, and it wasn't until . . ." His voice trailed off, his entire demeanor softening. "It wasn't until I met you that I knew that I was wrong. If you tell me to go tonight, I will, but it will be a doom too horrible to describe. It's not always such a blessing to be immortal as your people might think, and death . . ." Xandir stopped in a mournful pause. "Death is not nearly as bad as you make it out to be."

For a long minute, they both said nothing, and their eyes rested on the endless field of swaying vines.

"Come with me," he pleaded, his voice no louder than a whisper. "Leave this all behind. It is so fleeting. What I can give you will be forever. Wouldn't you rather have forever?"

Finally, she collapsed into his arms, her tears flowing freely.

"I can't, Xandir! I just can't. Please don't force me to make this choice."

Xandir's face tightened in frustration, but before he could reply, a silhouette appeared in the lighted doorway behind them—a young boy, one that they both recognized. The boy's eyes grew wide, and he gasped, ready to sound the alarm. In another instant, Xandir had lunged forward, seized the boy, and clamped his hand over his open mouth.

"No!" she cried. "Don't hurt him!"

Xandir met her gaze, his eyes wells of sadness. "Do you really think I would? I wouldn't hurt a soul of your family. Though I'm not sure that your father would extend me the same courtesy."

He drew his fingers over the boy's eyes, and he fell asleep. Gently, he lowered the boy to the stones, taking special care not to harm him. His fears temporarily allayed, he turned back to the woman who stood only a few feet away.

"I'm only going to ask you one more time. What will you choose? Eternity or drudgery?"

He extended a hand, his fingers stretching longingly toward her. His face remained impassive, but she could feel the intensity of his stare. Slowly, she advanced on him and brought her hands out to meet his . . .

The scene grew blurry, and Xandir quickly became aware of his present state and another voice cutting through the sudden darkness around him.

"Off to a bit of a rough start, are we? That was foolish to try to run from us. You may have survived the cave-in, but I can't say the same for your little accomplice."

Xandir squirmed beneath the crushing load above him, willing the memories to return and the voice to leave. There could, however, be no mistaking the burning sensation behind his ears and no mistaking Ganosh's haughty voice filling his mind.

"Okay, you've got me, Ganosh," Xandir called out, his voice filled with annoyance, "and I'm sure you're going to have some ridiculous conditions for letting me out, or a great I-told-you-so sort of speech. Well, trim the fat and give it to me straight."

But silence prevailed for several moments, and when it was broken, Ganosh's voice had not lost any of its smugness.

"That's the problem with you Heavenly folk. You think you're always at the vantage point to look down on everyone else and assume the worst. I'm a Giant; I believe in actions and not so much in pretty words. Don't you remember that? That was the root of our whole problem in the first place, but I digress. I'll gladly release you from your predicament, but I do have just one condition." He paused for dramatic effect. Xandir was hardly amused. "You must not go looking for the cherub."

Xandir did not reply immediately. He wracked his mind, but try as he might, he couldn't understand why the Giant would make such a request. After all, the cherub was hardly a figure of consequence or power. He was neither useful nor a threat. However, he couldn't shake the suspicion that Ganosh had another side to the story, one he probably wasn't going to share with Xandir.

"Now, of all the things you could ask for, why would it be that? Seems like a strange request that you'd be so concerned over such a little angel."

"Our concerns are not yours," Ganosh replied. "I don't want to leave you under there, but I will for as long as it takes to change your mind. I can assure you, he is alive and well, but I do not want you to go looking for him. My Master had not made me privy to all of his plans before, and I assumed that we would keep him here. But other opportunities have arisen, and that is no longer the case. Make up whatever excuse you want to tell your nose-in-the-clouds superiors, but give me your binding word, and you'll be free."

Xandir tried to squirm, gauging whether there was any chance he would be able to free himself, even if it might take some time. But he couldn't move at all, and the prospect of rotting in the darkness for weeks or months on end did not exactly appeal to him. There had been times in his life when no large pressing matters weighed on his mind, and then he might have even welcomed the break from his usual hectic pace. But now, as he gazed into the darkness, all he could see was his love's face, as crushed and heartbroken as the day he had flown from her balcony.

"Done," he blurted. "I give you my binding word. May the curse be upon my own head should I deliberately break it."

Xandir knew such a vow was probably something he should have taken more seriously, though he could have hardly restrained the words on his tongue. The consequences would be truly dire if he should break it.

"A wise choice," mused Ganosh. "You're not as thick as you appear at first glance."

Xandir, who was readying a witty retort, was caught completely off guard as his world of darkness was replaced by one of light and motion. His body shot upward at amazing speed, hurtling through stone and earth until he burst out of the ground and into the blazing sun. The sheer, stark blueness of the sky nearly blinded him after so many hours in darkness. Stunned, he tried to take flight but only managed to hover for a few moments before crashing unceremoniously to the ground.

As he opened his eyes, he became aware of a familiar figure brooding over him.

"How," Xandir muttered, "did you find me so quickly?"

The High Seraph didn't answer right away, allowing Xandir to stew in his indignation. "I surely hope you completed your assignment, Xandir," he began. "Where have you been?"

Xandir struggled for adequate words to describe the day's experiences but could think of no suitable sentence to even start with. "Let's just say that I've been in over my head," he finally managed. "In more ways than I care to elaborate."

The answer didn't satisfy the High Seraph. "I have also noticed to my dismay that you are alone. Where, may I ask, is Jarom?"

The High Seraph fixed his gaze on Xandir, his eyes boring into him like focused lasers. Xandir decided that frank honesty was the best course in this situation, especially because higher angels were almost impossible to deceive. "He has been taken by the enemy," admitted Xandir, rising to his feet and squaring his shoulders. "I have received reliable information that he remains alive and unharmed, but I have made a covenant not to pursue him in exchange for my release. Not an ideal situation, I know, but given the circumstances, it was the only course of action."

The High Seraph's face remained stoic, though his eyes glazed over with sadness. When he spoke again, his voice betrayed more emotion than Xandir had expected. "I see. That is most unfortunate. I sincerely hope what you have accomplished is worth the price you paid." The High Seraph stared into the distance. "Perhaps you would like to supply the details, or have you covenanted not to disclose those either?"

Xandir paused. "The details are not important, but the information that I obtained is. It would appear that the Giants won't leave me alone after all. They are living in seclusion, and Absalom was kind enough to lead me right to them."

Xandir hoped that the shock of his announcement would draw him away from the fact that he had dodged the question. To his relief, it had the desired effect.

"That is an absurd fabrication! The Giants were completely destroyed. I would know! I myself was at the head of the force that took care of the last of them!"

Xandir felt his rage boiling as old memories surfaced. He clenched his jaw and continued through gritted teeth. "And how could you ever know for sure? Sure, Sodom and Gomorra were destroyed, and everyone thought, for the longest time, that there were no survivors. But just look at old Lot. He has descendants to this day!" Xandir took a step forward. "That is, unless, the Almighty told you of the Giants' destruction himself."

The High Seraph squirmed as he formulated an answer. "No, he did not, but with something of such great importance, I am confident that I would have been informed."

"Why should you assume that?" yelled Xandir. "How does the old adage go? 'God works in mysterious ways'? He may be omniscient, but that doesn't mean he will always just give us all the answers. Not even to you."

The High Seraph's face flushed, and the glow around his being flared up. The two of them had sparred verbally before, but rarely had Xandir gotten the best of him to any degree. The High Seraph raised himself to his full stature. "He knows everything! Why would he allow them to remain? After all the terrible things we had to endure to accomplish their annihilation in the first place? I cannot accept this!"

Xandir raised a questioning eyebrow. "Presumably, he knew that Eve would eat the apple, but he commanded her not to do it anyway. And why? I'm not one to say, but do you think there might have been a higher purpose to that? It seems like it was meant to happen, part of the plan and all. Couldn't this be the same?"

The High Seraph stood still, his face wrinkled in intense thought. When he spoke again, his voice was devoid of emotion. "So what would you suggest that we do? If things are as you say, measures need to be taken right away to counteract whatever dark plans they have set in motion. I will need to make a full report."

Xandir shook his head decisively. "I wouldn't do that just yet if I were you. It might not reflect too kindly on you if the word gets out that you botched the job you were supposed to have completed centuries ago. Besides, I have a plan—a way to clean this up before things get out of control."

The High Seraph did not look amused. "I cannot wait to hear what you have conjured up. Allow me to guess: you want to enlist the Yeti and the Loch Ness Monster to mount a surprise offensive on their stronghold."

Xandir laughed the comment off. "Come now. You know I know the truth about those two, though I'm only personally acquainted with one of them. Actually, despite your scorn, my plan is no less exciting. I need to be granted access to Serche."

The High Seraph looked as if Xandir had just asked him to pardon the Devil. "And just what do you know about Serche? No doubt Giants have woven quite the tale. Serche is not your affair. I would not let you go there in a million years, not until Hell itself freezes over."

Despite the scathing reproof, a smile crept across Xandir's

face. "Do you really mean that? I mean about Hell freezing over?"

The High Seraph's face registered first shock then annoyance. "Yes, of course I mean it! What sort of insolent question is that?"

Xandir shrugged, his grin rising with his shoulders. "I'm just saying, you did give me at least one condition. Granted, it's not a likely one, but it is possible. Just remember, I'll hold you to it."

The High Seraph made to rise to the air, his face fixed in a scowl. "Very well, Xandir, very well. If by some twist of fate Hell really does freeze over, I shall take you to Serche myself. But now I have more important matters to attend to. Jarom's family must be notified, and allow me to say, you should pray that they do not find you before I do."

Xandir gazed skyward as he watched the surly Seraph disappear from sight. When he was gone, a wry grin broke across Xandir's face, a wily idea forming in his mind. He raised his hand and bounded skyward, hurtling in the opposite direction.

TWELVE

UNEXPECTED COMPANY

THE MAGMA FLOW, 2012

Jarom had finally found a cruise that he didn't like. In his previous residence while working with his father, he had often ridden along on the massive celestial vessels used in transporting the precious Ambrosia and other commodities across the many parts of the Heavenly Realms. The thrill of the ever-expanding vistas and the exhilaration of cutting through the clouds at high speed had always been something to look forward to. However, as this ship trudged through the molten river, he felt for the first time that such a voyage might make him sick.

He tried to keep out of the way of the ship's strange crew, most of whom were the tunic-clad Achillians. There were also others who looked much more like humans, were it not for their enormous size. They were, on average, about one and a half times the size of a regular human, with pallid skin and dark, bushy hair and beards that wreathed their heads.

To his relief, none of them seemed to pay him any attention, though either Jubal or Tubal kept a constant eye on him. Jarom spent most of his time peering over the side, staring at the swirling fiery river under them and letting his mind wander. If he thought really hard, he could imagine the succulent taste of Ambrosia, which almost masked the awful stench of brimstone wafting from the magma below.

A loud screech suddenly awakened him from his stupor, and

his eyes popped open just in time to see a trio of dark shapes rising swiftly from the lava below. With a cry of his own, he fell unceremoniously back onto the deck and covered his face as the shapes swooped up and over the ship.

"Verdemons!" cried one of the crew, gesturing at the shapes. The rest of the crew responded immediately, the Giants drawing swords and daggers while the Achillians opted for small slings and bows.

Jarom rubbed his eyes and focused on the Verdemons soaring above them. They avoided the crew, seemingly bent on damaging the ship, tearing and ripping at it with jagged claws and horns. Their spindly bodies were covered with sharp objects, from the trio of horns on their heads, clawed hands and feet, and barb-covered skin to a tail tipped by a sinister, spiked bludgeon. Each dark creature also boasted a full complement of fangs crammed so tightly in their mouths that none of them could completely close them.

The nimble, winged creatures were nearly impossible to catch. The Giants lumbered about, and the majority of their attacks cut only through the superheated air. The original trio was soon joined by another, and then another, until most of the deck was covered with writhing creatures, tearing, biting, and rending at every turn.

Tubal, however, soon made clear that he was the exception to his lumbering comrades. His sword snapped and whipped through the air with supersonic agility, causing everything else to seem lifeless in comparison. Several of the demons quickly fell to its sting, their lives severed by the flashing blade.

Caught without a weapon, Jarom crawled toward the ship's cabin, his hands covering his head and his lips murmuring a desperate prayer. He couldn't begin to imagine who had sent the mysterious attackers, but he could see that they were chipping away the ship's defenses. Without its outer armor, the ship would surely catch fire, and they would all be lost to the fiery depths.

The one person who seemed unaffected by the turmoil was Jubal. He leaned against the cabin door and withdrew his miniature harp from the folds of his robes, which grew much larger in his hands. For several minutes, he muttered musically to himself, strumming his harp so lightly that it couldn't be heard over the din. Then, as if parting a mighty sea with a wave of his hand, he stepped out into the middle of the deck, unfazed by the weapons and claws whirling all around him, and began to sing.

He strummed the harp much louder now, so that it mingled with his voice and carried off the smooth walls of the cavern. Strangely, the song drowned out all the other sounds of the commotion, though the turmoil did not stop right away.

As the haunting, melancholy chords continued their progression, the Verdemons sank to the deck one by one, followed by the crew, until each and every living thing on the deck, with the exception of Jarom and Jubal, was sleeping soundly.

Jarom raised his head, almost unable to believe what he was seeing. Where a battlefield had been only moments before, now a dozen sleeping bodies lay breathing peacefully as if nothing had happened.

Jarom fixed his gaze on the singing man who had just gone silent, the last note drifting off like a pleasant aftertaste. The cherub rose to his feet, his hands trembling a bit from shock. Music was a regular part of life in the Heavenly realms, and he had spent countless hours mixing his own harp and voice in song. He had not been good enough for one of the official Heavenly Choirs, but he still managed to uplift the spirits of his family and friends. But Jubal's ability was unlike anything he had experienced.

"Why didn't I fall asleep?" he whispered, not daring to raise his voice high enough to wake the sleeping creatures. Jubal smiled broadly, obviously pleased with his handiwork. He replaced the harp in his robes.

"Because," Jubal replied, "you were not fighting. Mystic songs will affect their listeners differently depending on the song's intended effect. I have other songs that could bring you, or even the Archangel Michael himself to his knees. That song was meant to break up a battle, and thus it only works on those who are actually doing the fighting. I'd call what you were doing something more akin to cowering." The pleasant look on his face held fast. "But no matter. Given the circumstances, there wasn't really much that you could have done. Not to demons of this sort."

Jarom's ears perked up, and he dared venture a few steps closer toward Jubal, taking care not to step on any of the sleepers. He glanced down at the grotesque black creatures and shuddered. He'd had his suspicions, but now he knew for sure. He had actually seen demons for the first time in his existence.

"What did they want?" he asked with a quavering voice. "Why did they attack the ship?"

Jubal's smile dipped slightly. "Sadly, I'm a musician and not a politician. I would very much like to know that myself. The last I heard, they were our allies, and I'm not aware of any change. The Verdemons are tasked with guarding this channel, but they aren't known for being the brightest creatures. But be that as it may, this was an unprecedented attack."

They stood in silence, pondering the field of sleeping bodies. "What do we do with them?" Jarom asked. "I know a good rest usually does wonders, but I'm not sure I trust them to wake up in a pleasant mood."

Jubal chuckled. "You are correct about that. They are miserable creatures who are only find delight in making others miserable. We must send them back to the stream. Come, help me push them over the edge. It won't harm them, but it will get them away from us—for a time at least."

Jubal led the way. He hoisted the nearest demon by the horns and flung it overboard with a single swift movement. Jarom followed with some trepidation, unsure what he would do if he accidentally woke one of them up.

He gripped the horn of the nearest one with a few fingers and rose into the air. The demon was surprisingly light, and he had no trouble taking it to the edge and throwing it over. It soared toward the glowing stream, landed with a satisfying hiss, and disappeared from sight.

The duo made quick work of the remaining demons, both dead and alive, and soon the deck was only covered with sleeping crewmembers. With the task finished, Jubal gave the young cherub an approving nod. "Well done, young one. Let us hope that we'll see no other incidents like this. Though to be sure, it does seem like an omen of sorts."

Jarom perked up, unsure of what he was getting at. "An omen? I hope you don't mind me asking, but an omen of what?"

Jubal peered into the distance, breathing in deeply, his eyes wide. "That we've almost arrived." Without another word, Jubal turned and returned to the darkness of the cabin.

Jarom clutched the side of the ship and peered into the lava. Somehow, a place that was only accessible by a lava river and guarded by terrifying horned demons did not seem like a place he wanted to go, even when protected by Giants.

He closed his eyes and tried to picture his home. Try as he might, he couldn't do it. Defeated, he opened his eyes, stared into the distance, and thought he discerned a faint glow just ahead. Jarom swallowed hard and tried to look away. No matter how bad the cruise had been, he had a feeling he would find the destination even worse.

THIRTEEN
THE GUARDIAN OF EDEN

NEW YORK STATE, 2012

Judy awoke in complete darkness, the faint ashy smell of burned paper permeating her senses and causing bile to rise in her throat.

An intense burning pain throbbed on her forearm, and when her eyes cleared enough to focus, she could see a sinister-looking red patch forming there. The surface of her skin felt sticky, and her hair was matted and generally disgusting, but miraculously, she was alive.

"Now who says soda is bad for you?" she muttered, brushing off debris and rising to her feet.

She groped around in the darkness and made her way to the desk. There she found a desk lamp that had not been knocked off in the course of the scuffle. She fumbled around until she found the switch and was able to cast a little light on her bleak surroundings.

She glanced at the trio of empty cans at her feet. Her mood quickly darkened as she thought of Eden. Frantically, she clawed at the debris carpeting the floor, revealing the face of her friend, gray as the ashes around her but still visibly breathing. She wasted no time in clearing the rest of the debris and propped her young friend up against the wall behind them.

"Eden, can you hear me? We've got to get out of here, pronto!"

Judy touched her cheek, trying to see if she could elicit a response. Eden stirred slightly but didn't open her eyes. "Come on, stay with me. I didn't give myself a soda bath just to let you give up on me."

She tried for several minutes more, but when Eden remained unresponsive, Judy decided to resort to other measures. She would have to try and carry Eden, even though she didn't want to draw any more attention to them than absolutely necessary. If she wasn't careful, people would start asking questions. What were they were doing behind doors where they didn't belong? Why was there a charred body in that office?

Cautiously, Judy crept over to the door and propped it open an inch or so. The hallway was now dark in every direction, signaling that most people had left for the day. "Finally," she muttered, "a spot of luck."

She quickly suppressed her grin when she heard footsteps approaching and the beam of a flashlight flickering off the walls. She quickly, but quietly, shut the door again. A security guard wasn't the ideal person she'd like to explain herself to.

Thinking quickly, she selected a solid paperweight from the debris scattered across the floor and propped open the door just enough so that she could see. She mentally crossed her fingers and drew back her arm and then threw the paperweight as far down the hall in the opposite direction of the exit as she could manage. The object landed with a satisfying thud, and she quickly replaced the door.

From down the hall, she heard the guard's startled reaction and the staccato of his hurried footsteps as he rushed past the door in the direction of the noise. As soon as she was sure that he had passed, she summoned up her remaining strength and hoisted Eden over her shoulder. Groaning quietly under the weight, she made her way back to the door and pushed it ajar. As she peered out, she realized that the guard was still busy further down the hall, and she quickly made her move.

Opening the door a little more loudly than she would have liked, she left the ill-fated room and continued down the dimly lit corridor toward the glowing green sign that marked the exit.

For the first few moments, everything seemed fine. She made her way quietly and quickly, despite the extra load on her back.

But her arm started throbbing with a sharp, burning pain, far worse than any she had ever experienced. She had to bite her lip to keep herself from crying out. She increased her pace and rushed toward the elevator, jammed the call button, and deposited Eden unceremoniously on the floor as soon as the doors opened.

Judy glanced down in horror at the ugly red welt on her arm, and she started feeling lightheaded. She had a sinking feeling that Eden wasn't the only one who needed to be rushed to the hospital. The question was, would the doctors be able to handle a bite from a supernatural snake?

Judy's forehead broke out in a stinging sweat, and instinctively, she undid the top button of her blouse in an attempt to bring more air into her constricting throat.

A short moment later, the elevator chimed, and the doors slid open on the ground floor, revealing the startled face of another uniformed security guard wielding a flashlight and a nightstick. He did a double take, as the person before him didn't look like the traditional cat burglar but more like an escapee from an insane asylum.

"Hold it right there!" the guard yelled. "Explain yourselves! You are trespassing in a secure area!"

The guard advanced slowly, brandishing his nightstick, still unsure of exactly what kind of intruder he was dealing with.

Strangely, the emotion that overtook Judy a moment later wasn't fear but a deep, inexplicable anger. It swelled up in her from deep within, boiling her blood and filling her with a nearly irresistible urge to lash out at anything she could reach.

The security guard never saw it coming. In a flash, the diminutive and usually reserved professor transformed into a human cannon ball, lunging forward with an unnatural cry and catching the hapless guard directly in the midsection. The guard went down with a thud, his nightstick and flashlight flying out of his hands and clattering noisily across the tiled floor.

Before she knew what had happened, Judy stood dazed above the unconscious body of the guard she had so expertly overpowered. Glancing down at the man, her entire body began to tremble. Aside from brandishing an occasional umbrella in

self-defense, she had never done anything remotely like this, nor
had she ever felt such rage. It just wasn't her.

"Am I losing my mind?" Her question remained unanswered
as she sunk to the floor, joining the security guard in unconsciousness.

As Judy she struggled to open her eyes, a dull throbbing pain
coursed through her head, and she fought just to remember where
she was and what she had been doing. When neither answer read-
ily came to her, panic took over, and she trembled slightly, a cold
sweat breaking out over her brow.

It reminded her of the last time she had felt so confused and
alone—the day the doctor visited her family's home, clad darkly
like some awful angel of death, and gave her mother the terrible
news.

Her eyes suddenly focused, and she glimpsed a figure dressed
in white, standing over her. Startled, she let out a cry and lunged
back, pulling a thick blanket over herself as protection. The doctor
smiled back at her, nonplussed at her adverse reaction. "Ah, Ms.
Meinecke, it's good to see that you've come to. I must say that we
were fairly worried about you for some time."

Judy peeked out from behind the bedclothes, abashed at her
extreme reaction. She glanced around, taking in the surroundings
of a sterile hospital room, an empty bed laying next to hers, and
an IV of clear fluid trickling into her arm.

The doctor lowered the bedclothes and straightened them out
in a more dignified manner.

"Just how long is quite some time, Doctor . . . ?" Judy asked.

"Forest," he supplied. "Dr. Forest. It's been about three days
since the incident. You've lapsed in and out of consciousness since
then, but you've never really been coherent. Now that you are,
we'd like to ask you some questions as soon as you're up to it."
His face tried to mask the gravity of the situation, but his bedside
manner was a bit transparent. "It appears that you are a very sick
woman, Ms. Meinecke, and unfortunately we do not yet understand why."

The shock of this grim pronouncement was softened as

another pressing thought entered her head. She shot up straighter in bed. "Eden! What happened to Eden? Eden Fortuna, she's my friend. . . . She was with me that night in the elevator!"

Dr. Forest held up a smooth hand. "She's just fine. We've been taking good care of her. She was also unconscious when we found her, but she came to much more quickly. It seems that her suffering is caused by a much commoner condition."

Judy leaned forward, narrowing her eyes. "What sort of condition? I didn't know that she was ill. Is it serious?"

The doctor smiled a sort of lopsided grin. "Oh, no, I assure you, it's something millions of women have endured and survived. She's carrying twins."

Judy shot forward in the bed, nearly ripping the IV from her arm. This changed everything. "What? Are you sure? Oh, my. How is she taking the news?"

The doctor's face turned darker, and his eyes clouded with unmasked sadness. "I'm afraid the news didn't go over well. I'm sure you're probably aware of the situation with her husband. We've been unable to contact him or his family." The doctor paused for a moment to let Judy digest the information. "The bottom line is that she feels desperately alone. I'm sure she would be thrilled to see you as soon as we can manage it. For now, however, we need to get on with some questions."

Judy fidgeted in her bed. The last thing she wanted to do was rattle off the answers to a laundry list of mundane questions. She also didn't want to offend the doctor with her indifference, as it was apparent that he was trying very hard to help her. She decided to mount her own offensive. "So tell me this, doctor, is it killing me?"

The doctor took an unconscious step backwards, blinking his eyes as if the question had bounced forcibly off of his forehead.

"Well," he managed, "it's a little premature to say. Your condition is, in a word, unique. Perhaps you might help us fill in the few gaps in your medical history to see if we can narrow down the cause."

He pulled over a chair, flipped up the first page on his clipboard, and took a pencil from an inside coat pocket.

The litany of questions bored Judy almost from the start. She started nodding off again, but she resisted the temptation to sleep. She didn't want to give the doctor the impression that she was sliding off into a coma again. She perked up a bit when he asked her about her studies abroad in the Middle East, but even that fascinating subject couldn't stave off her antsy feelings for long.

At last, the doctor's mild interrogation drew to a close, and Judy sank back into her pillow. Dr. Forest left without any further explanation of her condition, and she had the sneaking suspicion that they knew even less than they were letting on and that their lack of knowledge probably both scared and embarrassed them.

"Don't fret, my fellow scholars," she muttered absently to herself. "My advanced degree isn't helping this situation much either."

As she contemplated the strange turn of events, Judy's eye caught a glimpse of a bag lying on a brown cushioned chair near the side of her bed. With some effort, she managed to reach over and scoot the chair close enough to the bed in order to examine the bundle. She found it to be a small, black duffel bag with a note pinned to the top.

Squinting, she deciphered the slovenly script. "Blasted doctor's writing," she mumbled under her breath before coming to the conclusion that it read, "Ms. Meinecke's Personal Effects."

Judy pulled the zipper back and withdrew the contents of the bag. She fished out the clothes that she had been wearing the night of the incident, her wallet, car keys, and most important, the manila envelope with the papers that she had retrieved from Daren's office before the fire.

Her hands trembling a bit with anxiety, she unceremoniously cast the other items aside and withdrew the stack of parchment-type papers. At first glance, it seemed that the order had been changed, which probably meant that the papers had been riffled through. This didn't concern her very much, since she highly doubted that anyone would be able to make sense of any it.

Intent on reengaging her mind after such a long hiatus, Judy selected one of the sheets and set the others aside. The surface was covered with strange marks and glyphs that didn't immediately lend themselves to comprehension to the layperson.

However, as she stared at the characters, a faint burning sensation started spreading through her body, emanating from her chest and wrapping itself like wisps of smoke to the tips of her fingers. The characters glowed crimson in her field of vision, and understanding gradually dawned on her, the characters forming words in her mind, the patterns coming together as part of a comprehensive whole. She had barely been able to glean the gist of the message before, but now she could read as easily as a novel on a rainy afternoon.

She devoured the first page quickly, her mind reeling with newfound knowledge. Then, like a hungry hunter returning home to a feast, she tore open the envelope and began to read, her heart pounding an ancient rhythm in her chest.

Judy stared listlessly at the ceiling, her vision lapsing in and out of focus. A scattering of papers and parchment lay strewn across the white tiled floor, the only sounds coming from the faint humming of the medical equipment and Judy's shallow breathing. In her younger years, when she had been considerably fitter, she had once tackled a marathon and had done quite a good job of it. However, as she lay there, struggling to hang on to consciousness, she would have gladly traded her post-marathon exhaustion for her present state.

Though her body was completely worn out, her mind tingled with a wealth of tantalizing new information. It was so much that she could hardly focus her thoughts on a single subject long enough to make much use of anything. Individual thoughts flitted through her mind like mosquitoes gliding across the surface of a lake, and it took all her remaining strength just to try to maintain control.

Amid the maelstrom of jumbled thoughts, one particular notion burst through to the forefront: She needed to talk to Eden, and soon. If what she had just read was correct—and she suspected it was—her young friend was in greater danger than they could have imagined.

With concerted effort, Judy raised herself to a sitting position and reached over to the nightstand, fumbling around through the mess of papers for one in particular. When her search proved fruitless, she carefully leaned over the bed to look on the ground. At last, she located the ancient-looking sheet and nearly toppled from the bed in an effort to reach it.

Winded from the effort, Judy leaned back against her pillows, composing her strength and her thoughts. She glanced at the wall-mounted clock and saw that it was already 2:00 a.m., much too late for usual visiting hours. She closed her eyes and weighed her chances. She had overheard the doctor mention Eden's room number and had been to this hospital enough in her lifetime to have a decent sense of how to get around. Finding the room wasn't going to be the problem, though. Judy knew that the hallways were patrolled by security personnel at night, not to mention the numerous security cameras set up at intervals in the hallway, so avoiding being seen would be difficult, to say the least. Above all, her muscles were starting to tremble with exhaustion.

Judy closed her eyes again and imagined the route she could take to Eden's room. Eden's room was a floor below Judy's, down a flight of stairs, through a set of double doors, and halfway down a long hallway. Behind her closed eyelids, the characters of the document in her hand seemed to leap from the paper into her field of vision, their terrifying words burning brightly in her mind's eye like swathes of flame.

In an instant, she made up her mind. She strained to raise herself from the bed and succeeded after only a few seconds, finding the necessary strength in her new resolve. She stood for a few moments to steady herself before starting toward the door. She rested her hands on the doorknob, turned it slowly and quietly, and inched the door open, peering out through the crack into the darkened hallway. In the faint glow cast by the few remaining fluorescent lights, she saw that the hallway was deserted. She waited a few moments, resting her tired muscles.

"No time like the present," she whispered to herself, figuring that if she feigned grogginess, she could always claim that she had been sleepwalking.

Soundlessly, the door slid open, and she slunk out into the hallway. She tried to put on a convincing display for any cameras that might be watching, and she found that it was all too easy to swagger about and almost run into things.

She decided on using the stairs, as it would be somewhat difficult to pass off her taking the elevator while sleepwalking. As luck would have it, the nearest stairwell lay just across the hall, and the door opened with a push bar instead of a doorknob. Knowing that it was only a matter of time before someone came to fetch her, she tumbled through the door.

Opting for speed over caution, Judy took the stairs two at a time, rounding the flight in mere seconds. She reached the landing and pressed her ear up against the door leading out to Eden's floor. She hesitated as she heard an approaching squeak, like that of a cart whose wheels were in need of greasing.

Must be the janitorial staff, she thought to herself, the beginnings of an idea already forming in her mind.

The squeaking approached her door and stopped abruptly, close by. Judy slunk back, holding her breath and wondering if she'd been heard. She exhaled in relief when, a moment later, another door closed nearby. Whoever was operating the cart had entered another room. She seized the fleeting window of opportunity and chanced opening the door wide enough to get a view of the situation. It couldn't have been better.

A janitorial cart, laden with various dusters, mops, and cleaning solutions lay across the hall, abandoned by its owner who had just stepped into the bathroom next to it. A grubby blue vest and work gloves hung limply off the edge of the cart, just waiting to be utilized.

Judy rushed out from concealment, made her way to the cart, and donned both the gloves and vest to provide a makeshift disguise. She inched the cart forward, slowly at first, and quickly determined that it was one of the back wheels that was causing the awful squeak. Carefully, she lifted the back end of the cart so that only the front two wheels made contact with the ground. In this manner, she quickly turned the corner in the direction of Eden's room.

She was quickly compelled to slow down, her breathing heavy and her muscles aching. She was about to stop altogether when she glimpsed a figure approaching from the end of the hallway. Even from a distance, she could sense the air of authority about the person and deduced that it must be one of the night watchmen. Forcing her burning legs to continue moving forward, she kept her head down and the cart as quiet as possible, trying desperately not to draw attention to herself. The disguise would fool a casual passerby, but it would surely not stand up under scrutiny.

The person approached, and Judy could plainly see he was a burly man in a crisp uniform, his eyes scanning the hallway. She swallowed hard and fought to remain casual, trying to keep her speed constant and unhurried. However, as the man passed, he looked up, staring right at her. "Hey, where's Sealy tonight?"

Judy looked up ever so slightly, her blood turning to ice. "I-I think he called in sick. Kind of a last minute deal."

The man wrinkled his forehead in confusion. "That's odd. They usually tell me about these things. Come to think of it, I've never seen you here before. What's your name? Are you new?"

Judy's mind raced, perspiration forming on her brow. "Oh, yeah, I just started. My name's Justine, Justine Parmley. Pleased to meet you."

The man nodded, sizing up the much smaller woman, who was obviously nervous. After a tense few seconds of silence, he nodded politely and offered his hand. "Good to meet you too. I'll have to talk to the supervisor to make sure they keep me better informed. Just let me know if you need anything."

She tentatively shook his hand, gave a curt nod, and continued down the hall with a hasty thanks. The door she wanted was only a few yards away, and it took all her self-control to keep from sprinting. Bringing the cart to a stop a few doors down from Eden's door so as not to mark her whereabouts, Judy went to the door and grasped the knob. With a sigh of relief, she turned the knob, swinging the door into the darkened room beyond.

As lucky as her exploits had been up to that point, it all ran out in a millisecond. A blaring alarm shattered the stillness of the night, and the hallway filled with a bright flashing light. The fire alarm.

Judy slammed the door behind her and turned the lights on in the same fluid motion. The room's fluorescent lights flickered on, revealing a groggy Eden, her eyes barely open, her head still inches from the pillow. "Wha—?"

Judy held up a hand. "No time to explain," she cut in. "We have to go now. Can you walk?"

Judy didn't wait for an answer. She rushed to the bed and hoisted Eden over her shoulder in a fireman's carry. Eden remained groggy and limp, moaning softly, and offering neither help nor resistance.

With a single forceful gesture, Judy flung open the door and dashed into the hall. To her advantage, the fire alarm had roused many of the other occupants, and the hall was already crowded, providing some small degree of cover. Judy trotted as fast as she could with her extra load, pushed her way through the milling crowd, and located the stairwell that she had used to enter the floor. She kicked open the door and immediately leapt back as a wave of searing heat burst from the stairwell.

"Definitely not a drill," she muttered.

She went back the other way, hoping against hope that the stairwell at the other end of the hall had not been similarly blocked. But such hopes were dashed long before she reached the door.

"We're trapped!" screamed a woman in a hospital gown. "All the stairwells are blocked by the fire!"

Judy gritted her teeth, considering the situation. This was no normal fire, that much was certain, and if she sat around, the chances were that neither she nor Eden would last the night. With a grunt, she set off toward the nearest window and glanced down at the parking lot below. Fire engines blared in the distance, still much too far away to provide adequate hope. Fishing around with one hand, she undid the clasp of the window and considered the ground several stories down.

Spying an unused gurney through an open door to her right, Judy rushed in and lay Eden on it. Her friend had barely stirred during the whole ordeal, and a knot of fear that had nothing to do with the fire was clenching ever tighter in Judy's stomach. She whirled around and shouted to a group of terrified onlookers.

"You, there! Help me strip the sheets off these beds! We'll tie them together and let ourselves down!"

The frightened patients didn't move, seemingly unable to register her words. In frustration, Judy snatched a vase from the nearby nightstand and hurled it at the wall, shattering it instantly. This had the desired effect. The group was galvanized into action and tore through the adjacent rooms, grabbing every piece of bedding they could find and stockpiling it by the shattered window. Judy set quickly to work, tying the sheets together faster than she could have thought possible. Her adrenaline was pumping now, and all thoughts of weariness were forgotten.

Just as she bounded toward the shattered window to test the length of her makeshift rope, the row of sheets burst into flames beneath her grasp. She cast them to the ground, and they burned quickly and brightly, disintegrating before her eyes in a matter of seconds. She glanced down at her hands in horror and found them glowing bright red, blazing with heat, and tingling intensely. To her astonishment, though the heat was intense, it felt invigorating and pleasant instead of painful. The others around her gasped and fled in terror. Judy's eyes scanned the wall and quickly found what she had been looking for. She smashed the glass and extracted a fire extinguisher. Aiming it at the smoldering string of sheets, she depressed the lever and blanketed the flames with a thick layer of foam.

Unlike normal fire, the flames refused to die. They ate through the foam, reducing it to vapor in no more than a moment. Frantically, Judy tried again, carpeting the area with double the amount of foam, but it too disappeared with the ease of water vapor over a hot stove.

In despair, she flung the extinguisher aside and dashed back to the window. She glanced down at the drop before her and contemplated her options. They were several stories up, and a jump from this height would easily be crippling or fatal. The only other option seemed to be to burn to death in the unnatural flames. Swallowing hard, Judy glanced back at Eden and made her decision.

FOURTEEN
FLAMES AND FLIGHT

NEW YORK STATE, 2012

Xandir stood still, brooding over the metropolis he knew so well. The setting sun cast a warm glow over the city and caused the glass-covered skyscrapers to gleam like pillars of ice. From his familiar vantage point atop the tallest skyscraper, he could survey all that was going on below in the bustling city, though he paid it little mind. His thoughts lingered in the past and dabbled at the future.

He realized that in all the years of his service, he really hadn't learned much. The dilemma that faced him now wasn't so different than the one that had started his predicament. He was stuck on the fence that divided good and evil, both sides vying for his attention and exerting an ever-stronger pull. For the time being, neither side managed to tip the scale in its favor, and, once again, the choice was left up to him.

For the first time in ages, his hands didn't burn with incoming assignments. His mind remained silent of intruding voices. This came as both a relief and a bit of a surprise, though he figured he would discover the rationale soon enough.

"If I'm lucky," he mused, "I might just get Guardian Angel duty, shadowing a really boring person for a while." He wrinkled his face, thinking of the times he had been reprimanded before. "Then again, I might not be so lucky. Could be like . . ."

He recalled one particularly bad experience. He had been

sent to a little town called Nineveh to dole out what they had coming to them. Just as he was about to drop his black blade, a missionary—who was a little more than fashionably late— decided to show up and give the scoundrels one last chance. They had cleaned up their act, but the missionary changed his mind and said he wanted them to be destroyed anyway. Xandir couldn't have agreed more and was about to carry out the missionary's wishes, when he was accosted by an entire legion of angels who were sent to stop him from destroying the now-innocent people. He'd narrowly escaped getting one of the most severe punishments imaginable: banishment. Complete severance of ties and powers. This threat had worked wonders—banishment was one of the only things Xandir actually feared, and for the next century or so, he'd been a Saint.

A thin smile climbed his lips as he thought on how he'd actually appeared to a few peasants in the guise of some Saint or another a few times, igniting religious fervor across the countryside. Who was it he had claimed to be?

Xandir shook his head. This trip through his past was irrelevant. He needed to focus on other things. Things like Hell freezing over.

Maybe I could go about it in a roundabout way. Maybe I should focus on getting pigs to fly.

Xandir formed the picture in his mind's eye. Lava pits suddenly hardening over. Demons and tortured souls alike suddenly entombed in a massive slab of rock. Icicles forming off their little pitchforks. Snow-covered brimstone . . .

It was all speculation of course. Xandir had never so much as glimpsed Hell. It was a place his kind rarely dared to tread. He figured it was probably nothing like the typical accounts. He had known the being that had become the Devil personally, and Xandir was sure that he had neither horns, a forked tongue, nor a pointed tail—before or after his fall from grace.

Xandir's hand wandered upward, heading for the hollow place behind his ear. It was now or never, and it was up to him to set things in motion. As much as he hated allying himself with Ganosh, they seemed to have a common interest—for now.

A flicker of movement caught his eye a short distance below. He lowered his hand, watching the scene unfold beneath him. A man in a disheveled business suit stood on the observation deck of the building, inching himself precariously close to the edge. The deck was supposed to be off-limits to all except security.

The man inched ever closer to the edge, his gait slow but determined. He reached the safety rail on the edge and, with one fluid motion, swung one leg after the other over the rail. He glanced downward, his unkempt black hair tousled wildly by the wind.

Xandir had seen this many times before, and there was no doubt in his mind what was going to happen next. The man intended to end his life.

The man considered the drop, his head shaking and his hand rising to his mouth. With a whimper, he closed his eyes and stepped off into space.

Xandir deliberated for only a moment before withdrawing his white sword. This, however, had a vastly different effect than ever before. As the blade dropped, the ledge under Xandir crumbled, sending him plummeting down the side of the skyscraper. Apparently fate wasn't going to just arrange this one.

"Well, that was subtle," he muttered as he overcame the initial surprise and increased his speed in order to catch up with the falling man. With minimal effort, he glided to the man's side, watching in fascination for a second before extending his arms. "I wonder what he's thinking on the way down."

He slipped his hands lightly under the man's arms, slowing his descent. The man remained perfectly still in his grip, seemingly oblivious to his good fortune. Thinking quickly, Xandir searched the street below for a suitable place for the man to make his miraculous landing. As luck would have it, an open-bed truck appeared on the street below him, driving slowly and carrying mattresses. It was funny how his swords worked sometimes.

Xandir directed the man over the truck and released his grip, sending the man tumbling onto the stack of cushiony softness.

"Sleep tight," he whispered with a grin. "Don't spend that life of yours all in one place. And please don't turn out to be some sort of backstabbing business man or corrupt politician."

Xandir shot back up into the heavens, pondering how many times that had been the case. He'd saved the life of an Austrian art student once who had turned out particularly poorly. He had learned long ago to stop questioning why certain things were done. After all, knowing the *why's* wasn't part of his job.

Xandir stared disapprovingly at the ruined ledge that had been his favorite perch and once again hoped that saving that person's life was worth it.

He resumed his pondering on a ledge not far from his original one. There he sat until late into the evening, torn between visions of the Heavenly realms and visions of that beautiful face he loved so much.

Xandir had finally decided to leave when a brilliant shaft of light shot from the skies and landed on the ruined ledge. The High Seraph came into view, his haughty expression immediately erased as the expected ledge did not appear, and he stumbled forward down the side of the building for a few seconds before regaining his balance.

Xandir barely stifled a laugh. "You sure do know how to make an entrance, if not a landing."

The High Seraph glowered back. "I have had quite enough of your wit for the next century or so, so hold your peace and listen to what I have to say. I have a new assignment for you, though I am convinced that it is much better than you deserve."

"Hey, I've practically been a Boy Scout today. Didn't you see my good deed just now, or did you have your head in the clouds? Actually, it was more like a good dive, but really, it was spectacular—gold-medal worthy."

The High Seraph remained unconvinced. "Spare me the theatrics. I have not seen you this worked up since you tried to convince me to let you take care of that Egypt assignment. As I recall, you begged me even. Pathetic."

"Yeah," Xandir muttered. "But they still passed me over on that one."

"With good reason, I might add. You have always been reckless. If it had been up to you, you might have killed off the first *and* second born."

The High Seraph shook his head, regaining his balance on another part of the ledge that hadn't completely crumbled. "But, I digress. Your assignment."

The angel reached into his robes and withdrew a small roll of light-colored parchment tied with a scarlet ribbon. He carefully removed the ribbon and tucked it away, unraveled the parchment, and studied its surface.

He straightened up and read aloud with a booming voice. "Herewith I assign you, Xandir, Angel of the Second Order, the status of Guardian, for an indeterminate length of time. This you shall honor as your foremost priority, putting aside all other considerations. Violation of this obligation will bring about the harshest consequences imaginable with no possibility of appeal . . ."

Xandir realized that he was holding his breath, waiting for the name to be said.

"The name of your charge is Eden Fortuna."

Instantly, the scroll dissolved into a fine mist, which gathered around Xandir's hands. An image formed in his mind of a woman with full, red hair, the same woman he had rescued from committing suicide only a short time ago. A sharp burning spread throughout both hands, and Xandir's eyes shot downward, fearing they might actually be ablaze.

"What's wrong?" he gasped. "I haven't even had a chance to start yet."

The High Seraph's face darkened. "Your hands will burn when your charge is in peril. If you are in agony, then the peril must be truly great. Fly swiftly, or risk the wrath of losing your charge."

Xandir shot off the ledge, for once leaving without his trademark parting comments.

Xandir soared through the night sky, racing toward the billowing column of smoke and fire where the hospital once stood. It was as if he could feel the flames dancing across his hands. They pulsed with wave after wave of searing pain. He had only minutes.

Fire trucks and squad cars ringed the inferno, all trying futilely to fight back the flames. Xandir grimaced. He recognized the particular stench on the breeze. These flames reeked of demons and could not be extinguished by anything the firemen kept in their trucks.

He closed his eyes and reached out with his mind, probing the doomed building for a sign of his new charge. The flames dulled and muddled his senses, making him feel as if he were groping for a single brown pebble in the depths of a muddy pool. All at once, he caught a brief glimmer, which disappeared almost instantly. Flexing his muscles, Xandir braced himself and beat his wings with a new fury, spurred on by both pain and determination.

For once, he respected the High Seraph's threats.

Judy rolled Eden's gurney over to the window, cursing the chain of events that had led her to this desperate act. On the gurney, Eden stirred and sat up.

"What's going on, Judy? I feel awful."

"Eden! The building is on fire, and we're trapped. The only way out is through the window."

Judy glanced out of the window and saw that the rescue vehicles couldn't get close enough to the building to be of any help. Sweeping the ground with her gaze, she located a patch of bushes that she figured would provide the best landing she could possibly get. Eden joined her at the window and felt her already sick stomach take a turn for the worse.

"The other day, I convinced myself that I wanted to jump off a bridge. I didn't think I would get the opportunity again so soon."

"I'm no physics expert," said Judy, "but I think if we aim for that patch of bushes, the fall probably won't be fatal. Are you coming with me?"

Eden studied Judy for a moment and then ran a hand over her stomach. "The babies. Even if I survive, I could miscarry."

Judy placed a hand on Eden's shoulder. "I wouldn't suggest this if I saw any other way out. If it's our time to go, well, I for one can say that I had a good run." She gestured out the open window. "Well?"

Eden swallowed hard and nodded.

With a grimace, Eden hoisted herself onto the windowsill and hovered there for a moment, feeling the heat from the doomed building creeping ever closer. Its crackling enticed her, beckoning her to embrace the flames instead of taking her chances with gravity. With a cry, she heaved with all her might and leaped from the window.

Without waiting to see the result, Judy quickly followed suit and flung herself into the smoke-filled night.

Xandir soared through the air, shooting like a missile toward the building. The pain in his hands had become nearly unbearable. He ground his teeth furiously and expelled a roar of frustration and rage. He wanted nothing more than to place a tight fist into the High Seraph's face. Though he knew it wasn't polite to hurt the messenger, at least he knew it would make him feel better.

Time slowed, and a wave of potent déjà vu swept over him. He saw his target tumbling limply through the sky and sped toward her with outstretched arms. He grasped with one hand and caught hold of her arm. He let go of her immediately when he felt her shoulder dislocate, and she continued to fall. Cursing his luck and his aching hands, he barreled downward, smacking the ground so hard that it rippled and split under his feet.

He held out his arms, and this time, she landed snugly across them. He sighed in satisfaction as the pain in his hands finally subsided. He gazed down at the limp figure in his arms.

He stared down at her face and found that he couldn't pry his eyes away from her. The face looked so familiar, and not just because he had saved her life once before. With an unexpected tenderness, he studied her injured arm with his fingers and then reset it to its proper position. It would be sore for some time, but at least he hadn't broken any bones.

He frowned then, as a sensation of deep darkness washed over him. Something was very wrong with her, and it wasn't something that a hospital could do anything about. Xandir set her gently down on the dirt, his insides heaving and retching. Having lived the life he had, he had grown accustomed to darkness and its influence. But he had never felt anything like this before.

He backed away slowly, clutching at his chest and reaching for his ebony sword. "What is this? How could someone so beautiful house such incredible corruption?"

As he backed away, he noticed a second figure lying next to Eden in a charred depression in the ground. She had apparently fallen out of the window the same time as Eden. She twitched and groaned slightly, her hair and skin blackened by heat and smoke. Xandir's eyes opened wide. She was still alive. Xandir shook his head in disbelief for the second time in the last few minutes. Something very strange was happening. He sniffed the air and reached out with his senses. He wrinkled his nose, and twisted his mouth. "Demon," he seethed.

The stench was unmistakable and unbelievably strong. This normal-looking woman was most likely the source of this calamity. Narrowing his eyes, he inched the black blade out of its sheath.

The woman groaned and raised her head pitifully. Her eyes met Xandir's and grew wide, reflecting the flickering flames.

"Who are you?" she croaked. "You don't look like a fire-fighter. It's not Halloween, is it?"

Xandir narrowed his gaze, his temper rising with the surrounding heat. "So you can see me. All the proof I need."

"Of course," muttered Judy. "Why wouldn't I be able to see you? You aren't exactly a subtle character."

She studied the sword in his hand with growing alarm. "That's quite the prop for your costume. Really completes the ensemble. You mind putting it away, though? It's making me nervous."

The blade let off an ominous low rumble, and Xandir made no indication of sheathing it. "Give me one good reason why I shouldn't slice you in two, demon."

Judy's eyebrows shot up in alarm. "Because it would be a shame for me to survive a fall like that just to be cut in half a few moments later."

For once, Xandir wasn't in the mood for jests. "Wrong. Try again. One last chance."

Judy's face contorted in panic and confusion. "Please, I don't know what you're talking about or who you are. I'm a professor at the university, and believe me, I've been called some hurtful things, but never a demon! You're not a former student of mine are you? Because if you are, I'm sorry for whatever grade I gave you."

Xandir hesitated, sensing the truth in the woman's words. He held the blade steady for a tense moment, and then slowly returned it to its sheath. Stepping even closer, he concentrated all of his senses and probed into the woman's soul. He recoiled almost immediately as he met a blazing presence not far beneath the surface.

Grimly, he reached for his other scabbard and withdrew his other sword. "I'm very sorry. I'm not one of your students, and you aren't a demon. You just look like one for those with eyes to see."

"That's comforting and all, but the way I see it, you still have a sword in your hand. It's not as menacing as that black one, but I'm sure it chops just as well."

"Don't worry," said Xandir. "I'm not going to hurt you. You do, however, need some saving from yourself."

With no further warning, Xandir swung the sword in a high arc over his head and brought it down into the ground in front of Judy's face. Instantly, every muscle in Judy's body tensed up, and with a sudden spasm, she sank to the ground and lay motionless.

"There. You can sleep until I figure out what to do with you. Nothing else can catch on fire either."

Near them, the building groaned, threatening to buckle at any moment. Glancing about nervously, Xandir decided to take his two more pressing problems elsewhere. He picked up one woman in each arm and bounded back into the air. As he sped away from the scene, the hospital finally gave in, imploding nosily on itself in a cascade of sparks and smoke.

Though neither of the women was heavy, he strained to fly, barely able to maintain his normal altitude. He felt as if unseen hands were grasping his legs, pulling him inexorably back toward the earth.

He grunted. "The sooner I'm rid of you two, the better."

He altered his flight path, heading toward Eden's house. "No need to give me directions, sweetheart. Or a key for that matter. Looks like I'll be a regular from now on."

Xandir bit his lip as he thought of his greater task. He only had a short window of opportunity to carry out his plans, and unless he figured out a way to take his new charge completely out of harm's way, he didn't have a chance of accomplishing what he needed to do. He glanced up at the stars, reading the face of the seasons in their patterns. He shook his head. He should be halfway around the world by now.

He sighed as he realized what he needed to do. "The only way to make sure she's safe," he muttered, "is to leave her with someone that I can trust. Unfortunately, that means just one person."

He glanced down again at the woman's lovely features and wondered again if maybe, just maybe, there might be some connection. Americans, especially, had immigrant ancestors from all over the place.

With some effort, he landed on Eden's back lawn and made quick work of the door. Eager to be free of his burdens, he deposited one woman on each couch in the living room and started pacing the floor. There were plans to make, and none of them seemed to mesh with his original ideas very well. Not for the first time today, he wished that more beings of his sort resorted to the mortal practice of carrying a cell phone like an extra appendage.

In a flash, he stepped into Eden's bedroom, glancing fleetingly at the broken frame on the floor. "So she has a husband, it seems," he muttered. "Where is he in all of this?"

He stopped and lifted the frame, replacing it on the nightstand, and, for a moment, he recalled painfully why he avoided matters of the heart whenever possible.

With another quick bound, he entered the closet and selected what looked like the warmest clothing, stacking a few ideas on the unkempt bed. At last he had assembled a reasonably warm-looking assortment of clothing that, though it would not place in an Eskimo fashion show, would at least keep the frostbite off.

He glanced out the window at the position of the sun. After the trauma at the hospital, Eden could certainly use a few hours' sleep before taking on a new ordeal. He shook his head, coveting the hours as precious time slipped from his grasp. He sighed and returned to the living room, perching atop the mantel to start his vigil. As was so often the case, he really had no choice.

FIFTEEN

IMMORTAL NO MORE

THE MAGMA FLOW, 2012

Jarom woke trembling in the darkness. His dreams had taken him down roads he'd seldom traveled before—dark and menacing, filled with dancing demons, pools of lava and brimstone, wicked laughter, and painful shrieks. It took several moments for his vision to clear, and when it did, things were not much better.

He could hear voices, rasping and indistinct, floating his way through the open door. Curious, he rose to his feet and peered around the corner. Two large, dark figures stood hunched over on the deck, speaking with their faces only inches apart. Jarom leaned in closer to hear and recognized the voices of Tubal and Jubal.

"Are you sure about this, Jubal? Will he really be able to enter the city? I mean, I thought that the last attempt was a surefire one, but you know how that turned out."

"Relax," soothed Jubal, his voice like a crooning oboe. "I have it on the best authority. Besides, our angel accomplice is sure to come through, and once he does, the danger will be greatly reduced."

"Hmph," grunted Tubal, shifting his enormous girth from side to side. "You say *when*. I say *if*. I've seen him in action, and I don't think he's as talented as you do."

"It is not his talent I'm counting on," mused Jubal. "Though he does have some. It's his inspiration born of desperation."

Tubal pondered this for some time before answering, rocking

back and forth on his heels. "I still don't like it. Too unpredictable."

Jubal sighed. "You, brother, are completely hopeless. How would you do it, had you been endowed with such brains?"

Tubal shrugged. "I'm not sure. Something with a little more muscle involved. Are you sure we can't take the gate by force? You should see some of the weapons I've come up with since the last time. We would have a second Jericho!"

"You're a fool," spat Jubal, his words like three beats of a snare drum. "No weapon raised against that city can prosper, no matter how destructive. The Gates would only swallow up the energy, becoming stronger and stronger. No, we need a gentle approach, and that is the end of it."

Tubal reared up to his full height. "I shall show you what I think of a gentle approach!"

To Jarom's horror, Tubal lashed out with all his might, his huge arms swinging like oak logs through the air. Equally surprising was Jubal's swift feint. He leapt straight up into the air, gliding as gracefully as if he were a tiny leaf. At the crest of his leap, he lashed out with his foot, slapping several times against Tubal's face before landing back on the deck and rolling away.

The skirmish, however, didn't end there. Enraged, Tubal withdrew a morning star for each hand, the chains nearly as long as his arms. With a furious bellow, he lashed out with both weapons, nearly crushing Jubal.

Jubal leapt out of the way just in time. As he danced across the deck, he withdrew a gilded silver harp. Each string was stained crimson, as if dipped in fresh blood. Nimbly, his fingers lighted over the strings, plucking several of them at a time. Instead of the wistful tune of a normal harp, the instrument wailed and grated, tearing the air apart with the most appalling cacophony imaginable.

Jarom shoved his hands over his ears to silence the noise, which brought physical pain with every note. He couldn't believe it was the same musician who had played such an enchanting melody before. Jarom clamped his eyes shut and hummed a melody he had often sung with his own harp back home. The heavenly tune seemed to take the edge off the harshness of the other song.

Tubal didn't stop his onslaught but winced and howled as the harp assaulted his ears. Wooden splinters and shards of metal flew everywhere, coating both combatants with sharp debris.

Jubal whirled around the deck, hardly giving Tubal's eyes a chance to focus on his dervish opponent. Tubal lashed out blindly with both arms and legs and delivered blows that would have instantly crushed any normal being.

But even Tubal's resolve could not endure forever. In the middle of a wild attack, his eyes rolled up into the back of his head, and the mighty warrior fell with a resounding crash to the deck. The morning stars clattered after him, leaving twin craters in the deck.

Jubal sprang high into the air once more, withdrawing a dagger from within the folds of his robes. As Jarom forced himself to watch, the musician landed and plunged the dagger deep into his brother's chest.

For a moment, nothing happened. Then a trickle of blood oozed out from under the tip of the blade. Jubal gasped and quickly withdrew the knife.

"Impossible," he muttered. "You can't possibly be bleeding!"

Jarom screwed up his face. After such a fight, anyone was likely to be bleeding. But as he looked closer, he realized that although Jubal's face was flecked with sharp debris, none of the wounds produced even a trickle of blood.

Tubal slowly rose to a sitting position, clutching his chest. "Yet I am. I ate the fruit anew only this morning."

Jubal's face contorted. "Impossible. If you had eaten this morning you too would be unscathed. We have fought countless times for sport, and neither of us has ever come to any harm!"

Tubal shrugged, his former fury having vanished into humility. "It is true what they say, then. You cannot cheat death forever. You can run, you can pay him off, you can trick and fool him, but you cannot do so forever."

Jubal's normally gentle eyes burned with impassioned heat. "No! Death is all but conquered. He shall not rise again. You must be mistaken. Did you eat fruit from the ground again? Or did you simply lose track of time? You've done so before."

Tubal shook his head. "No mistake about it this time. My mortality is returning. Game over." He rose to his feet, leaving his weapons on the deck, and slunk back into the depths of the ship through another way. Jubal, still fuming, replaced the crimson-stringed harp and withdrew another, this one gold and green, with vines creeping around it. He struck up a tune so soft that Jarom had to crane his ears in order to make it out. As he looked on, the broken battlefield brought itself back together. The holes in the deck mended, the broken beams became whole again, and even the scuff marks on the ground faded to nothing. In a minute, the deck showed no sign of the violence that had occurred.

Jubal replaced the harp in his robes and closed his eyes, his face lined with the exertion he had hidden from his brother. His work finished, Jubal wandered over to the helm and gazed out into the distance. He remained silent for a long time, mulling over the night's events.

"Only hours," he whispered to no one in particular. "I only hope this time it works. It may be our final opportunity."

He took out another harp, smaller than all the others, and plucked a plaintive tune whose notes vanished into the darkness. He sighed, and the sound blended with the music.

"I am not ready for the song to end yet," Jubal said softly to no one. "There is nothing more tragic than an unfinished song."

He returned to silence and turned his head, staring directly into the darkness where Jarom hid. The cherub shrank back, turned, and ran as fast as he could manage to be swallowed again by the darkness of the bowels of the ship.

A few hours later, the boat came to a stop. Without the natural rhythms of the sun and moon to guide him, Jarom wasn't sure how long they had been traveling. He would have given anything to see even a dark storm cloud or a tiny glimpse of sunlight. The absence of the sun weakened him, and not just physically.

All hands wandered onto the deck, where Tubal and Jubal had assembled on the prow. Jarom hovered above the crowd and looked hard to see what had captured their attention. It didn't take long to find the source.

Before them roiled an enormous whirlpool of glowing magma. It turned slowly, emitting wave after wave of searing heat and ominous sounds—a combination of a high keening and a deep rumble.

Two jagged towers of rock jutted up from either side of the whirlpool directly across from each other. A series of stones, like massive teeth, lined the inward-facing surface of each tower, giving them the appearance of an enormous pair of jaws. In the center of the vortex sat a hole that, despite the eerie glow emitted by the rest of the lava, remained darker than Jarom had ever seen. He trembled despite the heat, unable to battle the dark feeling invoked by the sight.

Even stranger, however, was the scene just above the pool: an enormous floating city hovered precariously over the whirl-pool. It looked as if it could tip over and be swallowed up at any moment—it teetered and rocked from side to side but never touched the scalding surface.

A wall of luminescent blue stone surrounded the city, and many of the city's buildings were constructed of the same mate-rial. The slender buildings exceeded the height of the city walls and clustered around a central tower, which jutted up to a sharp point from the heart of the city. A group of other lofty buildings formed a ring around the central tower. The surface of each of the taller buildings was carved with an enormous symbol, whose metallic colors were tarnished with age. Some of the buildings had crumbled completely, which interrupted the otherwise satis-fying symmetry of the skyline.

A corroded metal gate flanked by two massive statues stood shut in a portion of the wall. The gate was decorated by large cir-cular stones, which reflected the surrounding light and intricate carvings, forming symbols and patterns similar to the ones found on the faces of the buildings. The statues resembled massive men holding elaborate spears. But their features seemed broader—their eyes wider, mouths larger, and faces longer than normal men.

The crew set course for the floating city, gradually slowing the ship's pace until it entered a holding pattern only a hundred yards from the gate. The ship vibrated but kept roughly the same position to the city. Jubal raised a hand, indicating the city.

"Behold," he announced to the crew, "the Doomed City, called in the old tongue 'Serche.' A city of such sin and corruption that it hovers precariously over the very Jaws of Hell. If not for its single righteous occupant, it would have long plunged to the fiery depths."

Tubal raised a hand and continued the narrative. "The gate is sealed, and no one has been in or out for thousands of years. Events are in motion, however, that will allow us to enter the city and claim what has rightfully been ours from the beginning!"

A rousing cheer rose from the crew, though it was mostly swallowed up by the tumult all around them. Jarom gasped as Jubal unexpectedly jabbed a finger in his direction.

"Jarom, come and take your rightful place at our side. When the time is right, you shall be the first to enter the city."

It took several seconds for the cherub to recover from shock and make his way toward the beckoning figure standing tall at the bow of the ship. He took his place between the two brothers. He couldn't help thinking he looked like a shrub at the base of a pair of towering oaks.

"How am I to do this?" he asked, his voice trembling. "You are all mighty warriors, but I have no advantage that might help me succeed where you would fail."

Jubal smiled, his eyes glinting strangely in the city's pallid glow. That is where you are wrong, my Ambrosia-fed friend. You have one thing that none of us have possessed for some time."

"What's that?"

"Innocence."

SIXTEEN

A MISSPELLED MONSTER

Xandir stared down at the sleeping woman, studying her face as closely as he dared. The evil presence that hovered around her had withdrawn a bit, allowing him to be more comfortable in her presence.

If only she would stay asleep. Too bad I'm not babysitting a hibernating bear.

His trip would take him halfway around the world through the harshest conditions, hardly something that this poor woman would take well right now. On the other hand, if he left her here and something happened to her, it would only cause trouble for himself, crippling him just in the moment when he needed to be in his prime.

Unlike most difficult dilemmas he had faced over the years, this one provided itself with its own answer. In this case, it was a voice from the other room.

"What the devil did you do to me?"

Xandir spun around, startled, which was a feeling he didn't often experience. He faced a bedraggled Judy, looking like she had just survived an avalanche. Xandir regained his composure and adopted a steely gaze. "I did what was best for all of us. To be blunt, you have a very serious problem."

Judy met his gaze and held it, adding some steel of her own. "That much is obvious. But I still don't know exactly what that

121

problem is, so if you wouldn't mind sharing some of your obvious insight into the matter, I would be grateful!"

Xandir frowned. "You really don't know? You weren't wounded recently? By a demon?"

Judy ventured a step closer. "And how would you know that? Are you a demon yourself?" She waited for him to speak but soon realized he wasn't going to continue without an answer.

"Yes," she said resignedly. "I was bitten by a snake. It looked like it was on fire. Since then, I've felt very strange, and violent things keep happening to me."

Xandir laughed without mirth. "Don't you think 'strange' is a little mild? You've been demon-blighted. It's like a poison that slowly spreads through your body; no, its more like a cancer that takes out your own cells and replaces them with demonic ones. Given enough time, you eventually will become one of them. Until then, it's like a shining vacancy sign, inviting demons to come in and stay a while."

Judy swallowed hard, trying her best not to show the turmoil just beneath the surface. "What can I do?" she asked, her voice low and pleading. "That isn't an option for me. I'd rather die than become like them."

Xandir's hand rested on the hilt of his black sword. "If that is truly your wish, I can help you accomplish it."

He drew out the blade a few inches and let it drop back into the scabbard. "But it isn't the only way out. There are those who might be able to help you. Unfortunately, they don't exactly set up shop next to the café or the salon downtown. No, such beings live in deep seclusion. The world at large does not understand them."

Judy's face fell to match the rest of her pitiful appearance. "Please, isn't there some way you could help me? This only happened to me because I was trying to protect Eden! You obviously have some interest in her as well, am I right?" Judy narrowed her eyes. "Would you mind explaining that interest?"

Xandir straightened to his full height, trying to put some dignity back into his face. "Haven't you heard of guardian angels? The name's Xandir, and I'm hers. It's a good thing I showed up when I did, because your version of protection seems to mean leaping from burning buildings. You didn't make my job any easier."

Judy took a step back and raised her hands. "I did the only thing I could do. I'm not your enemy."

"No," admitted Xandir. "Not yet, at least." He glanced down at the sleeping figure on the bed and then looked back at Judy. "I have a small proposition for you. I need to leave quickly on an important errand. It's my duty to protect her, and I chance harsh consequences if I fail. Where I'm going, there is the possibility that I might be able to find an elixir that would reverse the effects of the demon-blight on you. If you swear to remain here and protect her with your life, I will do what I can to bring you the antidote."

Judy nodded slowly. "But how do I make sure that I don't burn down her house? Things have a tendency to catch on fire when I'm around, but I can't control it!"

Xandir turned up one corner of his mouth. "Then I suggest you go someplace less flammable."

Judy blinked her eyes, mulling his words over to see if he was serious.

"No," admitted Xandir. "That's not the only thing you can do. The flames will only come when you are excited or in danger. Try to remain calm, and you shouldn't have any problems. So do we have a deal?"

Xandir extended his hand, standing solid as a statue. Judy nodded, stepped forward, and grasped the Angel's hand as firmly as her battered muscles could manage. "Done," she said. "Just don't take any detours."

"Never," he said. Then he spread his wings, bounded out the open window, and shot off into the sky.

Xandir continued his ascent into the upper atmosphere. Soon the city, state, and even the entire country looked like a child's puzzle below him. He coasted for a while, considering the seemingly trivial civilization below.

He flitted across the sea, staying high so as to reduce the friction generated by the atmosphere. The sea below was breathtaking, but he wasn't out for a pleasure cruise. Still, Xandir made a mental note to return as soon as all of this unpleasantness was over.

He stared down at the moon-frosted waves and thought he kept seeing Eden's reflection in the glassy surface. Try as he might, he couldn't get her out of his mind, and this bothered him immensely. It had been hundreds of years since a mortal had managed to get under his skin, and that had been so disastrous that he could barely think about it without feeling an ember of rage flare up in his chest.

He gazed into the Heavens at the blanket of glimmering stars. *Strange*, he thought. *How inviting the stars look. How peaceful and calm. But get up close, and they are vortexes of violence, ever burning and consuming themselves for millions of years until they finally collapse in on themselves in a cataclysmic explosion.*

He glanced back toward the earth. Some people are like that too: charming from afar, but when you get too close, that's the end of it. They burn themselves up and take you with them.

He shook his head in frustration. "Are you toying with me?" he shouted to the skies. "Did you give her to me to torment me? You know Eden looks just like her! Is this supposed to be some sort of twisted test, or are you just tormenting me for my mistakes?"

Not to mention that two-minute view of Heaven.

The skies gave no answer. He hadn't expected one. Suddenly, Xandir realized how cold it had become. He realized he was nearing his destination. For a moment, he forgot his frustrations and began his gradual descent, feeling frost clinging to his wings. Three peaks appeared in the distance, and he shivered despite himself. Drawing in his wings, he wracked his mind for the exact landing point.

A mental debate ensued in which two voices argued for the left peak versus the right peak.

Since when I have been able to trust my subconscious?

He opted for the peak in the middle. Through some fortunate circumstance, it turned out that he was correct. He landed gracefully on the snow near the peak and glanced around at the waist-high drifts.

He took a moment to survey his surroundings and located his destination. With a flourish, he withdrew the black sword and swung it leisurely in a figure-eight pattern in front of him. The snow in his path melted away as if fleeing before a dragon's breath, and Xandir walked through on dry ground.

It didn't take him long to reach the cave. He had been there many times before, though it had been a number of years ago. One hundred and twenty-four to be exact. Which was not to say he had seen absolutely nothing of his friend. No, intrepid mountain climbers had been catching glimpses of him for years and had assigned the most imaginative names to him. They had even gone so far as to use the word "abominable."

Xandir shrugged, picturing his old friend. Though the adjective could have been applied at times, it was hardly fit for general application. In fact, he was quite congenial . . . most of the time.

"The Congenial Snowman," however, would never make a good tabloid headline.

After only a few minutes, Xandir waited at the mouth of the cave, which jutted out from the side of the rock like some terrible creature's jaw frozen in granite. Xandir approached softly, not wanting to chance that his friend was in one of his fouler moods.

An echoing roar bellowed out of the mouth of the cave, sending the icicles around the rim flying and confirming Xandir's fears that this was of his friend's "abominable" days. Even so, he decided to see if his old friend's sense of humor had lasted over the years.

"Hey, Yearti, it's the twenty-first century! They've got medicines for problems like that!" Xandir stepped into the mouth of the cave and leaned against one particular icicle that spanned the entire space from floor to ceiling. "And if they don't, they have enough pills to make you forget the problem in the first place. It's a win-win situation."

The bellowing stopped, replaced by the crunch of heavy footfalls in the snow. A moment later, a huge, hulking figure completely covered in white fur emerged from around the corner.

"Do they also have pills to poison pesky tourists? That's what I really need. I'll take two if you have them." He motioned with one shaggy hand toward the entrance. "You just missed them. A pair of lovebirds poking around my mountain. With a . . . oh, what do you call it . . . a flashy, little box sort of thing . . ."

"A camera," Xandir offered. "Did they manage to get a close up?"

Yearti narrowed his eyes and bared all of his sizable teeth, lined up like minutemen ready to strike at a moment's notice. "I was sleeping," he seethed. "You know I only sleep about once a year. It's my indulgence every time my birthday rolls around. I had scarcely dozed off when I woke to a pair of nosey would-be adventurers shoving that blasted thing in my face and flashing it right in my eyes! If I had been fully awake, I might have taken the man's head off then and there, but you know how it is when I sleep. Takes me a while to wake up." He narrowed his eyes. "They got away, probably rolling back down the mountain in terror as we speak." His face relaxed, and he leaned back against a wall with a sigh.

Xandir nodded knowingly. "You ought to put up one of those signs like you see in hotels: Do not disturb." He folded his arms and cocked his head to one side. "Or better yet, beware of Yeti."

The fury returned to the creature's face. "Don't call me that!" he bellowed, punctuating his sentence with a roar. "You know how much that bothers me! See what I get from talking to humans? The one time I thought I would play nice and let someone in for a chat, it ruins everything. I told him my name was "Ye-ehr-ti", but he goes and shouts to the entire world that I'm the 'Yeh-ti.'"

Xandir narrowed his eyes. "After you were done with him, I'm surprised he remembered the letter your name starts with. What's a little syllable?"

Yearti rolled his eyes. "I don't fault you for your lack of knowledge about ancient languages, Xandir. You always did have your head in the clouds. In the ancient tongue of the mountain folk, Yearti means 'Mountain Sage.' In the same tongue, Yeti means 'servant who shovels manure.' "

Xandir winced. Such a slip was enough to give anyone a temper. Maybe the 'abominable' was a little more deserved these days than Xandir had thought.

"And another thing: those mortals cannot be trusted! I agreed with the rascal that he could talk to me as long as he didn't take an image of me on his . . . his . . ."

"Camera."

"Ah, yes, his camera. Anyway, we had a nice long chat about religion and philosophy, and I was just starting to think that maybe I'd misjudged humans as a whole." Yearti held one massive hand to his ear. "Then he took out this . . . calling device and said he needed to talk to someone."

Xandir winced, He could see where this was going. "Let me guess, he took a picture of you on his cell phone camera. You should have known, my friend. A cell phone could never get reception up here."

Yearti's face flushed crimson. "How was I supposed to know it had a camera in it? I thought he was joking when he pulled out a phone with no wires! That's the last that I had heard of them."

Xandir stepped closer, managing a sly smile. "You know, come to think of it, I think I saw that picture. Don't worry. It didn't turn out very well. Most people wrote it off as a hoax."

Yearti sat down again, a petulant scowl crossing his features. "I know. But is it too much to ask just to be left alone? Don't those humans have enough to keep them busy minding their own business? Last I heard, things were getting pretty complicated down there."

Xandir nodded. "It would take me months to give you even a condensed version. War is everywhere. The richer grow richer, and the poorer grow poorer. The line between good and evil is blurred into gray, and the faith of men is dwindling by the day. You know, the usual cheery prognosis."

Yearti scratched his scruffy chin. His eyes had changed from red to blue, an indicator of his mood. "That rosy, huh? Well, I'm not surprised. Can you blame me for wanting no part in it?" Yearti looked Xandir over as if seeing him for the first time. "So if you're here again after all of these years, it must mean that you want something."

Xandir smiled innocently and arched a single eyebrow. "Yearti, how could you assume such a thing? Can't an angel stop in at an old friend's when he's in the neighborhood?"

Yearti stared back suspiciously. "The neighborhood? There is no neighborhood. There's nothing here. Nobody of our kind comes here unless it's to see me. I know you've been upset about our last meeting, but did it really take a hundred years to get over?"

Xandir sighed, his resolve draining. "Okay, okay. I was being stubborn, and yes, I do need something. Something very important."

Yearti remained silent for several minutes, keeping perfectly still as his eyes probed into Xandir.

Xandir shifted nervously from one foot to the other but kept his face calm. At last he broke the silence. "Aren't you going to ask me what it is? Or don't you care?"

Yearti drew himself up to his full height. "Xandir, I've been here since the beginning, and I know what kind of path you've taken. I've seen you at your best and at your worst. You can be a great fool and, at the same time, a great friend. As long as your request doesn't tangle me in some harebrained time-travel scheme, I'd at least like to listen to it."

For once, Xandir allowed himself to look genuinely contrite. "I am sorry about all that business. I really thought we'd find that treasure trove in that British museum. But my current request is nothing like that."

"I'm sure thousands of Englishmen were sorry too. How far out did the ocean freeze while I was there? A mile? Two?"

Xandir nodded vigorously. "The entire Thames froze too. Quite the spectacle. I'll just be glad you're not a being of fire." Xandir straightened up, assuming his most diplomatic pose. "Yearti, how long has it been since you invoked a deep freeze?"

Yearti scratched his head, seemingly deep in thought. "I don't know, Xandir. Centuries. That business in England was close, but I stopped myself before it became full blown. You know, it can trigger an ice age for the entire planet if it completely runs its course."

"And am I right in saying that the longer you wait, the more powerful the ability becomes?"

Yearti nodded, the furrows on his face deepening. "Yes, but I don't like this chain of questioning. It sounds like you are planning to do something reckless. And with you, that doesn't take such a stretch of the imagination."

Xandir held up a conciliatory hand. "Wait, just hear me out."

Xandir advanced a few steps holding out both hands. "Reckless? Could the End of the World really be reckless? No, it's inevitable, and why shouldn't those who have the power simply help it along? I would once again have my freedom, and you my friend, would finally receive your solitude."

Yearti's eyes widened, gleaming pale and red in the low light. "You can't be serious! If I used the deep freeze now, it would slaughter millions. Contrary to popular belief, I am not a monster."

Xandir's face remained placid. "No, you're not, no matter what the tabloids print about you. And that's not what I am asking. I need to know if you can concentrate all that power on a specific location instead of letting it spread out over such a wide area."

Yearti nodded suspiciously. "I have never tried it, though it should be possible. But you need to tell me what this is about, quickly, before I decide to wrap you in ice and toss you off my mountain."

Xandir sighed, unaffected by Yearti's rising intensity. "Fire and ice. Fire and ice they used to call you. It fits. Just think of it as a bit of a challenge. The only thing that has to suffer is the pride of a bunch of demons. It will make them squirm for a while, and some poor tormented souls might catch their first break in, well, ever."

Xandir brandished his white sword, using it to point to Yearti like a finger. "Yearti, we need Hell to freeze over."

Yearti stared for a few seconds and then bellowed with laughter. "You want to . . . oh, my, that's really too good. Too good, Xandir. I don't know whether to fear or pity you."

"Do neither. Help me. You are the only one who can do it. Just name your price, and I will gladly pay it."

The old creature shook his head, flinging snow and ice from its furry face. "It's not a question of price, Xandir. Just think of all the havoc that would cause! I mean, how many people use the phrase 'when Hell freezes over'? It could cause untold chaos!"

Xandir's eyes perked up even more. "Oh, that's right. Hadn't thought of that. Now only if we could get pigs to fly as well. Maybe we can get certain sports teams to win while we're at it."

Yearti uttered a low growl. "I'm not fooling around. It really could bring about the End of the World."

"I really wish they wouldn't call it that," remarked Xandir. "It's misleading. When they say that, they really only mean the end of this particular civilization—the age of man as we now know it. It's not like there won't be anything left after it. There'll be a new order, and unless I'm gravely mistaken, a much better one. You were just complaining about how awful things have become—that's never going to change unless those with the power to do something actually do it."

Yearti leaned back against a pillar, steadying himself with one bulky arm. He said nothing for a long minute. "I just want to see one thing first, Xandir."

Without warning, the ancient creature drew himself to his full height, pounded his chest with both hands, and let out a thunderous bellow. The entire mountain shook and swayed at the sound, and in mere moments, a tidal wave of ice and snow sprang from the heights and went barreling down the mountain, sweeping everything before it.

"You have only seconds, Xandir. There are two humans on their way down the mountain right now. What will you do?"

In response, Xandir shot out of the cave, wings taut with exertion. Both blades glinted in the pale light as he dove forward like a falcon after its prey.

SEVENTEEN
BLAZING A TRAIL

NEW YORK STATE, 2012.

Judy kept a vigil over Eden all through the night, not daring to sleep herself. Though Eden's house remained still, Judy jumped at every little noise. She imagined she heard the crackle of flame or the mocking laughter of demons in the clank of the pipes and the hum of the furnace. She tried to relax, but the more she thought about relaxing, the tenser she got.

She glanced with sadness at the pictures of Eden and her husband. She hadn't known the man, but he looked like a kind, decent fellow. Surely he must have known about Eden's condition before they married. Eden wasn't the type to hold secrets from those she loved. All in all, something about the whole matter didn't add up, and as the night drew on, she only wished that Eden was conscious so that they could discuss things.

She wandered into the bathroom to splash some water onto her face and noticed a peculiar box near the sink. She picked it up and squinted to read it in the dim light.

"A pregnancy test," she muttered. She narrowed her eyes. The test showed a negative result, even though the doctor had been sure she was carrying twins. "How interesting."

Had Daren and Eden been trying long to have children? It was yet another piece of the puzzle Judy wished she could work on. Frustrated, she splashed cold water on her face and reeled as it made contact with her skin. The usual refreshing feeling was replaced by the sensation that something was peeling the skin off her face. Quickly, she turned the knob to hot and doused her entire head in the sink, covering it in scalding water. Relief flooded over her, and she lifted her head, groping blindly with one hand for a towel. This was going to take some getting used to.

Near dawn, Eden showed the first signs of stirring. Her eyes fluttered open briefly, and her lips parted slightly as though she wanted to say something. Judy squeezed her hand tightly and tried to make conversation, but Eden quickly fell back into a stupor. Undeterred, Judy sat constantly by Eden's side, watching for every possible sign of consciousness.

Throughout the morning, Eden became more and more coherent. At last, she managed to speak, like the voice of a drowsy child. "Where . . . where am I?"

Judy squeezed Eden's hand. "You're home, sweetie. In your own bed. It's me, Judy."

"Judy," she repeated. "We jumped. Are we okay?"

Judy paused, pondering if she should give her the straightest and most honest answer or the one Eden probably wanted to hear. She decided for something in between.

"We're fine, sweetheart. We've had a very rough day, but we've both survived, and that is a great blessing."

Eden's head rose, and her eyes momentarily met Judy's. "You look different," she remarked, a twinge of sadness entering her voice.

"I suppose I do," said Judy, settling back on the bed. "But then again, so do you."

Slowly and painfully, Eden rose to a full sitting position. With a sudden wince, she clutched her stomach, nearly doubling over from pain. "My insides feel like they're on fire." She shot Judy an earnest look. "And before you say anything, it isn't heartburn. It's a completely different feeling. It's not an ulcer either."

Judy nodded. "I know." She reached out and grasped her friend's hand. "Eden, I was finally able to read the documents we found at your husband's office. They speak of a series of Signs surrounding an ancient prophecy. According to these Signs, the End of the World is fast approaching. There were all sorts of strange and terrible things listed—it made the book of Revelation look like a children's fable. But there was one thing that stood out to me: it told of the birth of a set of twins, one who would serve good and the other who would serve evil."

She paused before continuing, unable to meet Eden's eye. "They said that the father would be a demon in possession of a man's body. The twins would grow to maturity quickly and usher in the Earth's final act." Judy raised her head. "Eden, you are carrying those twins."

Eden caressed her stomach, which was just starting to show the tell-tale swell. She shook her head. "What? That's impossible. The doctor did tell me I'm carrying twins, but all the pregnancy tests have been negative! I thought I was just putting some extra weight. And Daren, he's not . . . he's . . ."

The words caught in her mouth like a mouthful of stagnant water, which she couldn't swallow nor spit out.

"Possessed by a demon?" Judy offered. "Think about it. It would explain his strange behavior to a tee. His erratic, violent spells; the way he changed his habit; the strange phone calls. Heck, it's probably even why he wanted to eat all that spicy food. I know that's a lot to take, dear, but it also means that what has been going on is not your fault. These things are just beyond our control or understanding."

Eden's head rocked back and forth, and for a moment, Judy was worried that she was going to pass out. She leaned forward to steady her, and Eden collapsed against Judy's shoulder.

"How did this happen? Why did this happen? I've always wanted to be a mother but not like this! And Daren! We've got to find him. There's got to be some way to bring him back. We could start over again, put all of those unpleasant days behind us. If this is true, then it wasn't his fault. I don't know if it will do any good, but please, Judy, you've got to help me try."

Though Judy's stomach churned and everything inside her screamed in protest, her friend's pleading face and desperate voice struck a chord deep within her soul. She had to help. Like it or not, she had been drawn in, and once she had set her mind to something, there was no turning back.

"How do we find him? No one, not even his family, seems to have seen him. I thought for sure he'd go to his parents, but I guess it's not really him doing the thinking anymore, now is it?"

Judy nodded, mulling the problem over in her brain. "You said he didn't take anything with him? Anything at all?"

"No," replied Eden. "He left his cell phone, credit cards, even his clothes! I'm dying to see what he's managed to wear all this time."

Judy shifted her hand and, by accident, pressed a button on a TV remote lying on the nightstand. The TV across the room flickered to life, revealing a newscast already in progress.

"Firefighters are stretched thin in the state, as new blazes spring up almost every day. In the last few weeks, fires have taken out forests, hospitals, and entire residential neighborhoods. The police suspect an avid arson group given the frequency and general location of the fires. However, they report that as of this hour, they have no concrete leads. Joining us now is Fire Chief Davis from the scene of the latest fire."

Eden and Judy watched in fascination as the screen changed to a forest, showing a cluster of trees ablaze in the background, the air already heavy with smoke.

"Thanks for joining us Chief Davis. Can you give us an update on your crew's progress?"

The fire chief, a lanky, blond gentleman with a growth of stubble on his chin and dark bags under his eyes, responded loudly over the din. "We're having some trouble controlling the fire with conventional methods. Strangely, it is resisting water and our normal regiment of chemicals, which is not something we have seen before. Whoever set this one had some trick up his sleeve that I'd really like to know about. We're experimenting with some alternative methods, and we hope to get things back under control in the next few hours."

Eden leaned closer as the news anchor continued on. "I know that place! That's the woods up where Daren's family has a cabin. They visit every summer. I've been there a few times, and I recognize the name on the lodge. Do you suppose he could be there?"

Judy bit her lip. "It's probably no coincidence. You didn't see it, but the fire in the hospital was the same way—you couldn't put it out. Sounds like someone of the demon persuasion is up there causing trouble, and who knows? It could definitely be Daren."

"It's worth a look," Eden agreed. "It's better than just sitting around waiting for something to happen. Let's go."

Judy sighed, weighing her options. Xandir would definitely not be pleased if they left the house, and she was counting on the antidote that only he could provide. On the other hand, Eden needed help more than ever, and there was no telling how long Xandir might be gone.

"How far away is this cabin?" asked Judy. "We're not going to need a plane, are we?"

Eden shook her head. "It's only about an hour's drive. Probably even quicker since it's so late. No traffic."

"Except the emergency vehicles," corrected Judy. "I bet they have the whole place blocked off. We won't get anywhere near that place with all the firefighters running around."

Eden cocked her head to one side. "The cabin is a little ways away from the lodge. It may be the proverbial road less traveled, but we could still get to it by car, provided your suspension is good."

Judy smirked. "Honey, I once put a jar of cream on the passenger seat, and by the time I got to where I was going it was butter. We better take your car."

"Agreed," chuckled Eden. "We should go now, fire or not. I can't wait for them to decide when it's safe."

Judy heaved a sigh, seeing that there was no talking her out of this. "If you think you're up to it in your condition. Hiking is strenuous under any circumstances, much less when you're pregnant. Are you sure about this?"

Eden's eyes revealed a steely determination. "Yes. Help me up. I'm feeling better already."

With some effort, Judy pulled Eden to her feet. After only a few wobbly steps, Eden managed again on her own. Judy stared at her in concern.

"Now, if you even sneeze funny, I'm bringing you back. We can't risk anything happening to you, and I don't think we'll want to visit any more hospitals in the near future. Now, let's go, before I can talk myself out of it."

Eden and Judy took the longer route to the cabin. On the way, countless police, fire, and other emergency vehicles sped by them, taking little notice of Eden's unobtrusive car.

"They'll realize we're here soon enough," Judy said to herself, trying desperately to piece together some sort of plan for the coming hours. She couldn't seem to focus on any one idea. For some reason, all she could focus on were her flushing cheeks. She finally gave up trying to think, deciding that it was more important to stay calm. She didn't want to cause the firefighters any more grief that evening.

Eden kept quiet, speaking only to give directions. She seemed lost in her own thoughts, either staring out the window or absently caressing her swelling stomach. Judy could only guess what sort of skirmish was happening in her head, but she decided to let Eden decide when she wanted to talk more about it.

They turned off the freeway onto a side road and drove into the wilderness. The night sky was already choked with smoke and debris, blotting out most of the stars and moon. Judy glanced nervously at Eden as they approached an impasse choked with the glare of blue and red lights.

Judy nodded. "Are you sure there isn't another way in? They'll never let us through."

Eden sighed. "No, I don't think so. Unless this is secretly an all-terrain vehicle, we would have to use this path to get through."

Judy decreased her speed, trying harder than ever to think up some way to talk themselves out of this one. She gripped the wheel so tightly that the smell of melting rubber began to waft through the car.

In short order, a uniformed police officer stepped into the road, his hand gesturing for them to stop. Judy complied, and the officer dashed over to their window. "Ma'am, I'm going to have to ask you to turn back. This is an emergency zone, and it's extremely unsafe."

Judy adopted her best helpless look and stared at the distant blaze. "But officer, we were staying at the cabin. All of our belongings are there! We have to get them before the cabin burns. I'm not sure our insurance would will cover the damage!"

The officer shook his head. "I'm sorry. We have orders not to let anyone through for any reason. You go through there, and you probably won't come back alive. The smoke alone is enough to seriously jeopardize your health. For your own sake, turn back now."

Judy stood her ground, a plan finally forming in her mind. "We will not turn back. Please stand aside. We understand the risks, and we're going in."

She rolled up the window and placed her hands firmly back on the steering wheel. The officer, astounded by this strange turn of events, whipped out his firearm and pointed it straight at Judy. "Don't even think about it. I am authorized to use deadly force. Turn off the car, get out, and put your hands in the air!"

The sight of the gun and the officer's raised voice had the desired effect. Judy felt her blood boiling beyond the danger point. In one motion, she switched off the car and nearly ripped the door from its handles as she dived out of the car with a cry. The woods all around them ignited in an intense blaze, and the officer scrambled for cover. His firearm started melting in his hand, and he dropped it in horror. He reached for his radio and found that it too had become no more than a worthless hunk of metal. Seeing no other option, the police officer turned and ran into the blazing forest, judging his chances for survival better among the trees than facing the crazed woman.

Seeing her last-minute plan come to fruition, Judy hopped back into the car. She slammed on the gas, and the car shot down the smoky path, sending a cloud of gravel and debris shooting out behind it.

They made their way through the woods, and Eden indicated the path to the cabin. At last, the visibility grew so bad that they were forced to abandon the car and take to the path on foot. Judy thought it strange that they encountered no more officers on the path, but that was the least of their problems.

They came to a fork in the road, and the pair halted. Judy glanced over at Eden for guidance. Eden had brought her blouse up around her mouth to filter the acrid air seeping into her lungs. Eden glanced from side to side, seemingly unable to make her decision.

"What's the matter?" cried Judy over the noise and confusion of the blaze. "We need to keep moving! Which way?"

Eden continued to vacillate between the two paths, her panic growing by the moment. "I don't know! Everything looks different now. The smoke . . . it's getting to my head."

She rocked precariously from side to side, and Judy shot out her arms to steady her friend. Acting on impulse, Judy made her decision. The right path led uphill and would exhaust them faster. They would have to hope that the left path might hold something good in store for them.

"The smoke will kill us fastest if we stay put. We've got to take a path, one way or the other."

She steadied Eden against her shoulder, and started down the left path. Eden shrugged herself off and took up pace next to Judy.

"Thanks, I don't want to weigh you down."

They ran as low as they could manage, trying desperately to escape the effects of the choking smoke. Judy did this for Eden's sake. She didn't say anything, but the smoke had no effect on her; she breathed it in as though it were pure mountain air.

They scurried away as fast as they could, losing strength as they continued along their chosen path. The incline grew steeper and steeper, and sweat drenched them both as they crawled low to the ground, their progress fought inch by inch. Eden screamed as a canopy of burning foliage rained down on all sides, barring their way forward and backward. Judy tossed herself on top of her friend, shielding her from the brunt of the blast. She glanced up and saw only flames in every direction, creeping closer, cracking and popping like raucous laughter.

Judy rose and summoned every ounce of rage and frustration she could muster. Her thoughts flowed like roiling magma, threatening to spill over and consume everything around her.

If I am going to become a demon, I might as well make the best of it.

She closed her eyes, drinking in her surroundings, feeling connected to every crackling spark and shadow. She knew she had to try something. She stretched out her hands, spreading them like a maestro ready to strike up an orchestra.

"Flames, I am your master!"

The flames roared to attention, leaping to join their new leader.

EIGHTEEN
THE DOOMED CITY

Outracing an avalanche wasn't a problem. Xandir had beaten much faster opponents than barreling snow and ice. He'd once raced an angry cheetah whom he had insulted through the London underground. He'd done it on a dare from a clerical angel trying to liven up his day. No, the chase wasn't the issue—it was the dilemma of what to do when he got there that really distressed him.

In their scramble for survival, the tourist couple had gotten split up and was, even now, scrambling down the mountain as fast as they could. The avalanche roared for having been woken up, overshadowing the tourists' screams of terror.

Xandir withdrew both of his swords, and his mind tumbled over and over in a vain attempt to sort things through. Did Yearti wish him to let the tourists perish because of what they had done to him, or was he supposed to save them from the avalanche? Or, was he supposed to save one and leave the other, and if so, which was which?

His jaw clenched, and he glanced down and noticed that the man still clutched the camera in his gloved hands. The woman was rocketing perilously close to a sharp drop off, threatening to plunge to an icy death. Xandir took a deep breath and flung both swords, sending them hurtling in different directions.

The first sword landed at the top of the cliff toward where the woman was sliding and buried itself up to the hilt in snow. In an instant, a pair of gnarled trees fell in the woman's path and halted her progress. As soon as she stopped sliding, the avalanche roared over her, blanketing the trees with snow and debris before continuing on into a spectacular free fall off into space.

The second sword flew directly at the man's hands, snagged the camera by the neck strap, and tore it from his grasp. The camera sailed through the air and came to a sudden halt when the sword lodged itself into a towering wall of rock behind it.

The man continued to scramble down the mountain, all the time babbling and pleading for his life, when the earth parted beneath him. With a cry of terror, the man leapt forward, desperate not to be taken down into the depths with the rest of the snow. He tumbled free and rolled over and over. On the way down, he accumulated a collection of bruises, for which he would no doubt make up a multitude of adventurous-sounding stories.

The mountain continued to split, revealing a huge chasm. The bulk of the avalanche dove suddenly downward, as if a huge mouth had parted its lips wide to bite into a gigantic snow cone.

Though it took several minutes for the thundering to stop, the worst of it was over. The woman, guided by the line of the trees, poked her head out of the snow and climbed up to hang on to the upper branches. The man sat up, laughing with delight to be alive. A few moments later, his thoughts drifted back to his camera, which was nowhere to be seen. If his eyes had been sharper, he might have just been able to make it out, traveling erratically through the air up the side of the mountain, dangling from unseen hands.

Yearti sat with both his legs and arms crossed at the entrance to the cave as Xandir made his approach. Yearti's stoic gaze betrayed nothing as the angel landed and walked toward him, his footprints making barely any marks in the snow.

"That," rumbled Yearti, his eyes glowing a light green, "was an interesting performance."

Xandir shrugged, resting his hands on the hilts of his swords. "And by interesting, do you mean enjoyable? Crazy? Inspired? Come on, let's go ahead and talk about it on our way to Serche."

Xandir advanced, but Yearti halted his progress by raising one furry hand, and his eyes darkened to a steely gray. "We will discuss it, but we'll do it right here."

Xandir shivered despite himself. "Have it your way, Snowy. Just remember—I may be a lot of things, but I'm no snow angel. Let's make it quick."

"Fine," agreed Yearti. "I'm anxious to return to my sleep in any case. Tell me, why did you act the way you did just now?"

Xandir shrugged, barely masking his annoyance. If there was one thing he hated, it was trying to explain to others the reasons behind his actions.

"Surely you remember? As a destroying angel by profession, I really only have to make one decision in each case: mercy or justice." He withdrew his dark sword and stuck it in the snow. "I felt that the man deserved this one. After all, he had been the nuisance who had taken the pictures. And though he was a bother, his offense was hardly a capital crime, so he lost his camera but not his life."

With a fluid motion, he stuck the white sword next to its companion. "On the other hand," he continued, "the woman was just along for the ride. I felt that she deserved more lenience, and so I played the Mercy card with her. Other than having a little scare, she should be fine. At any rate, I doubt either of them will be back again, and they'll probably even warn away anyone else who will listen." Xandir pantomimed a monster raising its claws. "Look out for the abominable snowman! He's not very photogenic. You've confused him with the 'adorable snowman.'"

Xandir retrieved the dark sword and slung the camera's strap over the blade. He offered it to Yearti like a pair of socks worn for a week straight. "In the end, everyone is happy. The travelers are unharmed but scared out of their wits, you've maintained your privacy, and I've surely dazzled you with my indelible moral fiber and airtight reasoning."

Yearti remained silent for several moments, his eyes flickering between red and yellow.

"By the way," Xandir said, "I did manage to look at a few of these shots on the way up. They're actually quite good. You might really consider sending out Christmas cards this year."

A smile broke over Yearti's stony complexion, and his eyes lightened to a welcoming deep brown. "All right, give it to me. It might be useful. Maybe I'll surprise the next interlopers by taking a picture of them! Let them see how they like it!" Yearti's face grew serious again. "I accept your explanation. You may be reckless and foolish at times, but at least you still understand your duty. In return, I shall construct an object that will allow you to accomplish your task."

With incredible speed, Yearti's hand lashed out, snatching a single snowflake out of the air and grasping it between two claws. He drew his face in closer, opened his mouth wide and breathed heavily on it. The air around his hands twinkled with frost, which massed together around the original snowflake, creating an orb of increasing size. Yearti continued to breathe, and the frost whirled rapidly around the globe until it grew to over a foot in diameter. Yearti's eyes gleamed silver-blue, and the entire cavern vibrated with a swirling, drawn-out hiss.

At last, Yearti drew in his breath again and held aloft his shining creation. Its surface had become mirror smooth and clear, and it glowed in the pale light.

"I'm guessing that's not just a fancy Christmas ornament." remarked Xandir, thinking how much it looked like something to hang from a giant Christmas tree.

"No, indeed," said Yearti. "It's an ice orb. It allows me to focus my power wherever it is. Simply break the sphere in the intended location, and I will concentrate all of my energy into a deep freeze. I've given you what you need. Now all you have to do is find a way to get there."

Xandir stepped forward and took the sphere, which shrank in his grasp. He placed the orb in a safe place in his armor. "Oh, and while we are at it, can I ask one more favor? I need a little of your snow serum."

Yearti narrowed his eyes. "Why? I thought you didn't get sick. Or is the condition too embarrassing to talk about?"

Xandir ignored the barb. "Nothing so dramatic. I need it to counteract a demon-blight. As far as I know, your serum is the only thing that works consistently against it." Xandir held out a single hand, curling his finger. "So, how about it? I'd only need a little. It would help keep me motivated."

"I don't have any on hand. You'd have to come back later."

Xandir almost let a grunt escape his lips. It took years to brew the serum, and Yearti knew that. He didn't have nearly that much time. "Are you sure? Have you checked in the back? I mean, you must have some sort of emergency supply or something. Whatever would you use for yourself?"

Yearti bared a number of his jagged teeth. "I have a precious little, which I need. Unless you have something else to offer me, I won't part with it."

Xandir took a few steps toward the entrance, as if making to leave. "That's too bad, because even though I'm really fond of these little confections, I was thinking about sharing a few. But now that I see that you're not in a generous mood, I think I might just eat them all myself."

He withdrew a small clear bag of individually wrapped chocolate truffles. It had only taken a few minutes in central Europe to procure his backup plan. He meticulously unwrapped one and popped it into his mouth. "Mmm, I don't care what they say about Ambrosia—this is Heavenly. I hope that poor lady didn't mind losing these in exchange for her life: they really are almost worth dying for."

Yearti's mouth salivated, his eyes glowing bright green. "Xandir, you know I need that serum. It's the very last of the batch. Don't torment me like this."

Xandir's eyes widened, and his lips turned down. "I'll just be going. You know it's not good to eat such things right before you go to bed. I'm just looking after you as always, like any good friend would."

Yearti bulged like a dam holding back a torrent. "Let me have just one. Please."

He managed the last word only through clenched teeth, and Xandir had to admit, it sounded strange coming from the giant creature's mouth.

"I was planning on giving you the whole bag. I just need that serum. Think about it: chocolate for medicine. I'm sure anyone would agree you're getting the much sweeter deal."

In the end, Yearti's willpower lasted an admirable length of time, given the strength of the opposition.

He stomped off to the back of the cave in a huff and returned with a small vial of silvery liquid stopped by a tiny cork.

"Here, take it. You had better put it to good use."

Xandir grinned and took the vial, handing over the bag of truffles in the same motion. "I will. I'd recommend that you don't eat these all in one sitting. They'd probably do a number on you, even for someone with your constitution."

"Just get out of here," he growled, "and let me sleep. I have half a mind to send you on your way with a blizzard."

"As you wish," said Xandir. "Thanks again, old friend. I'll let you know what I find, and, at any rate, I won't wait a hundred years before I come around again."

Yearti's eyes turned a milky light brown. "Don't come back unless you have chocolate—the good stuff. Preferably like this stuff."

"Yearti, if this works, I'll make you an entire new mountain of chocolate." And with that, Xandir launched himself into the dim light of the Himalayan evening, searching his wildest imagination for a way he could fulfill that promise.

Soaring above a beautiful scene, Xandir was feeling good about things. That is, until he felt a familiar freezing from behind his ears that had nothing to do with weather. He cursed the poor timing. He had intended on returning to Eden and Judy before contacting Ganosh. If he waited any longer, Judy might be joining the ranks of the underworld in very short order. The feeling behind his ear intensified, completely destroying his ability to enjoy the breathtaking vista unfolding below him.

Grumbling, he alighted atop the nearest peak and reached behind his ears to answer the summons. "What? This had better be good. I don't get around this part of the world much."

Ganosh's hollow laughter echoed through his mind. "That's not my problem. I was actually hoping that you'd come visit a particular part of the Underworld, if you know what I mean."

"What's the rush?" moaned Xandir. "I have some other things

to take care of. I'll be there when I can."

"Don't trifle with me!" roared Ganosh. "Do not forget the leverage we have over you. Do I need to remind you who I work for? This is not a game, and it's now number one priority on your list." Ganosh paused for a moment to let his words sink in. "As we speak, Jarom is hovering over the Jaws of Hell on the threshold of Serche. You are to find your way in or else we'll toss him into the Jaws. That or I'll let Master Mahan's sons have their way with him. I don't know. Maybe I will flip a coin."

Xandir's rage frothed up inside of him as he grasped his swords simultaneously and then released them, realizing that they could do nothing.

"How do you suggest I get down there?" he growled through gritted teeth. "I've seen the stairway to Heaven, but I can't say anything about the other direction—an escalator perhaps?"

"Heh," grunted Ganosh. "Witty as ever. No matter. As you probably know, Heaven's Gates are connected to the earth by the conduit of Jacob's Ladder. It's a pathway through which angels and other heavenly beings can pass a series of rungs to bridge the gap between the mortal and immortal worlds. Only it doesn't stop there. Most beings are unaware that this ladder continues farther downward in a straight course to the Jaws. Though it doesn't have a single name, we've taken to calling it Jacob's Chute, since it drops off without the benefit of rungs. If you can locate it, it's the most direct way down, and you might still stand a chance of saving your friend."

Xandir stared off into the cloudy distance. It had been some time since he had seen the Ladder, visible only to immortal beings. He had longed to climb it, and had even tried once, but hadn't gotten any farther than the second rung when he was captured and thrown unceremoniously back to earth.

He had been mistaken for a shooting star as he plummeted to land in the Indian Ocean. The native tribes had taken this as an omen of impending doom and had fasted for a week straight. He wasn't about to start a mess like that again.

"Okay, so you're not going to clue me in as to its location? I assure you, it would be in both of our best interests for me to know. I have secured a way of entering the city."

Xandir could almost hear the sinister grin cross Ganosh's face. "Let's hope so. I would hate to have to harm your little lady friend. Like you, I've lived through countless centuries, and I must say, she's unrivaled. I've got half a mind to keep her for myself."

Xandir launched into the air, furiously slicing in random directions. His blades, however, only succeeded in severing snowflakes.

"If you as much as sneeze in her direction, Ganosh, I'll slice you back down to your atoms, you hear me? Not a hair out of place!" The sensation behind his ears had faded. Ganosh was gone.

Recovering from his tantrum, Xandir set himself back down on the peak. Suddenly his hands burned, signaling that Eden was in trouble. He cursed his luck. She and that other woman had likely decided to go wandering around again and had fallen back into the hands of the enemy, or worse.

He closed his eyes and conjured Eden's face, then that of his beloved. They were so strikingly similar. And now they were both in danger. Every grain that fell through the hourglass was another step closer to burying them for good.

"Can I save them both?" he wondered aloud. "And if not, which one?"

Not wanting to waste another moment, he shot up into the air and made straight for the stars. He had work to do.

NINETEEN

A DEMON'S RETREAT

NEW YORK STATE, 2012

The air around Judy glowed white hot. All the fire from the forest now swirled around her body, giving her skin a bright orange glow. She glanced down at her hands in amazement, both appalled and exhilarated at what she had done.

"If I can create this, can I also undo it?"

Concentrating all of her effort on the flames, she spoke again to all of them at once. "Go . . . to . . . sleep!"

At first nothing happened, but soon the flames reluctantly obeyed. They swirled up above Judy's head, forming an inverted funnel that ended with a brilliant point above her. They roared and hissed, then vanished in a puff of smoke and a shower of sparks. Judy collapsed to the ground, leaving the forest dark and silent.

From a few yards away, Eden picked herself up and ran over to her friend, expecting her to be dead or, at the very least, injured beyond recognition. "Judy, are you okay? How did you do that?"

Groggy, Judy sat up, her face flushed, and her hair nearly singed off. "It was a little experiment. I read it somewhere—in those documents we rescued from Daren's office. Demons have dominion over fire, and now that I'm, well, partially a demon, I thought I would see if that's true."

She glanced down at her tattered clothing and flushed skin.

148

"Didn't seem to completely protect my human side, but otherwise, mission accomplished. Come on, the flames might return any moment. I've got a feeling we're finally back on the right track."

The duo moved up the hill in silence, the sounds of the blaze falling away. The road leveled out, leading to a wide clearing containing a two-story cabin constructed of long, sturdy logs. Old-fashioned glazed windows and brightly painted doors lined the exterior. A brick chimney jutted out of the roof on one side, inexplicably spewing smoke into the already smoky night. Though the windows on the lower level remained dark, the windows on the upper level glowed with flickering light, accompanied by the sound of voices.

The pair crept up and took their places under the nearest window. They strained to catch a sample of what was going on inside.

"I'm guessing this isn't a family reunion?" whispered Judy.

"No," replied Eden. "No. Daren's aunt Ellen might have a funny laugh, but she couldn't make half the noises I hear coming from in there."

Though they couldn't make out the specific words, the voices were gruff and guttural and obviously speaking something other than English.

Judy summoned all her language prowess and still couldn't decide even what language it was. However, the more she focused, the faster the words took shape in her mind. She glanced at Eden.

"I think your hunch has paid off. Unless I'm very mistaken, they're speaking some sort of demonic language. I can't make out all of what they are saying, but I think I could if I got a little closer. I'm going in."

Eden was about to protest when a gentle voice, which she wasn't sure if she heard or felt, whispered, "Climb in the back window."

Eden cocked her head to one side, feeling compelled to repeat the instructions. "Climb in the back window," she whispered, trying to make sense of what had just happened. They made their way around the back and found the window wide open while all of the others had been shut.

"That's odd," said Judy, glancing through the window. "How did you know?"

Eden shrugged, already helping Judy through the opening and into the small kitchen area beyond. Judy then hoisted Eden through, and they crouched in the darkness.

From the cover of a table, they had a clear view down a hallway toward the entrance. There, two dark figures lurked, tall, muscular and brandishing curved blades, not standard issue for police or rescue workers.

Eden shivered. "I'm glad we didn't try the front door," whispered Judy, barely audible.

Near the entrance, a stairwell rose to the second floor, flanked by a wooden railing. Footsteps thundered down the stairs, followed by a few words in the demonic language. A dark figure, similar to the two guards, left the stairs and turned toward the kitchen. For a moment, the light spilling down the stairs fell onto the man's face, and Eden gasped. It was Daren.

"Send me to do their dirty work," he grumbled in English. "Not enough kick in the stew—well, I'll show them." He stumbled through the kitchen, tore open cupboards, and tossed their contents haphazardly onto the floor. Finally he flung open a cabinet filled with alcohol, and his eyes grew wide. "Here we are. How about some firewater?" He pulled a slim flask off the shelf and grinned. "This will kick them back to Hades."

His speech was raspy and slurred. It only vaguely resembled his normal voice. He was dressed smartly in a dark-colored suit and blazing red tie that caught the moonlight and shone different colors at different angles. His hair was slicked back against his head, and he sported a stylish pair of sunglasses and a close-trimmed beard and goatee. A gleaming gold watch and cuff links completed the ensemble, which made him resemble more a wealthy Casanova than the humble scientist he used to be.

Eden shook, calling on all of her restraint not to cry out. She watched as Daren selected a few more bottles and cradled them under one arm. He glanced both ways to see if anyone was around and surreptitiously sipped from one bottle. He did the same to a second and wiped his mouth on the back of his sleeve. He shook his head.

"Better quit now, or there'll be none for the stew. There's no need to make Dusteater jealous."

Both ladies shivered at dark images conjured by the name. Daren replaced the bottles under his arm, turned, and made his way back up the stairs, taking them two at a time. Judy seized the moment to shoot forward, hiding in the shadows by the stairs. Eden stayed back by the window, ready to bolt if things got out of hand.

The voices from upstairs resumed in earnest. Judy furrowed her brow as the words took shape in her mind. Unlike the majority of others she had attended in her lifetime, this was going to be an interesting meeting.

TWENTY
CHUTES AND LADDERS

OUTER SPACE, 2012

Xandir soared higher into the atmosphere, a light frost creeping over every inch of his weapons and armor. He smiled, reveling in the sensation. "This isn't cold. They haven't seen anything yet."

He cut through the clouds like a streamlined rocket, leaving the world behind. Soon, the entire planet sparkled beneath him like the crown jewel in a backdrop of diamonds. The few other times he had tried this, he had taken at least a few minutes just to admire the scene rotating beneath him. It had always amazed him how such a noisy and conflicted world appeared so peaceful when observed from above. It was a perspective he had often wanted to bestow on those below who blundered around in a rat race that nobody seemed to be winning.

He reached and checked where he had hidden the flask of serum. To his horror, it had vanished. He screamed in frustration, the sound vanishing into the void of space. There was no telling when he might have dropped it, and he couldn't spare the time to search for it. He would have to find another way.

Tonight his mission weighed on him with more than gravity ever had. He glanced around the vast space and located his destination. The smaller orb glowed pale in the reflected sunlight, rotating at a barely perceptible rate. He sped toward it, relishing the freedom of flying without the drag of the atmosphere.

With the finesse of an ice skater, he turned a corkscrew in

midair and lighted on the lunar surface. In the distance, he could make out a brightly colored flag planted in the soil. He smiled and decided to risk the diversion. With a bound, he hovered next to the flag, studying the deep rutted footprints so out of place on the undisturbed lunar surface.

"You know, they tried so hard to get here the first time, and for what? The landscape isn't exactly thrilling. Next time, I ought to give them something to talk about."

Working quickly, he withdrew his swords and carved a series of characters into the lunar surface. Drawing on his years of experience, he repeated the message in a variety of different languages, including a few dead ones. For good measure, he added some made-up nonsense. As a finishing touch, he reached as far back as he could remember and carved the message in ancient Egyptian hieroglyphics. "The moon is made of cheese."

"Now that will give them something to think about!" he announced, a devilish grin crossing his face. "Just wait until those conspiracy theorists catch wind of this." He screwed up his face and stroked his chin with his hand. "That is, if they do. Who knows when they'll manage to get back here?"

He made a mental note to try to arrange that at the first opportunity. The momentary diversion had given Xandir a chance to collect his thoughts. The task ahead of him would not be an easy one. In addition to inspiring poetry and regulating the tides, the moon also served as the first "rung" of many in Jacob's Ladder.

Travelers using the Ladder filtered in through this first rung on their way to other rungs. With its high traffic came a heightened level of observation. They were not yet aware of his presence, but if he got much closer, that was liable to change quickly.

He pictured the place in his mind: A sprawling structure of Heavenly metal and glass invisible to mortal eyes. It consisted of a hive of transparent cubicles, connected by a network of transparent hallways. The cubicles shifted and rotated as necessary, so that the building never maintained a definite shape. Xandir knew that the entire structure surrounded the actual pathway of the ladder, which appeared as a thin, golden pathway that snaked off into space, one branch toward Earth and the other toward the Heavens.

Now he needed to follow the path back to Earth, because, as Ganosh had informed him, the path down to the Jaws lay directly in line with the path of the Ladder. Now there was just the question of permission.

"Forget permission," he muttered, sheathing his swords. He was considerably stronger than the last time he had paid this place a visit, but he doubted that he could overcome so many Guards, who, unlike Guardians, were set to protect a specific place and not a specific person. What Xandir needed was a diversion, and he needed one quickly.

He recalled that he'd forgotten Mandarin Chinese in his message and rushed back to the spot. As he etched out his prank once again, an old proverb leapt to the forefront of his mind: "Those who live in glass houses shouldn't throw rocks."

"Unless," continued Xandir, "that pesky, shiny house is right in your way and mocking you."

He bent down and hefted a lunar stone several times as large as his head. He shot into the air and rocketed forward. He grinned as his target came into view. This was going to be more fun than he could have thought possible.

He built up speed, gathering up as much momentum as he could for his assault. His eyes roamed the building, searching for the point at which his throw would cause the maximum amount of destruction. As he made his second pass, a small voice echoed in his head. "Guardian angel. We have you in our sights. Please identify yourself."

He ignored the nuisance and went around for another pass, dipping down to collect another sizable stone for his other hand. The voice whined again in his ear.

"Guardian angel, please identify. Failure to comply will result in the use of Divine force and ejection to earth."

He didn't have much time now. Locating his best bet, he executed a hairpin turn and rushed at the building with all possible speed. A swarm of orange sparks erupted from the building, and Xandir knew they must have deployed the Fighting Cherubim, brandishing blazing swords and buzzing like a cross between a dragonfly and a hornet. They sailed toward him on a collision course, blades drawn. The time for negotiation was over.

Xandir didn't stray from his course or draw his own blades. Clutching the stone close to him, he spiraled like a bullet through space, rocketing like a bowling ball toward an assortment of brightly colored pins. The guards closed the gap rapidly, and the cherubim, flying in formation, raised their swords.

At the last moment, Xandir changed course, shooting straight up into the Heavens. At the peak of his arc, he let the stones fly. The stunned cherubim had no time to react.

The stones hit home with devastating force, each shattering row after row of cubicles and tunnels like a massive worm through the flesh of an apple. Great clouds of glass twinkled in the air, the low gravity relinquishing its hold on most of them and letting them slip out into space. The clouds swirled like a halo of diamonds around a wide, golden tendril of light that snaked out of the center of the facility, now more visible than ever.

In the midst of the confusion, Xandir seized his chance. He dove out of the sky, and flew into the glowing, golden stream of Jacob's Ladder. The light closed behind him, and he felt drawn toward the distant blue planet. Xandir flailed his arms and kicked out with his feet, but he found that he couldn't move any faster.

The flow, however, naturally picked up speed, and he soon barreled down the ladder at a dizzying pace. He gave a whoop, glancing back only once to leave a parting taunt. "That was for last time!"

And many, many other things.

Xandir's temporary elation faded with the light around him. He glanced up back the way he had come and cursed his luck. Somehow, they were shutting down the path behind him, and he had barely reentered the Earth's atmosphere.

He had not paid much attention to where the path was taking him. He glanced down, and found himself sailing toward central Europe. Then, as if a bubble had burst around him, the fingers of the path completely dropped him, leaving him tumbling headlong toward the landmass below.

His previous acrobatics forgotten, he struggled to regain control. His wings and arms felt like they had hardened into no more than dead weights, dragging him downward.

The landscape of rolling green hills loomed in his vision, and Xandir told himself that he had no choice but to brace for impact.

He hit the ground hard, crashing through the ruins of an old castle, and burrowing a dozen feet into the ground. Dazed, he squirmed around to an upright position and stared up from the hole.

"At least they're ruins," he muttered. "Can't really feel bad about knocking down something that's already broken."

Though he felt like rolling over and passing out, he knew that the cherubim with their stinging swords would be upon him any minute. Furthermore, he had not fallen far from the path of the ladder, which meant that he was still close to his original destination. With any luck, he could still locate the entrance to the Chute.

Groggy, he clambered out of the chute, flapped his wings to brush off the dirt, and gazed down. Though most mortals couldn't see him, he would be unable to hide the hole.

"An earth angel," he muttered, commenting on the shape of the impression he left. "That will have the locals talking."

Stepping away from the hole, he surveyed his surroundings. The ruins sprawled across the top of a hill and consisted of a series of crumbling walls, an intact main building, and a rectangular tower that jutted up from one side. The surrounding countryside was dotted with plains, forests, and tiny villages, outside of which were barely any signs of life. Xandir shot into the air for a better look, straining his eyes for anything that could cue him as to where to go next.

He scratched his head lazily with one hand. "Where did I land? 'Outer-nowheresville?' "

The revelations hit him simultaneously. First, he was no longer alone. A swarm of angry flickering lights descended like a glowing rain not far from where Xandir had landed. The cavalry was here, and they had called for reinforcements. Xandir cursed his luck a second time, admitting to himself that he might have carried his intended diversion a little bit too far.

Second, he noticed a familiar scent on the wind: brimstone. It penetrated every particle of the air, and for once he didn't wrinkle his nose. It was just the thing to let him know he was on the right track. He paused only a moment, trying to gauge which direction the smell was coming from. He made his decision and shot off at full speed. The swarm followed him; the smaller, white-clad angels easily matching speed and closing the distance with ease. Xandir flew closer and closer to the smell, but then the wind shifted without warning, erasing all trace.

He turned to the cherubim and held up a hand. "Now, wait just a moment. I really don't want to scuffle with you all. You might get your robes dirty. I just need some directions, and I'll be on my way."

The front row of cherubim answered with a volley of arrows from gleaming golden longbows. With unparalleled swiftness, Xandir brought both swords to bear, twirling them like twin tornadoes and stopping the deadly volley in mid flight.

Seizing the cherubim's momentary confusion, Xandir darted off in his original direction, hoping that the wind would shift again in his favor.

Unfortunately for Xandir, his pursuers decided to up the ante. A fully armored Guard Seraph emerged from the midst of the crowd, brandishing a menacing weapon. It was held by a grip in the middle, and a golden chain extended out in both directions. The chain featured lethal blades at even intervals and was tipped by a full-sized sword at both ends.

The Guard Seraph scowled and advanced on Xandir, his twirling weapon gleaming in the moonlight. His opponent lunged, and Xandir parried the blow and dived toward the ground, heading toward the cover of a grove of trees. The grove glowed a bit too much to be made of ordinary trees, leading Xandir to believe the grove might mark the way to his destination.

Xandir flew through the trees, and the glow vanished. He rubbed his eyes with the back of his arm. In his desperate hope to find his way, his mind was playing tricks on him.

Soaring back out of the trees, he turned to face his opponent and swooped away just in time to avoid the path of the Guard's deadly chain. Xandir struck back, deflecting the course of the chain and sending it flying toward its wielder.

The Guard brought the other end around, swinging the weapon with superhuman speed. Xandir shot off to the side and dodged several more blows, noticing to his dismay a ring of lights drawing closer around him in a tightening noose. He was just about to curse his luck for the third time that night when the wind shifted, bringing the scent of brimstone wafting back in his direction.

Xandir adjusted his course and sped off toward the scent, keeping his foe just barely out of striking distance. He spotted his destination and chided himself for not having seen it sooner.

A wide circle of darkness sprawled across an open field, a scar on the face of the earth. As he flew toward the shadow, the smell of brimstone grew stronger. He gathered every bit of strength out of his wings, not daring to look back in fear that it might break his concentration. Xandir kept both swords whirling at his side, partially deflecting the continuous barrage of arrows released by the attackers in pursuit.

A stray arrow descended from above and struck him hard in the shoulder. He lurched back, allowing the Guard Seraph to drive one of his blades into Xandir's wing. He screamed in pain and spiraled out of the sky, plummeting toward the large dark shadow. He hit the ground running, and let his momentum carry him forward, beating the air with his one good wing to help propel his body.

Seeing his opponents still gaining on him, Xandir reached into his armor and retrieved Jarom's Ambrosia. He bit into it, and tingling waves of relief washed over his body. Almost immediately, feeling return to his throbbing wing. With a grin, he took flight again.

Not bad for a doughnut.

As Xandir approached the darkened ground, the center of it opened up, creating a jagged gap like the open throat of a hungry beast. As he ran toward it, it grew wider and wider, producing scalding hot jets of smoke and steam. The Guard Seraph took one final swing at him before retreating, apparently too wary to get any closer to the gap.

Xandir glanced back with a grin. "Finally, a place where angels fear to tread. I guess this means I'm a fool."

He leapt awkwardly with one foot, somersaulting himself the last few feet and into the growing chasm. The stars fell away, and the sounds of the battle melted into the distance. Then Xandir's world went completely black.

TWENTY-ONE
EATING DUST

From their hiding place in the shadows, Judy translated the guttural language as quietly as she could for Eden.

"Now that our stew is properly strong, I think we can begin," said a first voice, coarse and rumbling like an idling truck. "I give the floor to our esteemed Dusteater, who I am sure, needs little introduction."

The room erupted with shouts and growls of approval and then fell silent as another voice began to speak, a smoother voice with a distinctly serpentine quality. "Honored colleagues, I thank you for your attendance tonight. The fires all around us should keep our meeting sheltered from prying eyes."

He paused, and the women could hear the crackle of flames filling the silence. "First," he continued. "I would like to hear the report that Sparkslinger has for us. I trust it will be most enlightening."

Another demon cleared his throat. "Yes, well, there's nothing much to report but that I was successful." It was the strange altered voice of Daren. "The children were conceived as planned. There is nothing that can stop us now."

"And what of your escape? Did you pull off a feasible cover story?" asked Dusteater.

"It was sufficient for the scenario. I told her there was another woman and that she would not see me again. Very convincing if I do say so myself."

160

Dusteater growled long and low. "Still, it would be better if there were a more permanent solution. Your departure still leaves doubt in the minds of those who knew this mortal vessel. They might come looking for him, and that could be most problematic."

"What? Do you mean you want me to give up this body already? Do you know how hard it is to possess the mind of such a strong-willed, able-bodied man? It took me months just to get my foot in the door. At least let me enjoy myself a bit first."

"Don't trifle with me, Sparkslinger! I have been in this business far longer than you! Do not forget who it was who beguiled the First Parents using the guise of a snake! The mission comes before everything else, even your 'fun.' There will be plenty of time for frivolity once this world belongs to us."

"What of the Fellowship of Nod?" asked another higher-pitched voice who sounded like he gargled nails on a daily basis. "Are we not to remain allies? The word is they are planning a massive offensive movement. Even now they've sent one of their magma ships to the door of Serche. That cannot bode well for us."

Dusteater laughed, the sound creeping over Eden like a horde of spiders. "They are fools to think they can enter Serche and take of its bounty. Let them try. Their efforts will come to naught, and they will have wasted their strength. They are still a formidable force, but in the end, whether they ally themselves with us is of little consequence. Once Caesar is born, they will cower at our feet.

"Now," Dusteater seethed, "I want to hear the other reports of the infiltration project. If Sparkslinger is to be believed, we have approximately seven months before everything must be in place. I would be most displeased to hear any complaints about such a generous time frame."

Another demon spoke, sounding like a normal young man with a cold. "I have just been around to the European contingent. They are making steady progress on all fronts. Seven months should be more than sufficient."

"I have similar progress to report in the Middle East,"

continued another. "The Legion will be well in place. Really, it seems almost too easy sometimes."

"This country is the easiest of all," announced a third, beefier voice. "I've just gotten back from Ryan Jennings' office, and he's under our complete control."

Five or six others gave their reports, each naming off their progress in various parts of the world. Judy and Eden exchanged confused glances. "Ryan Jennings," whispered Eden. "I feel like I should know that name."

Judy nodded. "You might have seen him on the news. He's a high-profile senior senator from New Jersey. Some are saying he's going to make a presidential bid."

When the rest of the demons had finished making their reports, Dusteater reclaimed control of the meeting. "Excellent," he praised. "I shall return to our Prince and let him know. Continue your efforts and stay alert. Sparkslinger, for your own good and the good of us all, you need to relinquish that body—tonight if possible. I'll personally see to it that you are supplied with an even better one."

Eden gasped and her hand flew over her mouth. She shook her head, as if the motion alone could influence the decision.

"As you wish," replied Sparkslinger, making no attempt to veil his disappointment.

"This meeting is adjourned," announced Dusteater. "We shall reconvene in a fortnight."

Eden's tears fell silently onto the darkened floor. She looked pleadingly at her friend. "What do we do?" she whispered. "That demon is going to kill Daren tonight. We've got to stop it."

Judy nodded, shrinking farther back into the shadows. "I agree, but the question is how? We've got to wait until the rest of them leave."

Eden's head sank, and she buried her face in her hands. "Maybe I can talk to him. There must be a part of my husband left in that thing. I know I could get through to him."

Judy bit her lip, watching the stairwell. "I don't know if that's wise. Chances are the demon has more control than you think. He'll be dangerous for sure. I mean, just look at what I've done."

Before Eden could protest, the first of the demons thundered down the stairs, growling and rumbling. The women had expected red-skinned, hunched beasts with menacing horns, but instead the group that met their eyes could have passed for well-groomed businessmen. They wore suits of various colors, with monochrome ties and brightly polished shoes. They all wore facial hair, some sporting full beards and others only goatees. Judy and Eden could have passed them on the streets of New York without the slightest idea of who they really were.

One by one, the group filed out the door, muttering parting words to the sentries posted nearby. At last, the sentries followed, shutting the door firmly behind them.

They waited in silence for several minutes, listening to the sounds of conversation fading into the distance. Eden glanced knowingly at Judy and gestured with her head up the stairs. Daren had not been among those who had just left.

"Okay," whispered Judy, "but I'm going up first. I'm at least part demon myself, and perhaps that will help."

They emerged from their hiding place and crept up the stairs. As they reached the top landing, a wave of heat assaulted their faces. Eden shielded herself with her hands while Judy smiled despite herself, relishing the warmth.

The door to the meeting place stood ajar, and the light beyond emitted a flickering glow. The entire floor had been covered with smoldering coals, but somehow the floor, walls, or ceiling hadn't caught fire.

Daren stood in the middle of the room, his eyes closed and his arms folded, the firelight glinting off his jet black hair. He reached into his suit coat pocket and withdrew a long, slender knife. The blade seemed to absorb the light instead of reflect it. Opening his eyes, he tossed the knife back and forth from hand to hand. With a sigh, Daren lifted the knife high above his head, the point aimed at his heart.

Judy leapt into the doorway. "Stop," she yelled, rushing forward with hands outstretched. Daren hesitated, lowering the knife harmlessly to his side.

"Who the Devil are you? We didn't invite any women."

Daren's eyes flared open, radiating hostility. "I can see you're nearly one of us," said Daren. "The demon's hold on you is growing rapidly."

"I was bitten by a fire snake," said Judy. "Ever since, I've felt myself slipping, becoming more and more like you."

Daren stroked his goatee with the hand not clutching the knife. "It's odd . . . you seem familiar somehow."

He then spat a command in the demon tongue, which Judy didn't understand. Instantly, her entire body flared with heat, and she felt like her soul was being sucked out of her. She stumbled a few steps toward Daren and fell to her knees, embedding them in the hot coals. A faint image of a beautiful but heavily scarred woman came into view in front of her. The woman moaned and gazed wistfully at Daren.

"That is because you know me well, Sparkslinger. It seems that despite my best efforts, fate has brought us together once more."

Sparkslinger gasped and dropped the knife. "Ashbreather, how can this be? Dusteater told me you were no more. You cannot be real. He told me he performed the deed himself!"

Ashbreather nodded. "Have you forgotten that he of all people can deceive? He is a master liar, second only to the Prince himself. He would make you believe that we can cease to exist." The woman laughed without humor. "To be sure, when he's through with you, it certainly looks that way. But no matter what he does, a tiny speck—a spark—remains. And if fostered long enough, that spark can rekindle the former flame."

Sparkslinger stepped closer with a trembling, outstretched hand. "It has been well over a thousand years. That long have I mourned you. That long have I lived under the shadow of this deception. Dusteater will answer for this!"

Ashbreather swayed mournfully from side to side. "No, you must not confront him. Would you like to taste firsthand the terrors I have been forced to endure? You are foolish to consider such a thing!"

Sparkslinger remained adamant, flames curling up around him. "Much has changed during the last thousand years. He has

grown weak and complacent. These days his mind is so preoc-
cupied by other things that he scarcely senses the dissent growing
in the ranks against him. I would not be alone in my opposition
of him."

He took several steps forward. Daren groaned and fell to
the floor as a ghostly figure rose out of his chest—a thin man
with stringy black hair, sunken dark eyes, and an impossibly
wide mouth. "Whatever we do, we must leave now! Dusteater is
coming back soon to make sure I have disposed of this body. We
need to be long gone by then."

After struggling through the demon's conversation, Judy
finally found her own voice. "Daren, your wife Eden is right outside, and she's anxious to have you back safe. Please, Sparkslinger,
can't you find a different host? You've done so much to them
already!"

Sparkslinger's razor thin eyebrows shot up in surprise. "My,
my—you are a strong one. Perhaps it would be better for you,
Ashbreather, to find a different host. She might resist you a very
long time before relinquishing control."

Judy continued, undeterred. "If you want to stand a chance,
you'll have to change too. When Dusteater finds out you've run
away, he'll know exactly who to look for. You'll need to disguise
yourself."

Sparkslinger wrinkled his face. "You might have a point,
mortal. But unfortunately, I know of no other suitable hosts at the
moment, so I'll think we'll stay put. Come, dear sister, let's put
some distance between us and that slippery snake."

At the mention of a snake, Judy caught sight of a flicker of
movement in the far corner. It lasted only a split second, but it was
enough for Judy to identify the source: a familiar crimson snake.
Her entire body burned with the painful memory. "Sparkslinger,
the snake! You've been discovered!"

The demon turned reluctantly, suspecting a trick. However, as
he turned, his face contorted in despair. "Dusteater, that vermin!
He is spying on us. Come, through the window."

In an instant, Sparkslinger flung himself back into Daren.
Daren leapt to his feet and made his way toward the window.

Before he reached it, however, the window imploded, scattering glass across the room. A bright flash of light ripped through the room, stunning everyone.

Struggling against the demon within her, Judy rushed for the door, which burst open with the window. She fell to the ground and watched in horror as Dusteater entered the room, grasping an unconscious Eden by the scruff of the neck like a disobedient puppy.

"Well this is a surprise, Ashbreather. It appears I didn't properly finish the job last time. How careless of me."

He wandered over and picked up the dagger Daren had dropped. "And you, Sparkslinger. I tried to tell myself that you could be trusted. I longed for it to be so. But you've just proved beyond all doubt where your loyalties lie."

He raised the dagger over the motionless Sparkslinger. His eyes lay wide open, though he could not move or speak. "Don't worry, Sparkslinger. You will not be forgotten. Your contribution has been great. For the sake of your final mission, I shall preserve your memory. No one else will know that you perished a traitor."

The knife slashed down through the air, and Judy screamed. The knife hung in midair, stopped by an unseen hand.

A warm, constant light flooded the room, emanating from the space between the knife and the fallen demon. Judy saw the outline of a winged figure holding a sleek blade against the dagger, halting it in mid-stroke. "Go!"

A resonate command rang from the figure, and in an instant, Judy regained control of her limbs. Eden dropped from Dusteater's arm as the demon strained against his new opponent.

Two other shapes shot through the window, one catching Eden in mid-stroke and the other joining its companion in combating Dusteater, now locked in fierce combat with his blade.

Drawing strength from desperation, Judy leapt forward and hoisted the much larger Daren onto her back.

I need to stop doing this. This old back of mine is going to give out any moment.

The second figure had already whisked Eden out the window, and Judy dashed to follow. Dusteater, noticing his prey escaping, dealt a scathing blow to his attackers and turned his attention to the escaping pair.

Dusteater hissed, and a dozen fiery snakes leapt up from the flames, carpeting the floor with a wriggling mass of death. The snakes leapt up onto Judy's legs, sinking their teeth into her through her clothes. Judy stumbled, her vision darkening and blurring. Her stomach heaved, and she fell to her knees, only inches from the window.

As she fell, her hands grazed the windowsill, and met with another set of fingers. The fingers gleamed pale in the moonlight, and they pulled Judy and Daren out through the window and into the night sky.

As she rose into the heavens, a few smaller winged figures fluttered around them with knives, flicking away the remainder of the fiery snakes. Judy didn't remain conscious long enough to see a plume of fire engulf the cabin, or the entire forest burst into flames.

TWENTY-TWO
A COLD DAY IN HELL

Xandir found his wings useless. His descent accelerated, and he tumbled recklessly from side to side, surrounded by complete blackness.

A scene burst into view so suddenly that it stung his eyes. Voices and chaos surrounded him from every direction.

He first saw himself, flying over a familiar Italian city, wincing as his burning hands called him elsewhere. Next, he found himself in a cove during a fierce storm where the woman he had fallen in love with had seen him for the first time. The storm had overtaken her fishing boat, and he had employed his white sword to rescue her from certain death.

The scene then flashed to their secret meetings by night—on the balcony, in the caves, near the ruined temples—every detail brighter and more vivid than any memory.

He winced as he saw the sword stroke that had crippled the peasant shepherd who had accidentally wandered in on them and had been attempting to flee. Disgusted with himself, he tried to shut his eyes but found them immovable. He tried to raise his hands but found them pinned to his side. Scene after harrowing scene flashed by, time and time again, one image meshing seamlessly into the next, driving Xandir to the point of near insanity.

"Where are all my good intentions? I thought the road to Hell was paved with them!"

Then the scene of Xandir breaking the glass building on the moon flashed by, playing back as if in slow motion. He watched every shard of glass fly off into space. He groaned and pursed his lips as he saw the individual terror on the faces of the hapless checkpoint employees as they scattered from their ruined offices. "I had to do it. They wouldn't have let me through otherwise!"

His cries fell on deaf ears, or rather, on no ears at all. As he fell, the Chute increased in temperature from uncomfortably warm to blazingly hot. Xandir couldn't be sure whether it was the actual heat or just the burn of his conscience eating a hole inside him.

He fell for what seemed an eternity, unable to move, and pinned by guilt on every side. Without warning, he burst out of the Chute and into a massive tunnel covered in a brimming river of magma. Directly beneath him gaped the Jaws, the churning whirlpool opening even wider to receive him. Out of the grip of the Chute, he struggled to regain control of his wings but found that he still couldn't move at all.

A sudden chill spread behind his ears, and a voice echoed in his head. "You don't want to go all the way down. Repeat the key word." He then gave Xandir the word, which didn't sound like any he had ever heard.

Only feet above the Jaws, Xandir yelled the word at the top of his voice. It reverberated throughout the smooth tunnel, and in an instant, his limbs were his to control once more. With only inches to spare, he swooped out from his collision course into the Jaws and skirted the surface of the magma, rising rapidly to the stalactite ceiling.

He drank in the whole scene, from the sleek black blot of the magma ship, to the mammoth form of Serche teetering close to the Jaws.

Xandir took a deep breath and reached behind his ears. "Thanks, but you really could have told me sooner."

"I told you soon enough," answered the voice with a growl. "I can't have you growing complacent. Remember, we are still in charge. Once they have your scent, the Jaws will hunger for you all the more."

"I'll be sure to stay clear of them, thank you. And you could have warned me about the trip down here too. Not exactly the scenic route."

"What did you expect? A leisurely stroll? It's the Chute to Hades! It serves to remind people that they deserve where they are headed."

Xandir sighed. At least it was over. "Right," he muttered in his best disinterested tone. "Now I've got the means to turn it all into a winter wonderland. Would now be a good time?"

"Yes, now!" spat Ganosh. "We've waited far too long already. Just get it over with."

Xandir reached into his armor and withdrew Yearti's orb of brilliant blue. It gleamed even brighter in the light of the magma, and already Xandir felt an intense chill sweep over his entire being. He gazed down at the Jaws and fancied that they were fixed in a grin. He responded with a grin of his own. He was going to enjoy this.

Hovering along the ceiling until he had positioned himself directly over the center of the Jaws, he held out the orb in his extended arm. For a breathless moment, he remained perfectly still, basking in the coldness amidst the relentless waves of heat. In an instant, he tossed the orb into the air, and before it could fall again, he withdrew both swords and shattered it with a devastating cross strike.

The orb released a blinding column of blue light that pierced directly down through the Jaws, writhing with raw energy. The orb's fragments scattered across the entire passage, creating a swift moving blizzard, the flakes fine and razor edged.

The stalactites frosted over to become icicles, and the river of magma cooled rapidly, sending up torrents of steam, which in turn froze in mid-air, creating ice crystals that clattered back onto the crusted magma and onto the deck of the now-stranded magma ship.

The whirlpool slowed and then stopped, freezing solid in a matter of seconds. The huge jutting rocks that formed the Jaws hardened into two brilliant shafts of ice, and even the floating city ceased its erratic movements and hung wrapped in a shroud of brilliant snow.

The entire transformation, drastic as it was, took place in mere moments. At last, the tunnel stood still, and Xandir nodded, pleased with his handiwork. He glanced skyward. "Yearti, if I ever see you again, I owe you one." A moment later, the tingling sensation behind his ears returned, and he placed his hands on one ear.

"Excellent! You do not disappoint, Xandir. Your resourceful-ness has been beyond our wildest imagination."

"Save the compliments for later. Just tell me what's next."

"Do you see the magma ship moored below you?"

"Kinda hard to miss," Xandir scoffed. "I bet they're in a bind. Am I supposed to help them?"

"Yes," replied Ganosh, "but not in the way that you think. Fly onto the deck. You'll meet someone there that I think you'll recognize. You'll receive further instructions once you arrive."

Not knowing how long he had until the Jaws thawed, Xandir wasted no time diving down to the ship and alighting gently on the ice-covered deck, which was completely empty of life.

As soon as his foot touched the deck, three figures emerged: the hulking Tubal, followed by the robed Jubal, and finally Jarom, his intended apprentice. Xandir's face brightened at the sight of the cherub, though his stomach churned at the thought of what they might be expected to do next. He fished for the right words.

"Well, Lil' Halo, I should have warned you that I hang out with a tough crowd."

The cherub flashed a smile, which faded almost as soon as it reached its peak. "Don't worry," Jarom said. "The company's been fine. I did always say I wanted to see some new places too. But I'm afraid I've gotten my wish fulfilled to the extreme."

"You're about to see one more new place," said Jubal, his voice melodious and low. "The condemned city that is, for once, enjoy-ing a respite from the constant heat."

Xandir was about to press his hands together to call the High Seraph when they suddenly flared with heat. With a flash of light, a small scroll appeared in his open hands.

Without delay, he unrolled the scroll, and a small, green, glass flask fell out. Jarom snatched the flask out of the air before it could clatter to the icy ground. Xandir's eyes scanned the parchment and recognized the High Seraph's flowing writing:

Xandir,

I shall not harbor any notions that the Jaws' freezing had nothing to do with you. I do not know how you managed it, but I am bound to keep my word, no matter how grudgingly. Rest assured that your movements and motives are under intense scrutiny, and you will be held fully accountable for whatever you may undertake in Serche. You are to take no one out, under the harshest penalty imaginable. Enclosed is the key to opening the gates. I suppose you are clever enough to get it working without my holding your hand every step of the way.

Elandael,
High Seraph of the First Order

Xandir raised an eyebrow. In all these centuries, Xandir had never known the High Seraph's given name, and it gave him a secret sense of satisfaction that he wasn't the only one with a strange name. He tucked the parchment away in his armor and turned back to Jubal.

"So, I have the key. What is it exactly that you want me to do while I'm in there?"

Jubal stepped forward, strumming a harp fashioned out of mother of pearl.

"First, you both must go to the gates. The nature of the task demands it. You must pluck an entire fruit from the Tree of Death located deep in the heart of the city. The fruit is poison to the touch of all but the purest in heart. As we all know, Xandir, you are no Saint, but we can't very well send the little cherub in alone, can we? He wouldn't last ten minutes."

Xandir grunted, holding back his will to protest. This wasn't how he wanted things to go, but it seemed that he had little choice. Apparently it didn't matter who he worked for—giving up his will seemed to be the eternal status quo.

"And how exactly are we supposed to find this tree? I can't

imagine they have street signs and road maps. Perhaps a billboard? 'See the noxious Tree of Death! Only ten gold pieces! Real fruit smoothies only two!'"

The corners of Jubal's mouth turned up slightly. "As the High Seraph said, you have proven yourself to be quite resourceful. I'm confident you will find a way, especially if you want to see your dear little Italian maiden again. She ought to provide ample motivation to get your brain working."

"Yes," agreed Xandir. "Plenty."

Jubal smiled wickedly. "Good. Then we shall wait here for your return—however long it may take."

Without another word, Jubal turned and beckoned for his brother to follow him into the darkness. They disappeared, the faint strains of a tune audible long after they had gone.

Xandir and Jarom flew the short distance from the deck of the ship to the forbidding gates of the city. Once there, Xandir studied the statues on both sides with a decided air of superiority.

"I've seen better," he announced.

Jarom, on the other hand, was trembling already. He had never seen anything like it.

"Relax, Lil' Halo," Xandir said. "I've seen cities like this before. They're too cheap or too scared to hire decent guards, so they fashion a really imposing gate. All squawk and no talons, if you know what I mean."

Jarom shook his head, his distress deepening. "Actually, I have no idea what you mean. The most imposing place I had to go before I met you was the Ambrosia Auditing Office, which, I'll have you know, looks like a candy factory in comparison to this."

Xandir sighed at his amateur companion. "Don't sweat it. We'll be in and out before the river starts to thaw. Serche's full of a bunch of old stiffs who have been hanging around for hundreds of years. How bad could this possibly be?"

Jarom remained unconvinced. "I don't know. I have heard stories about this place—none of them good. They say that a single good person who lives here is the only reason this place hasn't sunk completely. One good person!"

Xandir shrugged. "Stories are stories. If I believed half of the stories I've heard over the years, I'd take a nose dive into the Jaws and take my chances in Hades. We'll just have to get on the good side of that one good person, now won't we?"

Jarom bobbed his head in defeat, hoping silently that he wasn't going to have to use the phrase "I told you so" anytime in the near future.

"Now," Xandir muttered, "just how is that flask supposed to get us in to this place? It's not exactly your conventional key."

He unstopped the top of the flask and held the contents close to his face. "Smells like regular water. Though that doesn't really mean anything."

Jarom flew closer to the gate itself. Intricate carvings graced most of its surface, though he didn't see anything that resembled an actual keyhole either. Hesitantly, he touched the door with his bare hand. Nothing happened.

Then he looked closer at the characters that formed the frame of the door. Though he couldn't read them, they still looked vaguely familiar. He traced the pattern several times with his fingers to be sure his mind wasn't just playing tricks on him.

"Xandir, this language—it looks so familiar."

"What?" said Xandir sarcastically. "They teach ancient Serchean up there now? You really must have had too much time on your hands."

Jarom narrowed his eyes, groping around for the connection in his mind. "No, it's not that. But they do teach us the Original Tongue—you know, before all the languages got corrupted down here, they all spoke the same perfect language. Serche was around so long ago that maybe their language was still very close to the original."

Xandir glared back with a lifted eyebrow. "Well, professor, if that's the case, what does it say? Give us the rough translation."

Jarom squinted at the inscription for several long moments, all the while muttering to himself. Xandir flapped his wings impatiently and waited for the final verdict. When at last Jarom looked up, Xandir noticed beads of sweat on his young apprentice's brow from his exertion.

"Well?" prompted Xandir.

"As far as I can tell," Jarom said, "they're instructions about how to open the gate. They really couldn't have just made this easy, could they?" He cleared his throat. "Roughly translated, it says, 'The first bowl a drop of life's red sap, the second water in a trap. The third the vessel in the gap, then think upon the fourth— the cap.'"

Jarom traced the lines to where they formed a shallow impression in the door.

Xandir leaned in closer to see. "There's only one hole. It mentioned four."

Jarom shrugged. "I said it was a rough translation." He took a dagger, which hung by his side, and served as his sole means of defense. "I think this might do the trick."

He pricked the end of his finger with the knife, drawing blood, and placed it in the first gap. Immediately, a second gap opened up right next to it, and a handful of the carvings lit up, giving off a faint, crimson glow.

"Nice," Xandir muttered. "Life's red sap. Wasn't lost in translation."

The second hole was larger, and Xandir figured out quickly what belonged there. He emptied the whole flask into the space and stepped back. The water disappeared, and then a few more of the carvings on the door lit up, taking on a blue glow.

A third deep hole appeared and Xandir placed the now empty flask into the long slit. It slid snugly into place, bringing a third set of carvings on the door into golden life.

Jarom flew up and snatched the stopper from Xandir's hands. "I figured it out. I want to open it."

Xandir smiled and threw up his hands. "Suit yourself."

The stopper fit perfectly into the small depression that had formed at the insertion of the flask. The remaining carvings shone green, and a series of grinding clicks sounded from within the door. They both stepped back as the doors slid away in all directions, part of the gates sinking into the ground, part being carried up and over, and part shifting to the sides. In a matter of moments, a dark, somber passageway stood before him. Not a sound came from the forbidding darkness.

"Well, this is it. Unless you'd like to turn back."

Jarom shook his head. It was too late for that now. "No, like you said, let's just get this over with."

Xandir nodded and motioned for the cherub to follow. They both vanished from the view of the ship, melting into the frosty darkness.

TWENTY-THREE
TEA WITH TOBIAS

Xandir and Jarom passed through the corridor and emerged into a wide courtyard. It looked like no one had lived there in centuries, though they could tell that the place must have once been quite magnificent.

The entire courtyard had a certain symmetry to it, with fountains placed every dozen meters, topped with statues depicting winged and helmeted warriors wielding shields and weapons in heroic poses. Each fountain was connected to the next by a series of shallow canals coated with chipped flakes of fading enamel.

The buildings rose in terraces, each level supporting the next with intricately carved spiraling columns. The levels were connected by an elevator system, run by a series of weights and pulleys. The weights filled with water and emptied with the rise and fall of the lifts. They did so apparently of their own accord, without the benefit of passengers. The fountains spurted water only sporadically, and the water that spilled out would not have been fit to drink by any mortal.

A path made of green cobblestones cut straight from the entrance to another gate, similar to the first. They approached, glancing around nervously.

"Looks like no one told them to leave the light on," muttered Xandir.

"Where do you suppose they all went?" added Jarom.

Xandir shrugged, glancing over his shoulder. "Maybe there is a nightlife scene here—Club S, the Happy Demon, something like that."

Jarom rolled his eyes. "Or they're thinking about ways to ambush and torture intruders, should they ever come along."

Jarom scanned the surface of the second gate, looking for the same strange writing, which might give them some clue of how to progress through the city.

"There's nothing here," he cried. "Just pictures. It seems they wanted to let visitors in to rot!"

"Keep your voice down," said Xandir. "It doesn't look like anyone's around, but rest assured, they're lurking somewhere."

"What an awful word. Lurking sounds so sinister," said a new voice from the shadows. The voice was old but smooth, as if it had much practice wheeling and dealing its way out of tight situations.

They whirled around, Xandir drawing both blades to hover at the stranger's throat.

The man didn't appear to care half as much as he should have. "A little high strung, are we? Why don't you come in and have a spot of tea? That'll be sure to calm your nerves."

The man was short and of medium build with a tangle of pathetic gray hairs flopping over the side of his mostly bald head. Deep wrinkles and pockmarks marred his ancient face, though angel and cherub both noticed that the man miraculously still had all of his teeth. His eyes darted to and fro quickly, never resting on one place for more than a few seconds. He wore a dark green robe, stained with years of dirt and grime.

Over the robe a cloth fell down both his front and his back with a hole just big enough for his head cut out of the top. Though the cloth must have once been white, it was now stained with dark spots that looked like splatters of blood and ink. Xandir wrinkled his nose at the sight of it. He couldn't imagine why the strange man would ever keep such a garment, especially when it looked easy to remove.

"You do want to pass through the gate, don't you? You'll need help for that. And if you want to get any farther than the first gate, you'll surely need a guide. The city is vast and perilous, and you'll need someone who knows all its ins and outs."

Xandir lowered his swords a few inches. "And I take it you're volunteering for that position?"

The old man nodded vigorously. "Why, yes. My name is Tobias, and I would be an ideal candidate."

He grinned in a way that made Jarom think of a snake inviting a rabbit into its hole.

Xandir scoffed, withdrawing his swords still further. "I have a feeling you aren't offering anything out of the goodness of your heart. I can't imagine we'd have anything you want, so I want a straight answer. What's your price?"

Tobias's perfect teeth glinted in the low light. "Well, there is one thing. Once you are finished here with, oh, whatever errand you've set out to do, I ask only one thing: take me with you. Take me out of this wretched place."

Jarom glanced warily up at Xandir, torn between their immediate needs and the future consequences. "Xandir, you remember what the High Seraph said," Jarom whispered. "We might be better off muddling through alone."

Tobias laughed full on, the sound echoing through the empty streets. "You two are either exceptionally brave or exceptionally foolish. You're not going to be able to solve all the problems that lie ahead with those oversized butter knives."

Xandir narrowed his eyes and stepped closer to Tobias. "We need to get into the heart of the city as quickly as possible. If you can deliver us there and back in safety, I'll figure out a way to get you out of here."

Jarom sighed. Xandir had completely ignored his input, as most people did. Just how was Xandir going to smooth out bringing a Serchean out of the city? Jarom realized he wasn't the copilot in this operation—like it or not, he was simply along for the ride.

"Come inside," Tobias repeated. "There are some things you should know about the city before we head out."

He motioned them through a dark archway covered by a dingy curtain. Then he parted the curtain, allowing a dim glow to spill out onto the cobblestones. Xandir enterd next, followed reluctantly by Jarom.

They entered the darkened room and took seats around a low table on thinly padded cushions on the floor. The man set down three chipped teacups and pressed a lever on the edge of the table. With a grinding of gears, a trapdoor slid back in the center of the table, revealing a miniature fountain shaped like a dragon with four heads. When the fountain had risen to its full height, each head spewed a stream of steaming water directly into each of the cups. The streams cut off with a sputter, creating a short but violent storm of scalding water on the table around it.

Tobias grinned sheepishly. "Doesn't work as well as it used to," he apologized. "Just like most everything around here."

He reached behind him into a cupboard and retrieved a small satchel with herbs. He placed a small amount in each cup, and the hot water turned deep amber and released a sweet aroma.

Xandir raised the cup to his lips and took a sip. He bobbed his head in satisfaction. "That's really quite good. Aren't you going to drink any?"

Jarom eyed his cup suspiciously but made no motion to lift it. He shifted his gaze to Xandir, sizing up his reaction to the brew.

Suddenly, Xandir's face paled, and he fell backwards, clutching his throat. Jarom leapt into the air, making for the door.

Tobias rose and blocked the exit. "Stay where you are, little one. Your friend is fine. I know a prankster when I see one."

Jarom turned about, fearing the worst, and found that Tobias had spoken the truth. Xandir sat upright, sipping his tea, obviously trying to stifle a laugh.

"It's just tea, Lil' Halo. Now sit down and relax before I have to tie you to the table."

With a scowl, Jarom fluttered back down and landed on his cushion. He took the teacup in his hand and sipped from it. Then he nodded and set it back on the table.

"So," muttered Xandir, "what is it you wanted to tell us? I hate to be rude, but we don't have all the time in the world."

Tobias took another sip of tea and set his cup down. "Ah, yes, let me just explain a few things, and we'll be off." He reached behind him in another drawer and withdrew two strips of white cloth with a circular hole in the middle, much like the one draped over his own clothing. He offered one to Xandir and one to Jarom.

"Thanks for the souvenir, I guess," muttered Xandir, "but fashion has changed a bit since you all got stuck down here." He turned the cloth over in his hands. It felt and looked like normal fabric in every way.

"Put them on," urged Tobias.

Xandir raised an eyebrow. "I can't say it goes too well with my armor. Is there a reason I should ruin my signature style with this strange-looking thing?"

Tobias nodded. "You won't be able to get through any of the following gates without one. Put them on."

Xandir slipped the cloth over his head. It came down to only about the middle of his chest. Jarom's, however, spanned the entire length of his body. No sooner were the clothes over their heads than they began to change. Ghastly red and black blots spread across the surface of their bodies, creating a grotesque picture of chaos. Xandir swatted and brushed off the cloth, but the stains were already deeply imbedded and weren't even smudged by his hands.

"What just happened?" demanded Xandir. "I definitely do not look good in red."

"Forgive my reluctance to tell the whole truth right up front." Tobias held out the cloth and they watched as another red blotch about the size of a small coin formed near the bottom. "These clothes are called Sin Shrouds. They are a punishment for all those who enter Serche: a visual record of all your outstanding misdeeds. The red blots represent sins of commission—sins of action, if you will—and the black ones represent sins of omission or inaction."

Xandir glanced over and saw that Jarom's shroud was immaculate compared to his own, which looked rather like an explosion in a pen factory.

"As I mentioned before, none of the gates in the city will open to a person without one. Furthermore, the front gate won't open again for someone wearing one."

"What's the problem in that?" asked Xandir. "Can't we just slip them off?"

In answer to his own question, he tried to pull the cloth back over his head, and found that the more he tugged, the tighter the cloth constricted around his neck. He finally gave up altogether.

"No, it's not that easy," warned Tobias. "The cloth can only be taken off when it is completely clean—spotless. Seeing that the city's entirely populated by sinners, it is a pretty effective way of keeping everyone inside."

Xandir glanced over his shoulder, trying hard to mask the mounting panic swelling up in his chest. "We need to get out of here eventually. Please tell me there's some sort of heavy-duty laundry facility in town."

Tobias shook his head. "You could scrub all day. Those stains are deep and lasting. There is a way, however, to get them clean. If you wash the shroud in the Pool of Divine Tears, they will become clean."

Xandir rolled his eyes. "So I suppose we'll have to navigate a labyrinth, fight off legions of guards, solve ridiculous riddles, and tame and ride a pair of local three-headed monsters in order to find this pool? Isn't that usually the way this works?"

Tobias chuckled, pointing toward the exit. "Ah, thankfully not. The pool is located in a small covered pavilion not far from the main gate. That will be the easy part."

Xandir sat down, trying to calm his nerves with another sip of tea. It was Jarom's turn to be inquisitive. "Why does it have such a strange name? What's so special about it?"

Tobias sighed and began. "Many thousands of years ago, Serche was a heathen nation who believed in a whole legion of gods. The legend was that the pool shows visions of that which is lost. Even the gods visited the pool and mingled their tears with the water as they stared at the tormenting images. Back then, we Sercheans were a moral and enterprising folk, more prosperous than any other people under the heavens. We developed technology centuries before its time and generally enjoyed a life of extreme luxury unparalleled in the entire world."

"But after a while," he continued, it seemed like our little world was simply not enough. Our leaders reasoned that such a superior race had a right, nay, an obligation to spread its influence to all those they could reach. They launched a massive and highly successful military campaign against the known world.

"With our superior technology, we easily overcame nation after nation, spreading our influence far abroad. But even that wasn't enough for King Mardan. Secretly, the king made a pact with the Devil himself. Together, they planted the Tree of Death, a cruel mockery of the great Tree of Life. The king wanted to use the tree to eradicate those who would not conform to the Serchean ways and to secure his conquest beyond all reasonable doubt."

Tobias hung his head, causing his feeble strands of hair to dangle in front of his face. "That's when the city started to sink. Fortunately for the world, Heaven could not let the Serchean conquest continue. The city first sank to the bottom of the ocean, where it was guarded by a powerful being who did not let anyone in or out. But he didn't stop our leaders from trying, all the while missionaries poured in, intent on saving our souls and salvaging the city. In the end, they all left except one, and it is for his sake that the city now hovers over the Jaws instead of plunging headlong into them. Even now, he walks among the worst of us, trying to get us to mend our ways."

"Do you think we'll see him?" asked Jarom, his interest piqued.

"Perhaps. He lives near the tree itself, so there is always a chance. After the city's fall, it was organized into levels according to our crimes. Here, in the Lower Court suburbs, you'll find the 'best of the worst'—those who are only petty criminals. We'll pass through the second gate into the Den of Thieves. If we're able to crawl through the den, the third gate will take us into the Bed of Iniquity, and if we manage to squeeze past those wretched dogs unmolested, we'll find ourselves with the murderers in the Dome of Death. From the Dome, we can take the tunnels into the laboratory where the tree was created, just within the Realm of the Traitors. Once you've done your business there, we can escape through a shortcut into the Tower of Pride, where you can take a trolley back down to the main gate and the fountain."

Xandir nodded, ingesting this information with the rest of his tea. He set the empty cup down and drew the back of his hand across his lips. "Well, I think story time is over, as enlightening as it was. When do we leave?"

Tobias downed the last of his tea and stood. He slipped a satchel from its peg and slung it over one shoulder. "No time like the present."

The old man led the other two out of his residence to the front of the second gate. To their combined surprise, it opened freely as they approached.

Tobias stepped forward, beckoning the others to follow. "This is the easy gate. You just have to be wearing a shroud. Watch your pockets—anything that isn't nailed down is up for grabs."

Xandir placed a protective hand on each sword, and Jarom simply swallowed hard, wondering again just how he had gotten mixed up in all this insanity.

TWENTY-FOUR
DEN OF THIEVES

Xandir, Jarom, and Tobias stepped through the gate, and the dim light fell to almost nothing. Occasional torches flickered on the dusty streets, revealing rows of ramshackle houses, none of which boasted four upright walls. Xandir's first step landed him in a pile of rotting garbage, and he wrinkled his nose. The next step didn't fare much better.

"Stay airborne, Jarom. You won't like what you land in."

Jarom wrinkled his own nose, swatting at the cluster of gnats swarming about his face. "It's not much better up here," Jarom said. "I'll never complain about those American cities again. At least they have places where you can come up for air."

Tobias sighed. "I wish I could say this was the worst of it. It really is tragic how low we've sunken. Your eyes get used to the darkness though. Just give it a few minutes."

They waited in silence, watching ghostly shapes weave in and out of the dark corners and alleyways. True to Tobias's word, their eyes adjusted, bringing the dilapidated suburb into a clearer focus. They didn't like the view.

Straight ahead of them, the third gate loomed large. Its surface was completely smooth except for a tiny keyhole slightly off to the left. The polished metal looked completely out of place in the dismal environment.

Xandir's eyes brightened. "Well, that looks easy. Just insert the key, and we'll be on our way. No need to go messing about with thieves."

Tobias laughed, wiping his brow with his filthy shroud. "Sure, it will be easy. Nothing could be simpler."

Jarom groaned as a deep red splotch blossomed on the end of Tobias' shroud.

"Okay, okay," Tobias admitted. "I guess I can't lie. This is going to be a bit tricky. We had best find an unoccupied shack and claim it."

"What?" Xandir seethed. "We're not going to stay here! We don't have time!"

Tobias shook his head. "You're lucky you weren't around when they were handing out life sentences. They would have put you in the Passage of Patience. The victims are trapped in a cell with 365 stone blocks between them and freedom. They each have a pick ax and can see just the one block ahead of them. Together, they work on chipping themselves out. The catch is that if they so much as touch more than one block per day, the tunnel caves in with a complete set of new blocks, bringing them back to the beginning."

Jarom's eyes grew wide. "They have to wait a year to get out? I don't know if I could resist the temptation."

Tobias nodded, gesturing toward a nearby lean-to, which looked a bit larger than its neighbors. "Do you see the point? The punishment is tailored to the crime. The only way they could ever escape is to overcome the flaw that got them in there in the first place. It's the same principle here. Among all these thieves, the key changes hands constantly. One thief is always taking it from another, and they never seem to learn that the key will only work in the hands of someone who didn't steal it."

Xandir narrowed his eyes. "Just how many people live here?"

"Thousands, my dear angel. Thousands of greedy, grubby little hands."

Even Xandir's countenance fell. "Thousands?" he gasped. "How are we supposed to find the key?"

"We wait," insisted Tobias. "You see, patience comes in handy down here too."

186

They sat down, clearing out the debris from the shack. They found why it had not been claimed: it was home to a putrid corpse, its flesh half eaten away.

Jarom covered his mouth with his hands. "We should bury him, don't you think?"

Tobias kicked the corpse, sending it sprawling onto the street. "Why waste the time? He can't be helped."

Jarom retreated to the back of the shack, and Xandir kindled a rudimentary fire.

Once their basic camp was set up, they turned to their plans. "We've got to be subtle. Find out where the key is and track it," suggested Tobias. "Once we know who has it, we could find some way of convincing him to give up the key."

Xandir withdrew a few inches of his ebony sword. "Oh, I'll convince them. My friend here is very persuasive."

"No!" protested Tobias. "That's just the sort of thing we mustn't do at any cost! If we obtain the key by violence, it will be useless!"

"Then what do you want us to do? Run up to one of them and ask him nicely? The only thing you'd get is a beating."

Tobias sat back with a rattling sigh. "That will depend on who has it. Remember, patience."

They set out that night, each taking a concealed position at a different point in the city. Xandir took turns intimidating the various passers-by, flashing his swords and demanding information. Unfortunately for him, most of the inhabitants were genuinely clueless.

Jarom stayed in the shadows, calmly eavesdropping on various conversations. His efforts were also met with frustration. Though whispers of the key were frequent, few people spoke in specifics.

Tobias's tactics fell somewhere between the other two, at times lurking, at times applying his own considerable pressure to those weaker than him. Several times, Jarom spied him speaking in low tones to wretched creatures in the alleyways.

The three met every night for the next several days to touch base and share their progress. Xandir grew surlier with each day and spoke only in terse sentences. Jarom also stayed uncharacteristically quiet, though his demeanor didn't reflect Xandir's negative attitude. For Tobias, it was simply business as usual.

On the evening of the fifth day, Tobias brought back more promising news.

"Listen to this! I've convinced one of my old contacts, who owes me a great deal, to tell me what he knows of the key. He said the key has been missing for some time and that the word on the street is that someone is hiding it, keeping it from everyone."

Xandir scoffed. "Well, does the word on the street also tell you just who's run off with it?"

Jarom chimed in, pleased that he actually had something to contribute. "Well, yes. From what I've heard, it's probably Lucio. It seems like he was the ringleader of one of Serche's largest organized crime organizations before the city fell. I can't go a day without hearing a dozen new stories about his exploits. You'd know all about him too, if you would stop busting heads and start doing something useful for a change."

Xandir scowled, barely containing an outburst. "Yeah, I've heard of him. And a few of his thugs have certainly heard of me."

"This isn't helping," complained Tobias. "Perhaps we can bargain with him."

Xandir rolled his eyes, his voice dripping with sarcasm. "Oh, with what? I suppose you've got a secret stash you've been sitting on? You know, that would be nice, because money is so useful around here."

Tobias drew up to his full height. "I am still a wealthy man!" he snapped. "Just a few days before you came, I won an enchanted jeweled amulet at a game of chance."

"Well," challenged Xandir. "Where is it? It can't be worth more than your freedom."

Tobias shrank back. "Ah, it was stolen. Three thugs robbed me in an alley while I was scavenging for treasure. You still find good little undiscovered morsels once in a while."

Xandir leaned his head back and clenched his eyes shut.

Jarom could take it no longer. "Ah—just listen to you two! Bickering like babies while nothing is actually getting done. I don't know about you, but I'm going out to look for something we can bargain with. Feel free to stay here and debate for the next few hours if you like."

Jarom buzzed out of the shack, leaving the door to swing closed. Tobias and Xandir resumed their heated conversation as if the cherub's outburst had been little more than an annoying public service announcement.

Jarom fluttered along the streets, passing only the occasional bum. For once, the air was hot and steamy, and no one seemed in the mood to cause him much trouble. In a stroke of luck, he found an abandoned stick not far from their shack, bone dry and the perfect length for a torch. He kindled it on another torch mounted to a wall and continued his search, checking one alleyway after another.

After finding nothing but refuse and waste stacked in every corner, Jarom's spirits began to droop. He had never felt so far away from home, where every breeze brought the pleasant smell of baking Ambrosia. The days were always bright, and the temperature hovered at a constant state of pleasantness, day in and day out. Jarom gazed toward the ceiling and saw only the blanket of blackness that enveloped the city. He thought of his father and pictured his smiling face, which always used to lift his sadness.

"Father, what would you do?" he called to the Heavens. "We can't delay much longer, or we'll never get out!"

Though no voice answered, a warm calmness swept over him. Somehow, he felt as if his father was watching him, though he knew his father could hardly be farther away.

He continued his search, turning over even remotely promising leads—trash bins and boxes, empty food containers, and gutted window wells. Although his search remained as fruitless as before, he felt a little better about things. At least it was something to do.

As he crossed the street to examine a rundown row of buildings on the other side, he stopped in the middle and hovered there for a moment. Something had glinted below him. He slowed his wings and fluttered to the ground, trying to locate the shiny object.

"Nothing shines here," he told himself. "At least, nothing I've seen so far."

He saw nothing on the ground but a pile of rotting fruit pits and a sewer grate. He fluttered into the air, wondering if he had been looking so long that his mind was starting to play tricks on him.

Again, the object glinted below him in the torchlight. He landed again and realized he'd been looking in the wrong place. The light had not originated from the ground but from below it.

Jarom lowered the torch next to the grate and saw a circular object peeking halfway out of a puddle of grime, glinting invitingly in his torchlight. With his free hand, Jarom tugged at the grate, which refused to budge. He reached his arm down inside, wincing at the thought of plunging his hand into the sewage. Unfortunately, his arms fell far short of his glittering prize.

Jarom pursed his lips, sinking deep into thought. If he was going to retrieve his prize, then brains—not brawn—would have to win the day.

Hovering over the hole, Jarom drew back his wings as far as they would go. With a sudden thrust, he flapped them hard in unison, creating a strong gust of wind, which sent the water in the grate billowing up in an impressive splash. He glanced down into the grate and saw that the object had moved.

Heartened by his progress, he tried again and again, beating his wings until his face flushed red with exertion. Finally, his shining prize broke free and flew into the air, its chain wrapping itself around the bars of the grate. Exhausted, Jarom thudded back to the ground, his tiny hands untangling the chain.

Once the object was finally in his grasp, Jarom took several minutes to admire its handiwork. By the cherub's estimation, it was a handsome object and well worth his time and effort to find it. Its entire golden surface was covered with depictions of various flowers and herbs, all surrounding a bright blue, multi-faceted jewel. Best of all, it emitted a faint, cloying fragrance, which served to mask the ever-present stench of the slums.

Jarom stuffed the prize into his robes. If anyone else got a glimpse of it, there would be trouble. Just to be sure, he stooped down, reached for a handful of mud, and smeared it all over the surface of the amulet, masking its shiny appearance.

Slowly, he fluttered back toward the shack where they had set up camp. He glanced around, trying to remain calm and appear inconspicuous. However, the more he tried to blend in, the less he succeeded. He jumped at every sound, saw sinister shadows in every alleyway, and cautiously drew every single breath. When at last he arrived back at the camp, he found the shack deserted and slipped inside.

The fire had gone out, though the fumes hung in the air. He didn't bother to light it. No light meant his prize could neither glint nor glow, and that was how he liked it.

Jarom sighed and laid his head down on the bundle of smelly rags that served as his makeshift pillow. He could tell the others about the amulet later. With any luck, the amulet would be enough to buy off Lucio so that they could keep moving.

"Anything's got to be better than here," muttered Jarom, his eyelids drawing to an inexorable close.

Jarom awoke some time later to the sounds of a struggle. The room shook as something heavy slammed against the outer wall. Jarom winced as the entire structure threatened to collapse.

"I told you, we don't have anything!" barked Xandir. "Leave us alone, or I'll make you sorry you dropped by."

"We know it's in there," replied a raspy, strangled voice. "We saw the little one take it. Give it back, or it is you who will be sorry."

A cry burst from Xandir's lips, and Jarom could hear the metallic hiss as Xandir unsheathed both swords. Pressing his face against a crack in the wall, Jarom saw Xandir and Tobias surrounded by an entire gang of thugs. Their leader, who had addressed Xandir, waved a wicked spiked club in the angel's direction.

The leader was a tall man clothed in a hodgepodge of dirty rags and wrappings, giving him the appearance of an unfinished mummy. From his face, only his dark eyes were visible, and they burned with hatred as he launched himself forward to counter Xandir's opening attack.

The club rang against the ebony sword, scattering sparks into the dark air. In another moment, the club burst into flame, startling Xandir and sending him momentarily on the retreat. The leader advanced boldly, swinging the club in a series of deadly, glowing arcs.

The gang advanced on Xandir, swinging clubs wreathed in flames. Xandir kept them at bay with strokes from his dark sword, his face contorted in rage and frustration.

"Justice! You all deserve the sting of justice!" cried Xandir.

With every connecting blow from the dark sword, the enemies' hands blossomed in oozing sores. They dropped their clubs and fell to the ground, rolling around in shock and agony.

"Try stealing again with those hands!" taunted Xandir, continuing his grisly work.

Tobias joined the fray, flicking out his short dagger with surprising speed. His face contorted in pure rage as he stabbed without remorse. Several of the gang fled from him, rejoining the fight against Xandir.

With a signal from their leader, the entire pack leapt at Xandir at once. The angel had just enough time to launch himself into the air, barely avoiding the fiery barrage of clubs.

Not missing a beat, the thugs hurled their flaming clubs into the air. Several of their clubs met their mark, scorching Xandir and forcing him back to the ground. The leader leapt at him, dealing Xandir a crushing blow across his chest. Xandir fell back and crumpled. Enraged, Tobias leapt forward and was similarly silenced by a flaming projectile. They both lay in a heap on the ground, unmoving.

Jarom knew that he had to act. It was his fault that they were in this predicament. He reached into his robe and withdrew his slender, golden bow and nocked an arrow. He found the largest crack in the planks and stuck the point through. He squinted in the low light, trying to adjust his aim. This tactic would only work once.

The leader strutted over to Xandir, his arms raised in a gesture of triumph. "Who is sorry now, you foolish winged beast? I am not usually a patient man, but I'm feeling generous today, so I shall give you one more chance. Where is the amulet?"

Jarom drew back the bow and let the arrow fly. It was small but sleek, and it cut through the air without a sound. The arrow flew true, striking the man a few inches below his heart. Caught completely off guard, the thug leader reeled, fell back, and dropped his flaming club on top of himself in surprise. His clothes and bandages ignited, engulfing him in pitiless flames.

A moment later, Xandir rose to his knees, sliding out his white sword. With a painful grimace, he thrust it into the ground next to the burning man. "What a coincidence. I'm feeling merciful too."

Instantly, the flames vanished, leaving the scorched man groaning and writhing on the filthy ground. Xandir rose, and the rest of the gang fled, casting their clubs aside.

Sensing the battle was won, Jarom burst from the shack and shot to Xandir's side.

Xandir shot him an intense glance, full of praise and reproof. "Tell me that this man was lying. And don't try any lying yourself. You wouldn't want to tarnish that unblemished shroud of yours."

Jarom reached into his robe and withdrew the muddy pendant. Xandir nodded, his face grim. "I'm guessing you're the one who shot that arrow too."

Jarom nodded. "It was a lucky shot." He offered the amulet to Xandir. "I found this in a grate, and I thought we might be able to use it to bargain with Lucio. I didn't think anyone saw me."

Xandir shook his head, wincing a bit from the pain the movement caused. "This place is full of suspicious eyes. Nothing is done completely in secret. You should have told me."

Jarom hung his head, unable to glance up at the body-strewn battlefield. "I know—I'm so sorry. None of this should have happened."

Xandir sighed and indicated the defeated man at his feet. "Lucky for you, there might be an upside to all of this. Unless I'm gravely mistaken, this unfortunate fellow is none other than Lucio himself. It seems your antics coaxed him out of hiding. That's why I spared him. We could probably still use his help."

Tobias groaned and raised himself to his knees. The entire

front part of his robe sported an ugly gash where both cloth and flesh had been singed.

He crawled toward the two angels, his hand outstretched,

"That . . . that amulet! It used to be mine! It has healing properties! Quick, give it to me! I will not survive if you don't."

Eager to comply, Jarom flew over to the injured man and placed the amulet in his trembling hands. Instantly, Tobias pressed the amulet with the jewel side toward him against his chest. It emitted a soft glow and a pleasant hum as the burns lessened and quickly disappeared from his skin, leaving only a reddened patch no worse than a minor sunburn. Tobias tossed the amulet to Xandir, who applied the healing powers to his various wounds.

At last, he returned the amulet to Jarom, who dangled it out in front of himself, eyeing it closely. Without a word, he flew over to Lucio and started tending to his wounds.

"Hey, what are you doing?" protested Tobias. "The amulet has only so much power! We should save it for ourselves."

Jarom shook his head and continued his work. Tobias lurched forward to stop him, but Xandir raised a sword in his path, ending the argument.

Lucio's groans ceased, and his now-exposed face settled into a calm expression. "Thank you," he whispered weakly. "Why did you do that?"

Jarom withdrew the amulet, whose glow had weakened considerably. "Because this was my fault," he explained. "No one should have to suffer on my account. I was doing what little I could to make it right."

"How do you know I won't attack you again? I would have been down for good if you hadn't intervened."

"I know," replied Jarom. "The right choice isn't always without risk, but I stand by it anyway."

Lucio remained silent for several moments, then he rose slowly to a sitting position, his arms resting on his knees. "Well, don't worry about that. I won't cause you any more trouble. It is so rare to see any mercy in this place that I hardly know how to react."

"You could start by telling us what you know about the key. Rumor has it that you're the man to ask."

Lucio nodded, drawing himself up a bit more. "Fair enough. Valuables have a tendency of slipping through one's fingers here. No matter how hard you try to grasp them, there's always a crack. Take this key, for example. Most people here consider it the most valuable object in this part of the city. I would have to agree, and it has passed through my hands no less than five times. I tried locking it up in vaults, burying it underground, hiding it in various places, and changing my residence, but nothing seems to work. Someone always stumbles onto it, or figures out the location, and takes it from me again. At last, I decided that there is only one place to keep it where I can always be sure of its location, and that is on my person."

He lifted his arm, revealing a jagged scar. With a flick of his knife, he slashed open the oozing scar, drawing blood, as casually as if he were slicing bread for a sandwich.

Without a flicker of pain on his face, he set down the knife and extracted the key, wiping it on his grimy clothes and then offering it to the cherub.

"Here. It might smell bad, but I admit that I'm actually glad to be rid of it. Though my plan worked for some time, I could always feel it moving around in there, like it was struggling to break out. It was driving me insane."

Jarom nodded his thanks, his lips showing only the faintest hint of a smile. He pocketed the key and then removed the amulet from around his neck and deposited it in the man's hands. "Here, a little something for your trouble. Try not to lose it."

The man nodded, took the amulet, and applied pressure to his bleeding arm. "That's kind of you. Now get out of here before I change my mind."

Xandir and Tobias had already turned around and were headed toward the gate. Before joining them however, Jarom fluttered up to the man and whispered something in his ear. The man's face went from surprised to delighted as the cherub floated off to join his companions.

Xandir gave Jarom a sidelong glance as he caught up. "What took you so long? I don't think he was joking about changing his mind."

Jarom shook his head, grinning broadly. "No, I just thought of something that might prevent him from trying his hand at amateur surgery in the future. I told him that after we used the key, I would hide it in a certain spot, so he could retrieve it at his leisure. Since I'm practically giving it back to him, it won't be stealing, and he can finally use it."

Tobias raised his eyebrows, obviously impressed. "That was a very generous gesture. The Lower Court will never be the same. All he'll have to worry about now is cleaning off that filthy shroud of his. I wonder if he'll ever manage it. Those stains don't come off without a fight you know."

Xandir glared at him. "Why do I have the feeling you're not telling us everything about these shrouds? Hasn't anyone ever managed it before?"

Tobias shrugged, avoiding Xandir's eyes. "Oh, I don't know. Probably. It's not like I spend all my time at the pool, watching everyone who tries. I mean, even if they do get the stains out, where are they to go? There's a sizzling stream of magma as far as the eye can see."

"Well, it better be possible," muttered Xandir, "or I will invent some tailored punishments of my own."

Jarom held up the key, ready to insert it into the keyhole. Suddenly, something struck him as odd. "Wait, Xandir, how does he know about—"

Xandir cut him off with a wave. "Just insert the key already. I know this isn't Hell, but it can't be much better."

Jarom obeyed, and the gate melted away like a lump of butter in a hot skillet. Working quickly, he flew up and placed the key under the roof board of a nearby lean-to. The three of them rushed through the door and were immediately blinded by a brilliant flash of light.

TWENTY-FIVE
RIPPLES IN THE POOL

THE FALLEN CITY OF SERCHE, 2012

The party had been expecting another scene of desolation and depravity. So the scene that met their eyes was more shocking than anything they could have imagined.

The city in front of them burst with light. The houses here were constructed of both stone and wood. Bright, multicolored lanterns adorned every window. Raucous laughter echoed down the street, mingled with singing, shouting, and the scuffling of large crowds of people moving about.

Xandir's eyebrows knitted together. "Are you sure we're still in the same city? I haven't seen a party like this since I helped destroy Sodom and Gomorrah."

Tobias nodded, indicating that they should move away from the gate. "A fairly good comparison. It's every bit as sleazy and has even more ways to lose yourself, thanks to the advance of technology." A twisted grin snuck up his face. "In short, this is my kind of place."

Jarom gazed into the faces of the people rushing by and wrinkled his brow. "I don't understand. Everyone here looks so happy. I don't think I saw a single person smile in the Den. These people look like things are great."

Tobias sighed. "That is what it looks like. But the truth is, they are a wretched, miserable lot. They're always trying to drown their sorrows with the latest diversion and putting on a face to show everyone else how ridiculously happy they are. The mind can only take it for so long. Many of them have gone completely insane."

"Great," muttered Xandir. "We're probably better off with all those kleptomaniacs. The sooner we ditch this place, the better. Where's the gate?"

Before Tobias could answer, a man in gaudy yellow robes stepped out in front of them. His black hair was pulled back in a ponytail, and his fingers and ears sparkled with an assortment of rings. When he grinned, he displayed an entire row of false teeth. "Welcome, fortunate travelers! You must be weary. Why don't you come sit down for a little diversion?"

Tobias pushed himself to the forefront. "They're not interested," he said. "We're just passing through."

The man's sickly smile only broadened. "Oh, I think they can speak for themselves, can't they? You there! You look like a man who enjoys the finer things in life."

He pointed to Xandir, who stared back coldly. "Yes," he agreed, "and I know where to find them all by myself. The way I see it, you've got nothing to offer me."

Xandir pushed ahead past the man and continued down the street. It wasn't long before the offer was repeated from both sides of the street by similarly dressed, insistent Sercheans. They smiled broadly, though their eyes did not reflect their mirth.

The three travelers ducked into an alley, trying to lose a pack of provocatively clad women who had tailed them for the last several blocks.

Jarom's eyes grew wide, his face flushed. "I thought things were bad above ground."

Xandir bobbed his head. "It won't be long before the Earth catches up, the way things are headed up there. I've seen all sorts of sleaze before, but you're right—I've never seen so much in one place."

"To be sure," muttered Tobias. "They certainly weren't after me."

Jarom glanced uneasily down the alleyway, hoping they had managed to lose their pursuers. "What did that first man want us to do, anyway? I couldn't read the sign over his business."

Tobias shook his head. "A bit over your Heavenly head. That man runs a Pleasure Parlor. Mind-altering drugs, liquor, and Pleasure Pools."

"Pleasure Pools?" asked Jarom. "I've never heard of those."

"You stand in a Pool, and it shows you whatever you want to see. In the case of most of these lunatics, the vision isn't exactly a bedtime story. Some people go in and never come out again. I once lost myself in one for three days. Best not even to set foot in the front door."

Jarom nodded, a curious itch forming in the back of his mind. Could the Pools really show him whatever he wanted?

"Well, this is not my kind of party, anyway," muttered Xandir. "The question we should be asking is how do we get out of here? I'm guessing there's some ridiculous restraint in place to make sure people don't get out."

"Yes," confirmed Tobias. "The gate is hidden in a building on the other side of town. You might call it a night club. Those who fancy themselves the most attractive and interesting gather there to waste their time together. The gate itself is guarded by three Pleasure Pools, each with a specific purpose."

"Such as?" questioned Xandir impatiently.

"I have no idea. I've never been up that way. The club is restricted to members only, and as you can see, I'm not particularly attractive or interesting."

"Perhaps they'll find that I make the cut." Xandir withdrew his swords a few inches.

Tobias waved him off. "We're not just talking burly, bad-tempered guards here. The place is riddled with mystical defenses. Let's see your swords slice through those."

Xandir paced up and down the alleyway. "So what about the restriction on stealing? Does that apply here?"

Tobias nodded. "Yes. Unfortunately, a stolen proof of membership will not let you pass. They all wear a blue dolphin ring on their left hand, and they are tailored to the specific person. It can't be stolen or forged."

"They really have thought of everything," Xandir grunted.

"I don't suppose you've heard of any way around this unfortunate road block, have you?"

Tobias glanced down the alleyway, saw that the coast was clear, and gestured for them to follow. "Yes, I do have an idea. Follow me. We can talk about it somewhere safer."

He led them down brightly lit streets to a towering building with rows of circular windows. A pair of crouching lion statues flanked the entrance—a scarlet curtain with golden trim. Tobias disappeared inside and could be heard speaking with a man inside.

He emerged a few minutes later, his face fixed in an expression of extreme annoyance. "Follow me up! It's blatant robbery what they're charging, but I've secured us a room for the next few days."

Tobias led Xandir and Jarom through the curtain and up a flight of stairs. They slunk down a dim corridor and stopped in front of a painted wooden door. Tobias withdrew a key from his pocket and let them in.

The room beyond was small but decadent, with a fancy canopied bed, a ring of overstuffed velvet chairs, a table, and a porcelain washbasin. They hurried in and locked the door behind them.

Xandir slumped down in one of the chairs while Jarom lay on the bed, his wings folded in snugly.

"So what's this master plan?" Xandir asked. "Do you really think I couldn't just bust my way in?"

Tobias seated himself and leaned toward the reclining angel. "Well, it goes something like this. You are a unique figure. I'm betting you can make an impression on the society here. If we get you seen in the right places, we might be able to get you accepted into the proper circles, who have the power to grant you a pass."

Xandir raised one eyebrow. "This place looks too much like other cities I've leveled."

Tobias grinned. "You won't have to do anything too drastic. I was thinking we might get you into the gaming scene. This place is full of crooks, so if you bring along your justice sword, you can constantly tip the odds in your favor! They all deserve to lose!" Tobias wiped his brow on a plush towel hanging by the basin.

"Win some games and attend a few parties. Just to get you seen. What do you say?"

Xandir leaned his head on one hand. "I say this better work. I don't want to stay here one more moment than I have to."

"Where do I fit into all of this?" asked Jarom. "I look like a child, and I doubt anyone here is going to take me seriously."

"They'll take your patronage," offered Tobias, "but they definitely wouldn't take you seriously. Or us for that matter, if you were seen with us. I'm sorry, but you'll just have to stay here. You wouldn't last a night out there."

Jarom groaned, sinking deeper into the luxurious bedding, quickly succumbing to sleep. "Have fun mixing business and pleasure. I'll hold down the fort."

The following days crawled by for the cherub. He did little but sit in the room all day, the monotony broken only by the occasional meal brought up by Tobias. Though angels didn't technically need to eat, the food was a pleasant diversion and much better than anything they had scrounged up in the Den of Thieves.

He slept often and dreamt about the Pleasure Pools. Waves of guilt slammed him every time he woke from one of those dreams, so he tried desperately to drive them from his mind. As the hours stretched on, he felt his mind wander again and again, invariably ending up back where it started.

Xandir and Tobias checked in periodically, though sometimes they stayed away for days at a time. Jarom buzzed around his prison, burning off his pent-up energy. As more time passed, his thoughts of the Pools increased in frequency and intensity until they monopolized his consciousness. At last, he could take it no longer.

He waited for Xandir and Tobias to return with inevitable stories of their grand exploits. Xandir had made a splash in the gaming circles, using his uncanny luck to empty the purses of his opponents. They bragged about the parties they had crashed, and despite his original reluctance, Xandir appeared to be enjoying himself. Jarom tried to tell himself that this meant they were making progress and that they would soon be leaving this place, but he couldn't completely dispel the jealously tugging at his heart.

"Did you see the look on his face?" laughed Xandir over one of his recent exploits. "You would have thought I'd just taken his right hand instead of his money."

Tobias grinned, showing all of his teeth. "I just love that moment when they realize all hope is lost!"

Xandir laughed, but Jarom felt that he might be sick. He could see the dark colors creeping across both of their Sin Shrouds, much denser than when they had entered.

"Are you sure about this?" offered Jarom. "Is this really what we should be doing? Isn't there any way to become popular here without being . . ." He stumbled for a word. ". . . evil?"

Xandir laughed. "Evil? It's really just a bit of harmless fun, Lil' Halo. Right, Tobias?"

"That's Tricky Toby to you, Xandir. Soon enough they'll have a name for you at the tables too."

Xandir rubbed his hands together. "I could take another round right now. I think tonight might be our night. There's a fish in my future."

Jarom was about to protest that dolphins were not fish, but the pair had already departed.

Well, if they can have some "harmless fun" in the name of the mission, then so can I.

Jarom fluttered up to the circular window and withdrew an arrow from his quiver. "He was glad that the arrows all found their way back to his quiver by themselves over time. Otherwise, he would have run out long ago." Using the slender head, he unfastened the seal around the window, carefully removed the pane, and placed it under the bed.

Without another look back, he shot off through the window, rising to the rooftop to get his bearings. With little trouble, he located the gate where they had entered this portion of the city and flew off in that direction. The Parlor was there, and at last he would have a chance to tame his nagging curiosity.

He landed at the Parlor entrance and glanced both ways before slipping into the building.

He landed himself in a haze of sickly sweet smoke and lapsed into a coughing fit. Without thinking, he fluttered lower to escape the worst of it, and had to squint to see through the artificial fog. Before he could get too far into the shop, the gaudily dressed proprietor stepped in his path.

"Welcome, little man. How might I help you relax today? Perhaps you'd like to sample our Serchean spirits? I guarantee, even those wings have never taken you so high."

Jarom waved a hand in rejection. The man continued undeterred. "Then perhaps a little companionship? Come to think of it, I've got someone just your size."

Jarom shook his head even more emphatically. "No! I . . . I just want to see the Pools."

The man smiled toothily and gestured with a heavily ringed hand. "Well, why didn't you say so? Step this way."

The man led Jarom through the haze and laughter to a small, circular basin, much like an ornate birdbath. It was filled nearly to the brim with shimmering, clear water, lit from somewhere below.

The proprietor gestured to the bowl. "Since you're a first-time customer, your first hour is free. After that, our rates are very reasonable."

"What do I have to do?" Jarom asked nervously.

"Just step onto the platform, place your finger in the water, and let your thoughts wander. And don't be shy—no one else will be able to see what you see. When you're finished, simply step off of the platform. Any questions?"

Jarom shook his head and nodded a quick thanks, but the Proprietor spotted another group of potential customers and had scurried off to tempt them with his wares.

Jarom trembled as he floated up onto the platform. "I'll only take a quick look," he rationalized. "I'll just see what it's like and then go back to the room."

Mustering up his courage, he reached out and touched the surface of the pool. The surface rippled and shimmered, glowing as if with an electric current. Jarom cried out as the current shot through his body, every hair standing on end. The sensation was both terrifying and exhilarating. It numbed the guilt and dispelled the crushing boredom that had been his constant companion for the last few days.

He gazed into the rippling surface and voiced his wish. "I want to see my father."

The pool rippled and changed, the ripples smoothing out into flat viewing surface. In a moment, a three dimensional image of his father leapt from the surface.

His father sat around a huge circular table, in deep conversation with a group of other robed figures. Some he recognized from his time in the family business, and he even noticed a few familiar faces from the Manna bakeries, which were set up adjacent to his own family's. Though sound came through, he could barely make anything out—too many voices were sounding at once.

He concentrated on his father's image, and the pool honed in on him. His father's words became clear. "But what of these reports? We must investigate them to find if they are credible or not! If the Fellowship of Nod is actually showing themselves again, they will certainly be a force to be reckoned with!"

Someone replied, but the words were lost in the din. "Yes, I'm aware they haven't been spotted for hundreds of years, but that's exactly what makes me nervous. They would have had that long to pool their resources and let their schemes simmer. I certainly don't want to be around when they finally serve what they've been brewing up all these years."

His father's face was drawn with pain and frustration, and it took all of Jarom's resolve not to look away. Clutching the edges of the basin, he stared even harder, trying to figure out to whom his father was talking. His view broadened, and his breath caught in his throat as he noticed who presided over the meeting.

It was Michael, the Archangel. He stood like an exquisitely sculpted statue, a head taller than all the rest, dressed in the full splendor of his battle armor. His armor shone white and gold, its reflective surface constantly changing color as it rippled and roiled with inner light. At his side hung a flaming sword so brilliant that Jarom had to look away. If he led the council, then the matter at hand must be grave indeed.

The chief of the seven Archangels drew himself up to his full height and raised a hand for silence. For the first time, the entire room fell silent.

"I have heard many different opinions in this council, and I thank you all for your input. After taking in all the facts, however, I still abide by my original plan. We must dispatch the final fleet of Whisperers. They will cover the whole earth, warning all who will listen to be ready. We must have faith that my brother will come through in his role. Only then will things proceed as they are supposed to."

Jarom's father stood and spoke with reverence. "But, your grace, your brother does not even know . . ."

Suddenly the picture dimmed and faded to blackness. The pool once again rippled back and forth. Jarom cried out in frustration, willing the image to return. But the pool refused to obey and remained as black as a crow against a starless sky. In his rage, Jarom splashed an entire hand into the pool, scattering water in wide droplets across the floor. He then gawked in amazement as the water floated off the ground of its own accord and assembled itself back into the pool.

Must be some sort of security measure. They probably have ways of knowing they are being spied on.

Since he figured that he hadn't been in the Pool anywhere close to an hour, Jarom thought of something else to divert his attention from his current situation. Out of curiosity, he turned his thoughts to the magma ship to find it still stuck in a sheet of ice.

Quickly leaving the unpleasant scene, he directed his thoughts to home: the Elysian Fields and the sweet sight of the Ambrosia makers going about their daily business, harvesting the trees and fields, flying their wares around in great golden chariots, talking and laughing with one another.

The image appeared so vividly that he could almost smell the Ambrosia wafting temptingly in the wind. The golden fields sparkled in the eternal sunlight, the rivers beckoned to him with the soft lapping of water against their white-sanded shores, and the shining, towering dwellings of the other Cherubim greeted him like old friends.

Why did I ever leave? Just to sit in an inn while others do the important things? It doesn't make sense! It's not fair!

Jarom found himself leaning in closer to the water, willing the waters to swallow him whole and insert him into the idyllic scene. However, as his face met the water, the image instantly faded, and he was left with a dripping face.

He conjured the image again and again and stood spellbound, unable to take his eyes off the placid water.

TWENTY-SIX
DROWNING IN PLEASURE

Xandir and Tobias staggered back to the hotel room, dizzy with excitement. They had been at an extremely exclusive party, where, after a night of wining and dining, it had been announced that Xandir had been granted his dolphin ring. He wore it proudly out in front of him like a war trophy, letting it catch the light every chance he got.

As they entered the inn, he glanced down and got a good look at his Sin Shroud. The last stripe of white down at the very end of the cloth had now faded into a violent splatter of black and red splotches. His spirits fell like an anchor cast from the side of a cruise liner. Tobias had made it sound like there was no other feasible way to leave the city. Still, Xandir couldn't completely beat back his nagging doubts, which his conscience constantly hurled to the forefront of his mind whenever he had a quiet moment.

Interesting that I can still have an active conscience after all of these years. I thought I got that under control decades ago.

Every glance at the Sin Shroud brought back the harrowing display he had endured while falling through the Chute. Though he tried to compartmentalize these thoughts away in the corner of his mind marked "Irrelevant," he couldn't help wondering how the blotches on the Shroud would translate to images in the Chute. He glanced down at the dolphin ring again and laughed coldly. How many times had he laughed at humans when they had

207

sold themselves for trinkets like this one?

Xandir shook his head. He had to stay focused on the task at hand. He would sort the particulars out later, provided there was a later.

Xandir and Tobias reached the door and stopped cold. The door had been flung wide open, obviously with some considerable force, and the room beyond was in shambles. The bedclothes had been ripped to tatters, the bed itself cleaved cleanly in two, and the rest of the furniture demolished beyond repair. Huge, gouging holes appeared in all of the walls, and the far window was missing every shred of glass.

"Jarom!" gasped Xandir. "He must have been here when this happened."

Tobias glanced around and wagged his head. "No, I don't think so. There would be some sign of a struggle with him—cherub's blood or a feather from his wings. No, I think by some strange twist of fate, he wasn't in the room."

Xandir unsheathed the black sword. He was in no mood for mercy should the perpetrators return. "Who would have done this? Why? Were they targeting him or us?"

Tobias brushed away a pile of debris and sat crossed legged on the floor. His eyes glazed over for a moment, and he sank into deep thought.

"The affluent and popular always have enemies, especially the so-called rising stars such as you. Perhaps someone believes you are a threat to his standing. The best course might be our own swift retaliation."

Xandir rolled his eyes. "If only they knew. I don't plan on staying in this town one second longer than I have to. They can have it."

They scoured the room for any other clues as to what had taken place. After several minutes of silence, Tobias bolted upright, straighter than he had ever been. "Xandir, look."

He had moved a broken cupboard out of the way to reveal a roll of parchment, tacked to the wall with a shard of multi-faceted green crystal. The letters glowed crimson, as if ringed by fire, though it smelled of sweet perfume.

Most Honored Sir,

We regret to inform you that your acquaintance, the cherub known as Jarom, has incurred a debt for which he cannot provide any suitable capital. You have been named as a possible benefactor who might be willing to settle the outstanding balance. Payment should be made as quickly as possible in order to ensure the safety of your colleague. Terms can be discussed in person at the Gateway Pleasure Parlor.

Yours respectively,
Philo Schlimme,

Proprietor,
Gateway Pleasure Parlor

Xandir read the message several times over, unable to believe what he was reading. Of all the people he expected get stuck in such a predicament, Jarom was surely the last.

He turned to Tobias with narrowed eyes. "Do you think it could be some sort of trick? Are they drawing us into an ambush?"

Tobias sighed and snatched the paper off the wall. "No, I don't. These people put profit over pounding. They only resort to violence when it helps them collect on their debts."

Xandir raised an eyebrow. "So do we bring some pounding of our own, or do we play nicely? We do have our winnings."

"That's true. They won't do us any good once we leave this area of the city. We go any higher, and money isn't an object. It wouldn't hurt to keep one hand on your sword, though. It could get ugly if they aren't satisfied with what we bring."

Xandir was already out the door, reaching into his armor for his money pouch. "Let's go."

He only made it a few steps down the hall when he stopped, his hand still halfway into his pocket.

"What is it?" questioned Tobias. "We need to go!"

His hand slipped back in, assuring himself that it was really gone. For a moment, Xandir's face flared with frustration and disbelief. "It's just that there . . . isn't as much money as I remembered."

Tobias cocked his head, sensing that he had just heard a poorly veiled half-truth. "All right, whatever you say."

Xandir grimaced as a pea-sized red blotch blossomed at the bottom of his Sin Shroud.

The Pleasure Parlor still hummed with activity, the flashing lights and playful shouts mingling with the haze of sweet smoke.

Seeing the two figures enter, the Proprietor rushed to the front only to have his own parchment thrust in his face.

"I believe we have some business to discuss," offered Xandir.

The Proprietor's usually broad grin slackened a few notches, his eyes glinting. "Ah, yes, the cherub. It's hard to imagine a person of your status having anything to do with a being like him."

"Who we deal with is our affair," said Xandir, raising his voice. "I want to see him. Now."

The proprietor's grin resumed its usual broadness. "Certainly. Right this way."

He led them past the various patrons—who all seemed oblivious to their presence—through a curtain in the back of the Parlor.

They entered a dark room filled with cushions and extravagant paintings. With his gaudy clothes, the Proprietor blended in so well that if he sat still, he might be mistaken for one of the cushions. He seated himself on a massive orange and pink striped cushion in the center of the room and folded his legs toward him. He clapped his hands twice, and two slender guards dressed in pale robes emerged from the shadows. One handed him a bulging bag made of animal hides, and the second stood at attention and waited patiently for a command.

"Bring in the delinquent," the Proprietor commanded. The guard rushed out of the room and soon returned with Jarom in tow, his hands bound with metal manacles.

Jarom hung his head, unable to meet Xandir's gaze. The guard tossed him roughly to the floor in front of the main cushion, and the cherub adopted a contrite pose, face to the floor.

"So," muttered Xandir, "what is the nature of the debt?"

Philo lifted his eyebrows in overplayed severity. "Fifteen.

Seems he greatly overstayed his welcome."

Xandir fingered his swords, deciding which one would better fit the situation. Neither seemed to work. If he picked Justice, the Proprietor would have to punish Jarom for the debt, which might include slavery and other untold horrors. If he chose Mercy, they might still be in trouble, as Philo might feel that he had been robbed and attack them. The movement wasn't wasted on Philo, who narrowed his eyes and reached into his bag, extracting a slender green shard like the one that had been used to pin the note.

"Just in case you are thinking about trying something stupid—I'm an expert shot with these. They're filled with an interesting hallucinogen, powerful enough to drive the victim to the brink of insanity. I don't want to have to use them, so here are my terms: pay up, or get out and never come for this miserable wretch again."

Xandir fingered the bag in his right hand. The sum Philo named was enormous, and he was several thousand short. For a moment, his mind reeled, trying to imagine how one little person could have racked up such an exorbitant debt.

He offered the bag to Philo. "There's about eleven. I can pay you the rest in a matter of days with interest. My luck at the dice tables is legendary. You won't be disappointed."

Philo's eyes flashed with disapproval. "Do you take me for a fool? What's to keep you from skipping town with the rest of my money? No, either you pay me in full now, or you've missed your chance."

Xandir glanced at Tobias, who made a simple gesture. Xandir narrowed his gaze. "What?" he whispered to the old man. "After all we've been through? We can't just give it away!"

Tobias pursed his lips. "Do you see any alternative? Rest assured you'll never see your precious 'Lil' Halo' again if you let him go now. This city has a way of swallowing people whole."

Xandir sighed, feeling defeat come crushing in on him like the avalanche he had stopped only days before. "We don't really have a choice here."

He hated that worst of all. He was supposed to have a choice. Even if it was only one.

Xandir turned about and removed the ring from his finger. With no expression, he reached out his arm and offered it to Philo. "I think you'll find this is worth the entire debt in itself. Perhaps you would consider it in lieu of money."

"Now that's not something one gives up lightly," the Proprietor mused. "I do already have one, but I wouldn't mind another. Let me examine it."

Xandir let Philo examine it from a distance. The wiry man's eyes glistened with greed.

"Tell you what . . ." he began, his face lighting with a slimy grin as he held up another piece of parchment written in crimson letters, in which both Philo and Jarom's names were clearly visible. "I'll take the ring, all your money, and give you a sound beating to boot. That should send the proper message."

Xandir's eyes narrowed. "Oh, is that how negotiation works here? Well, if you want it, come and get it."

Both swords flared out, slicing through the air just as a green shard of jagged crystal shot toward Xandir's face. The blades caught the shard in mid-flight, scattering glass and poison in every direction. Xandir whirled around as the guards launched their own volley from the shadows, and he turned their projectiles back on them. One crystal bounced back whole, striking a guard straight in the chest. The man lapsed into convulsions, screaming and clawing frantically at the air as if warding off a swarm of stinging hornets.

Xandir swiveled and tossed the gold bag to Tobias. "Get us a diversion!" he barked, swinging back around to deflect more flying darts.

Tobias wasted no time. As Xandir backed toward the door, Tobias plunged his hand into the money bag and flung the coins in the crowd of patrons. Immediately, a cry went up, and the mass of patrons rushed at the door. Seizing his advantage, Tobias melted into the crowd. Xandir, however, saw that Philo had taken Jarom by a heavy chain and had pulled him back out of his reach.

The contract once again caught Xandir's eye, and in a moment, an idea formed in his head. Waiting for a small break in the onslaught, Xandir rushed forward with both swords raised, and stabbed down hard with both swords into the contract. The blades bit hard into the parchment, causing the letters to flare and writhe on the paper like living things. "I assume the debt!" Xandir cried. "He shall pay me instead!"

At the same time, Xandir threw down the ring, which melted into the strange parchment. The parchment exploded with motion as a pile of gold coins flew from the surface, clinking to the ground at Philo's feet. At the same time, Philo's fiery signature melted away to be replaced by Xandir's. Before Philo could react, Xandir already had the blades at his throat.

"Call them off," Xandir barked tersely. With a wave of the Proprietor's hand, the attack ceased, and Xandir lowered the man to the cushion once again. "You can't claim that I'm cheating you now. That gold is enough to cover the debt. I claim what is rightfully mine: the cherub."

Philo didn't speak. He gestured toward the door, where his shop was being ransacked by a horde of greedy pleasure seekers. His grip slackened on the chain, which Xandir sliced in two with a flick of his sword. In another second they were out and into the air, soaring above the rabble of the crowd, slicing through the smoke like a flaming arrow.

They shot out of the shop as from a cannon and continued rocketing down the street. They had just time enough to hear the angry cries below, but in an instant, they were safely out of the range of danger.

"What are we going to do now?" wailed Jarom. "I mean, I appreciate the rescue and all, but we just gave away our ticket out of here!"

Xandir shook his head, already making his way toward the club where the next gate stood. "Nope. We just gave away Tobias's ticket. Observe." He opened his palm to reveal another dolphin ring, exactly like the first.

Jarom's eyes opened wide. "You mean they gave him one too? That wrinkled old man?"

Xandir shrugged, a half smile creeping up his face. "You'd be surprised. He's actually the life of the party once he gets out of his shell."

"Won't we need him? I mean, we promised to help him get out!"

"We'll meet up with him later," reassured Xandir, "back at the pool. He says there's another person in the next part of town who should be willing to help us. And if you ask me, I think it's that one person who's keeping this whole place from going under."

"The missionary?" questioned Jarom, a tinge of confusion entering his voice. "Why do you suppose he's living with the killers? It's the last place I'd go."

"Maybe he likes a challenge." Xandir slowed and landed in front of the door. "Here's our stop."

He made as if to enter but turned around at the last moment. "By the way, you're welcome. Believe it or not, I've grown a bit partial to you, Lil' Halo."

Jarom smiled weakly and followed Xandir through the doors. The guards took a look at the ring, and Xandir spoke to them briefly, explaining Jarom's presence to their satisfaction. They hustled into the club, which closely resembled the one they had just left, only on a grander scale.

Gold-plated Pleasure Pools surrounded the perimeter of the vast room, and the center was occupied by variously shaped tables, from stars to circles to rectangles and other completely amorphous shapes that didn't answer to anything at all. Waiters in bright blue uniforms poured glass after glass of intoxicating concoctions and brought plate after plate of sumptuous food.

From a raised dais in the center of the room, a five-member musical group played soft, atmospheric music on instruments that only resembled distant cousins of those Jarom was used to. The smiles plastered on every face sent chills up Jarom's spine. He had never seen anything so rehearsed in his life.

Jarom swallowed hard, trying not to stare at the strange scene. "Okay, we're in. Now what? Where's the gate?"

Xandir scanned the crowd, not letting Jarom know what he was looking for. "He said, it would be pretty conspicuous," he muttered. "Something very—"

Xandir's hand flew to his forehead, as the idea struck him. "Of course," he announced pointing in the right direction. "Look at that. It couldn't be plainer."

Jarom had to agree. Near the back of the room, a cascade of water fell from ceiling to floor, silhouetting a broad archway behind it. They jostled their way through the crowd, Jarom clinging to Xandir like a second shadow. They refused a dozen offers for drinks and at least as many offers to join groups already dining.

They hesitated only a moment in front of the waterfall before taking the plunge through it to the doorway beyond. Instantly, all the sounds died away, replaced by the steady roar of falling water. Ahead of them stretched a vast dark space with a single long flight of illuminated stairs slicing through the middle.

The stairs were divided into three sections by circular pools of water, which served as landings at equal intervals. They jogged up the first section of the stairs in silence and hesitated before the first pool.

"It's one of those Pleasure Pools, all right," whispered Jarom, cringing back from the rippling surface. "I wish I never had to see one again. I'm so ashamed."

Xandir leaned over and considered his reflection in the pool. "Don't worry about it. I've done some things here that I'm not proud of either. We just need to keep moving. My guess is that this one doesn't let you look at whatever you want but instead shows something to you. Probably a method to keep unwanted travelers out."

"I wonder if we both have to pass the test," murmured Jarom, still unwilling to move any closer to the pool.

"There is only one way to find out," said Xandir. "I'll go first."

He bent over without hesitation and dipped his finger in the cool water. The surface bubbled, and the entire room changed, revealing a large estate house atop a hill. They stood in a tranquil cove below, rocking back and forth in a fishing boat, already containing a full net from a recent cast. Jarom wrinkled his nose, but Xandir appeared elated.

"Where is this?" asked Jarom, edging himself away from the fish. "It has to be some sort of illusion."

Xandir reached down and took a fish. "Feels real enough to me. Even my nose is fooled."

"Where are we then?"

"Pompeii," replied Xandir. "Well, pretty close to it. This is a private villa on the coast."

Jarom raised his eyebrows. "Isn't that the city that was destroyed by the volcano? Why are we here?" Xandir's face adopted a grave expression, his eyes glazing over as if trying to part the mists of memory.

"Jarom, I suppose there isn't any way to keep this from you now. Many, many years ago, I met a mortal woman who entranced me like no being has before or since. I knew that such associations were forbidden, but I didn't care. I met her secretly for years, and we kept getting bolder until we slipped up and were discovered. Though people usually can't see me, once I made myself visible to her, I became visible to all. Everything ended in tears after that."

Jarom stared up at the larger angel in disbelief. "They told us at school that it's forbidden because of something to do with Azazel and his Two Hundred Watchers, but no one had really explained why. I . . . I'm sorry to hear that."

"Well, I can fill in those holes for you. You see, I was pretty much Watcher Number One. We were a group that had been set apart after the War in Heaven for being fence sitters. They sent us down to Earth after the Creation of Man to observe them and to tend to all the menial affairs of the new planet. They wanted to keep an eye on us where they figured we wouldn't cause any trouble."

Jarom's face wrinkled. "Well, that obviously didn't go as planned. What happened?"

Xandir sighed, long and deep. "We became fascinated with Mankind. Many of us abandoned our posts as observers and attempted closer associations. By and large, they were awed by us, and after seeing that reverence, some of our number got careless. They started revealing secrets that were to be kept in Heaven—how to make weapons and wage war for example. Not only that, but many of them paired off with mortal women. They lived with them and treated them as wives."

Jarom stood speechless, shaking his head. Xandir continued. "It wasn't so much the association with mortals itself that was so bad. It was what resulted from such unions: children. Somewhere between mortal and immortal, they were unpredictable and powerful. They were hard to hide. Even the smallest of them grew to be larger than the tallest mortal. Most people called them Giants."

Jarom's face grew grave. He had heard stories of the exterminations of the Giants but had never really paid much attention to the details.

"We were each punished severely. They scattered our number across the earth and gave us new tasks. Most they stripped of their immortality, but for some reason, they simply reassigned me. Though I didn't take a mortal wife at that time, it was a temptation that stayed with me, one I never indulged until centuries later."

A shadow passed over Xandir's eyes. "They made me destroy her entire city in punishment. They thought they finished all the Giants off—but apparently not. I met one just the other day."

"This just keeps getting stranger. Why would the pool take us here?"

Xandir shrugged and noticed for the first time that the stairs inexplicably remained part of the scene. They extended from the side of the boat and continued into thin air until they leveled off at the second pool. He took the stairs two at a time, reaching the second landing in a matter of seconds. Xandir peered down and placed his finger in the pool.

In a flash of light, a gold, jeweled crown materialized in his hands, emitting a brilliant golden light. The center of the crown held an ornate crest centering around a character that Jarom recognized as being from the Pure language.

For the second time, Xandir's face lit up. His hands ran tenderly over the surface. "It's my Crown!" he cried. "They took it when I fell! I had forgotten what it looked like . . . it's . . . so brilliant!"

Jarom had never seen Xandir look so happy. He had seen many Crowns before but none so ornate or impressive. The Crown was bestowed on angels who reached a high standing, and its complexity mirrored the angel's accomplishments and position. Once placed on the head, the crown materialized into a glow around the head and face, which had lent the popular halo look adopted by painters and sculptors. Without a crown, any particular angel couldn't tap into his entire power and was completely stripped of his standing in society. Xandir without his Crown was a force to be reckoned with. With it, he would be nearly unstoppable.

Reverently, Xandir placed the Crown on his brow, and it blossomed out in a brilliant ring of golden light. His face shone with a new luster, and his entire figure seemed to grow several inches in each direction. Emboldened by his new power, he bounded up the final flight of stairs, leaving Jarom far behind.

When Jarom reached the balcony at the top of the stairs, he found Xandir with a beautiful woman in his arms. Her hair cascaded down her back like a shimmering waterfall, her eyes glowed with rapture, and her olive skin reflected the glow from Xandir's face.

For several minutes, Xandir remained oblivious to Jarom's presence. They held each other closer and kissed, staring longingly into each other's face. Jarom blushed, unsure of what to do. He was witnessing something deeply forbidden and could do nothing but stare on in shocked silence. His heart burned within him, and, for a moment, he longed to be feeling exactly as Xandir felt just then.

As the spell drew him in, his attention suddenly broke off as he noticed something he hadn't before—the gate. It stood at the end of the balcony, inching open invitingly, willing him to dash forward and slip through.

Jarom shot forward, hands outstretched, aching to leave this strange, twisted place behind. His face planted itself painfully against the bars of the gate. Groaning, he reached up and rattled the bars, a cry of rage leaping from his throat. The bars refused to budge.

"Xandir," he cried. "Forget the girl for a second and help me open this gate!"

Xandir turned, silencing Jarom with a look. "Can't you see I'm a busy? Open it yourself."

Jarom reeled back, cowering under the raw power that had entered Xandir's voice. His glow intensified, and Jarom was sure that the villa would catch fire at any moment.

Suddenly, the hours in the Parlor came rushing back to him. He had been completely absorbed by his senses. True, these were much more complex than the Pools he had used earlier, but they were Pools nonetheless. This was all an elaborate illusion, and if he didn't do something soon, Xandir might fall forever captive to it.

Mustering all his courage, he dashed forward with an out-stretched hand. "Xandir, we have to go on. Don't you see that this isn't real? These things are to keep you from passing through the gate. You've got to let go."

Xandir whirled about, his eyes blazing like twin stars. "I said leave me alone! This can't be an illusion. I think I would know the difference."

He swatted Jarom away, and Jarom hurtled back through the air, the grill of the gate digging into his back. He slid to the floor, dark shapes swimming before his eyes.

He rose to a sitting position. "Xandir, how can this be real? You said so yourself—you destroyed Pompeii! She's only a ghost!"

Xandir turned, his eyes dimming. "You're wrong. She lives. They . . . they saved her . . . ."

His voice trailed off, and he let go of his love. She looked so real. He wanted to believe. But in that moment of recollection, he realized Ganosh would not have let her go.

Xandir turned and stepped toward the door, wishing he could silence the voice of reason.

"I don't care!" he roared. "I don't care if it is an illusion! It feels real to me. You're just jealous because I might actually have the chance to be happy for once."

Xandir advanced on the gate, bent on silencing the cherub for good. But several steps from his goal, the entire scene flickered out of focus, like a poorly adjusted camera. He turned back and saw the face of his love obscured. The light from his Crown dimmed, and his heart seized within him.

"No!" He leapt back toward the beautiful woman. Her face once again snapped into focus.

"Xandir, you must have seen that! You'll never really be happy living an illusion. Remember all of those people down there in the Parlors? Come back toward the gate."

The woman reached out her hand, beckoning for him to stay. Xandir clamped his hands firmly over his ears and shut his eyes fast. The clear voice of reason called from one direction, while the sweet voice of pleasure beckoned from the other. The strain threatened to pull him in two.

One voice had to go.

He lunged with swords outstretched, hurtling himself toward the gate. He raised one sword and brought it down with supersonic speed, aiming to silence Jarom's voice for good. Jarom screamed, his fate sealed.

The scene faded into black, leaving only stairs. At the last second, the sword's arc shifted, slipping through the tip of Jarom's wing instead of his head. Jarom writhed and fell to the floor.

Xandir glanced back, his mouth open in a silent wail. The voice of reason was right. He clutched the bars of the gate, and saw the scene fade until it was barely visible. He reached up, and removed the Crown from his head, letting it clatter to the floor. It disappeared in a puff of smoke and sparks, and the gate slid open a couple of inches.

He swiveled about, clenching his stomach as he met the gaze of the woman he loved while she faded into nothing more than a specter. She floated toward him, humming an enchanting melody that brought drowsiness to his eyes.

He glanced back at the gate, and for the first time he noticed that as the gate had opened, it had revealed a new panel on the side of one of the thick, metal bars. It contained a single slender object—a sleek silver dagger.

"No," he moaned. "No, I can't! I already did it once—I can't do it again!"

The spectral woman advanced on him, her song increasing in volume, casting a net of slumber over Xandir, drawing him into unconsciousness. "Come, Xandir, join me in slumber."

He reached for the dagger and gripped it in his trembling

hand. He turned to face the approaching phantom. "My love, wherever you are, forgive me."

Darkness gathered round him, and he fell forward into the specter's embrace, lashing out with the knife.

The knife slashed through the ghostly figure, and she vanished in a violent splattering of water. The gate leapt open, drawing both Jarom and Xandir into the darkness beyond. The pull of the gate drew them in, and they tumbled through the blackness, down and down, toward the heart of the fallen city.

TWENTY-SEVEN
A TOUCH OF THE DIVINE

NEW YORK STATE 2012

When Judy and Eden awoke, they realized they were back on the bed in Eden's master bedroom. Daren lay between them, his eyes still closed, his face pale and lifeless. If not for his slow, measured breathing, they would have already considered him dead. He neither moved nor responded to any of Eden's desperate words or touches.

It took them some time before they could convince each other that their entire adventure in the woods had actually taken place. But as they surveyed the bandages all over their bodies, there could be little doubt.

Snatches of the memories of their return trip trickled back. They remembered the soft hands and luminous faces—the beings whose very presence filled them with peace. The feelings remained long afterward, and they were sure that some of them lingered around the house.

"Do you think they have something to do with that Xandir character?" Judy asked. "You know, that angel who saved you? Where is he anyway?"

Eden shrugged. "Maybe. But from what you said, Xandir seemed so troubled and conflicted. These seem to be the opposite of conflicted. I suppose it's appropriate to say that only Heaven knows where Xandir may be."

Judy sighed and sat back down on the bed. The presence of

the angels had driven back the demons inside, but she knew it was only a matter of time before the Demons fought their way back to the surface.

They placed Daren on a cot in the bedroom and took turns watching over him. As time passed, he began to mutter in his sleep. Judy recognized the demon language, although he spoke so softly that she often couldn't make out the words.

In such a short time, Eden's stomach had swelled, and she had to spend more time in bed and in the bathroom than watching over her husband. Her skin had grown warmer to the touch, and even at this early stage, she could feel the babies shift and sway within her, as if locked in a miniscule wrestling match.

That night, as Eden was enjoying a rare absence of nausea, she sat by the open window in her bedroom, gazing out at the stars. The moon was full, and as she peered into the darkness, she could sense the angelic figures stronger than ever, circling her house in a solemn vigil.

"There must be a reason I'm getting such protection," she whispered to herself. "I can't imagine everyone has this many Guardian angels circling their property. But then again, what do I really know?"

She gazed Heavenward and caught a glimpse of the brilliant North Star, shining out brightly among the rest. She closed her eyes and made a wish.

Suddenly, one of the floating shapes broke from its circular formation and rose rapidly toward her window. Eden gasped and stepped backward.

The figure entered the room, bathed in a soft light, like moonbeams. The figure of a woman appeared in front of Eden. She wore long, flowing robes. Her plaited hair was dark, in stark contrasted to her pale skin.

The woman raised a hand in greeting. "Fear not," she breathed, the voice more felt than heard, "and be ready. We have been with you and will not forsake you. You have heard our voices whispering in your heart. Your feet have been placed on a dangerous path, and you have had the courage to follow."

Eden thought of the subtle voice that had guided her back at the cabin and smiled. She wondered if they had had something to do with her being led to the cabin in the first place.

A second figure appeared beside the woman—a smaller personage with round, childish features. He floated toward her and placed a single hand on Eden's shoulder.

All feelings of fear and anxiety fled. For once, the children within Eden ceased their struggle. Her racing heartbeat slowed, and her anxiety was replaced by a soft, warming glow that started from deep within and radiated outward, filling her body to the extremities with shimmering light.

Both figures smiled and turned in unison to go. They faded into the night sky, leaving Eden to ponder the strange occurrence.

TWENTY-EIGHT
DEATH DIAMONDS

Xandir awoke in a puddle riddled with dark crimson streaks. As his eyes focused, he saw that the streaks were blood, and he felt about his chest, taking it to be his own. However, as his senses cleared, he could find no wound, and he finally realized that it was the wrong color and consistency for angel's blood.

The actual victim lay only a few paces to his left, facedown in a gutter. The man was dressed in a loose, black robe, flecked with grime. A jagged tear in the back of his robe exposed a gaping wound, from which the blood trickled.

Xandir approached the man and used the hilt of his sword to flip him over. The man's pale features and unblinking eyes told it all: he was dead.

Xandir backed away and jumped as an object clutched in his palm vibrated. He opened his hands and narrowed his eyes. In his palm lay an immaculately cut diamond, the size of a small fist. It was without blemish and would have fetched a fortune. The diamond's vibration increased, drawing Xandir's hand toward the slain man.

As he drew close, the blood from the man began to rise, congealing in the air into a single mass. From the ground, the man's clothes, and even from Xandir's wings, the blood rose, leaving nothing behind.

Suddenly, a single drop broke off from the main mass and sped through the air toward the heart of Xandir's diamond. In an instant, the drop of blood had stained a tiny part of the diamond a deep crimson, while the rest of the blood swirled about and then funneled back in to the man through the wound from which it came.

In a few moments, the blood had all disappeared, and the wound had sealed itself, becoming no more than a faint scar on the man's back.

The person stirred, groaning and cursing under his breath. He rose to his knees, snarling and brandishing an ax. He eyes met Xandir's and bore into his like a beast.

"That," he snarled, "was a dirty trick. I'll teach you to go around shooting people in the back like a gutless coward!"

The man advanced on Xandir, brandishing his ax. He swung three times, practically slicing the air in two with the ferocity of his blows. Xandir leapt backward and parried with both swords, reluctant to deal any damage to a man that had just come back from the dead.

A cry rang out from the other direction, and a group of rough men in dark blue robes emerged from the shadows.

A short, stocky man with a shaved head rushed out in front and thrust an accusing finger at Xandir. "Thought you could steal our drop, did you? Well, you'll be giving us more than one of your own by the time we're through with you."

The band launched their attack from the other side, brandishing an assortment of multi-bladed throwing knives. The knives whizzed past, and Xandir dodged them only with a beat of his wings that propelled him into the air. The knives sailed past with a whine, missing Xandir and embedding into the ax-wielder.

With a cry, the ill-fated man once again fell to the rough, dirty floor. The bald man rushed forward, holding his own diamond aloft and collected a single drop of blood.

Their original prey taken, the band turned their attention back to their new target. The men clapped their hands smartly, and the knives returned to their owners as if on invisible strings. Xandir winced. He didn't know how these people miraculously sprang back to life after taking fatal wounds, but he didn't want to wait around to find out.

Xandir weaved in and out of a storm of knives, figuring that an offense might be fruitless. The dark glass ceiling curved around at a gradual angle, forming a dome. Below him, a twisted maze of corridors, dead ends, stagnant pools of water, and crumbling statues covered the floor. Xandir moved toward the center of the dome, flying to the point where the ceiling rose to its peak. The knives finally fell short, and the racing mob gave up the pursuit.

However, just as Xandir was about to sigh in relief, another shape struck out of the darkness. A man on giant mechanical wings shot toward him, shooting bullets from miniature cannons attached to each arm. The flurry hit Xandir head on, knocking him out of the air and sending him spiraling toward the ground. He landed with a spectacular splash in a crumbling fountain, the water coated with dank black algae. In an instant, a dozen other shapes leapt from the shadows, squabbling with each other as they closed in for the kill.

Xandir peered up from the water just in time to see a massive drill descending toward his face. There was no time to move out of the way.

A second before impact, a blast of white flame spilled out of the passageways behind the oncoming attackers. The rabble scattered, clutching their eyes and scrambling about in confusion, yelling and screaming.

In the midst of the light, a short figure emerged, his body robed in white and his face swathed in white hair. At his approach, the rest of the mob scattered, disappearing into the holes and cracks from whence they came. Xandir rose the rest of the way out of the water, propping himself up on the rim of the fountain.

The approaching man smiled, his expression radiant and pure. Clearly, this was the one light in a sea of wickedness.

Xandir brushed back his sodden hair out of his face. "You must be the missionary."

The man nodded and stretched out a hand in greeting. "Yes," he confirmed. "My name is Johannes. I have been waiting for you for some time."

Xandir started to form a question, but Johannes silenced him with a wave of his hand. "No, no, we should not talk here. Come, we must move quickly."

The old man flew through the tangle of mazes at a speed that caught Xandir by surprise. Though he seemed aged, his spirit was so brimming with life it could scarcely be contained in a body a fraction of his age.

Johannes led Xandir to an open space near the edge of the dome. It contained a marble shrine. Short carved columns held up a domed roof that sheltered a circular altar, a bed roll, and a small bundle of supplies. Xandir noticed a handful of scrolls lying around the back of the shrine, well-worn from constant use.

Johannes beckoned him to enter. "It's a good thing I found you. I might have mistaken you for another one of the locals if it hadn't been for your little friend."

Xandir's head whirled around. In all the commotion, he had not seen any sign of the brave cherub. Apparently, he had yet another thing to thank Jarom for.

The cherub came fluttering out of the back of the shrine, grinning broadly, his wing bound in a fresh bandage.

"Glad to see you're in one piece, Lil' Halo," Xandir said. "Looks like you've been taken care of. They didn't exactly roll out the welcome mat, did they?"

The cherub's grin broadened even further. "If understatement was a sin, you would be locked in here forever."

"I suppose that's true. The Dome of Death, if I'm not mistaken. It's aptly named."

"Yes," muttered Johannes sadly. "The work of death continues every minute of every day. There is hardly a more wretched place anywhere."

"Is there a method to all this, or are they all just butchers?" asked Xandir, keeping his eye on the maze.

"They've deceived themselves. They think that the killing will gain them their freedom," replied Johannes. "You see that crystal you have in your hand? It's called a Sanguine Diamond. Every time someone in here slays a foe, the diamond collects a single drop of blood. The more blood, the more powerful the bearer of the diamond becomes. They think if they keep collecting blood from one another that someday they will grow powerful enough to unlock the door that leads out of the Dome."

Xandir cocked an eyebrow. "Is that true? I mean, is that what we're going to have to do to get out of here?"

Johannes shook his head. "Yes and no. It is true that the diamonds open many doors. But what these people don't understand is that in order to pass through the doors, they have to give up their own blood."

"That makes sense," Xandir agreed. "That would effectively keep them all in here. Their own blood is the last thing these murderers would give up."

Johannes sighed, deep and long. "I have tried so hard to get through to them. I have wandered all of the levels, especially this one, to try to get them to change their ways. Even when confronted with certain doom, there is no love in their hearts or reason in their minds."

Johannes perked up, his eyes still radiating hope. "That isn't to say that I should give up. I would count myself a success if I could reach even one soul in this city."

"What about Tobias?" suggested Jarom. "He may be crooked, but at least he agreed to help us."

Johannes's eyes narrowed, and his face darkened. "Did you say Tobias? You have met him?"

"Yes," answered Jarom, a bit flustered. "In the Lower Court. We left him on the last level."

Johannes paused for a moment before continuing. "Tobias is a very dangerous man. He is one of the very few who has found the way to navigate all of the levels as he pleases. The security here is tight, but it isn't foolproof. Not for someone as crafty as he is."

Xandir dared to ask the question that fought its way to the forefront of his mind. "Was he originally locked in the Dome? He was pretty handy in a fight."

Johannes shook his head. "No, he was even further up: the Realm of the Traitors."

Now they all fell silent. From Tobias's description, only the vilest of all had been consigned to the Realm of Traitors, the citadel in the very heart of the city. Xandir tried to imagine what

Tobias had done to earn him that distinction.

"That seems ridiculous," muttered Xandir. "I just can't imagine him being worse than all these cutthroats."

"That is exactly why he is so dangerous. He doesn't look the part. Do you think the Devil comes rushing up on his victims in a fiery column of flame, dashing his hooves and swinging a pitchfork? He's much more subtle than that. He doesn't have any of those things, by the way. To look at him, he's actually rather handsome and charismatic."

"Well," sighed Xandir, "I'm glad that we're rid of Tobias then. Though, we're supposed to meet him on the way out. He thinks we're his ticket out of the city."

Johannes's head shot back and forth. "You must not let that happen! I'd rather see the entire lot of the Dome unleashed on the world than see him roaming free. It would be a complete disaster."

"Then what do we do?" moaned Jarom. "Are you going to help us get out of here?"

To his surprise, Johannes nodded. "Yes. I have foreseen your coming for many years. I have watched and waited, and now I am very glad to see you actually show up. I know what you are seeking."

"You do?" Xandir asked, raising a single eyebrow. "And you are still willing to help us?"

Johannes indicated the scrolls at the back of the room. "These scrolls contain the writings of a vision I had many years ago. It talks about the End of the World and the calamities that might occur before the End finally comes. It's all been carefully thought out, and we each have our roles to play."

He stooped down, picked up a scroll, and unrolled it in front of Xandir and Jarom. The writing was faded but still legible.

"See? It tells here of great catastrophes that will slay millions. They are not pleasant to read about, but that doesn't lessen their reality. When I first discerned the reason of your coming, I rebelled at the idea and thought that you should be stopped at all costs. But the more I pondered it, the more I see that it is simply part of the grander Design. I do not know why you must do what you are going to do, but I do know that it must be."

"Old Hebrew," whispered Xandir in amazement. "You wrote this? They only have this stuff in museums now. Just how long have you been around?"

Johannes withdrew his lower lip and bit down. "I stopped keeping track of the years long ago. Suffice it to say, I'm here until the End, which, by the looks of it, might be coming sooner than we all supposed."

"I've heard that one before," said Xandir. "It can't happen soon enough, in my book."

"Why don't we just focus on getting out of here?" Jarom suggested with a hint of desperation. "I don't think those ruffians would have any qualms about mixing in a little cherub's blood with the rest."

"Don't worry, little one," reassured Johannes. "You are quite safe as long as I am with you. Only the boldest would even dare approach the shrine."

He folded up the scrolls and replaced them at the back of the room. "Come quickly. The Dome goes down many levels. Only I have access to the lift that will take us down far enough."

Johannes adjusted his robes and left the shrine, beckoning them to follow him into the darkness. They followed a dizzying path through the hedges of stone and over pools of foul-smelling water. They passed gangs of men and women in different-colored robes who ceased their fighting only long enough to let them pass.

After an hour of walking, they reached a massive, rounded stone in the shape of a cylinder, which stood at a right angle to the ceiling. Johannes ran up to the pillar and placed both hands against it, muttering softly as he did so. The stone groaned, and a metal door emerged from the rock.

Johannes turned and gazed earnestly at Xandir. "Cover me," he commanded, his fingers working at the door. "It will take a moment for me to get this open. The truly desperate ones would take any chance to get on this elevator."

Sure enough, a ring of combatants had already formed at the edges of the clearing. They advanced with weapons drawn, their mouths hanging open in anticipation.

"Stand aside," barked one. "Let us down, or we'll gut ya!"

A dart whizzed through the air, and the clearing filled with acrid smoke. Dazed, Xandir backed himself against the smooth column, keeping his eyes on Johannes as he worked at coaxing the door open.

"I just need a minute!" he pleaded. "Don't let them get too close."

A trio of shapes emerged from the darkness, striking in unison with sharpened scythes. The blows whizzed past either side of Xandir's neck, severing locks of his hair on both sides. Xandir responded in kind, countering with his Justice sword. Immediately, the trio fell to the ground, and three bright crystals rolled onto the ground next to them, shattering into thousands of crimson shards. The attackers howled in agony as their winnings rose into the air and evaporated from sight.

"Anyone else?" Xandir challenged.

A rain of arrows answered, and he had just enough time to raise his sword to block a few. Unfortunately, two landed square in his arm, sending a bolt of pain streaking through his body.

Jarom flew up to Xandir's defense, releasing a volley of his own, flinging arrows with incredible speed and accuracy. Xandir snapped off the two arrows and threw them back through the lessening fog. He raised both swords and winced as another volley of arrows struck home, grazing his left leg in several places.

He readied himself for another strike when the creak of metal against stone sounded behind him and echoed through the Dome. He turned briefly to see the elevator door standing wide open and Johannes already inside, drawing Jarom in after him.

"Come, Xandir! You have only a moment!"

Xandir leapt into the space, absorbing a final volley of arrows to his back and wings as he went. The door slammed shut after him, silencing the clamor of the crowd and leaving them in total darkness. Xandir sank to his knees in painful exhaustion.

"How bad is it?" asked Jarom anxiously. "They aren't going to get your blood, are they?"

Xandir winced as he withdrew another shaft. "No," he whispered. "They won't have me today. Though I admit, I have felt better."

Johannes placed his hands on Xandir, and a quiet peace settled over Xandir's body. He relaxed and sat back as the elevator began its decent.

"Don't worry," said Xandir, withdrawing the last of the Ambrosia cake. "Lil' Halo's donut came through before. I think I'm going to need the rest of it though."

He popped the last of the cake into his mouth and leaned back against the wall to let it take its healing effect.

"Once you cross the door, you'll be in the deepest part of the city and the most dangerous. I have not yet been there, but it is said that only one person remains, the former King of Serche, who whiles away his days in misery in the shadow of the Tree of Death."

"I can't imagine he'll be too happy to see us," thought Jarom aloud. "Isn't there any way around him without having to fight?"

Johannes sighed. "I wish I could say yes. Even in life, he knew nothing but the language of violence and war. I can't imagine that his long imprisonment has done much to improve his disposition. You will have to summon all your cunning if you are to defeat him."

They passed along in silence, and the elevator slowed to a halt. The door swung open to reveal a narrow, dimly lit hallway of black stone. At the end lay a gate constructed of silver, wreathed by torches of blue flame.

In front of the gate on a raised pedestal lay a massive diamond, larger than the angels had ever seen. Its heart remained clear, and its facets glinted eerily in the blue light. They approached it.

"Do not worry," counseled Johannes. "I assure you that we are quite alone. It is a rare thing indeed for any to venture this deep."

Xandir gazed at the diamond, spellbound. He couldn't conceive what power might have constructed such an incredible object as this.

"What must we do? Am I correct in assuming that this is also a Sanguine Diamond?"

"Yes," confirmed Johannes. "The largest there is."

"It's beautiful," whispered Jarom, unable to take his eyes off it.

"But it must hold millions of drops of blood."

"Indeed, millions. But here's another secret: Not all blood is counted equally. As angels, your blood is more potent. Blood of an innocent person has much greater strength than that of a vile sinner, and blood freely given is more powerful still."

"It doesn't look like there's a single drop in it though," observed Xandir. "Hasn't any one tried before?"

"Oh, yes," confirmed Johannes. "There have been some over the course of the years. But as soon as it stops being filled, the blood slowly runs back out of the diamond and is lost. No one is sure where it goes, only that it is nowhere man or angel can see."

Jarom eyed the gem, his inner tension mounting. "What exactly do we have to do? Do we give it our own blood?"

Johannes indicated two holes on the side of the pedestal. "An offering can be made by placing both hands through these holes. The diamond will draw your blood until the hands are retracted."

Jarom shuddered at the thought. It was almost too grisly to think about. For a long time, Xandir and Jarom simply stared at each other, each unable to suggest how they might proceed.

Suddenly, in a moment of determined decision, Jarom stepped forward, baring his bare arms. Xandir's arm shot out in front of him.

"No, I can't let you do this. I'll do it. I'm stronger."

Jarom shook his head. "It's not all about strength, Xandir. We are both angels. But look at your Sin Shroud. It is plain to see that I'm the more innocent of the two. And I give my blood freely. Maybe that will make it powerful enough to satisfy this thirsty diamond."

"That," added Johannes, "and you are the greater warrior, Xandir. If you are to stand any chance against the King, it would be best if you, Xandir, went through."

Xandir's face fell. He had hoped it would not come to this, that he would have to finish things alone. It was all he had ever done for centuries upon centuries, and now, he was finding that it was a sorry way to work.

"There has to be another way. There has to be!"

"There is no other way," said Johannes, his eyes glistening.

"For this to work, it must be either you or him, and I think reason is on his side."

Jarom stepped forward, his arms trembling. Sweat broke out across his brow. "Let's just get this over with."

Xandir caught his arm one more time. "Thank you, Lil' H— Jarom. Thank you."

Jarom nodded and thrust both arms into the holes. The diamond lifted from the pedestal to hang several feet above them in the air. A single drop of red swam through the pedestal and rose through the air to meet the hovering diamond. Other drops leapt up to join it, forming first a queue and then a steady stream. The crimson spot grew to a ribbon inside the diamond and blossomed into a sanguine rose. Jarom rocked and groaned, great beads of sweat popping out like an advancing army across his forehead.

Xandir forced himself to divide his time between the darkening diamond and the silver gate, which slowly inched open, equal to the progress of the diamond.

Jarom's body trembled, and one of his knees gave way. He sank to the ground but managed to keep his arms firmly rooted in the dual holes. He grunted and rocked and finally screamed as the diamond continued to fill with the essence of his life.

Johannes stepped forward and placed both hands firmly on Jarom's shoulders. He spoke softly and urgently, whispering a prayer of help and strength. Xandir stared at the diamond, seeing fewer and fewer spots where the redness had not taken over. He held his breath as the silver gate creaked open, beckoning him to enter.

Jarom's head sagged, and his eyelids fluttered rapidly. He had lost the strength to cry out but gritted his teeth through unspeakable pain. The gate creaked open, nearly providing a gap large enough to slip through.

A burst of red light erupted from the diamond, which was now completely immersed in red. The gate flew open wide, revealing the passageway beyond. Jarom, completely spent, slumped forward and slid down the face of the pedestal. Xandir turned to return to him, but Johannes raised a warning hand.

"Go, I will see to him. The diamond is already beginning to drain."

It was true. The stream was already falling in reverse, returning the blood to the pedestal from whence it came. The silver gate crept shut again. He wasn't going to miss this chance.

With a single bound, Xandir flapped his wings and shot through the opening. His body suddenly took on a feeling of great speed, and the corridor melted to a blur around him. He stopped abruptly in front of another door, this one constructed of pitch-black wood with a metal handle. One more door and he would finally reach his destination.

He gripped the handle and took a moment to bow his head. "Jarom," he whispered, marveling at the sacrifice of the little angel. "I may never know your fate. If we never meet again in this world, may it be a happier reunion in the one to come."

He gripped the handle and turned.

TWENTY-NINE
GEARS AND ROOTS

THE FALLEN CITY OF SERCHE, 2012

Xandir shivered. The scene before him held none of the frost or snow usually associated with cold. Instead, the chill seemed to come from every lethargic particle of air. It was as if no living thing had breathed or disturbed it for centuries. The darkness let in only the tiniest particles of light by which Xandir made out the towering edifice in front of him.

The citadel stretched up from the very bowels of the city like a jagged backbone of glossy black stone. A massive arched portal graced the front, whose door hung a foot off the ground, pried open by gnarled, darkened tree roots. They looked as if they had been blackened by fire, though they still lived and writhed with a will of their own. Dark sap trickled down the roots, emitting a noxious odor into the chill air. Xandir looked back and saw the rest of the city lay motionless and dead.

He approached the door and withdrew his swords. Tentatively, he poked at a gnarled root and was rewarded by a rumble from deep within the tower. He glanced up at the door and saw more of the Serchean writing from the gate into the city. He thought sadly on the memory, wondering how long it had been since Jarom had helped him crack that code.

"If only he could be here now," he sighed.

He placed a hand on the door, and to his surprise, it lit up under his touch. A bright crimson light flowed from his hand

and spread throughout the door in ripples and cracks. He tried to remove his hand, but the door held him fast. The smooth surface of the door parted in a dozen directions, leaving him touching a single stone obelisk. A voice spoke from the center of the obelisk, which still glowed red under his hand.

"Look into the light," the voice prompted in a penetrating whisper. "Only the treacherous may enter. We must see into your soul."

Seeing that he had little choice, Xandir gazed into the pulsating red light, which grew until it filled his entire field of vision. The events of his stay in Serche passed in an instant before his eyes, filling him with anguish. The images faded, and he couldn't help but ask himself if all this was worth it, even if it was for her. He shook his head, trying to clear his thoughts. He would just have to see.

The obelisk clicked and whirred, retracting into the floor.

"Evidence of treachery confirmed. You may proceed."

Xandir stepped into the corridor, making his way through tangled masses of roots and vines. They covered every surface, curling and writhing, groaning and swelling. Xandir lashed out at them with his swords but found that this more often than not brought painful retaliation as the nearby vines whipped at him at welt-inducing speeds. He feinted and dodged, weaving from side to side in a desperate effort to remain unscathed.

The tunnel fanned out into a large, open room, and Xandir paused as he glimpsed his destination for the first time. The true Tree of Death stood rooted in the center of the tower, its twisted, black trunk coiled into the sky like two misshapen snakes wrapped around each other. The branches stretched the length of the tower and contained glossy black leaves, bursting with clusters of pear-shaped fruit the size of basketballs. Other branches swayed under the weight of prickly crimson blossoms that exuded a pungent, sweet odor.

A flight of stone steps led from the platform on which Xandir stood down to the base of the tree. Xandir flew down the pathway, his wings blazing.

His heart soared as he approached the tree undisturbed and he picked up speed, ready to launch himself to the upper branches to pluck a fruit from the tree's wooden fingers.

He stopped. There in front of him stood a man, taller and more muscular than any he had seen. He stood with a calm expression, his arms crossed behind his back. He was dressed head to toe in battle regalia of dark blues, greens, and grays, which devoured the light around it. His hair and eyes were dark and flawless, in stark contrast to his smooth, pale skin. His lips formed a thin line and held almost no color at all. When he spoke, the voice wormed its way into Xandir's mind and blanketed out all else.

"Welcome, fellow traitor. Have you come to prune my tree with your flashy swords?"

Xandir stood tall and advanced on the king. "I'm Xandir, and these swords aren't for gardening. I've come here for the fruit."

"Have you?" asked the king, the faintest glimmer of a smile gracing his lips. "That is a foolish pursuit."

Xandir crossed his twin blades in front of him. This wasn't the time to negotiate.

"Foolish or not, it is coming with me. Stand aside, or I shall make you taste pain as you never have."

The king did not flinch. "No. First I will give one last warning: I am the greatest mind that ever lived. I stand supreme among even the vilest traitors, and all who have seen me fight have their end."

Xandir held his gaze. "I do not fear you."

"Very well, then. You shall not live to regret it."

Suddenly, the image of the king flickered out, leaving only empty air. Xandir glanced up along the height of the tree and saw it for the first time: a giant, mechanical mass, a crude representation of a man with four arms tangled among the branches. With a metallic roar, the mechanization broke free of the branches and plummeted toward the ground.

It landed with a tremendous splash in a pool of murky water at the base of the tree, sending up a vile mist as much of the water evaporated on contact.

The figure stood twice Xandir's height, with the same mysterious color scheme of the king's armor. The skeletal figure afforded a view of the creature's inner workings: dozens of pounding pistons, whirring gears, and torrents of steam, which erupted from every orifice. The face was fixed in a perpetual glare, with three malicious glowing eyes piercing the darkness. Though it carried no visible weapon, Xandir quickly found out why.

The king pointed his arm at Xandir, and it rocketed toward him. Xandir dodged it by only inches. The arm swung of its own accord, balling itself into a fist, and pummeled Xandir across the back. It moved on, only to be joined by a second fist.

Xandir slashed out with his swords, putting all his strength into a crushing blow. The blades skittered harmlessly off the metal, leaving barely a mark. The arms returned to their master, and the king lumbered forward, detaching one metallic leg in mid-stride and brandishing it like a broadsword. The two arms fastened themselves seamlessly without hindering the advancing machine.

Xandir flew into the defensive, parrying the blows with strokes of his own and flailing to find some sort of weak point. He struck out at the creature about the head, but the blows glanced off. In response, the king removed its head and lobbed it like a boulder in Xandir's direction. The head exploded into a thousand pieces, peppering the angel with deadly shrapnel.

Xandir recoiled and fell to the ground. Immediately, the Tree's tangled roots latched on to him, squeezing and coiling as if to press the life right out of him. Xandir lashed out blindly, severing the roots and bringing himself upright.

The warrior angel watched in horror as the headless abomination grew a second head, identical to the first, from the bowels of its mechanical maze. It fixed its eyes on Xandir and shot out three of its limbs in pursuit.

Xandir took to the air, just barely able to outrun the speeding limbs. He twisted back around through the air, thinking of bringing the limbs back on a course toward their own master. They sped along without swerving, and for a moment, it looked as if they would slam into the king. However, Xandir's hopes evaporated as the arms simply snapped back on with a clang, primed for the next assault.

The flyby, however, had one positive effect. Xandir had glimpsed a pulsing heart amidst all the mechanical workings, and he knew he had a new target.

Xandir shot higher into the air, making his way toward the interwoven branches of the evil Tree. The king followed, shimmying up the trunk with incredible agility and grasping the branches with all four of his arms. Xandir lunged at a dark, sticky piece of fruit. The king barreled toward him, his legs twirling so rapidly they created a whirlwind. The gale-force gust tore Xandir from his flight path and sent him sprawling downward. The king followed him, spinning his appendages ever faster.

Xandir fell once again into the groping mass of roots. The king stopped the column of air and hovered motionless for a moment over his prey. Xandir seized the moment, reaching into his armor and extracting an arrow he had saved from those that had struck him in the Dome. With a quick flick of his wrist, he sent the arrow flying between a gap in the metal and into the machine's beating heart.

The king shot backward, obviously surprised. However, instead of crumpling, he let out a scornful laugh. He reached one of his arms inside his chest, plucked out the heart, and flung it down at Xandir with full force. Xandir pressed himself deep into the roots of the Tree, shielding himself from the brunt of the attack. The heart caught fire and exploded like a grenade, peeling back the cover of roots and unleashing the smell of rotting wood. The surrounding roots reared up in protest, lashing about and flailing to grasp their attacker.

It took several moments for Xandir's vision to clear, and he knew that when it did, he would see that the creature had grown a new heart. In a moment, he had to come to grips with the fact that this sinister creation actually had no conventional weak spot and that he would have to change his tactics if he expected to survive.

The rise of the vines presented him with an idea. Though the king was powerful, the Tree itself presented a still greater source of strength. It was only a matter of harnessing the Tree's power to achieve the correct result.

Rising again from the floor, Xandir rushed toward the trunk

of the tree, followed in hot pursuit by the king. Xandir drew his blades close together, and with a swift chopping motion, he brought them down time after time on the surface of the ebony trunk. In response, a bundle of roots from the base rose up, working frantically to ward off the attacker.

At the same time, the king launched all six of his appendages in a deadly swirling formation. Xandir held his ground until the last second and then darted swiftly out of the way, allowing the tree to take the full force of the attack.

The tree rocked back and forth, leaves scattering and blossoms shedding their sanguine petals. A huge mass of roots reared up, swallowing the collective appendages whole. The limbs struggled and writhed, but as more and more roots joined the mob, the king's limbs slowly capitulated, disappearing into the depths. The king let out a piercing scream as he realized what had happened. He flailed about without his limbs, struggling to rise into the air.

Taking a cue from his foe, Xandir shot up above the king and beat his wings as fast and as hard as he could, driving the king down into the expectant vines. Sheathing his swords, Xandir withdrew the remainder of his arrows, flinging them down into the Tree's vines, working them into a frenzy.

The king roared and thrashed, but in the end, he couldn't resist the inexorable pull of the roots. He vanished with a gurgle beneath the surface, and then all faded to silence.

Xandir slipped in and out of consciousness, his entire body aching from exertion and pain. However, with his goal in sight, he forced himself to ignore all of it and shot toward the canopy.

The nearest cluster of fruit loomed large above him, held to the tree only by a fragile stem. With one swipe of his sword, the cluster fell free and into his outstretched hand.

He recoiled and nearly dropped the fruit as the skin burned his flesh, eating through like acid. Quickly, he slid his hand up the side of the fruit, grasping it loosely by the remainder of the stem.

Behind him, the Tree roared to life. It had obviously not taken too kindly to having its fruit stolen. Xandir beat his wings in a flurry of motion, heading toward the tiny opening in the wall from whence he came. The branches swayed downward, creeping constantly toward him as the roots from the floor rose up, creating a jagged cage around him.

He hacked repeatedly with both swords, clearing the way in front of him barely fast enough to stay ahead of the advancing vines. He burst into the tunnel, which closed in around him like a swollen windpipe. Roots crawled over his skin, tangled in his hair, and beat his body, slowing his progress more and more with every passing second.

Gritting his teeth, Xandir focused hard on the opening at the end of the tunnel. He had not come this far just to have his plans thwarted by a mere plant. With a renewed burst of speed, he threw every last bit of energy into a final hacking charge. He reached the door just as the tangle of roots closed in around him, trapping him halfway in and halfway out the portal.

He writhed and squirmed, but he could not free himself. On the upside, he found that the roots were also not trying to pull him in either. With a frustrated wail, he closed his eyes and put all his strength into one final attempt—to no avail.

He held the forbidden fruit at arm's length, dangling like rotting carcasses. The pungent odor of rot and decay wafted from the bunch, adding to Xandir's intense discomfort.

To Xandir's surprise, he didn't remain alone for long. In minutes, a hunched figure rocketed up from below to stand on the edge of the platform in front of him. The figure approached and came into a dim patch of light in front of him. Xandir drew in his breath as he recognized the figure: Tobias.

"Seems like you've gotten yourself in a bit of a bind."

Xandir rolled his eyes, uncertain if he was happy to see his new visitor. "Cut with the bad jokes and get me out of here. How did you get here, anyway?"

Tobias smiled wryly in a way that made Xandir's stomach take a nose dive. "I have my ways," he whispered. "I would love to get you out, but you see, I've never really been much for gardening."

He walked forward and examined the fruit in Xandir's outstretched hands. "Well, what do we have here? Not exactly the freshest pick of the vine, but I think they will do."

Xandir snatched the fruit out of Tobias's reach. "Johannes was right about you. You were playing us for fools the entire time."

Tobias sighed. "Yes, yes, we did have some good times, didn't we? You showed me what I needed to know—that you could actually take on the king and the Tree and succeed. Though I have certain powers of my own, I wouldn't have stood a chance against that pile of junk."

Tobias drew his eyes together and flicked his hands toward himself. With a small rush of air, a single piece of fruit ripped free from the bundle and flew into his outstretched hand.

"I only need one. It's got plenty of seeds."

Xandir renewed his struggle to break free. Each hand was only inches away from a sword. He would only have to grasp one hilt or the other to draw on its power. "What are you going to do with that? You said it yourself—you can't possibly get out of here!"

Tobias shrugged, wincing at the touch and odor of the fruit. "That was then, this is now. I've found myself a way around the conventional rules, and as it turns out, there's even one around the way out."

Xandir strained, his face contorted with pain. "Oh, yeah, and how's that? I might want to take it myself one of these days, provided I do get out of this mess."

Tobias shrugged. "I guess there is no harm in that. You see, the only way to get around the rule is if the alternative is so bad that nobody will take it."

"You have my undivided attention."

"Thank you," he sneered. "Now think about it—what is the one predicament that this place is bent on avoiding?"

Xandir rolled his eyes. "Falling into the Jaws, I get it. Could you just get to the point already?"

A belly laugh burst from Tobias's gut. "Oh, I'm sorry! Did you have somewhere to be?"

"Tell me," Xandir seethed, his eyes boring into the old man.

"Fine," he muttered. "The long and short of it is that you are allowed to leave if you cast yourself directly into the Jaws. They must figure that that's where you're headed anyway, so if you just want to speed up the process, all the better."

"I don't understand," moaned Xandir. "How does that help you? Nobody gets out of there once they're in—nobody."

Tobias tossed the fruit up and down in his hand, gaining a short reprieve from the fruit's caustic affect.

"The Prince of Darkness himself has had his eye on this fruit for a long time. I made a pact with him. I would retrieve this for him in return for certain favors. I've taken a little bit longer on my task than expected, but I imagine he'll still be happy to see me."

"You piece of filth," spat Xandir. "I guess you won't be helping me out of here after all?" He writhed, straining both of his arms toward the grip of his swords. He managed to get a bit closer but still found himself out of reach.

Tobias shook his head, his face a mask of contrition. "No, sorry. You might be tempted to go see the Devil yourself. He drives a hard bargain, but he doesn't care who he drives it with. I'll let other people know you're up here though. You might become a pretty popular attraction if anyone else manages to reach you." Tobias considered this for a moment. "Or perhaps I should let you be the first to have a taste of this succulent little fruit. Find out if it's the real deal."

Xandir shrugged. "Just as long as you don't make any awful jokes about how it's 'to die for.' In my book, bad humor is almost worse than death."

Tobias advanced with a murderous gleam in his eyes. "Suit yourself, Xandir. Open wide."

He brought the fruit out in front of him, squeezing to release the foul juices. Xandir tried to back away, already regretting his words. Perhaps the plant would get the best of him after all.

He closed his eyes for a moment and thought of all those counting on him—Jarom, Eden, and most of all, the woman he had loved all his life. He would not let this be his End. With a prayer in his heart, he stretched out one more time, giving all his mental and physical energy to the task.

The foul fruit moved closer and closer, and Tobias's face grew wilder, gleaming with the glow of impending murder.

Xandir's fearful expression masked his secret elation—his hand had closed around a sword, but his opponent didn't know that yet.

Xandir bided his time, waiting for the exact moment to leap out and strike. A moment before he actually made his move, a brilliant bolt of white light erupted from behind Tobias, lancing through his back and continuing out his front. The fruit, cradled in his outstretched hand, exploded, coating Tobias's hands and face in foul, steaming liquid. Tobias shrieked and clawed at his face, running around blindly in terror and pain. He shot backward and fell from the platform, plummeting into the city below.

Drawing on the power of his swords, Xandir shot out from the roots like a cork from a bottle, raising his swords to deflect another attack. None came. Before him stood Johannes, a many-tongued whip glowing in one hand, and righteous indignation in his eyes.

"Johannes!" Xandir cried in relief. "How did you—?"

The old sage shook his head and raised a silencing hand. "There is no time. Quick, we must get you out of here at once. Word of your exploits has already spread throughout the city. You'll be hunted by every crook and creature."

Xandir's eyes flitted back and forth, scanning the air around Johannes. It was empty. The little cherub had not come with Johannes, possibly because he couldn't. Xandir had clung to the hope that Jarom might have survived his ordeal with the blood diamond, but he realized now that he would probably never see his apprentice again.

He lowered his head and gazed briefly on his spotted shroud. It was the blood of another innocent on his hands.

Trying to shake off the thought, Xandir glanced down at the Dome far below them and the other roofed levels of the city beyond. "I couldn't possibly go back the way I came, can I? What about the other way Tobias was talking about?"

Johannes shook his head once more. "There is still another way. No gates at least, except the front one. Follow me!"

He ran to the edge of the platform and indicated a deep canal cut into the stone a dozen feet below. "Watch this."

He withdrew a flask from his robe, much like the one they had found at the front gate. He unstopped the top and poured the contents into the ravine. In an instant, the ravine filled with clear running water, rushing off several hundred feet and then becoming a cascading waterfall. Xandir had to admit, this was one trick he had never seen.

"That's pretty and all," he mused, "but what good does it actually do us? I mean, I guess I am a bit thirsty."

"It is no mere waterfall," insisted Johannes. "It is a transport system. Once you touch the water, you will become water yourself, for a time. The locals would use this route all the time, but now I have one of the only remaining working specimens. This route flows all the way from the top of the city to the fountain at the front gate. There's no easier way."

Though he had his reservations, Xandir didn't voice any of them. With a quick smile of thanks to Johannes, he leapt from the platform and dove into the water. The sage called something after him, but his words were lost as he splashed down and vanished beneath the rushing waters.

Suddenly, he was Xandir no longer. Instead he had become part of the surging stream. He tumbled over and over himself, rushing forward with blinding speed and fluidity. Colors and shapes whizzed by, though he recognized nothing concrete. In a matter of moments, his watery journey came to a triumphant end as he burst into the air from the top of the fountain and scattered into pieces.

The next minute was spent getting himself back together. It took a while for all the water to float around and congeal in one place. He came back to his senses gradually, and when he snapped back to full consciousness, he found himself sitting waist deep in the bowl of the fountain, soaking wet. He stood and shook himself to dislodge all the water.

"Phew," he muttered. "So that's what it feels like to be water? It's exhausting!"

He glanced around and, to his relief, found himself at the lowest level of the city once more. He located the pavilion that marked the Pool of Divine Tears and worked his way toward it, trying to walk as nonchalantly as possible.

Strangely, he reached the building—a dome supported by

simple columns—without incident. Inside stood only a rect-angular pool of calm, clean water, fed gently by clear streams, which issued from the eyes of a statue of a robed woman at the far end.

Silently, he moved over and dipped his shroud in the clear water. The waters sullied as the red and black ink swirled away in wavy tendrils. A voice echoed from the statue at the far end.

"Your sins are many," it whispered, electrifying the air. "What shall you offer as penance?"

Xandir's breath caught in his throat. True to form, Tobias had said nothing about this.

"What can I offer? I simply wish to leave the city. I'm not a Serchean."

"Your sins are many," the voice repeated. "Only a great sac-rifice will do."

Xandir rose, panic welling up in his chest. "What do I have to give?" he shouted back at the statue. "I know I've made some poor decisions—but I did them all to help the woman I love! That must count for something!"

"You must pay," said the voice, growing sterner. "Justice cannot be mocked. Your sins alone deserve eternal banishment."

Xandir drew his sword, backing away from the pool. "Ban-ishment? What's the point? I'll take my chances here. You won't take me against my will!"

"No, Xandir the Archangel. We cannot do that. But we also cannot let you leave until penance is paid. You must take this burden or find someone else willing to take it for you."

Xandir narrowed his eyes. "What? I'm no Archangel. None of this makes any sense."

He backed away from the pool and turned to go but found that all the portals had shut behind him.

Xandir ranted in frustration. "Let me out! You have no right to keep me here. Of all people, I know that one cannot defeat justice, but I've also learned that one cannot forget mercy either. Only together do people get what they really deserve."

He drew out both of his swords and placed them side by side, blade crossing blade, so that they seemed to flow into one. He raised the hilts high above his head and held them there, the sword tips pointed at his heart.

"So be it. If I must be banished, it will be by my own hand."

He raised the blades higher, and plunged them simultaneously into his chest. The angel gasped and fell forward into the pool, which turned darker still with the taint of his blood.

At the far end of the room, a single portal parted, allowing a small figure to flutter through. He was dressed in a completely white robe and bore a spotless Shroud dangling from his neck. Silently, he flew over to the water and dipped the Shroud in it. It quickly absorbed the liquid, taking stain after stain onto its white surface. The stains crawled and writhed over the immaculate material like splattered bugs, miraculously returning to life. They festered and boiled over the surface, raging about like a torrent of bubbles tossed by a whirlpool.

However, as quickly as the stains appeared, they disappeared, overwhelmed and absorbed by the white fabric. As the Shroud grew full, the water trickled back down off the saturated fabric, once again pooling crystal clear in the depression in the floor. After several minutes, both Xandir's and the newcomer's Shrouds were perfectly unblemished.

The small figure reached down and retrieved the swords from Xandir's chest. "Come on, Xandir. You know it isn't time. Not even your blades can slay an angel."

Xandir opened his eyes, every one of his senses drinking in the clear coolness of the water. He felt clean, lighter than air, and completely at peace. Slowly, he sat up, and a smile broke across his face.

"Jarom," he cried. "You're alive!"

The cherub smiled back, his face beaming with heavenly light. "Yes, Johannes saved me. The diamond returned my blood, and I was spared an awful fate. In fact, it has helped us in more ways than one."

He pointed to his chest, indicating his Shroud. "My great personal sacrifice wiped my Shroud clean. I was then able to stand in for you."

"Not that you had many spots to begin with, Lil' Halo. I

know you're supposed to be my apprentice, but right now, I'm feeling like the weak one here."

Xandir rose to his feet, and Jarom extended him his swords. As Xandir grasped them, however, they glowed momentarily with intense light and heat. Before his eyes, the blades fused together, melding their colors and shapes to become one seamless blade of brilliant silver. One side still held a white edge while the other a black edge, but the center was a complete perfect blending of the two.

"The gray blade," Xandir muttered. "How fitting."

Jarom smiled and nodded his approval. "What will you do with your other sheath?" he asked.

"I don't know. Get another sword? Just for show."

Jarom glanced over his shoulder and indicated the exit. "We should go. We have much to do." He glanced down at the fruit that Xandir had retrieved from the side of the pool. "Are we still going to give it to Ganosh and their lot? They certainly aren't going to do anything good with it."

Xandir pondered for a moment, then nodded slowly. "Yes, but remember what Johannes said? It is supposed to be. It is part of a greater mosaic, of which we are only two tiny stones, like the two swords I had. The logical part of me breathes a warning, but the rest of me feels that it is what we must do."

Jarom sighed and headed toward the door. "I was afraid you might say something like that. Come on, the gate isn't far."

Together they floated out of the building and stood in front of the gate. Their spotless Shrouds glowed momentarily and then the great, rusty gates swung open wide. A crowd of onlookers rushed forward, trying to reach the gates before they swung shut for good. No one made it. No one, that is, but a pair of weary angels.

THIRTY
THE FIRST OF THE LAST

NEW YORK STATE, 2012.

Eden gazed at the TV screen in disbelief. She called across the room, beckoning for her friend, unable to take her eyes off the screen. "Judy, what was the name of that senator they mentioned in the demon meeting?"

"Jennings," she called back, approaching from the other room. "Why?"

Judy entered the room, and Eden indicated the television screen.

"In a surprising comeback, Senator Jennings of New Jersey has upset his opponent, Senator Phelps of Alaska to win the Presidential nomination for his party. Key states such as California and Texas, which were largely thought to be pro-Phelps, threw their support behind Jennings, securing his victory. As they say, he's just got one more river to cross between him and the White House, and based on the numbers we've been seeing lately, he might want to get used to the title Commander in Chief. In other news . . ."

Eden switched off the TV and slumped into the couch. "This feels fishy," she whispered. "I don't think it could just be a strange coincidence. Somehow, they've gotten to him too, and that means we might be electing a demon for president. Who knows what sort of damage he could cause?"

Judy nodded, her face grave. "And this country might not be alone. It sounds like they are working on multiple fronts to possess

251

world leaders. That would effectively make them the puppet masters, with the strings attached to our backs. I don't like that idea at all."

Suddenly, a rustling from the bedroom propelled them both from their seats. Behind them, framed in the doorway, stood Daren, an expression of smug satisfaction spread across his face. "I've had a pleasant nap," began Daren in a voice laced with his demon counterpart, "biding my time, conserving my power for the right moment. I know now that it is time, and I am delighted that I should be here to witness the fruits of my labors."

Eden backed away, realizing that the Daren she knew was still not in control. "What do you mean? Get away from me. You know this place is surrounded. Those angels will help us if you try to do anything!"

Daren shrugged, gesturing nonchalantly to the window. "I'm sure they would. But I'm not here to do anything of the sort. Let's just say things are about to get interesting, historic if I do say so myself, and I want to be around when it happens."

"What are you raving about?" spat Judy, placing herself between Daren and Eden.

Daren rolled his eyes, stretching his hands toward Judy. "It's time for you to wake up as well, Ashbreather."

Suddenly, Judy clutched at her chest and writhed in pain as the demon fought for control of Judy's mind and body.

"It is difficult," Judy wheezed in Ashbreather's voice. "She has a strong will, and I am still greatly weakened."

"Draw strength, dear sister. They shall be here soon, and you shall have strength enough. Try harder!"

Judy writhed and twisted, fighting an internal struggle against an unseen powerful opponent. Flames sprouted from her fingers and leapt from her mouth, scorching the furniture and carpet, igniting little blazes all across the room.

Daren continued to goad her on. "Come, I will need all your strength. Only one child must be allowed to live!"

At his words, Eden doubled up in pain, clutching her stomach. Her eyes grew wide with terror. "The babies are coming, quickly. I can feel it starting even now."

Judy's eyes looked up in despair. "How is that possible? You are nowhere near nine months pregnant."

"Do you think these are normal children?" asked Daren, a note of contempt entering his voice. "You'd be naïve to think so. No, they will come now, and they will come quickly. The wait wasn't as long as usual, but long enough for me. And that fool Dusteater wasn't even going to allow me to savor my triumph."

Judy glanced about with what free will she had, trying desperately to find some way to call for help. Just then, all the windows and doors in the house burst open, admitting a flood of beings into the room. On one side, a league of angels flowed in through the windows, some bearing bows and spears, others clasping harps and other instruments. A group of seven angels with glowing swords formed a ring of protection around Eden, standing still with their blades outstretched.

From the other side, a band of people burst through the door, the visages of demons etched on their features. They glowed red and menacing, howling and cursing with rough, raspy voices as they pressed in, surrounding the ring of angels around the woman in travail.

Judy stood beside Eden, sinking to her knees and trying to assist her friend, though her hands often trembled and jerked unexpectedly from side to side. Eden cried out in pain and fear, clutching desperately at the carpet.

Two angels entered the ring, and Eden recognized one of them as the one who had given her comfort all those nights before. She again touched Eden on the shoulder, and a wave of peace and calm rippled through her, stilling her frazzled nerves like a rush of cooling water on her skin. The angel glanced down and smiled broadly but said not a word.

The second angel, smaller and childlike with a loose robe of azure cloth, hovered in front of Judy, holding out a small flask in his hands. From the flask dangled a note written in elegant handwriting. It read simply: "Antidote—from Xandir."

Judy's eyes widened and for a fleeting moment, hope swelled in her heart like a hot air balloon taking flight. She undid the stopper and started to raise it to her lips.

The blue angel held out his hand. "Stop," he commanded gently. "You do not know what you are doing. For this I do not blame you, but let me explain. The two children who will now be born are very important to how the following years will unfold. One of them is destined to lead the forces of evil, and the other the forces of good.

"The one child has the unique ability to hold the hundreds of demons inside him all at once, a legion, as they say, and some of those present are here to try to claim that chance. The others wish to possess or destroy the other child before he has a chance to oppose them. So you see, the antidote you hold in your hand is best not used for you, but for the children! It will halt the progress of the demons, spare the good child, and weaken the powers of the one that would be used for evil."

The blue angel gazed into Judy's eyes with brilliant blue irises to match his robe. "Still, it is given to you to choose. If you take the antidote, you may still be able to repair the damage that has been done to you. If not, you may never be whole again. I implore you, choose wisely. These children bear the fate of millions, and your decision now will contribute to whatever happens to them."

Judy stared at the open flask in her hand, which trembled and shook, sending constant ripples through the liquid. She drew it closer, gazed at the life-giving draught, and found herself trapped in a web of indecision.

"This was meant for me. Xandir got it for me for helping him. Why shouldn't I drink it? I have struggled so long and so hard and for what? To give it all away? Of course not!" She lowered the flask slightly. "But then again, who am I to judge the fate of so many people? Who knows what may happen to them? Is my life really more important than the fate of the world?"

She moved the flask back and forth, unable to drink but unable to put it down.

THIRTY-ONE
ALWAYS AND FOREVER

THE MAGMA FLOW, 2012

Xandir and Jarom shot out of the gates, unable to put distance between them and the doomed city fast enough. The cavern still glittered and sparkled with thick sheets of ice and snow, and the magma ship loomed near. Xandir brought his hand back behind his ear and was rewarded with a familiar voice. Jarom held the fruit, immune to its caustic effects.

"Xandir," Ganosh sighed. "At last. We were beginning to think that even you couldn't escape the city alive. Do you have it?"

"Yes," shot Xandir. "I've got it. Where you do you want it? Let's get this over with."

"Board the magma ship," came the swift reply. "It will take you where you need to go.

"Oh, and do not attempt anything tricky," he added as an afterthought. "If the fruit doesn't arrive safely, your little darling won't last long either, and I must admit that no one wants that—not even me."

Xandir's arms shot forward, severing the connection. He extended one arm and pointed toward the empty bow of the ship. "Aren't we lucky, Lil' Halo? After our little vacation in the city, it looks like we're taking the pleasure cruise."

Jarom moaned. "Minus the pleasure."

They hovered over the deck of the ship. Xandir withdrew his

sword and slammed it hard down on the deck, sending a spider web of cracks rippling through the ice pane. He landed on the deck, his weight shattering the remaining ice under his feet.

"Nice of you to leave the light on for us, Harp Boy. Now get out and get this old rusty tub moving before the century is out."

Nothing stirred. His temper boiling to the surface, Xandir crashed forward, forming jagged holes in the ice. "I said, get out here, or I'll scrap your ship and find my own way back to Nod if I have to."

In response, the first few notes of an intoxicating melody wafted from the open cabin door. Immediately, Xandir felt his eyelids droop, and he sank to one knee. He shot back up, brushing off the shards of ice that clung to his clothes.

"Oh, no you don't. I see what you're trying to do, and it won't work!"

"Sing something else," urged Jarom, remembering his earlier encounters with Jubal's music. "You can try to counteract the music with something Heavenly."

Xandir's head lolled from side to side. "I never was any good at singing. I tried once, and it caused a thunderstorm. I'm surprised they didn't add that to my list of offenses."

Xandir leapt into the air, intent on escaping the allure of the sound. He made it only a few feet when the sticky fingers of song snatched him again. Jarom opened his mouth wide and belted out a hopeful counter melody, singing with all of his remaining strength.

They that sat in darkness have seen a great light. He shall lead us living fountains of waters and shall wipe all tears from our eyes. There shall be no more death, neither sorrow, nor crying, neither shall there be any more pain, for former things are passed away.

For a moment, it appeared to be working, and both of them made some ground in taking to the air. Jarom's voice grew hoarse, yet he sang on, his eyes streaming with blinding tears.

Jubal, however, redoubled his efforts. His song rose in volume and tempo, increasing its already potent draw to an almost irresistible pull.

Xandir's last vision before losing himself was of Jarom hitting the deck hard beside him, an arrow falling limply from his hands, his voice cut off in mid syllable.

The music didn't stop when they fell asleep. It crept into their subconscious, lying in wait for their dreams and smothering them in nightmares. Its sweet notes twisted into dissonant, grinding chords and harsh, pounding rhythms. Though they tried to escape, sleep held them fast and would not release them. Whether hours or days passed they could not tell, but when they finally awoke, they found that their slumber had been anything but restful.

"Welcome back," soothed a familiar voice. "It appears you've had a long trip."

Xandir tried to stand and sunk back down halfway through the attempt. His head was throbbing, and the colors of the room appeared soggy and wet.

"Please tell me we're back in Nod," he mumbled sourly. "I don't know what you call jet lag on a boat, but—"

Ganosh chuckled softly. "It's not the jet lag, Xandir. Don't worry; the song's effects will wear off presently. You'll be back to your sword-swinging self in a matter of minutes."

"You didn't answer me." Xandir managed, groggily reaching for his sword. "Where are we?" His eyes scanned the room and his nose wrinkled as with a rancid smell. "And where is Jarom? If you've harmed him—"

"Of course we're in Nod, you big lummox. Where else? You'll see your precious little cherub soon enough. Come, there is someone who very much wants to see you. He will deal with your persistent questions."

Xandir stumbled along, waving his sword out in front of him like a child's toy. They walked through an endless series of torch-lit tunnels that twisted and turned nonsensically until Angel and Giant stopped in front of a simple iron grate.

Ganosh pressed in a small section of the wall, and the grate rose, revealing a hallway leading to a wooden door.

"Here you are, Xandir, the end of your long journey. Our Master is waiting inside, along with someone I know you'll want to see."

Xandir, whose wits had trickled back to him, only grunted and made his way cautiously down the hall. He stopped at the door, and inhaled deeply. He had the distinct impression that he was waltzing into a trap. He had been so elated when he thought he had her back the first time in the Pleasure Pool. Could the Giants be planning something similar? Could they really deliver all they promised?

He placed his hand firmly on the handle. Whatever transpired after he walked through this door was meant to be. He turned the handle, and the door fell away, revealing a room with a low ceiling beyond. A formidable figure stood in the center, his arms crossed and his eyes fixed on Xandir. Though he had never seen the man before, he radiated such a tangible feeling of malice that there could be no doubt that this wasn't a Heavenly being.

In the center of the room, balanced in the middle of a raised dais stood the only person Xandir had ever truly loved, locked tight in her statue form.

"Master Mahan," muttered Xandir. "Let her go."

The man grunted, narrowing his eyes. "That all depends on you, angel. Do you have what I requested?"

Before Xandir could answer, Jarom fluttered into the room, grasping the fruit with both hands. Xandir released the breath that he had been holding, and a grin crept up the side of his mouth before fading again. The cherub appeared unharmed.

Master Mahan nodded and pointed at the fruit.

"The seed," he commanded. "Reach in and extract the seed. You are the only one here pure enough to do so."

Jarom's gaze wandered to Xandir, seeking reassurance for an act that might destroy millions. Xandir nodded, his face blank.

The cherub plunged his arm into the fruit and broke out in a coughing fit as its stench hit his nostrils. Seconds later, he withdrew his hand, bearing a misshapen lump that might have resembled the heart of a dragon. He offered it to Master Mahan.

The Master withdrew a long flask with a stopper and sealed the seed within. A grin crossed his face so malevolent that Jarom averted his eyes.

"It is yours," said Xandir. "Now give me what is mine."

"But of course," Master Mahan soothed, his voice curling around Xandir like tendrils of incense. "Did you think we would do otherwise? Here."

Master Mahan extended a hand and touched the statue. He muttered under his breath and then spit forcefully onto its face. The spittle trickled down the statue, and it began to dissolve, collecting on the dais in a steaming puddle of sludge. Under the sludge, hair, skin, and clothing appeared. As more and more fell away, the entire beautiful figure became visible, sending a thrill of delight coursing through Xandir's body. Her cheeks were rosy, her complexion fair, and she didn't look a moment older than the fateful day when he had been forced to doom Pompeii forever.

The last bit of sludge fell from her body, and for a moment, she hung there completely still. Next, she gasped, taking her first breath in centuries. She fell forward suddenly, her white robes billowing out like silky wings, and Xandir rushed to her aid, catching her lightly in his arms.

Her eyes widened, and she glanced up at him in amazement. "Xandir, it's you! What happened? There was so much fire and noise and smoke! I thought we were all doomed."

For a moment, Xandir could not speak. He stroked her hair and smiled—a genuine, heartfelt expression that felt foreign to his face.

"There were all those things, but you are safe now. I'm here, and I don't intend to let you out of my sight again. I will always be with you, Sempre."

He spoke her name for the first time since that fateful day, then drew her up and kissed her. He held her close, reveling in the warmth, the joy, and the impossibility of it all. This was no mere illusion. It was her—really her, living, breathing, and whole.

Reluctantly, he released her and stared into her deep, brown eyes. "We must leave this place, quickly." He turned to Master Mahan. "How do we get out? I don't want to spend a second longer here. I am grateful for our arrangement, but it ends here. I want nothing more to do with you or any of your people. Just let us leave, and I promise you, I will not cause you any trouble in return."

Master Mahan stood rooted as an ancient oak. Then his head shook from side to side. "It cannot be."

Xandir's blood raced to his face. "And why is that?" he spat.

Master Mahan arched one bushy eyebrow. "Because, you see, your dearest is in no condition to travel."

Xandir glanced over and found that it was true. Sempre was kneeling on the floor, doubled over and clutching her stomach. Xandir rushed over to her, fire in his eyes and flowing through his veins.

"What have you done to her!" he bellowed, his teeth clenched.

Master Mahan retained his composure. "Nothing at all, Xandir. Strangely enough, it is a matter of what you have done."

Xandir withdrew his sword and advanced on Master Mahan. "Tell me now, or I will cut you to pieces."

Master Mahan arched a bushy eyebrow. "If you must know, I have been around for a long time and have spies in every corner of the globe. You see, they possess all kinds of strange and marvelous powers, and it just so happens that my son Jubal has the uncanny ability to sense life, wherever it is. He's very useful when tracking someone, but in this case, his ability provided us with another interesting bit of information."

He pointed to the woman, writhing on the ground. "You see," he continued smugly, "when he looked at her, he sensed a greater life force than any human he had ever laid eyes on. At closer inspection, he discovered why."

Master Mahan's grin suddenly fanned out to cover the full length of his twisted face. "The woman was with child—and not just any child. A Giant."

Xandir lashed out with his sword, positioning it directly under the man's bushy beard. "You're lying!" he screamed. "You did something to her. Tell me what really happened."

Master Mahan did not flinch. "Xandir, surely you remember something like that. You know it's true. Just ask her. She hid it from everyone well with her billowing robes, but yes, she is carrying your child."

Xandir dropped to his knees, hit harder by the words than any other blow he had ever taken. Memories, bright and vivid, flashed through his mind, memories of the night some months before he had been forced to destroy her city. The memory brought with it a flood of both pleasure and horror as he realized that the crafty man in front of him spoke the truth. He drew himself over to her side and cradled her in his arms.

"Sempre, is it true? Is this our child, or is it possible that it is another's?"

Her head bobbed slightly, her face streaked with sweat. "Yes, it is ours. There is no other explanation," she managed. "I wanted to tell you. I had been meaning to tell you for so long, but I just couldn't find the words. You had told me what had happened to such children in the past, and I . . . I was afraid."

"I understand," soothed Xandir. "I understand."

Now that she was lying down and her robe lay flat against her, Xandir noticed the bulge of her stomach. Feeling himself drowning in remorse, he clutched her hand tightly and stroked her hair with his other hand.

She squeezed his hand with all her might as the pains of labor took her with full force.

The baby wasted no time coming into the world. Xandir held Sempre's hand, shocked and horrified at the feelings of powerlessness that taunted him from all sides. He cried out in pain in unison with her, unable to do much more than watch. Jarom hovered around them both, whispering words of comfort and encouragement.

"Ever think this would be part of your job description, Lil' Halo?"

"No," said Jarom. "But then again, I thought I would be an Ambrosia baker my whole life. It hasn't been the most pleasant ride, but I'm still glad we took it."

Before Xandir could reply, a throaty cry rang out in the chamber.

Xandir reached down hoisted the baby girl in his arms, at least twice as large as the largest human baby. She cried and bellowed and shivered in the cold of the cave. Master Mahan stood by as a casual observer, his arms crossed and a smug expression on his face.

"Congratulations, Xandir. A beautiful young girl. The race of Giants shall be perpetuated. And with this seed, I shall make sure that the race of Men will not be around to trouble us this time."

Speechless with shock and loathing, Xandir looked down at his dearest love with pity. Her face was deathly pale, and she was barely breathing.

He leaned down and kissed her forehead. "What shall we call her?" he whispered tenderly. "I need to know."

Sempre gasped for breath, and it was a long minute before she could muster the strength to answer. "Her name . . . is . . . Clara . . . for she . . . shall be . . . a bright spot in this darkening world."

Xandir placed Clara near Sempre's heart and held them both, as if trying to prevent Sempre's soul from slipping away. "I've waited so long. I won't lose you again, not now!"

She glanced up at him and smiled, and Xandir thought that he had never seen anything so angelic. She spoke again, her eyelids barely parted. "Oh, Xandir, don't worry. This isn't good-bye. I've . . . done my part . . . but I feel the world . . . still needs you."

She squeezed his hand a final time and whispered so softly that he could barely make out the words. "I . . . love you."

Gently, her head lolled backwards, and her eyelids closed. Her breath seeped out one last time, and her broken body lay still. For the first time in hundreds of years, Xandir allowed a single tear to make its course down his cheek onto hers.

Sword in hand and fury in his eyes, he bellowed with rage and shot toward Master Mahan, intent on cleaving him in two. From nowhere, Master Mahan brought his own substantial sword to bear, a dark, jagged blade, stained with layers of blood and grime.

"This is your fault!" bellowed Xandir, slashing over and over again with his gray blade. "You knew she would die, and you tricked me into helping you. You'll pay for this!"

Master Mahan stepped aside, parrying each blow as if dancing with a child. "You don't understand, Xandir. You're dealing with someone who does not fear death. I am beyond it. Behold the mark I bear."

He reached up with a hand and pulled back his hood from his forehead. The surface bore a crimson mark, intricately etched right into his skin, bearing ancient symbols and characters that Xandir couldn't even begin to decipher.

All at once, Xandir realized with utter certainty whom he was facing. "You! You are the first Murderer—Cain."

"Very good, Xandir. I thought you'd recognize this mark. You know what it means if you hurt me. The retribution on you will be swift and tenfold what you do unto me."

Cain snarled and then drew his lips up into a wicked grin. "Your child will live with us. She is the key to reviving the race of Giants."

Xandir stepped back, holding his sword at the ready. "Don't you even think about it. She's mine, and I won't let you monsters have anything do with her."

Cain's face adopted an expression as if he had just drawn the right card in a high-stakes game of chance. "Really? And how will you protect her? You know she's a forbidden child. She'll be hunted and persecuted all the days of her life if she is discovered. There are those who would not hesitate to destroy her on sight. Is that what you want?"

Xandir continued to give ground until he stood again over his fallen love and the child still nestled at her chest. Her mother's features stood out so starkly on her face that it robbed him of breath. First one knee buckled, then the other as Xandir realized that Cain had spoken the truth.

Xandir shot to his feet and fixed Cain with a withering gaze. "You snake! You filthy dog! There isn't a word vile enough for your kind of evil!" He looked down on the sweet face of his daughter, leaned down, and kissed her gently on the forehead. "I can't stop you from taking her, but mark my words. I will be back for her! I will make sure she won't forget who she is."

Cain sheathed his sword and brought his fingers into steeples in front of his face. "And as for you, don't think you're getting off so easy. Though you have done us a great service, you know too much and have seen too much for us to be letting you simply wander off just yet. Don't worry, after a few years down here, things will settle down. Then it won't matter what happens to you. Maybe they'll even mention you in the new history books I'll cause to be written. We have thousands of Achillians waiting at our command and other allies besides. This world won't last long."

Xandir looked Cain full in the face and spat, "It would seem that you've underestimated me as well. I'm leaving now, and I'll be back for my daughter. Take care that she remains unharmed."

With that, he bent down tenderly and scooped up his fallen love. His eyes then turned to Jarom and an unspoken understanding passed between them. His child would not be completely without friends in this bleak place.

He then withdrew his sword and let out another fierce, echoing bellow, giving voice to all the pent up rage and sadness within. He shot through the air like a comet, tearing past Master Mahan and through the door.

Ganosh instantly leapt at him, bearing a club in both hands. Xandir rolled and set Sempre to the side and whirled about to face his new opponent. A pair of blows landed just next to him, and he countered with a glancing blow of his own, knocking the Giant sprawling. Before Ganosh could recover, Xandir dealt another blow to the ceiling directly above his fallen opponent. The ceiling buckled and in seconds, Ganosh disappeared under a mound of rubble.

"I've seen the Jaws, Ganosh, and you'll see them soon." Xandir picked up Sempre and hurtled forward. He twisted through the tunnels of the compound, barreling past dozens of Achillians on his way toward the surface.

Tubal leapt from the shadows, his massive sword slicing through Xandir's hair and nicking his skin. Xandir drew up his own sword to block the next blow, and the air rang with the clang of metal on metal. Tubal's blows fell so hard, they forced Xandir back down the passageway. Xandir set Sempre down a second time and renewed his own assault.

"So what if I need both hands?" Xandir screamed, aiming for Tubal's head. He dodged the blow but caught the tip of the angel blade against his cheek. Startled, Tubal shot his hand to his face and felt a trickle of blood from the wound.

"How does it feel to bleed?" hissed Xandir. "How about turning the other cheek?"

Tubal dropped to one knee, his eyes gleaming with new fear. "Go," he whispered, the sound echoing in the close quarters. "The fountain has failed me, but I am not ready to die."

Xandir withdrew and hoisted Sempre's body under one arm. Without giving Tubal a chance to change his mind, Xandir sped past him and flew upward.

A brilliant light appeared ahead, and Xandir could feel the stale air growing fresh. Just when he thought he would escape unmolested, a final shadow filled the exit. Xandir pointed his sword and did not slow. Nothing would stand in his way now.

A sharp note rang through the tunnel, followed by another and another. Each note ripped through him like a bullet that passed clean through. Xandir's vision blurred, and he stumbled to the ground. The notes swelled, and soon, Xandir couldn't hear or feel anything else.

All at once, the notes stopped, leaving a ringing silence. Jubal approached displaying a single hand, red and throbbing. "You see Xandir, this hurts me as well as you. I hope you are more willing to listen now."

Xandir raised his head and pried his eyes open. Sempre lay sprawled out by his side. "What do you want? You got your cursed fruit!"

Jubal withdrew another harp and strummed it as if they were going on a summer stroll. "You see, Xandir, you always were a fence sitter. We cannot have you reporting back to your superiors. And who knows? Perhaps in time you would come around to our way of thinking."

Xandir shook his head. "Let me guess, another deal? Forget it. It took me thousands of years, but I think I've finally learned my lesson."

Jubal chuckled in time with his lilting song. "Music can do wonderful things, Xandir. Things you couldn't even imagine."

"What do you mean? I've lost so much I don't really care for your tricks anymore."

Jubal indicated the motionless woman next to him. "Her soul is not far. Just say the word, and I will call her back."

Xandir gazed over to his fallen love and felt himself sinking into a dark and lonely place. He closed his eyes against the image, and suddenly, the streets of the Heavenly Realms materialized in his vision. She stood there, radiant as he had ever seen her in life. Their gazes met, and she shook her head as the image faded from sight. The message was clear. He knew what he must do.

"No," rasped Xandir. "She has gone to the place she was always meant to be. She's been delayed far too long already."

Jubal sighed and placed the harp back in his robes. "Very well, Xandir. I'm only sorry that I can't grant you a last request. This song will have to do."

He withdrew the first harp, ebony with crimson strings. Without warning, his fingers flew over the strings, picking out a jagged melody that saturated the air with excruciating noise. He wished at once for Jarom's comforting voice to drive back the noxious sound. Xandir's vision drew in so that all he could see was his love's face.

An arrow shot through the tunnel, and struck the deadly musician in his playing hand. The music ceased, and Xandir's head shot up. A new voice rang through the tunnel. "Fly, Xandir! She's safe with me."

With effort, Xandir rose to his feet and caught a glimpse of the cherub, cradling a bundle in his arms.

"Lil' Halo? How did you—?"

The cherub's curls flew wildly around his face. "Just go! Before I have to come up with an embarrassing nickname for you."

Xandir snatched up Sempre's body, and both Xandir and Jarom darted off in opposite directions.

Xandir broke through the surface and shot into the overcast heavens, trailed by a cascade of dirt and debris. He soared straight up, flying high enough to ensure that no mortal could follow. He rocketed forward for hours, not pausing to think or to feel before descending and landing hard on a grassy hill, overlooking a sweeping plain.

He inhaled in astonishment, as he recognized the terrain. It was the same Italian countryside he had often visited in his original days with Sempre.

He leapt into the air again and flew hard and fast, finding

his way almost without conscious thought. He came to rest atop another familiar hill. Gently, he lay Sempre down under an olive tree where they had spent many evenings together. He set to work with his sword, carving a place for her in the soft soil. He sighed as he finished and lowered her into the ground, humming a melody that she had often sung to him.

He didn't allow himself a tear this time, though he felt that his often stony heart was now splintered and riddled with cracks. He took one last look at her face and then replaced the dirt, marking the place with a large stone on which he carved her name with the tip of his sword.

"I don't have to remind you, what your name means, my love," he whispered, his mouth suddenly dry, "but this shows that I have not forgotten." He knelt down and caressed the surface of the stone, tracing the single word with one finger. "Always."

THIRTY-TWO
THE LAST ARCHANGEL

ITALY, 2012

Xandir was about to take flight when a shaft of light materialized behind him. The High Seraph stared at Xandir for a long moment, saying nothing. To his surprise, Xandir saw none of the indignation he was sure would be there.

Xandir spoke first. "So, are you here to punish me? I suppose I deserve it. Though I can't think of anything worse than what has already happened."

"Xandir," spoke the High Seraph, ignoring Xandir's self-pity. "It is time for you to take on a new assignment."

Xandir, his head bowed, didn't meet his gaze. "Anything. Send me to the lowest pit in the darkest corner of the world. Destroy me if you wish. I don't care anymore. I'm tired of fighting."

"There are other ways to fight than with your sword," continued the High Seraph. "And you'll be getting used to them instead in your new role: a mortal life."

Xandir's head shot up. Of all the assignments, this was the only one he had not considered. "What? Why? My exile was to be until the End of the World."

"The End is here, Xandir. It isn't a certain day or a precise moment. It is a period of Time, during which you are released from your Angelic service and are slated to reenter Earth as a mortal, immediately. This is both a blessing in light of your heritage and a trial that will in some small way compensate for the many poor decisions you have made during your pervious assignment. Come, there is no time to waste." The High Seraph stepped forward and extended his hand. "I will take you across the divide."

Xandir extended his hand and clasped the High Seraph's, and they took to the sky. A rush of light enveloped them, and it was as if a rusty cage deep in Xandir's mind flew open, setting free long-fettered memories.

"I remember who I am!" Xandir exclaimed joyfully. "I scarcely knew that I had forgotten."

The High Seraph smiled, a long suppressed warmth entering his face. "You shall no longer bear the name of your exile. Welcome back, Archangel Uriel. The council of Archangels will be seven once more, and now that the End is truly near, you are the last of them to enter mortality. You shall enter the world as a mortal child into a family that I think you already know."

Uriel's world swelled as large as the Universe and then suddenly collapsed into an unimaginably small space.

"Good luck, Uriel. Good luck."

NEW YORK, 2012

The angels around Eden pressed back the thronging hordes of demon-possessed people, reeling at the sheer volume as they came wave after wave. They represented people of many races, nationalities, and ages, clawing and pushing their way toward the forefront. Eden's cries of pain vanished in the tumult as her labor progressed, and she was shielded from sight by the ring of angels.

Angel reinforcements arrived constantly, flinging away demons with glowing swords and spears. The demons pressed back, each wave growing fiercer than the last. The angels remained silent, their mouths set in hard lines, while the demons screamed, their faces twisted and their eyes unblinking.

Judy forgot for a moment about the demons and attended to her friend. Eden was sweating and breathing heavily, unable to speak from the pain. The comforting angel held her tight, whispering words that only Eden could hear, while other angels assisted in the actual birth. They pressed vials to her lips, sang softly, and whispered into her ear.

"Some good my PhD is doing me now!" called Judy, her eyes meeting Eden's. Eden managed a tight smile for her friend. "Thank you, Judy," she whispered. "Thank you for everything. I'm sorry that I drew you in to all of this."

Judy's breathing quickened, though the smile remained on her face. "Well, I needed something to spice up my old age. All that scholarship was starting to get downright boring."

Eden's pain intensified and overwhelmed her ability to speak. Judy watched in horror and fascination as first one child and then another entered the world.

The first had dark eyes, orange tinged skin, and a shocking amount of unnaturally long black hair running down his back. His first breath rushed out in a menacing growl of anger and pain. The demon in Judy writhed, leaping back and forth, as if worming its way out of her skin.

The second baby was fairer skinned with the same unnaturally long hair, flowing a brilliant white down its back. As Judy looked on, she couldn't help but think that he reminded her of someone. In contrast to his brother, this baby cooed softly, looking up at the unfolding scene with childish curiosity.

The demons clawed forward in earnest as a spectral form rose from the flailing dark child on the floor. It looked like a single person with many faces, all of them twisting in sinister smiles.

"I am the New Caesar, the great Emperor. Let the worthy among you rise to join me!"

The crowd of demons roared as they leapt from their host bodies, shedding them like empty husks or discarded snakeskins. They flew through the air at the gauntlet of angels, who fought bitterly against the advancing horde. The angels lashed out with swords and spears that glowed as if they had just been removed from a blacksmith's forge. Many of the demons fell victim and blew apart, reduced to ash and smoke.

Despite the valiant efforts of the Angel defenders, the most powerful of the dark horde forced their way through to reach their destination. Those who succeeded disappeared into the demon child, though some, in their confusion, made their way toward the other child, who flailed and screamed at their approach. Smoke filled the room, blanketing the ceiling and pouring out of every opening.

Eden had lost consciousness on the ground, and Judy crawled over with the last of her ebbing strength, removed her jacket, and placed it over the spent woman. She glanced down at the children and realized that despite the Angels' efforts, the demons were making headway with both of them. She knew what she had to do.

She popped off the stopper and dangled it over the first baby's mouth. Her hand jerked back and forth of its own accord, willing her to bring it to her own mouth or spill its contents onto the floor. She gritted her teeth and wrestled control back from the demon inside of her.

"I won't let you stop me," she growled through gritted teeth. The demon gave no reply but writhed even harder, burning her up from the inside. Judy felt her strength sapping away as Ashbreather continued to draw on her energy. She knew she would hold back the demon only minutes at best.

With great effort, she tipped the flask, dropping a stream of large drops into the demon baby's open mouth. The child sputtered and gagged but was forced to swallow as the liquid made its way down his throat.

In that moment, she relaxed her grip, and the bottle clattered to the floor, spilling a few precious drops to vanish uselessly on the carpet. The rest of Judy's body followed, losing consciousness as Ashbreather wrested total control and then cast her body aside. Judy's skin had turned dark with burns, and she wheezed and gasped for breath.

The last thing she ever saw was a pale pudgy hand grasping a flask of blue liquid. She smiled and closed her eyes, greeting her final release from all pain.

EPILOGUE

NEW YORK STATE, 2012

Eden lay still on the floor, breathing deeply. All around her were the strewn bodies of the formerly possessed in various states of consciousness. Some had not survived the melee, while others clung desperately to life. Among the fallen lay Judy, who, though she had met a terrible end, appeared as peaceful as if she was finally enjoying a good night's rest for the first time in months.

From her prone position, Judy's spirit sat up and surveyed the grisly scene. The demons had taken the dark child with them. A circle of angels still hovered around Eden and her other baby, tenderly tending to both.

Suddenly, Judy turned as a robed figure floated through the front door, wearing a grim expression. A mass of red hair framed his face, and a deep frown etched his features. He swung his head around and caught Judy's gaze. Then he held out a hand in a gesture of peace.

"I'm sorry, but I'm afraid your time has come."

Judy narrowed her eyes. "I'm beg your pardon?"

"I am called Jertel. It has been my task to watch over you during your life, and it is now my privilege to escort you to the other side. Xandir managed to obtain the antidote but then lost it again. Looking after your best interests, it was I who arranged to find the flask and have it brought to you as Xandir intended."

"Xandir?" asked Judy. "I was wondering how he managed it. I didn't see him here."

"He wasn't. At least not as you know him."

Jertel stared down at Eden, and his serious face grew even grimmer. "It is amazing she survived such a punishing ordeal."

Judy glanced down, her face taut. "Will she live? What will happen to the baby?"

"That I do not know. But your friend is in good hands."

"And no longer in mine," sighed Judy in resignation. "What do we do now? I'm new to this, of course."

"There is nothing to fear," replied Jertel. "Come with me. We cannot stay."

Judy only glanced back once as she followed Jertel out the door and into the night. "Who knows," she whispered. "Maybe they'll let me be your Guardian angel someday."

Eden slowly opened her eyes, her body throbbing all over with pain. The luminous figures still filed around her, silent and grave. Seeing her awake, one of the silent figures extended his arms to her, holding the baby in his arms out to Eden.

"Your child," he said warmly, placing him in Eden's embrace. "He is indeed special." The angel backed away and smiled. The baby slept on peacefully.

"We will be near you," continued the angel. "You will not always be able to see us, but we will always be here. We will take you from this place to a safer one. The child must be raised away from prying eyes."

He extended a pale hand and placed it on the child's forehead. "He will not grow up like most children. Neither shall his brother. It will be startling at first, but just remember, this has all been foreseen."

The angel helped her to stand just as another figure rose to his feet. Eden gasped and clutched the baby tighter. "Daren? Is it you? Or am I still talking to that . . . demon?"

Daren looked as if he'd been crumpled up into a wad like a paper doll and then smoothed out again. His bloodshot eyes bored into her, desperate and wracked with pain. "He didn't take me," he muttered. "He found me lacking."

Eden stepped forward and slapped Daren full on the face, knowing that the demon still had its hold. "What more do you want with me and my husband? You made me believe he had gone crazy, that he was now violent and unfaithful. You buttered me up with gifts just to get me to play into your hands and then dropped me. I almost committed suicide because of you! Leave us alone!"

"Please," wheezed Sparkslinger from within Daren, rubbing his cheek. "You don't understand. I can help you."

Eden backed away, flanked by the angel. "Yes, by leaving my husband's body. Now."

"No!" he cried, shaking his head. "His body is too weak right now. If I don't sustain him with my energy, he will die."

Eden turned to the angel, her face twisted with pain. "Is it true?"

The angel nodded, his mouth a rigid line. "I am afraid so. I would be wary about trusting him though. He is a demon, no matter how desperate or broken he seems at the moment."

"Please," muttered Sparkslinger. "I don't want this body anymore, but I can't leave yet. I don't want to be without one, and right now, he can't survive without me. Just let me stay until I can find a new one."

Eden retreated into thought. She had no way to know if he was lying, but it was too good a chance to pass up. She might actually get her husband back, and they could start again. Perhaps.

The angel flapped his wings. "Eden, we must go," he said, glancing toward the window. His usually calm face twisted suddenly in surprise. "What in the world?"

As Eden's gaze followed the angel's gestures, the sight turned her heart ice cold. The full moon had turned a deep crimson as if coated with fresh blood. All around it, the brightest and thickest meteor shower Eden had ever seen streaked violently across the skies.

Her jaw trembled as she fought for the words to say. "What is that? What's happening?"

The angel now stared directly at the phenomenon. "It is a Sign to herald the birth of your children. It is the Sign of the End."

Eden shivered, finding the sight both terrifying and spellbinding at the same time. "Please, lead the way out of here. I understand that we are not safe."

She turned reluctantly to her husband and managed a tight-lipped smile. "You too. For now."

He nodded and followed Eden and the angel out the door and into the night. Holding their hands, the angel took them both high into the night's sky, trailing a flame that fully engulfed the house, reducing it to ashes in minutes.

A gust of wind ruffled the baby's blankets, and he squirmed in his wrappings. For the first time Eden noticed a strange mark on the baby's chest. At first she thought it was a smudge of ash and tried to wipe it away. However, she found instead that it was a birthmark, part of the baby's skin: two gray lines forming an X.

She glanced down at her child and smiled. Though he had just arrived, she felt that this little person seemed familiar to her. "Don't worry, little one. I'll do everything I can to protect you."

Suddenly, the baby's eyes opened, and he smiled broadly, his face quite unlike any infant's she had ever seen. His eyes twinkled in the strange light of the red moon, and somehow Eden could tell that he knew that it was true.

THE REALM OF NOD, 2012

Jarom huddled in the darkness, willing the child who was already almost as large as he was, to keep quiet. He reached into his bag and withdrew the last of his Ambrosia cakes. Clara's eyes lit up as she spied the treat, and in seconds it had disappeared into her expectant mouth.

The cherub sighed and brushed the crumbs from his hands. "I don't suppose you eat rocks, do you?"

The baby chortled in response as if she had understood and then curled up in a ball and fell promptly asleep.

A thin smile crossed Jarom's strained face. It had been several weeks since Xandir's escape, and so far they had eluded capture or discovery. They had made their home in a cave containing a pure pool of water, secluded from most of the main tunnels. He didn't know how long they could continue this way, but somehow, the entire endeavor felt right. It was as if he could imagine his father smiling down on him, wishing him luck.

Jarom's smile grew as Clara yawned in her sleep. So many awful things had happened since coming to Earth, but looking back, he did not regret any of them. He leaned down and caressed the child's hair. "Now that you're my new apprentice, I'll just have to come up with a name for you. Isn't that what I'm supposed to do?"

His brows knit together as he discarded half a dozen possibilities outright. Somehow, any version of "Lil' Halo" didn't seem to fit.

At last he gave up and settled back against the wall, the beginnings of a Heavenly lullaby on his lips. He would have to work at this master/apprentice deal, but there would be time for that. "Just Clara then," he said. "My little light."

THE HIMALAYAS, 2012

Eden strolled to the window and threw open the curtains, letting in a refreshing blast of mountain air. The peaks rolled on into the horizon, and the effect of the moonlight on the snow never ceased to thrill her. A streak of light, like a star fallen to earth, passed by below, signaling the round of the patrol assigned to guard her. But instead of passing by like normal, the light turned, and before she could think, the light flitted through the window and hung before her in the air.

The light took form, assuming the shape of a person Eden knew well. Her glasses were gone, and she had adopted a new hairstyle, but there was no mistaking her.

"Judy," cried Eden. "What are you doing here?"

Judy arched an eyebrow. "Aren't you happy to see me? I've come a long way to see you."

Eden gestured to the window. "Anyone would have to travel a long way to see me. We're halfway to Shangri-La."

Judy chuckled and approached her old friend. "Is it true? You and the Yeti are next-door neighbors?"

Eden shot Judy a severe glance. "Whoa, don't let him hear you say that. It's Yearti, and yes, he's two peaks over. He stops by once in a while to make sure we're okay." She paused and ran a hand through her thick hair. "And to see if we have any new chocolate. Guess I'm not the only one with a weakness for it."

The women shared in a laugh, and Eden shook her head. "So what does this mean? I didn't think I would see you again."

Judy leaned in. "You remember when I told you I'd be your Guardian angel? Well, after I finished off my last assignment, they agreed to let me."

Eden broke into a broad grin. "Just when I thought my life couldn't get any stranger." She cocked her head to one side. "Out of curiosity, what was your last assignment?"

Judy's head flew from side to side. "You really don't want to know. Suffice it to say, it entailed a police officer, a hobo, and the creative application of a wishbone."

Eden narrowed her eyes and leaned forward, then decided not to pursue it.

"And the family?" asked Judy. "How are they adapting to mountain life?"

Eden's countenance fell. "Daren has managed to keep the demon at bay, especially with Yearti's help. It's slow going, but we are starting to patch things up. He's still so frail, but he's going to try to make dinner for me tonight." She paused, and some of the warmth returned to her face. "And Xandir is . . . Xandir."

"I had heard about that, though only whispers. Hard to imagine that big shot angel in a little body."

"Yes," agreed Eden, "and I don't let him near anything even resembling a sword yet. You wouldn't believe how quickly he's grown or how fast he's progressing—already running around and saying the strangest things. He tells me he doesn't remember anything about being an angel, but I'm not taking any chances."

The two made their way to the window and gazed at the stars and the moon, still tinged red.

"What's going to happen, Judy? I've lost track of time up here, and I don't have a clue what's going on in the outside world."

Judy shrugged. "You may count that as a blessing. Jennings

was elected president, and things are looking pretty bleak, though it seems a shame to talk about such things on such a brilliant night."

"Agreed," said Eden. "We've got a lot of catching up to do." Eden glanced down at the slopes below and then back up at her friend. "So, are you allowed to ski as an angel?"

Judy shook her head disapprovingly at the steep declines. "I suppose if you attempt any of those slopes, I would be obligated to follow you."

Their combined laughter echoed across the snow, and for a moment, they were both able to forget that there was anything wrong with the world.

ABOUT THE AUTHOR

Michael is a graduate of Brigham Young University with a degree in German teaching and a minor in music. He puts his German to good use by working to build online German courses for high school students. Though he grew up traveling the world with his military father, he now lives in Utah with his wife, Jen, and his two sons. Michael enjoys acting in community theater, playing and writing music, and spending time with his family. He played for several years with the handbell choir Bells on Temple Square and is now a member of the Mormon Tabernacle Choir. His first book, *The Canticle Kingdom*, was released in February 2010 through Bonneville Books. Michael is also the author of the inspirational short story, *Portrait of a Mother*. His work has also been featured in various online and print magazines such as *Mindflights*, *The New Era*, *Allegory*, and the *Ensign*.